the

SURRENDER

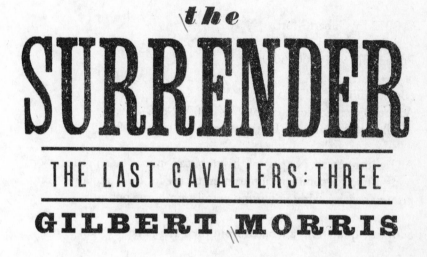

the SURRENDER

THE LAST CAVALIERS: THREE

GILBERT MORRIS

BARBOUR
PUBLISHING

© 2012 by Gilbert Morris

Print ISBN 978-1-60260-909-9

eBook Editions:
Adobe Digital Edition (.epub) 978-1-60742-828-2
Kindle and MobiPocket Edition (.prc) 978-1-60742-829-9

Scripture quotations are taken from the King James Version of the
Bible.

This book is a work of fiction. Names, characters, places, and incidents
are either products of the author's imagination or used fictitiously.
Any similarity to actual people, organizations, and/or events is purely
coincidental.

Cover design: Faceout Studio, www.faceoutstudio.com
Cover photography: Steve Gardner, Pixelworks Studios

FIC.

Published by Barbour Publishing, Inc., P.O. Box 719, Uhrichsville,
Ohio 44683, www.barbourbooks.com

*Our mission is to publish and distribute inspirational products offering
exceptional value and biblical encouragement to the masses.*

Printed in the United States of America.

PART ONE

CHAPTER ONE

Miss Mary Anna Randolph Custis walked out onto the porch and paused, as she usually did, to look around and savor the day.

It was a hot, hard, bright morning in August of 1829. The sky was a deep blue with no cloud puffs to soften it. Below the gracious home on the hill was the lazy Potomac River and just beyond lay the city of Washington, DC. The distance mellowed the outlines of the shabby town, and heat shimmers made it appear dreamlike.

Mary lifted her head and sniffed appreciatively as she caught the elusive scent of roses, the last blooms in the luxuriant rose garden by Arlington Mansion.

She went down the steps and surveyed the pony cart waiting in the drive. A slave held the mare as Mary inspected the eight large baskets in the cart. Filled with sweet cherries, they glowed a glorious crimson in the glaring sun. For a moment Mary considered parking the cart under a nearby oak tree so she could paint it: cart, horse, slave, cherries, and all. They made a wonderful picture, and one of Mary's loves was painting. She was a gifted artist.

Finally aloud she said, "No, I suppose the hands will enjoy the cherries much more than I would enjoy painting them." She came around to pet the mare's nose and asked, "Did you get the things I wanted for Bitty, Colley?"

The slave, a small somber man, nodded. "Yes, Miss Mary. I put the mugs and the pitcher and the ice block under the seat, all packed nice in sawdust. But don't you want me to go fetch one of the boys to drive this around?"

"No, I'm taking it," Mary said firmly. "But I don't want to bounce around in the cart. I'm just going to walk." She pulled the mare's reins down and wrapped them once around her hand.

"But Miss Mary, it's hot, and it's probably a two-mile walk all around the quarters," Colley said helplessly as Mary started walking down the drive.

"I'll be fine, Colley. Stop fussing. You're as bad as Bathsheba," she said over her shoulder.

Colley returned to the house, muttering, "That Miss Mary's got a stubborn streak wide as that river! Ain't no telling her nothing!"

Mary heard his muttering, and a fleeting smile crossed her lips. She had heard such dire imprecations all her life—from the helpless entreaties of her mother and father to mutterings and grumblings from house servants like Colley, who were prone to taking more liberties than the farmhands.

Only twenty-two years of age, she was already finding that she understood some of their care for her, particularly her parents' concern. Mary Lee Fitzhugh Custis and George Washington Parke Custis had had four children, and Mary Anna was the only one to survive infancy.

She was tiny, her frame as small and delicate as a bird's, and she was fragile. She had dark brown hair, thick and curly, and her rich brown eyes were probably her best feature, wide and fringed with thick dark lashes below the smooth oval of her forehead. She was not pretty, she knew: her chin was too pointed, her nose too long, her mouth not full and pouty as was the fashion. But she was attractive, particularly to men, as they found her interesting, amusing, and vivacious. Though she was small, she had a fire within her, and it showed in her alert, quick expression and her sparkling eyes.

Walking down the path to the south slave quarters, she savored each moment. The grounds surrounding the house were a clean, solemn forest, cool even in the hottest of summers. It was quiet and peaceful. Accompanying the creaks of the cart and the mare's plodding steps were the cheerful calls of birds. Everywhere Mary looked was a shade of green, mottled only by the lichen-gray stands of boulders that were allowed to stay in the much-manicured woods.

When she reached the first cabin, she saw with dismay that the elderly slave Bitty wasn't sitting out on her porch, as she always did in fine weather. Tying the mare's reins to a porch post, she knocked on the door and called softly, "Bitty? It's me, Miss Mary. May I come in?"

"Yes, ma'am, miss." She heard faintly.

She went inside and saw the woman on her small bed, struggling to get up. Quickly she went to her side and laid her hands on the woman's shoulders. "No, no, Bitty, don't get up. I heard you weren't feeling well, so I came to see about you." She propped up a pillow so Bitty could sit up. "I brought you some things. I'll just be a minute."

From the wagon Mary got a tin pitcher and two covered mugs and then went back to get the ice block. It was sitting in a small crate filled with sawdust and covered with a linen cloth. When she had all the items on the kitchen table, she pulled a chair up to Bitty's bedside and asked, "How are you feeling, Bitty? What's wrong?"

"Touch of catarrh is all, I guess," she said tiredly. "Dunno how I got it in middling of summer, but here it is. Sneezing and coughing and sniffling like it's dead winter. Cold one minute and hot the next."

Mary nodded. "That's the fever. I brought just the thing for you, some wine whey, and it's still warm. It'll break that fever, and then maybe you'll feel like having some fresh cherry cordial. I even brought you some ice so you can have it nice and cold." Mary brought her one of the covered mugs and a spoon. "Here, this will make you feel so much better, Bitty."

"I'm just not very hungry, Miss Mary," she said wanly. She was normally a hearty woman, thickly built and sturdy, but now Mary could see that she had lost some weight and looked drawn.

"None of that," Mary argued. "Either you eat it, or I'm spoon-feeding you."

"Yes, ma'am," Bitty said resignedly.

Though Bitty had been a farmhand, Mary Anna, along with all the slaves, was aware of her strong will. After Bitty took a few cautious spoonfuls, Mary could see from the slave's reaction she liked wine whey, which was basically milk boiled with white wine.

Mary continued to watch her, hawklike, until Bitty finished.

Taking the mug and spoon, Mary efficiently washed them up and laid them by the sink to dry. "Father bought forty bushels of sweet cherries," she told Bitty as she chipped ice to make her a small cordial. "I'm taking a bushel to everyone. Would you like me to leave yours, Bitty, or would you rather that I take them back and have the kitchen put them up for you?"

"No'm, I love cherries. I'd like to have them," Bitty said, her eyes brightening. "And please tell Mr. Custis my thank-yous. And to you, too, Miss Mary."

After making sure Bitty's cabin was in order, Mary went back out to the wagon and continued her long circular walk around the Arlington property, stopping at each cabin to give the families the cherries, greeting all the children by name and asking all the women—the men were working—little details about their families and their work at Arlington. Finally her cart was empty, and it was almost a half-mile walk back up to the house. Though it irritated her, Mary admitted to herself that she was tiring, so she drove the cart back home.

As she pulled up to the gracious portico, her maidservant

Bathsheba came hurrying out of the house, scolding with every breath. "There you are, all hot and wearied. Your hair all down, and your dress smudged all 'round at the hem! Ain't a bit of sense in you going wandering all over this place like a peddler, but can a body tell you that? No, ma'am!"

"No, ma'am," Mary smartly repeated as she climbed down from the cart. "I wasn't wandering, Bathsheba. I was going around to the quarters, taking everyone some cherries. It was a very pleasant walk."

As Mary went into the house, Bathsheba followed her, making shooing motions. Bathsheba had actually been Mary's nursemaid and was now a woman of forty, round and plump, with a jolly disposition, although she was often as severe with Mary as she had been when she was a willful child. As she followed Mary up the stairs, she said, "Now you knew you was having a caller this evening, Miss Mary, and what did you do? Go traipsing off and get hot and get your dress as dirty as an urchin, and what happened to those nice curls I did this morning?"

"They melted," Mary answered shortly. "I got hot. I want a sponge bath, Bathsheba, and then I'll change clothes. I still have plenty of time."

"No, you ain't," Bathsheba argued. "How is it you're such a smart girl, and you can't tell time for nothing? You know Mr. Robert is always right on spanking time to the minute, and you always keep him shuffling his feet and fidgeting, talking to your mama and daddy."

As they went into her bedroom, Mary turned and smiled mischievously at her maid. "Oh, Mr. Robert will wait," she said. "He always waits."

❧

Robert E. Lee passed the apple orchard, the overseer's house, Arlington Spring, and the dance pavilion and turned up the wide drive to Arlington Mansion. He felt like the object of a master's painting of a soldier riding at ease. He hoped he also looked the part.

Perfectly erect in the saddle, he sat the horse so easily it was as if they were one. He wore the dress uniform of a lieutenant in the United States Army, Engineer Corps. His gauntlets were of the softest yellow kid. A simple dark blue frock coat with a single row of brass buttons, the somber grandeur of a military uniform was evoked by the high collar with a wreath encircling the single star of a lieutenant embroidered in gold thread and heavy gold epaulettes. His trousers were plain blue, and he wore spotlessly shined boots. His spurs were gold. The US Army regulation hat for officers was a low-crowned, wide-brimmed blue with gold braid trim. It was called a "slouch hat," but there was nothing at all about Robert E. Lee that might be called slouchy.

At twenty-two years of age, Lee had reached full maturity. According to many young ladies he had become an exceedingly handsome man, but he was not so sure himself. His wide brow lay beneath black hair so thick and glossy and wavy that many women desperately envied it. His eyes were well set, of a brown so dark that sometimes they looked black. He had a straight patrician nose and a wide mouth, slightly upturned at the corners, which gave him a habitual expression of goodwill, though his jaw and chin were very firm.

Passing through the farm fields, he came to the grounds of the estate, which had been left so heavily wooded that it was called "The Park" rather than the grounds. Ahead he relished the first glimpse of Arlington House, as he had each of the many times he had visited this home. Set up on a gentle hill above the river, the wide veranda with eight great Doric columns made the house look more like a Greek temple than a private dwelling. It invoked a feeling of serenity and peace.

When he reached the house, a servant appeared to take his horse, and Colley opened the door to him. "Good afternoon, Lieutenant Lee," he said, taking his hat and gauntlets. "If you'll just come with me, suh." Colley led him into the drawing room.

George Washington Parke Custis and his wife Mary, who was called "Molly," greeted him warmly, and soon Robert was installed in a comfortable armchair, sipping a cherry ice.

As with all the rooms he had seen in Arlington House, he thought the parlor was elegantly appointed, the furnishings lavish, but it was still a comfortable room. The two tall windows had white linen shades, which were opened to the east. The fireplace had a brass fire screen fashioned as a peacock, with brass andirons in a holder with the same design. A large rectangular looking glass was over the George III chimney piece. A Dutch oak bookcase, a gold velvet camelback sofa with matching armchairs, and two William IV rosewood carved round tables made a comfortable corner for visiting.

"Mary will be down soon, Robert," Molly said. She was a pretty woman, with a blue-eyed-blond English look. "George bought enough sweet cherries for the entire plantation, and Mary took them around to everyone. She returned a bit later than she intended, I'm sure. I apologize for her tardiness."

"Please, Mrs. Custis, there's no need for apologies," Robert said, his dark eyes twinkling. "To know Miss Custis is to wait for Miss Custis. I would be afraid she was unwell if she were on time."

"'S truth." George Custis harrumphed. Short, balding, tending to plumpness, and generally of an amiable temperament, he still was impatient at times. "That girl will be late, no matter what I or her mother do or say. So, Robert, you cut quite a dashing figure in your shiny new uniform. Have you received any orders yet?"

"Yes, sir, I'm ordered to the Savannah River in Georgia, to Cockspur Island," he answered eagerly. "The US Army has decided to construct a fort there."

"Georgia?" Mr. Custis repeated darkly, as if he had never heard the word. "Cockspur Island? Sounds dreary and troublesome. I don't believe we have family in Savannah, do we, Molly?"

"The Edward Carter family and the James Randolph family

live in Atlanta," she said thoughtfully. "But no, I don't believe we are connected to Savannah."

George Custis was George Washington's step-grandson and a descendant of Baron Baltimore. The Parke and the Custis families were among the original colonists of Virginia. Mary Custis's maiden name was Mary Lee Fitzhugh. She was Robert's mother's cousin. The Parkes, the Custises, the Lees, and the Fitzhughs were all Founding Families, the aristocracy of America. George Custis in particular was so proud of his step-grandfather that he had collected much of George Washington's possessions and displayed them proudly at Arlington. Northern Virginia was his birthright, Arlington was his home, and he very rarely thought about any such obscure hinterlands as Savannah, Georgia.

Mary came in, tranquil and with slow grace in spite of the fact that she had kept Robert waiting, a breach of etiquette that she often committed with no apparent regret. Robert rose as she entered wearing a white dress patterned with small pink roses and a green sash encircling her small waist above the bell-shaped crinoline. Her cheeks were delicately flushed, her eyes were glowing, and the warmth in her smile of greeting was unmistakable. She held out both her hands, and he took them and bowed. "Mr. Lee! I'm so happy you called. It's good to see you again. How long will you be here this time? Where are you staying?"

Settling back in his chair, Lee replied, "I was just telling your mother and father that I'm assigned to Savannah, Georgia, but I don't have to report until the middle of November. I'm staying at Eastern View." This property was owned by one of his Carter cousins and was just outside of Alexandria, Virginia.

"Oh, good. Then you can call every day," Mary said with a mischievous glance at her father.

George Custis said, "Don't be foolish, Mary. Lieutenant Lee doesn't have time to call here every day and sit twiddling his thumbs waiting for you."

"Perhaps he does," Mary said. "Perhaps we should ask him."

She turned to him, eyes sparkling. "Mr. Lee? How is your schedule these days?"

"I've set aside plenty of time for thumb-twiddling," he replied. "I was sure to include it on my calendar, Miss Custis."

Molly Custis looked amused, while her husband made a slight grimace.

Robert knew Mr. Custis liked him and thought him a fine-looking man with an impeccable manner and noble bearing. But while the Lees were one of the most prominent families in Virginia, they were also poor, and Robert knew it was difficult for George Washington Parke Custis to envision the heiress of Arlington as living on an army lieutenant's pay. For years now the bond between Robert and Mary had grown from childhood friendship to one of mutual affection and esteem. Now that both were in their twenties, Robert knew the master of Arlington understood very well where his daughter's wishes lay, but Robert was not sure her father could be glad for her.

They talked for a while about small things: family, mutual acquaintances, and the army. As it grew later in the afternoon, Molly suggested, "George, I'd very much like to sit out on the portico and watch the sun set. Mary, Lieutenant Lee, perhaps you would care to join me?"

Mr. Custis decided to join them, too, and as the ladies collected their fans and instructed the servants to bring tea and cakes, he began to tell Robert about a new addition he had just acquired for the conservatory, a rare orchid.

As the four went out onto the veranda, Mary took Robert's arm, and the moment there was a lull in her father's raptures, she said, "Yes, Father, the orchid is interesting, and perhaps after we watch the sun set you might show it to Mr. Lee. But I noticed this morning that the last roses have bloomed, and I know he would like to see them."

"Yes, sir," Lee said instantly to Mr. Custis. "Perhaps you would give Miss Custis permission to show me your roses? Arlington

House is, after all, quite famous for the grounds and the gardens. I haven't toured the rose garden since last spring."

"Of course, of course," he said, smiling happily after Robert mentioned Arlington. "Mary, hurry on, so Lieutenant Lee can get the full benefit of the last light."

They walked down the steps and around to the north side of the house, where the large rose garden was situated. As they got out of the view of the veranda, without any signal passing between them, Mary clasped Robert's arm tighter and drew closer to him.

Robert slowed his pace so they walked very slowly down the rows of rosebushes. Though many of the bushes were already bare of flowers, some of them still had lush blooms on them. The garden's sweet scent enveloped them.

"You must miss your mother terribly, Robert," she said in a low voice of sympathy. "Please tell me, how are you coping?"

The last time she had seen him was at his mother's funeral, about a month and a half previously. Robert had nursed his mother through years of debilitating illness. "I do miss her very much," he said. "But she was a godly woman, and she is with her heavenly Father, well and whole and joyful. I couldn't wish her back." Brightening, he pointed to a red rose in full bloom, almost as big as a dinner dish. "That indeed is a glorious rose, Mary. Now I won't worry too much that I was exaggerating about Arlington's rose garden just so we might have a few moments alone."

"You? Exaggerate or prevaricate? Nonsense! There is not a shred of vanity or guile in you," she said, squeezing his arm. "And while I do understand that your code of honor as a gentleman would never permit you to even think of any dishonesty, I don't understand how you've kept from getting vain. You're perfectly lovely, Robert."

He flushed. "Men aren't lovely, Mary. I can't imagine why you would say such a thing about me. It's ridiculous."

"I think not. My cousin, Katherine Randolph, told me that she heard that at West Point they called you the 'Marble Model.' Perhaps I should call you that instead of lovely."

His face must have reflected a curious mixture of confusion, vexation, and embarrassment, as Mary laughed. "Never mind, Robert. I don't mean to embarrass you. If I did, I would have said that in front of my parents."

"Yes, I know, and I'm very grateful to you for sparing me that at least," he said with exasperation. Then, raising his eyebrows and cocking his head, he said, "I've heard gossip about you, too, Miss Custis. I heard that you've sent away several beaus this summer, among them congressman Sam Houston. And now the word is that Mr. Lynville Fitzhugh is actively courting you."

"Pah, he doesn't do anything *actively*," she said dismissively. "I understand that ever since Beau Brummel became an *arbiter elegantiarum*, languor of manner and contrived boredom are all the fashion on the Continent these days. I couldn't conceive of marrying such a silly man. Besides, he has a cast eye. And he's my cousin."

"Everyone in northern Virginia is your cousin, Mary," Robert said. "I'm your cousin."

"That's completely different," she said stoutly.

"How? Why?"

"Because you have the elegant and polished deportment of a gentleman, you are intelligent and accomplished and cultured, you are energetic and hardworking, and you don't have a cast eye," she finished triumphantly.

"I see," he said lightly. "I had no idea I was such a paragon. But I am beginning to see that it could definitely be to my advantage."

"To me you've always had many advantages over other men I've known, Robert," she said.

He stopped, turned, and took both of her hands. His dark, intense eyes searching her face, he said quietly, "And to me you've always been the most intriguing, the most charming, the most gracious, and the most captivating woman I've ever known."

"Do you mean that?" she asked breathlessly.

"Every word," he said firmly, "and every sentiment. But you

do understand, don't you, Mary, the position I'm in right now? I only graduated West Point in June. Now, thanks to the mercy and goodness of the Lord, my mother is at rest. I'm in the army, and I haven't even performed my first duty yet. I feel that I have a new life, and it is just beginning, just now."

"I understand, Robert," she said. "I understand everything. I'll be here, you know. When you've learned your new life, I'll be right here."

He bent to kiss her then for the first time, a mere brush of his lips against hers. When he raised his head, they exchanged brief smiles. Though it was unsaid by either of them, that kiss was a promise that they would keep.

CHAPTER TWO

Lieutenant Jack Mackay adjusted his wide-brimmed slouch hat so as to channel the heavy cold rain away from his neck. Then he continued the conversation. "But Robert, I really think my sister has become extremely attached to you. Don't tell me you haven't noticed!"

Lieutenant Robert E. Lee looked up quickly in alarm. "Jack, you don't think I've been misleading Miss Eliza, do you?"

"Of course not," he said dismissively. "And neither does she. But she does find your attentions very welcome. I can tell."

"I enjoy her company very much," Lee said, "and also Miss Catherine's. Both of your sisters are amiable and pleasant ladies." He resumed walking slowly along the earthen embankment, occasionally stopping to plunge a sharp stick into the side.

In the previous month, November, a gale had destroyed part of this earthen wall, and the site for the fort had flooded. Due to illness and then rambling bureaucratic shuffling in Washington, the major commanding the site was not there. It had been up to Lieutenant Lee to supervise the repair of the breach and to strengthen the entire protective mud wall. He inspected it several times a day when it was raining, even on a dismal and cold day such as this.

" 'Amiable and pleasant,' " his friend repeated. "That could be said of every lady of our acquaintance. Robert, I don't like to intrude, but may I ask you a question of a personal nature? Rude of me, I know, but I hope that you'll excuse me because of our long friendship."

Lee and Jack Mackay had been at West Point together, and they had been at Cockspur Island now for over a year. Somewhat to Mackay's surprise, Lee grinned at him. "You're going to ask me about why I've never courted anyone."

"Well, yes. Certainly you've had ample opportunity. The ladies all adore you. Barely notice I'm in the room when you're there," he added, grumbling.

"Nonsense," Lee said crisply. "Anyway, the answer to your admittedly rude, though forgivable question is that I have been courting a lady for a long time now."

Mackay nodded. "Miss Custis, isn't it? I know that every summer you spend most of your time up around Arlington House. And I know that you write her often."

"It is Miss Custis," Lee admitted readily. "It's always been Miss Custis."

❧

The new commanding engineer reported to Cockspur Island just after Christmas. By spring, he had made his best evaluation: the plan for the fort would not do, and it must be redesigned. In April, Second Lieutenant Robert E. Lee was reassigned to Fort Monroe in Hampton, Virginia. Although it was almost one hundred eighty miles to the gracious home on the hills above Alexandria, it was still much closer than Savannah, Georgia.

Lieutenant Lee reported to his new post on May 7, 1831. Now with certainty in his course, he secured a leave of absence and made his way again up that long slope to Arlington House.

It was a gorgeous day, balmy with occasional cool breezes that carried the sweetest scent of all, jasmine. The cherry trees and dogwoods in the park were blooming, their virginal white flowers bright against the cool green of new leaves. Northern Virginia was in her best dress, that of a sunny spring.

He was greeted happily by the family, at least by Mary Custis and Mrs. Custis. George Custis welcomed him but was perhaps a touch less effusive than his wife and daughter.

Lee, of course, noticed this, but it made no difference to him. He knew Mary Custis as well as any person on earth can truly know another, and her thoughts and desires were the only thing that mattered to him.

They sat on the veranda for a while sipping lemonade and talking mostly about Arlington, for Mr. Custis invariably brought the conversation around to his much-beloved home. As he and Lee talked, Mr. Custis soon warmed up to him, as he always did. Robert E. Lee was cordial and pleasant, and he had a quick and curious mind. He never feigned interest in any of Mr. Custis's topics, whether it was George Washington or some scheme Mr. Custis had for an agricultural enterprise or news of the economy in England. Lee was truly interested in all of these things and many more.

Robert was invited to dinner, and just after sunset, they all repaired to the dining room. As it was still cool in the evenings, a fire had been lit, but in Robert's opinion it did little to make the formal room more inviting. It was a magnificent room, grandly furnished. A very long Charles X mahogany table was centered in the room, covered with the finest French damask cloth. Intricately carved mahogany Chippendale chairs lined the walls, except for the four set at the table. An enormous George II serpentine-front sideboard was on one wall, the fireplace on the other.

A slave, dressed in a dark suit with a tailed coat, white vest, and spotless white gloves, stood behind each chair. Robert saw with an inward sigh that he was stranded at one end of the long expanse of the table. Mr. Custis said grace, and the servants began to prepare each dish for the diners from the sideboard.

Before her father could monopolize the conversation again, Mary asked, "Mr. Lee, please tell us about your new position. I've never been to Hampton Roads, though I've heard it's a most pleasant holiday spot."

"Hampton Roads may be, but I'm afraid Fort Monroe isn't quite as congenial," Robert said. "At least there is actually a fort, which is more than can be said for Cockspur Island."

"And what is to be your work there, Lieutenant Lee?" Molly asked.

"Construction on the fort itself is pretty well complete. It houses a garrison, and in fact, they have just begun artillery training there. But the outerworks still aren't finished, and it's been decided to build an adjacent fort just offshore, on a rock bank sunk in deep water. I'm rather excited about the project," he said, warming to the subject. "I do hope I'm assigned to work on the new fort, and not just finishing the outerworks on Monroe."

"Good heavens, Mr. Lee, you've practically spent the last two years chin-deep in that swamp in Georgia," Mary said spiritedly. "To this day I cannot imagine how you kept from dying, either from some noxious swamp fever or from catching a deathly chill in the winters."

"I must have a strong constitution," he said. "Do you know, I've never been ill in my life, except for the usual childhood things."

"Yes, I know," Mary said so assuredly that her father gave her a strange look. "But most mortal men do get ill at one time or another in such an environment. I'm glad that you'll be better situated at Fort Monroe. So since it sounds already well established, I assume that they have adequate housing there? You know, officer's quarters—and married officer's houses?"

George Custis choked slightly on a bite of roasted pork, Molly Custis smiled knowingly, and Mary stared at Robert, her eyes sparkling, her expression challenging.

Robert E. Lee was definitely a man to squarely meet a challenge. "Oh yes, Miss Custis. Naturally I was most interested in the housing available. I saw several homes for officers. In fact, I am very partial to one of them. It is small, but it could be made into a comfortable home, I think, with the right touch."

"A woman's touch, I'm sure you mean," Mary added mischievously.

"Of course. Could any house be called a home without the right woman's touch?" Robert said with aplomb.

At this Mr. Custis felt it was important to intervene, so the rest of the dinner conversation revolved around Arlington and tidbits of family news.

After dinner they retired to the formal drawing room, which adjoined the dining room. Mr. Custis talked to Lee for almost two hours. They found themselves talking about the Revolution, and about George Washington as a general, and of course about one of his most trusted young cavalrymen, General "Lighthorse" Harry Lee, Robert's father. As the men talked, Mrs. Custis sewed and Mary read.

At length Mr. Custis said he was going to go to his office and go over some papers and excused himself.

Mary laid aside her book, and Robert asked, "What are you reading, Miss Custis?"

"*Ivanhoe*," she answered promptly. "I like Sir Walter Scott very much. I know that you don't care much for novels, Robert, but would you please read to me? My eyes are growing a bit tired."

"It would be my pleasure," Robert answered. He had a low, melodious voice, and with his warm manner, listeners found his recitations very enjoyable.

"Chapter fourteen begins with a poem by Warton," Robert said, and quoted with feeling:

" In rough magnificence array'd
When ancient Chivalry display'd
The pomp of her heroic games

And crested chiefs and the tissued dames
Assembled, at the clarion's call,
In some proud castle's high arched hall.

Prince John held his high festival in the Castle of Ashby. . . ."

After he had read for about an hour and was about to begin a new chapter, Molly Custis said, "Lieutenant Lee, it is such a great pleasure to hear you read. But I'm sure you need some refreshment. Mary, why don't you take Lieutenant Lee into the dining room and get him something from the sideboard?"

"Of course, Mother," Mary said, rising and going toward the dining room.

Robert followed her, but they had only taken a few steps when Mrs. Custis said, "Mary?"

"Yes, Mother?"

Molly Custis never looked up from her sewing. Quietly she said, "I had Colley set up refreshments in the family dining room, dear."

"Oh?" Mary said in surprise. "Oh! Of course. Come along, Robert."

Instead of going back into the formal dining room, Mary led him across the hall to a much warmer, more pleasant room. It was a large room. Two-thirds of it was taken up by a plain rectangular wooden table that held six places. At the other end of the room was a cozy family parlor. It was a much more intimate setting than the grand drawing room.

Mary led him to the sideboard, took a plate, and put a piece of fruitcake on it. "Tea? Or—"

He put his arm around her, turned her to him, and drew her close. "Mary, I don't want to wait for tea or cake or anything else. I love you, Mary, I love you so much that I can't imagine life without you. Would you do me the very great honor of marrying me?"

"Finally," she murmured and put her arms around him. They

kissed, a long, lingering, sweet kiss.

Robert E. Lee and Mary Custis both felt a rush of joy, for at last they were home.

❧

Truth to tell, George Washington Parke Custis was hiding.

His office was more like a library—a comfortable room with a mahogany barrister's desk, three walls lined with filled bookcases, and a window that looked out on the lawn and the park. By this window in summer he placed his favorite chair, perhaps the only piece of furniture in Arlington House that was shabby. It was a solid leather wing chair, overstuffed, with a matching hassock. Mr. Custis could spend hours in this chair, reading, looking out the window onto his magnificent grounds, or dozing. But on this early morning, he sat uneasily, trying to concentrate on a Dickens novel, but more often looking out the window, his brow furrowed.

A peremptory knock sounded at the door. "Father?"

"Come in, Mary," he said resignedly.

She came in, and he noted that she was looking particularly well this morning, wearing a sky-blue dress and matching ribbons in her curled hair. Her color was high, and her dark eyes were fiery. "Father, I can't believe the way you treated Robert! How could you?"

He stood slowly, laid down his book, and said in a kindly voice, "Mary, dearest one, please come sit down with me. Please?"

She looked rebellious, but then relented and followed him to the corner by the fireplace, where there was a sofa and loveseat. She took her seat on the sofa, and her father sat by her.

Taking her hand, he said quietly, "I didn't refuse Lieutenant Lee, you know."

"I know that. It wouldn't have done any good if you had. What I don't understand is your attitude of clear reluctance, Father. Robert isn't offended, because he is so kind and understanding. But I am offended for him," she said ardently.

"Mary, I like Robert. No, that's not quite correct. I hold him in very high esteem. But I do have two objections to your marrying him. One I told him of, and we spoke of it at length. The other I said nothing about, but of course he would be aware of my concerns."

"It's all that malicious gossip about his half brother, isn't it?" Mary said with disdain.

"It's not just gossip, my dear. The story happens to be true," Mr. Custis said gently.

Robert E. Lee had an older half brother, Henry Lee, the son of "Lighthorse" Harry Lee's first wife, who had died. Henry Lee had inherited the Lee family mansion, Stratford, and had married a neighbor, a young woman of means. Her sister, a seventeen-year-old girl, had come to live with them. After the death of their first child, Henry's wife became addicted to morphine, and Henry and his wife's younger sister had an affair. All of this had happened many years previously, but it had only come out that year, because President Andrew Jackson had appointed Henry Lee as consul to Algiers. He and his wife, who had recovered from her addiction and reconciled with her husband, traveled there. But all of Henry Lee's past, instead of merely being whispered about, was now soundly denounced on the floor of the Senate, and every senator who voted went against his confirmation. He had moved to Paris that summer of 1830, and the couple now lived in obscurity there.

Mary argued, "I don't care if it is true. It has nothing whatsoever to do with Robert."

"But it's his family," Mr. Custis said. "Even his father, an esteemed general and friend of my grandfather's, with so many opportunities, went to debtor's prison and left his family penniless."

"Yes, it is a terrible thing what happened to Robert and his mother and brothers and sisters," Mary said evenly. "But his mother was a strong, determined, godly, loving woman who passed on all of those qualities to Robert. And she taught him self-reliance and frugality and self-control. His other, nobler qualities, like personal courage and sense of duty and honor are in his blood, Lee blood, and he is proud of it. It is an honor for me to marry this man, Father. Can't you see that?"

His eyes wandered to the window, that window that he had looked out on with such pleasure for over thirty years. "I suppose I do, Mary," he said at last. "You're right, of course. I've known Robert all of his life, and perhaps I have grown so accustomed to him that I have forgotten his finer qualities as a man." He turned back to her and continued in a tone now tinged with worry. "But Mary, he is poor, and I can't help but worry about that, and I addressed my objections to Lieutenant Lee. You've never been poor, child, you've no idea what it's like. You, living in officer's quarters in a fort? I tried to tell Lieutenant Lee that I would like to be allowed to help, but he—"

Mary burst out laughing. "Oh Father, dear Father. For a moment there I really thought you were coming to understand us. Don't you know Robert E. Lee at all? Don't you know *me*? Neither Robert nor I would ever accept your charity under any circumstances. And no, we didn't discuss this last night. Of course we talked about Fort Monroe and economies that would have to be made and so on, but neither of us ever mentioned asking you for help. We didn't have to. We both knew that it was impossible."

"But Mary, a fort?" he protested weakly.

"Yes, a fort," she said firmly. "And in spite of my ignorance, I happen to know that there are many people that are much worse off than that. I am so blessed, so exceedingly blessed, and I'm so happy! I want you to be happy for me, too, Father. I believe that in time you'll find that Robert will be just as treasured by you as if he were your own son."

He sighed. "That may be. He is a man that I admire, I freely admit. But it may take some time for me to be positively giddy about your marriage."

She squeezed his hand. "Not too much time, Father. Because I have told Robert that I've waited for him long enough. I refuse to have a long engagement. We're going to be married next month."

the SURRENDER

~

On June 30, 1831, Robert E. Lee married Mary Anna Randolph Custis at Arlington House.

It was a stormy day, and the Episcopalian minister had arrived soaking wet through and through. Mr. Custis loaned him some clothes that were ill fitting, but his vestments gave him an appropriate grand solemnity.

Robert waited by the fireplace in the formal drawing room. Six of his friends stood with him. About forty people, all of them relatives to one degree or another to the Lees and the Custises, were in attendance. He looked expectantly past them to the door into the dining room, where his bride, with her six attendants, was to enter.

Jack Mackay, his old friend from West Point and Cockspur Island, leaned forward and whispered, "Robert, it's the first time I've ever seen you look pale. Are you all right?"

Lee looked slightly surprised. "I'm pale? How very odd. No, I'm fine. I thought I would be more excited than this, but I feel only calm."

Mary's attendants started coming through, but Robert only had eyes for his bride. Somewhat to his consternation, she looked very nervous. He mentally made a note to write of this day later to a friend not in attendance:

> *The minister had few words to say, though he dwelt upon them as if he had been reading my Death warrant, and there was a tremulousness in the hand I held that made me anxious for him to end.*

But Mary recovered from her jitters as soon as the ceremony was over.

The happy couple stayed at Arlington for a week then started making the rounds of nearby friends and family, all of whom had large estates and gracious homes.

Robert E. Lee was the happiest of men. He and Mary had played together as small children, when he had come to love her as part of his extended family. They had teased each other and argued with each other and flirted with each other all through their teenage years. And now he was a man, and in the footsteps of the immortal Paul, he had put away those childish things.

He loved Mary Anna with a devotion and loyalty and respect so deep that it would never waver, never falter. He knew he was blessed, for he had married the greatest love of his life.

❧

Mary Anna had to admit that, despite her insistence of her worldly knowledge to her father, life at Fort Monroe came as a great shock to her. The enlisted men who were assigned to the artillery school were a raucous, belligerent bunch of men who got drunk as often as possible and fought with each other, reeling drunk or rock sober, almost every day.

Looking up from her book, she watched Robert with affection. He sat at his small camp desk, lit by a single lantern, sketching out mechanical drawings for breastworks. His handsome face was a study in total concentration, but it was not indicated by frowning or chewing his lip or any other facial gesture. He was expressionless, except for his intense gaze, and he was motionless except for his drawing hand.

The room was small, a tiny parlor that barely held a sofa, two armchairs, and Robert's desk. At the other end of the room was the kitchen, which consisted of a cookstove, three cabinets, and an oak table that served both as a worktable and a dining table. The door on the right-hand side of the room led to their bedroom, the only other room in the apartment. This shabby little second-floor flat was as far from Arlington House as two structures can possible be and still be called houses. But Mary didn't care about the house. To her, home was where Robert was, and that made her happy.

Robert finally looked up from his work. He rose and smiled

at his wife. He came to kneel by her chair and took her hand and kissed it. "You know, I knew that our home would be happy, no matter how much of a setdown it is from Arlington. But what I didn't really realize was what a good soldier's wife you would become. This life is so different from your world."

"You are my world, Robert," she said simply. "You have been my whole world for a long time."

He studied her then said warmly, "I love you, Mims. I thank the Lord for giving you to me. You are my treasure."

She smiled at him. "Robert, how would you like to have another treasure?"

"Hm? What?"

"An addition to our world. A small, noisy one that I fervently hope looks like you."

He took both her hands and stared up at her, his eyes so dark they looked ebony. "You're pregnant? We're going to have a baby?"

"Yes, we are," she said happily. "In September, I think."

Robert E. Lee laid his head down in her lap and, in quiet reverent tones, gave thanks to the Lord.

❧

He was born at the fortress on September 16, 1832. They named him George Washington Custis Lee.

To Mary's joy, even as a newborn, the boy had the aristocratic male handsomeness of the Lee men. Mary bore the birth well, and Custis was healthy.

In her journal she wrote:

The voice of joy, and the voice of gladness,
The voice of the bridegroom, and the voice of the bride,
The voice of them that shall say,
Praise the Lord of hosts:
For the Lord is good;
For his mercy endureth forever.

CHAPTER THREE

Life at Fort Monroe was pleasant for Robert and Mary. Robert's immediate superior was a man named Captain Andrew Talcott, and they made fast friends. He married one of Mary's cousins, a girl named Harriet Randolph Hackley, and the two couples enjoyed many good times: picnics in the summer, riding to Hampton Roads, and dinner parties.

But extremely good news came to the Lees in the fall of 1834, when he was assigned to Washington as assistant to the chief of engineers. That meant that they would only be across the Potomac River from Arlington. Though Robert tried to find suitable lodgings for them in Washington, it was impossible to find a nice home for a couple with a son in the overcrowded city. So he rode back and forth to work every weekday from Arlington, and though it was difficult, he and Mary were blissfully happy to be back at the gracious home.

Although Lee was happy with his home situation now, he intensely disliked his work. The politics in Washington—the bickering, the petty dislikes, the favoritism, the double crossing—

irritated to the extreme his finer sensibilities. And he was exceedingly bored with office work.

In the spring of 1835, a boundary dispute arose between Ohio and Michigan, and the young lieutenant eagerly applied to the Topographical Department to be assigned to the survey team. To his delight, his old friend Captain Talcott was commanding the team, and he immediately left Arlington for the Great Lakes.

Mary and two-year-old Custis were sorry to see him leave, but Mary knew very well how he felt about his clerk's position in Washington, though he never complained. She was pregnant again, right at six months when Robert left, but she was in good health. Custis was a strong and energetic child, and they were in the tender care of her parents and, of course, Bathsheba, who was like a lion with her cubs. And so Mary was happy for Robert, that he was able to get out in the field, which he loved.

The surveying mission lasted the summer, and the final determination wasn't made until late September. Robert had enjoyed the mission intensely; it was interesting, complex work, and Captain Talcott was a lively, obliging friend. They had even begun a friendly "rivalry" concerning their children, for the Talcotts had had a boy soon after Custis Lee's arrival, and then in winter of 1834, both Harriet Talcott and Mary Anna found they were expecting. Lee was "betting" he'd have a girl and Talcott would have another son, while the good-natured Talcott bet the opposite.

Robert E. Lee won the bet. In July, news reached him that Mary had given birth to a girl, whom they named Mary Custis Lee. Robert was concerned because the child was a bit earlier than they had predicted, and Mary's letters said she had not had such an easy time as before, with Custis. But she wrote that the baby was thriving, and though Mary was ill, it was nothing serious, and she was recovering.

In September, Robert brooded over her latest letter. The tone of the letter was lighthearted, with descriptions of the leaves turning their glorious fall colors, with Bathsheba's latest vocal antics, with descriptions of Custis's mischief and baby Mary's beauty. But Robert knew his wife as well as he knew his own soul, and he worried over the last paragraph:

> *I am not recovering as quickly as I would wish, for Dr. Waters says I have some sort of infection, and it vexes me to the extreme, for on some days I must remain bedridden. On the good days I enjoy little Mary and even Custis' rowdiness so much, I hate to miss a minute of their days. But don't trouble yourself, please, Robert, for I'm sure that by the time you're back home I shall be my old cranky self.*

Both Robert E. Lee and Mary regarded complaining as a personal weakness, and so he suspected that Mary was downplaying her illness. When he received his orders to return to Washington in October, he was much relieved.

❧

Mary stared at her reflection in the mirror. She was now twenty-eight years old, but she looked fifty-eight. Her face had gotten so thin in her prolonged illness that she looked positively gaunt, with deep purple shadows under her fever-dulled eyes. Her complexion had no hint of color; she was deathly pale.

Sighing, she looked at her hair. Not one strand could be cleanly pulled from the mass of tangles, no matter how long Bathsheba and her mother tried to brush it out. Her mouth tightening, she picked up a pair of scissors, grabbed a huge tangled mass, and cut it off. In only a few minutes she was surrounded by great hanks of hair, and what was left on her head stood up in bizarre spikes of different lengths.

"I don't care," she said defiantly to her sickly reflection. "It feels so much better." But walking from her bed to her dressing table—all of four steps—and cutting her hair had exhausted her. She rested her forehead on her hand for a few minutes before she made the effort to go back to bed.

The door opened and Bathsheba flew to her side. "Oh, Miss Mary! Look what you done! Oh, Miss Mary, how could you have cut all your pretty hair!"

"It wasn't pretty. It felt like I was lying on a scratchy wool rug," she retorted. "I'm glad I cut it. I already feel so much better, and I want it washed right now."

Bathsheba crossed her arms against her massive breast and said knowingly, "Mm-hmm. You look like getting your hair, or at least your head, washed right now. I better git it done in a hurry 'fore you fall over dead. You just had to get up and come over here and cut all your pretty hair off, didn't you? Me and your mama tole you ten thousand times not to try to get out of bed by your own self!"

Mary said wearily, "I am sorry now, Bathsheba, I admit. I'm not feeling too well. Would you please help me back to bed? Maybe after I rest awhile I'll feel more like having a bath."

Bathsheba almost carried her back to bed, which she could have done easily since Mary probably weighed no more than ninety pounds now. Tucking her in, Bathsheba clucked over her much as she had when Mary was a child. "You rest now, baby girl, and I'll go have Cook fix you some sweet creamed rice, and then we'll get you cleaned up, and I'll give you a nice alcohol rub. You know, Mr. Lee is comin' in tomorrow, so maybe you'll get a good night's rest and feel better when he gets here."

"I'll feel better when he's here anyway," Mary said. "I've missed him terribly."

"I know dat, and I know Mr. Lee's missed you something fierce, too," Bathsheba said soothingly. "So you just stay in this here bed, Miss Prance-About, till I come back to sit with you."

"I will," Mary promised.

Bathsheba bustled out, and Mary immediately fell into an exhausted doze.

She only rested for about half an hour, however, and woke up knowing that her temperature was rising, and that in about an hour she would have a debilitating fever. In her melancholy, a sudden thought came to her. She visualized her husband riding up to Arlington—his handsome, clean-cut features, his immaculate uniform, and the gladness and appreciation so plain on his face every time he came home.

And then she remembered that awful reflection in the mirror. She looked twice his age, old and ugly, and now her hair was grotesque. Even a ruffled housecap wouldn't cover the bald forehead and sides. What expression would she see on Robert E. Lee's "Marble Model" face then?

❧

Robert E. Lee loved his mare, Grace Darling. She could walk all day long over the roughest terrain and never jolt him. But she wasn't a racer; she couldn't travel at a strong canter for long. Nevertheless, he pushed her as soon as he reached the Arlington property and galloped right up to the wide portico.

A servant came rushing out of the house to take his horse, followed by Mr. and Mrs. Custis. They greeted him warmly, but he could tell that they both looked strained, and his heart plummeted.

Mrs. Custis said, "Please, Robert, come into the drawing room before you go up to see Mary. We'd like to talk to you."

He followed them into the room, and a maid offered him lemonade or a cordial, but he asked for iced water. Molly Custis seated herself on the sofa and patted the seat beside her for Robert to take. Mr. Custis stood in front of the fireplace, fiddling with the ornaments on the mantelpiece.

After Robert had had a few sips of water, Molly Custis said quietly, "Mary is very ill, Robert. She was adamant that when we wrote to you none of us would give you a hint about exactly how grave her condition is."

In a voice of pure misery George Custis said, "Dr. Waters says that she—that this infection—that—" He choked slightly.

Robert turned to his mother-in-law. She looked straight into his eyes and said, "Dr. Waters has prepared us for the worst."

Robert's eyes closed in pain, but in only a few moments he looked back at Molly. "No, I don't believe that Mary will be taken from us," he said firmly and clearly. "Deep in my heart I've always known that when God gave her to me, we would have a lifetime together." He stood up and went over to lay his hand on Mr. Custis's shoulder. "Sir, Mary has the strength of heroes' blood in her veins, and she has fire, and she has heart. Please don't mourn. Just pray for God's assurance and comfort."

Mr. Custis's head was down because he was fighting tears, and it embarrassed him. But he nodded.

George Custis had had a complete turnaround about Robert E. Lee in the three years that he had been married to his daughter. Mary's prophecy had been right. To him Robert had proved to be the best in a son—honorable, loyal, and as dutiful toward him and Molly as any son of blood could be. Robert even helped him tremendously with his complicated business affairs.

Robert asked, "But how is baby Mary? How is she faring?"

Molly smiled. "She is thriving, Robert. She's just fine. Apparently this infection that Mary is suffering from had nothing to do with her pregnancy or the birth, and it didn't affect baby Mary. Dr. Waters is of the opinion that Mary would have these abscesses whether she was pregnant or not."

Overwhelming relief washed over Robert like a dunking in clear, cool water. He felt guilty enough being away when Mary was ill, but if it had been caused by her pregnancy, he thought he would never be able to recover from the remorse. But his face merely showed relief, and he managed a small smile. "Then I'll go up to see my Mary now."

Molly said, "There's just one more thing, Robert, that I think I should tell you before you see her. Yesterday she cut her hair. It was terribly tangled and matted. Bathsheba and I both kept working on it, trying to get it combed out, but Mary didn't have the strength to let us brush it for long. Apparently it was so uncomfortable that she just cut it herself."

George Custis had recovered enough to say, "Looks like she whacked it off with a hatchet. Impetuous girl, always has been."

"And always will be, I suspect," Robert said. To the Custises' surprise, he looked amused. "But thank you for telling me first." He went upstairs to their bedroom, and the door was open.

Mary was sitting up in bed, wearing a pretty white ruffled bedjacket and a morning cap. She held her arms out, and he hurried to sit on the bed and pull her up into his embrace.

"How I've missed you, darling Mims," he whispered, kissing her cheek, her mouth, her forehead. "I try not to be impatient, but it seemed the days were endless, waiting until I could hurry home."

She pulled back from him and searched his face hungrily. Then she opened her mouth, tried to speak, but couldn't make the words come out. Swallowing hard, she tried again, and tears filled her eyes and began running down her cheeks in a flood. "I cut my hair!" she said, almost sobbing.

He gently drew her to him again, and she wept against his chest. She felt as fragile as delicate china. She was so thin, and her bones so small, yet her tiny body threw off heat because she had a fever. "I'm glad you did, my dearest, because I'm sure you're more comfortable."

"You are?" she asked dully. "But I look—"

"As beautiful as ever to me. Mary, you are the light of my life. How could I see anything but beauty when I look at that light?"

She cried a little more against his breast, but Mary was not a woman that dissolved into tears very often. Finally she pulled away from him and sat back against her pillows. "All of that salt water is going to tarnish your shiny brass buttons," she said drily. "I would hate for the impeccable Lieutenant Lee to have dull buttons on his uniform."

"So would I," Lee admitted. "But in this case I think you may be forgiven for tarnishing my buttons. Now, where is my daughter? I'm going to take care of you, my dear, from now on, but first I must see little Miss Mary Lee."

"I'm sure Bathsheba is listening outside the door," Mary said in a loud tone. "She'll take you to the next bedroom."

The door opened slightly, and Bathsheba said in an offended tone, "I was just waiting to make sure you didn't need anything, Miss Mary. Hello, Lieutenant Lee. We've just put the baby in the spare bedroom next door, and Master Custis is waiting to see you, too."

The sturdy three-year-old Custis ran to his father and grabbed him around the knees.

Lee bent to hug him fiercely. "Is this my son? This big sturdy lad? Let me look at you. You are a fine-looking boy, aren't you? Have you been a good boy?"

"I'm good sometimes," he said in his little-boy lisp. "But Mother says sometimes I'm not, sir."

"I see," Lee said. "Well, now that I'm home, we can talk about all of that, man-to-man."

Custis brightened. "Yes, sir. Please, sir."

Lee went over to the crib where the sleeping baby lay. She was four months old now, and already Lee could see the long thin nose and the stubborn chin. She opened her eyes and considered him gravely. He picked her up, and she kept her eyes trained on his face.

"Come along, son," he said to Custis and went back into Mary's bedroom and sat on the bed.

Mary managed a smile at her son and patted the other side of the bed. Eagerly he climbed up. "How do you feel, Mummy?" he asked worriedly.

"I am already feeling much, much better since your father is here," she said, glancing at Robert. "I know I haven't been able to see you much lately, Custis, but soon I'll be well and we'll be able to go out in the sled when we have our first snow, and we can visit your friends, and we'll have a wonderful Christmas."

"That's right," Robert said. "Baby Mary's first Christmas is going to be a happy one. She's just beautiful, Mary. She looks like you."

Tears welled into her eyes again but didn't fall. "Thank you, Robert," she said simply.

"No, thank you, wife," he answered. "Now, as soon as you feel strong enough, Mims, we're going to Berkeley Springs, in Bath. I think it will be so good for you. I don't know much about the medicinal properties of the springs, but I know that a holiday in the mountains will be a treat for all of us."

"All of us?" Custis repeated quickly. "May I go, too, sir?"

"Of course," Robert answered. "All four of us, my beloved family, are all going. I've been away so long I couldn't think of being separated from you again anytime soon."

❧

Mary was very ill indeed, and it was the next year before she was able to travel to the old hot springs resort. The town was named Bath after its English sister city, founded by her father's grandfather, George Washington.

In all the long months of her illness, Robert E. Lee had cared for her day and night, just as he had cared for his mother for most of his teens and early twenties. These two women, though they were weak and sickly in body, imparted to Robert E. Lee some of the most forceful and virtuous qualities that are found in the best of men. He learned self-sacrifice, the highest form of that virtue in that he was never conscious of it. Putting others before himself became such a natural part of the fiber of his being that it was difficult for him to recognize a lack of it in others.

Though his father, "Lighthorse" Harry Lee, had been a man of audacious courage and fiery élan, Harry was an undisciplined man, flighty and careless in business and in caring for his family. He had died when Robert was eleven, and during Robert's life he had barely known his father, for Harry Lee was always traveling and had spent more than two of those years in debtor's prison. Anne Carter Lee had raised her children practically single-handedly. In stark contrast to her husband, she was intelligent, level-headed, dutiful, and loving. She taught Robert frugality without being poor-mouthed; the visceral rewards of always fulfilling any duty, no matter how small, to the utmost; a Christian warmth and care for others; and above all, self-control.

For all his life, when Robert E. Lee's closest friends were describing him, the two words they most often used were *honor* and *duty*. These two excellent virtues were the primary forces of Robert E. Lee's character.

The years of 1835 and 1836, when Mary was so ill, became a clear turning point in Lee's life. Always before he had had a lively disposition, much given to teasing and laughing heartily at jokes he found funny, his demeanor generally bright and cheerful. After the Lees returned to Arlington from Bath, a friend wrote, "I never saw a man so changed and saddened."

But because of his unselfishness and his iron self-control, Lee never showed any hint of distress or upset to Mary or his children. With them he was always happy, buoyant, playful, and merry.

It was with others that his demeanor, while not cold, became more dignified and decorous. Always gallant with the ladies and unfailingly delighting in the company of children, he nevertheless had an air about him that set him apart from other men. And because of the noble qualities that had been so firmly set in him by his mother, and the genuine deep love and caring that he had learned from his life with Mary, he did indeed become a man above other men.

CHAPTER FOUR

Mary Lee wrote in her journal:

July 1, 1848. Although Robert only returned two days ago, he has been ceaselessly playing with the children. Tonight, again, he is allowing them to stay up very late, telling them stories.

She looked up from her writing to watch her family. Mary had borne Robert seven children in fourteen years. Now Custis, the eldest, was fifteen years old, while baby Mildred was only two. Blissfully "Milly" sat on her father's lap, resting her head against his broad shoulder. It was the first time she had met her father.

As Mary's gaze rested on her daughter, Mary Custis, she sighed. At thirteen Mary was blooming, and she was turning into a lovely young girl. She was hearty, too, the healthiest one of the four girls. It was odd that she had been born so strong, since her birth had been a nightmare for Mary. It had been after Mary Custis's birth that Mary had cut her hair. A small smile touched her lips as she recalled that even then Robert had insisted that his wife was beautiful.

SURRENDER

Custis and Mary sat on side chairs next to Robert's armchair. The other children, except for Milly, sat on the floor around their father's footstool.

Rooney was eleven, a fine strapping boy who from the time he was first able to talk had insisted he was going to be in the army like his father. When he had been eight years old, they were stationed at Fort Monroe, and Rooney had decided he was going to go to the stables, where they were bringing in a load of hay for the horses. He proceeded to grab a straw cutter to help trim the stalks and managed to cut off the tops of his left forefinger and middle finger. It was an hour and a half before a doctor arrived. He had sewn the tips of Rooney's fingers back on, and they had mended with no muscle damage or nerve damage. The officers present had marveled at the young boy, who sat stoically on a hay bale waiting for the doctor, bleeding profusely, without a word of complaint or any sign of pain. He was very much like his father, and he was as handsome as Robert E. Lee, too.

Next in ages had come "The Girls" as the family called them, for they were only eighteen months apart in age, and Robert and Mary had purposely named them as one might name twins: Annie and Agnes. Annie had been born with a reddish-pink birthmark on her face, and Mary reflected that that might have made a girl very shy. But her father affectionately called her "Little Raspberry" and told her all the time how pretty she was, so she had grown to be outgoing, vivacious, and mischievous unfortunately. At five years old she had been playing with a pair of scissors and had sliced part of her left eye and eyelid. Her vision was not much damaged, only the peripheral vision in that eye, but the accident had left a ropelike scar on her eyelid and socket. Still, it seemed that her father had made her feel so secure that she didn't seem to let her disfigurement affect her. She had been delighted when her sister Agnes was born. In fact, Annie had left off playing with any of her dolls, for Agnes had been her "baby doll" until she was a year old. The two girls were as close as twins.

Robert E. Lee Jr. was now five years old, and of all her children, Mary knew he was going to be the most trouble for her. In fact, he already had been the rowdiest child, ever since he started to walk at ten months old. From that day he was into something, anything, hiding from servants and his mother and grandparents, running in the house, yelling at the top of his lungs, balking at food he didn't like, often attempting to hide green peas under his plate. However, on the rare times his father had been present, Rob behaved perfectly.

Now Rob was taking his turn tickling his father's feet. Robert loved taking off his slippers and socks and having the children tickle his feet as he told stories. They liked for him to read to them, too, but they enjoyed it most when he dramatized the stories. On this warm July evening he was telling them the grand story of "The Lady of the Lake," basically paraphrasing the poem by Sir Walter Scott, for the language was too difficult for the younger children. However, he often quoted memorable simple passages.

Mary thought that this poem, above all, represented all things that Robert loved. It was a story of chivalry, of true nobility, of familial love and loyalty, of self-sacrifice, and of course, of bravery and courage in war.

Just then Robert lifted his head and quoted in deep ringing tones:

"And the stern joy which warriors feel
In foemen worthy of their steel!"

Mary thought with a touch of regret, *That's the part of him I will never understand—the warrior. He is so gracious, so warm and kind, so gentle. I suppose no person, man or woman, who is not born a soldier can understand that stern joy.*

All at once, Rob, Agnes, and Annie all started talking loudly. "Papa, don't stop! More story about Ellen and Roderick and Malcolm! Please, Papa!"

With mock gravity he said, "Rob has been lax in his duties. He stopped tickling my feet. No tickling, no story."

Mary laughed with the children, marveling at the difference in Robert E. Lee's public persona and his playful demeanor with his family. No matter what problems arose, no matter what the circumstances, he was unfailingly jovial with them, teasing her as much as he ever did when they were young, playing even infantile games with the youngest children, laughing with delight at their antics.

Rob resumed his duties, and Agnes pitched in by taking one foot while Rob took the other. Lee started his spellbinding story again.

Mary returned to her journal:

> *Robert is telling the children the story of "The Lady of the Lake," and my thoughts went back to the nightmares I've had for the last twenty months since Robert went to fight the Mexican War. I always knew that being a soldier's wife would mean moving often, postings to strange and lonely places, being away from home. But what I didn't understand until 1846 was what it was like to be a soldier's wife when he was in war. It was agonizing, struggling daily—sometimes hourly—to stop thinking of Robert getting wounded or even killed. I pray, dearest Father God, that my husband will never have to fight a war again. Thank You, my Lord, for this homecoming was of all most blessed.*

Even as she wrote the words, she thought that this time may actually have been the most difficult for Robert himself. Mary, who had never been completely healthy in the years since Mary Custis had been born, had grown steadily weaker in body in the last two years. Though she had downplayed her decline in her letters to Robert—as she always did—by the time he returned, rheumatism had so drastically invaded her right side that she was barely able to walk, and often she couldn't write or paint.

She knew it had been a shock to him when he had first seen her. But the only way she knew it was because she was his wife, and in the seventeen years they had been married they had in many ways become two halves of a whole, and she knew him as well as she knew her own soul. His face showed nothing but joy and love when he greeted her, but deep in her spirit Mary knew he was grieved. As she was, for she knew that Robert had spent most of his young life caring for his invalid mother. And now his wife was an invalid. But Mary was determined that she would do all that she could, for as long as she could.

Though the servants and the older children had begged her to get a wheeled chair, she flatly refused. She knew that day was coming, but until it did, she courageously either walked with help or even with crutches on the days she was strong enough to manage them. She was even beginning to teach herself to write with her left hand, though on this night she wrote in a strong script with her right. In fact, she had felt very well the last couple of days—probably because Robert was home.

Idly she leafed back through the previous pages of her journal. Mary didn't write in it every day. By nature she was a gregarious person, taking after her father, who loved having a busy social life. Mary took great interest in all her friends and extended family, and she loved receiving visits from them and visting them. She concerned herself with all parts of their lives, not in a busybody way but because she truly cared for their well-being and wished happiness for all of them. She also loved nature, taking long walks, studying the flora and fauna of the Park, and tending all the gardens, even the kitchen vegetable patch.

Her painting was probably her favorite pastime, and she was extremely talented in landscapes and still life, both in oils and watercolors. It irritated her that she had no aptitude at all for portraiture, but then she thought wryly that perhaps that was a good thing, for if she were good at it, she would probably never do anything but portraits of her handsome husband.

the SURRENDER

Mary was an active, busy woman, and oftentimes her journal was the last thing she thought of, especially since Robert had left for Mexico. During that dark time the only private thoughts she had were of fear, and she had no desire to journalize such things. She turned back to 1847, where she had written a short entry:

This was reported in the Richmond Times.

A newspaper clipping was pressed between the pages:

General Winfield Scott, commander of the Army in Mexico, is quoted here in an excerpt of his battle reports to the War Department in Washington. Colonel Robert E. Lee, married to Mary Randolph Custis Lee of Arlington House, was particularly singled out by his commanding officer:
I am impelled to make special mention of the services of Captain R. E. Lee. . . . This officer, greatly distinguished at the siege of Vera Cruz, was again indefatigable during these operations, in reconnaissance as daring as laborious, and of the utmost in value. Nor was he less conspicuous implanting batteries and in conducting columns to their stations under the heavy fire of the enemy.

The only other entries Mary had made during the Mexican War were:

Commissioned August 1846, Major, for gallant and meritorious conduct in the battle of Cerro Gordo.

Commissioned August 1847, Lieutenant Colonel, for gallant and meritorious conduct in the battle of Churubusco.

Commissioned September 1847, Colonel, for gallant and meritorious conduct in the battle of Chapultepec.

And now, she thought with satisfaction, he was showing his gallant and meritorious conduct to his family, at his own home.

∿

In a couple of months, Mary took her journal and sketchbook and paints and crutches to Baltimore, where Robert was stationed for construction of a new fort on Soller's Flats, which would become Fort Carrol. He was pleased Mary enjoyed their time there—which turned out to be four years—for they were close enough that they could visit Arlington often, and they had many friends and the ever-present Fitzhugh, Carter, Hill, and Lee cousins in Baltimore.

In September of 1852, Colonel Robert E. Lee was appointed as superintendent of the United States Military Academy at West Point. He was a superb administrator, but he was an even better leader of young men. The classes that were fortunate enough to attend the Academy during his tenure were better educated, better disciplined, and had a more deeply ingrained sense of honor and duty than ever before. Mary loved it, too, for she mothered all of the young cadets, while her husband was to them the best in a father, strict but always fair.

The only thing that marred their three years there was the death of Mary's mother, Molly Custis. Since Robert had been young, she had loved him like a son, and now he mourned her almost as much as he had mourned the loss of his own mother twenty-four years earlier. The entire Lee family missed her terribly, and Mary and the older girls made several prolonged trips to Arlington to take care of her father, who was desolate.

But 1854 was a good year, for in June George Washington Custis Lee—Robert and Mary's eldest son—graduated from West Point at the head of his class. Both of them were very proud of him, for he had become a brilliant scholar; a dedicated, well-disciplined cadet; and a strong and purposeful man. All these qualities made Robert E. Lee especially proud of his son. He never realized that all of Custis's best qualities were mirror images of his own. Born to follow in his father's footsteps, he immediately joined the Engineer Corps.

Though he thoroughly enjoyed his role as an educator and life-teacher of young men, Robert E. Lee's second love, after his wife and family, was the army. In 1855, because of the increasing Indian uprisings in the West, Congress authorized the formation of two new regiments of infantry and two of cavalry. Colonel Robert E. Lee had high hopes, though he said nothing to his wife. On March 13, 1855, Albert Sidney Johnston was named colonel of the new 2nd Cavalry, and Robert E. Lee was named lieutenant colonel, as his commission as a colonel was brevet only.

To Lee, service in the line meant a healthful, vigorous outdoor life, which he loved. The superintendency at West Point was a high honor, but it was mostly confining and dull office work.

In April, Mary and her younger children moved back to Arlington. Though he would miss his Mary, for the 2nd Cavalry was to be sent to Texas, he was glad his family would be back at Arlington House. Although Robert and Mary had made each little place they had lived into their own home, they both now regarded Arlington as their true home, the center of their family, regardless of where they lived or where Robert was assigned.

Since Molly's death, George Custis had been terribly lonely, and he often complained that he didn't feel well. He was in very good health, however, so Mary and Robert knew that his ailments were mostly from emotional upset. Robert did not, perhaps, love his father-in-law as deeply as he had loved Molly Custis. But he was very devoted to Mr. Custis and felt a son's duty toward him. He, too, was glad that his wife and girls would be at Arlington House with his father-in-law. As a conscientious and caring son, he determined that George Washington Parke Custis should never again be left alone.

❧

The Indians were courageous and daring fighters, but they were not stupid. They would attack small villages and single homesteads and a group of farmers that might be daring enough to hunt them. But they weren't foolish enough to attack a numerous force of trained professional soldiers in the field. In April of 1856, when Colonel Robert E. Lee reached what he was to call his "Texas home"— desolate and crude Camp Cooper, more than 170 miles from the nearest fort—all the Comanches had disappeared, fleeing farther west to hide in the mountains.

At this time Lee was charged with the most unpleasant and troublesome task he ever knew in the army: court-martial duty. Dispensing justice, which must at all times be perfectly fair and impartial, was an onerous burden for a man like him.

Robert E. Lee was apparently born with true aristocratic sensibilities, without the usual accompanying qualities of superciliousness and vanity. He believed that all men were created equal before God, but he also knew that all men must be governed by rules.

Robert E. Lee's rules were in truth a high and noble code of honor, which few men could ever attain, but because of his modesty he never realized that. In his mind men made choices, and often the choices they made were not the correct ones, and then they disobeyed the rules and must bear the consequences. But they, like he himself, were simply on a journey toward harmony with the Lord, and people were in different places along that long road. At heart he was a simple man.

❧

"I believe that Texas dust is probably the best, most comprehensive and complete dust there is," Major George H. Thomas announced grandly.

Colonel Lee chuckled. "Do you, now? I was unaware that it was of such exalted quality, although I'm sure I've dealt with a ton or so of it about my person and belongings in the last two and a half years."

"Oh yes, it has to be the ultimate, as dust goes. It comes in all colors, from orange-red to dull gray; all textures, from gravelly grit to the finest sand. Regardless of its composition, it's able to invade every single object that exists, from your mouth and eyes and ears to your books and clothes and coffeepot. And it never dies. It only disappears temporarily when you brush it away and then returns as soon as you put your brush away."

"The same dust, you think?"

"And its cousins."

They rode in silence for a time. Both men were saddle weary, for this was their third day of hard riding. George Thomas, at thirty, was a full twenty years younger than Robert E. Lee, but he slumped in the saddle, his shoulders rounded wearily, his hands limp on the slack reins. As always, Lee kept a beautiful, erect posture in the saddle, and his eyes and face were alert and watchful, continually scanning the empty desert landscape.

Now Lee stood up in the stirrups, shielding his eyes from the blazing setting sun on his right. "I think I see the willow bank ahead. It should be Comfort Creek."

"Thank heavens!" Thomas exclaimed. "The little pool there is the only place within five hundred miles of here to get a good bath." Sitting up straighter, he said, "What do you say, Colonel? I think the horses may not mind a little gallop for a long cool drink of water."

The two broke into a canter that brought them to the creek, a welcome oasis on the hard-bitten plains of south Texas. Willows lined the banks of Comfort Creek, providing a cool, freshly scented shade beside the bubbling cheerful stream. An old tributary splashed over a six-foot-high ridge to form a pool that through the ages had gotten to be several feet deep. It was indeed the most welcoming stop for weary travelers between Fort Mason and San Antonio.

When they reached the banks, both of them dismounted and let the horses wade out into the cool water. They knelt, splashing their faces and drinking deeply.

Through Lee's silver beard, droplets of water trickled, turned crimson by the glare of the dying sun. He stood and faced due west, narrowing his eyes. "The dust is cruel, Major Thomas, but I think that it is the reason for these spectacular sunsets. I've never seen anything like them."

"Neither have I," Thomas agreed, wetting his gold neckerchief and scrubbing his face with it. "And I'll treasure the day I see the last one of them in this country."

Lee waded over to his horse, the solid, hardworking mare named Grace Darling, led her to the bank, and began unsaddling her.

Thomas joined him. "Don't you agree, Colonel Lee? Surely of all of us you have the most reason to despise this place."

"I? The most reason? Why should that be?" Lee asked, puzzled.

Thomas grimaced. "Because of this court-martial duty. I know it must be most distasteful to a man of your sensibilities."

Lee shook his head, easily lifting the heavy saddle from the mare's back and placing it up against a deadwood log on the bank. It would be his pillow for the night. "Somehow you've got the wrong idea, Major Thomas. The only sensibilities I have about being a tribune are the responsibility I feel for the men being tried, and that their rights are fully respected, and that justice, fair and impartial, is done them. This is my duty as I see it, and there is no question of finding an honorable duty distasteful."

Thomas put his saddle next to Robert's, and they began currying the horses. Both the mare and Thomas's gelding were covered with foam and grit. Thomas said, "But wait, Colonel. You said your responsibility to the men being tried? What does that mean? Surely you feel no responsibility to those men? You don't even know them!"

"That makes no difference," Lee said. "God has placed me in a position of authority over them. Having authority over another person makes you responsible for them. Certainly there are degrees of responsibility, according to the situation, but one must always be mindful that with any power comes grave responsibility."

"But what can you do?" Thomas demanded. "You can't possibly influence these men in any way or even help them."

Lee said quietly, "I can pray for them."

After a short silence, Thomas rasped, "Oh. Shot me right between the eyes, Robert. Again."

Lee grinned. "You're just a bumptious youth, and you need advice from your elders."

"Hmph!" Thomas grunted. "You never gave anyone advice in your life, and now I guess I can see why. The responsibility, eh? Aw, I don't want to talk about this anymore. The trouble with you, Colonel Lee, is that you refuse to complain. It's just like with the dust. I spend half my time here grumbling about it, and all you have to say is that it makes for beautiful sunsets. But you can't possibly like it here. Can you?"

"I don't like anywhere that's away from my wife and family," Lee said quietly. "And I like anywhere I am with them. If they were here, I would be perfectly content."

They finished brushing out the horses and let them graze on the raggedy prairie grass growing underneath the willows. Both men bathed in the pool, spluttering and shivering a little.

It was the first week in October, and although the days were still burning hot, the nights were cool. They made a campfire, and Major Thomas fixed them some gravy in a small frying pan he carried. One of the ladies of Fort Mason had given them a dozen biscuits for the five-day ride to San Antonio, and in this arid country they kept well.

After eating and doing the little bit of washing up, they spread out their bedrolls, leaned up against the saddles, and gazed up at the millions and millions of stars in a perfect moonless night.

"This is another thing I like about Texas," Lee murmured. "This land, it's so flat that the sky seems to go on for eternity. Very little of earth, much of the heavens."

"Despite all that nonsense about you being my elder, I have learned a lot from you, Colonel," Thomas admitted. "There is a certain stark beauty here, if you look. I guess I haven't bothered. But I will."

Lee nodded. "Then you'll see it. And it helps a man to know

there's beauty around him, especially when he's lonely."

"So you are lonely?"

"Oh yes, there's no shame in that. A man's not complete without his wife and children with him. Anyway, by the time we get back, I should have several letters waiting for me," he finished, smiling. "The next best thing."

Two days later, on October 21, Robert reached headquarters in San Antonio, and the first thing he did was check his mail. He only had one letter waiting for him, and it was not the next best thing. His father-in-law, George Custis, had died suddenly on the tenth of October after a short severe illness. Colonel Robert E. Lee asked for leave and started the long journey back to Arlington.

CHAPTER FIVE

It was the saddest homecoming of all.

Robert E. Lee reached Arlington on November 11, 1857, a month after his father-in-law had died. The funereal pall cast by George Custis's death still remained over Arlington. Even the slaves mourned.

Mary, dressed in black from head to toe, was melancholy in her greeting to her husband. "It was so abrupt," she said as they talked in the family parlor. "I still feel much of the first shock. Countless times a day I think that he's still here."

Lee took her hand—her left hand. Her entire right side had become so crippled by arthritis that she was almost paralyzed, and she was in constant pain. The realization had been an additional blow to Robert, for she had, as always, downplayed the severity of her condition in her letters to him. He hadn't seen Mary or his children for twenty-one months. Sadly he realized that his wife was now an invalid.

"It's not surprising that you still feel him here. He was such a part of this home, our home," he said. "I think that we'll always be reminded of him here, and I know that in time the Lord will give us His perfect comfort so that the memories will be joyful. But it will take time, dearest."

She nodded and grasped his hand tightly. "You're right, of course. Oh Robert, in spite of the circumstances, I'm so very glad you're home! I've missed you terribly. This is the longest time we've been separated since we were married, you know."

"I know all too well. I've been very lonely without my Mims. But now I'll be here for a long while. I've been granted six months' leave, and I promise you that I'll work very hard to make sure Arlington remains our beloved home."

A quick spasm of pain crossed her face as she moved to stroke his hand with her swollen, misshapen right hand. But she managed a small smile. "Robert, wherever you are is my most beloved home."

Six months' leave was not nearly long enough. George Custis had left an extremely complicated will, and Robert E. Lee was the executor. Custis had several other properties besides Arlington, and he was what was called "land poor," a common condition when people had large tracts of land and sometimes several homes but had very little ready cash.

Mr. Custis's will also stipulated that all his slaves be freed within five years of his death. Lee approved of this in principle, but he found it impossible to implement immediately. As it turned out, Lee had to take over two years' leave to straighten out the Custis legacy, and it took all his time, energy, and the meager savings he had managed to accumulate. Those two years, from winter to winter, 1857 through 1859, were perhaps the bleakest of his life.

Although he was on extended leave, Colonel Lee was, by General Winfield Scott's order, considered on "active duty" because he still held the position of a military tribune and attended several courts-martial in the two years at Arlington.

Late in May of 1859, he returned from a trial at West Point, and to his surprise and pleasure he saw that Mary was sitting out on the veranda, and she had shed her mourning clothes to wear a light blue muslin dress with satin trim. He rode up and dismounted and hurried to lift her hand to his lips and bow to kiss it. "Mrs. Lee, you look as pretty as nature herself today!"

"Get on with you, silly man," she scoffed, but her expression was pleased. "Such foolishness."

"I have many faults and failings, but I don't believe I'm a fool," he said lightly. "I'm going to wash and change. Do you think that you'll be able to wait here for me?" He could still be quite boyish, at least with Mary.

"I'm staying here until night falls," she said firmly. "Perhaps it's the benevolent weather, but I feel much better today, and I want to enjoy the outdoors as long as possible."

He hurried off and soon returned. Arlington had several cane lounge chairs and glass-topped tables for the veranda, and he and Mary sat companionably close together by a table that held lemonade and tiny sandwiches. Robert ate two of the triangles then reached for a third. "Is this one that fish kind?" he asked, lifting it to his nose.

"Can't you tell? They do have such a distinctive odor," Mary teased.

"Yes, I know, but after you've had one you can't smell them anymore. I forget, what is this fish kind?"

"Anchovy paste. This half of the platter is anchovy paste, and the other is cucumber for me. Don't worry, I'm not going to take your sandwiches, Robert, and I'll thank you to stay out of mine."

"Yes, ma'am," he said obediently.

They both ate for a while, and then Mary asked, "How was the trial?"

Robert grew sober. "It was disheartening, Mary. I suppose they all are. But when the defendants are officers, and supposedly gentlemen, I find it so distresses me. It is very difficult for me to understand how these young men can behave so irresponsibly."

"Yes, Robert, I know that you find it difficult to understand," Mary said quietly. "That is because you have never done an irresponsible thing in your life, and I doubt that you ever will. In fact, I doubt that you could even think of something feckless to do. It's not in your nature."

"I could be feckless," he said mockingly. "I can be, right now. Watch this." He took one of the little triangular sandwiches and threw it out onto the drive. "See? See how irresponsible and capricious that was?"

Mary laughed, and Robert reveled in it. Though she was not ill-tempered, she rarely laughed out loud, mainly because she was so clever it took something very witty or absurd to amuse her.

"It was, Robert, and I am shocked to the core of my being!" she said, her dark eyes sparkling. "I'm so proud of you!"

"Are you? Gracious, I must be monstrously boring if it takes something like that to make you laugh."

"Don't worry, I laugh at you all the time, dear. You just don't know it," she said slyly. "No, you are not at all boring."

"I'm gratified to hear it."

"Good. Now that I've complimented you for the day, I'm going to proceed with telling you what to do."

"Now I know that we have indeed returned to normal." He sighed. "What can I do for you, my dear?"

She looked out over the gracious Park. "Do you remember when Father used to have the spring sheepshearing here?"

"Of course. It was such fun. And he would always use President Washington's tent and display all of the artifacts."

"Yes, and we did it for so many years. I know that Father truly enjoyed the party, but I don't think he could actually bring himself to have such a large party after we got married, and I wasn't here to help."

"I'm sure that's true," Robert agreed. "He did love social events, parties and dinners and outings, but I know that you and your mother were always the ones to plan and organize them. So, Mims, you want to have a sheepshearing?"

"No, I don't think people have sheep as they used to. But I would like to have a party in the Park, with dancing at the pavilion. And like the old sheepshearing days, I'd like to make it semipublic, instead of simply by invitation. You know, word used to get around quite easily. I think if we choose the date carefully, we can get the boys here."

All four of the Lees' daughters were at Arlington, although thirteen-year-old Milly was attending daily academy in nearby Alexandria. Custis was in the army. Rooney had married, and he and his wife were living at White House Plantation, a property left to him by George Custis. Rob, now sixteen, was at boarding school.

"I long for us all to be together again," Robert said. "Christmas was so wonderful this year."

Mary looked down, and her crippled hands clasped in her lap. "And I think we both would enjoy a big party and seeing all of our friends and family, Robert. To forget for a while our troubles."

He nodded. "You're right, Mims," he said quietly.

His eyes searched the city beyond, across the Potomac River, and he thought of the chasm of differences between the politicians there, the underlying hostility between abolitionists and the men representing the Cotton South. Lee abhorred politics and paid as little attention to the political matters of the day as he could possibly manage and still stay knowledgeable. But he could see that the slavery issue was slowly going beyond politics, and the chasm was growing dangerously wide and deep. It was beginning to dawn on him that that rift may in fact cause a tearing asunder.

He dreaded to think of it, and he shunned too much reverie on the subject. And so he agreed with his wife, though the troubles he wished to escape from were not just those of managing Arlington and in fulfilling all of George Custis's last wishes. He wished to escape the creeping fear that it may be his world that was in danger of being torn asunder.

◦⁖

"Marse Robert," Perry said apologetically, "I found Miss Mildred over there in the apple orchard. And she's climbing a tree."

Robert merely sighed, but seated next to him Mary rasped, "Good heavens, Robert! How is it that all of our children are full-grown, but they're still like a flock of wild geese!"

It was an exaggeration, for Custis was performing his duties as a host admirably by dancing with every lady attending the party. Rooney, his wife Charlotte, and Mary Custis were sitting on a pallet right next to the Lees' lounge chairs. "The Girls," Annie and Agnes, were also dancing, although eighteen-year-old Agnes had disappeared from her father's hawklike gaze, and Robert had asked Perry to find her along with Milly and Rob.

"Did you find Rob?" he asked Perry, his manservant.

"Yes, suh. He's right with Miss Mildred, a-egging her on."

"All right, I'll come," he said resignedly.

But Rooney got to his feet, grinning. "Never mind. I'll go get them, Father. And Mother, I'm a little surprised at your indignation. What was that story again about the fall from the apple tree. . . ?"

"Never you mind that, Rooney," she sniffed. "I was only a child. Milly is thirteen and should comport herself in a ladylike manner."

"I believe you were twelve years old at the time," Robert said innocently.

"Twelve is not thirteen. Rooney, stop standing there gawping and grinning. Hurry up before she falls and breaks her head."

Rooney went across the plantation road in the direction of the apple orchard.

Mary returned to her knitting, and her pleased composure returned. "Oh Robert, this is wonderful. I'm so glad we decided to have this party. We simply must start entertaining again."

"It does seem to be a success. It's good to be back in touch with the family." Between Robert's family and Mary's family, they were related to practically all the First Families of Virginia. Although they had literally hundreds of cousins, neither Robert nor Mary viewed any relation as "distant" or "close." If people were related to them in any way, they were family.

Rooney soon returned with his younger brother and sister in tow. Milly and Rob came to stand in front of Robert and Mary, their heads bowed, their hands crossed in front of them. Robert reflected with amusement that they looked guiltier than many criminal defendants he had seen.

Mary said in an even tone, "Milly, what were you thinking? Climbing a tree?"

Without looking up, she said in a small voice, "But Rob said I couldn't, and I knew I could, but I had to prove it to Rob."

Rob faced his father, his cheeks crimson. "It's true, sir. I teased her into it, and it's all my fault."

"But it's not," Milly argued. "I decided to do it. It's my fault."

"You're both right. Both of you are responsible, and I'm glad to see you own up to it. Now go on with you. It's too pretty a day for me to be fretting over my children acting like circus monkeys." Mary settled back in her chair again, her mouth twitching.

"How do you know what circus monkeys do?" Robert asked. "You've never been to a circus."

"I've read about them," Mary said indignantly. "And I wish I had seen a circus. If there is ever one near here, Robert, I would very much wish to go."

"You never fail to surprise me, Mims," he said with amusement. "You, at a circus! But if one does come here, it would be my honor to take you, my dear."

Perry appeared again and slid in front of Robert. "Marse Robert, suh, Miss Agnes, she's in one of them little sailboats, chasing around in circles and giggling, it appears to me."

"Is she by herself?" Robert said alertly.

"No, suh, there's a young gentleman with her. I b'lieve it's that Taliaferro boy."

Robert relaxed. "That's fine then. Thank you, Perry."

Mary Lee hummed. "Circus monkeys."

Mary had chosen a glowing day for the party. The dance pavilion that George Custis had built many years before had received a new coat of white paint, and it gleamed brightly in the benevolent sunshine. They were at the foot of the hill that Arlington House was built upon, on the banks of the Potomac River. Just across the road was the apple orchard and the stretch of actual farm fields belonging to Arlington.

During George Custis's time they had lain fallow, for he was not a man to be a dedicated farmer. He was interested in agriculture, and often had grand plans for crop rotations or watering systems or new methods of fertilization, but implementing these imaginative ideas was too mundane for a man with such a mercurial mind.

In the previous year, however, Robert E. Lee had managed to bring in a corn crop that actually made the estate some money. Now the corn plants were only knee high, but they were verdant and shone as if they had been polished.

Just by the dance pavilion was Arlington Spring. It was not at all connected to the river, for the water bubbled up clean and icy cold. Cheerily it splashed into a small pool that had an underground outlet, for the pool stayed always about six feet in diameter.

George Custis had collected large rocks and had made a border around the fountain-like spring and pool, arranging them artistically rather than functionally. It was the kind of project he loved and would stick to until the end.

For the party, Robert had had low benches built to set around the pool, and now at least twenty young people sat there, catching mugs of water to drink and sometimes splashing each other. "I think there must be about fifty people here," he told Mary.

"I'm sure more will come along," she said with satisfaction. "All I did was tell the Fitzhughs, the Bollings, and two of the Carter families to spread the word, and I see many more of our cousins here."

Most everyone had arrived by boat, for sailing and punting on the river was a favorite entertainment of the young people that lived on both sides of the river. Arlington was a well-known stopping point, to get a drink of the refreshing spring water and rest or picnic in the shade of the pavilion. George Custis had always intended the landing to be semipublic, for he had enjoyed visiting with anyone who happened to stop at the landing.

It was not just young people who had come, however. So far there were four carriages lined up behind the tea tent next to the barn. Close by Mary was her aunt Fitzhugh, who lived in the fine country home of Ravensworth; her cousin Melanie Byrd; and another cousin Katrina Page. Other older couples were dancing or were sitting on one of the many canvas pallets that Arlington provided. Though the sun was bright, it was not hot even at high noon.

Mary glanced up the road and then shaded her eyes. "There's a crowd coming up the river road now, Robert. I wonder who that could be."

"Six people, one of them a black boy," he murmured after searching the distance. As they drew nearer, Robert said, "Oh, it's Edward Fitzhugh and his two daughters. I haven't seen him for at least two years. I must go and meet them."

He got to his feet, but before he walked away he gave Mary a sly glance, and she almost, but not quite, made a face at him. This was the Edward Fitzhugh who had been courting Mary for two years before Robert E. Lee had become her fiancé. He had seemed gravely disappointed when he found out that Mary was engaged to Robert, although Mary had never given Edward the least reason to suppose that she would consider marrying him. Even now, twenty-eight years later, Robert still gently teased her about Edward Fitzhugh.

He went to meet his guests and saw that Edward's two daughters were riding, both dressed in attractive riding habits. A man on a giant black horse accompanied them, along with a black boy riding a fine mare.

The company turned up the plantation drive road. Edward and the other two men dismounted, and Edward greeted Robert with obvious gladness. Shaking hands heartily, he said, "Robert, it's so good to see you. I didn't even know until last week, when Aunt Fitzhugh told me about this party, that you were still here at Arlington. For some reason I'd got muddled and thought you were back in Texas. Certainly we would have called before now. You remember my daughters, Frances and Deborah? And may I introduce to you our friend, Mr. Morgan Tremayne? Mr. Tremayne, this is Colonel Robert E. Lee."

Robert shook hands with him and "took his measure" in the few seconds their eyes met, a gift of discernment he had that he was completely unaware of until he had been told he possessed it.

Tremayne was about twenty-five, with a slim build but with wide shoulders. He was distinctly patrician in looks and bearing. His auburn hair was thick and carefully styled, his dark blue eyes were well spaced under neatly arched brows, his nose was thin and high-bridged, and his mouth was as full and well shaped as a woman's. However, he was as tanned as a farmhand, and the hand that clasped Lee's so firmly was rough and calloused. His eyes were keen and quick, surveying Robert and the surroundings alertly.

"Welcome to Arlington, Mr. Tremayne. Edward, please, come sit with us. Mary is anxious to see you, and Aunt Fitzhugh is here. Miss Frances, Miss Deborah, are you ladies going to ride the bridle paths or come to the party and dance?"

The girls looked gratified at Colonel Lee's courtliness. Their father, Edward Fitzhugh, was very plain, and he still had his cast eye, but he was a kind and gentle man, and he had won the heart of a beautiful woman. His two daughters took after her, with lush chestnut hair, heart-shaped faces, velvety dark eyes and complexions like magnolia blossoms. Frannie was nineteen, and

Deb was seventeen, and they were very close.

Frannie said, "Oh, Colonel Lee, I simply must show off my new mare, so I don't want to disappear into your lovely forest. May I ride her over on the other side of the spring?"

"I want to show mine off, too," Deb said. "May we ride them over there, sir?"

"Of course, if you feel confident of controlling them," Robert answered. "They are both very handsome, I must say." Admiringly he stroked Frannie's mare. Her coloring was distinctive, a uniform silvery gray, which was rather unusual. Deb's horse was a dark chestnut, almost a mahogany-red color, with dramatic black points. Both mares had small neat heads and petite alert conformation.

Edward murmured, "Oh, I don't know, Frannie. You've only had them for two days."

"Father, we've been riding since we were four years old," Frannie said lightly. "And besides, Mr. Tremayne's horses are so well trained and behave so admirably, I'm sure there won't be a problem."

"All right then." He relented.

Morgan turned and said to the black boy in a low voice, "Go with them, Rosh, and bring them up to the barn when the ladies are through with them."

"Yes, sir," he said and handed the reins of both his horse and Tremayne's stallion to Morgan. Then discreetly he followed the ladies around behind the gatherings of partygoers and the tea tent.

"Those are your horses, Mr. Tremayne?" Robert asked, puzzled.

"They were until two days ago, sir," Morgan answered good-naturedly.

"I bought them for the girls," Edward said. "Both of them love to ride, and I admit I'm proud of them. They are excellent equestriennes."

"They are," Morgan agreed. "It makes me very happy to know when my horses have good owners."

"Come," Robert said, "I'll walk with you to the barn. In the back is a lean-to roof where we're tying up the horses." He loved horses. Everything about them interested him, and he wanted to talk to Morgan. "Edward, will you walk with us?"

"By your leave, Robert, I would like to go visit with Mrs. Lee and Aunt Fitzhugh. And, I admit, have a nice cup of tea. Mr. Tremayne, would you mind taking care of Rutherford?"

"Not at all, sir," Morgan replied, taking the reins of Mr. Fitzhugh's horse.

"Go on then, Edward. We'll join you shortly," Robert said, and he and Morgan turned toward the barn.

❧

Morgan Tremayne was glad he was getting an opportunity to look over the horses of all of those present. In his business, it was important to know what horses people liked and thus bought.

Eyeing the stamping, snorting stallion behind them, Robert asked, "And so you are in the business of selling horses, Mr. Tremayne?"

"I have a horse farm, and yes, sir, for the last two years I have done well," Morgan answered.

"That great brute behind us is one of your horses, I take it."

"Yes, sir. This is Vulcan. He's my prize sire. The mare is from my farm, too." Vulcan tossed his head so far that Morgan almost lost all of the reins he held.

Hastily Robert said, "Here, Mr. Tremayne, perhaps I'd better take Edward's horse." After fumbling around until the reins were straight, he went on, "I assume Vulcan is acting up because of the mares."

Morgan rolled his eyes. "Sir, for Vulcan this is not acting up. This is fairly calm for him."

"Really? You must have spent many hours training him, if he's this manageable around mares. He's quite a striking horse. If you're selling his bloodline, he must be very good advertisement for you," Robert said shrewdly.

"Yes, sir, he is, when he behaves like a civilized horse," Morgan said. "That chestnut mare that Miss Deborah is riding? Vulcan is her sire, by a fine brood mare named Bettina that I have. In my opinion, their offspring are the best of my breedings."

They went on talking as they watered the three horses then tied them up in the shady lean-to. Morgan quickly checked the other four horses there and saw with satisfaction that they were geldings. Vulcan wouldn't be too pleased with his company, but at least there were no other stallions. Morgan knew that Vulcan would almost certainly start a fight if there were.

Robert led Morgan back under the great spreading live oak tree where the lawn chairs had been placed for the older people. Robert said, "Mary, I want you to meet Mr. Tremayne. He is a friend of Edward's. Mr. Tremayne, this is my wife, Mary."

Morgan bowed over her hand and said all the usual pleasantries.

An empty chair was next to Mary, and she motioned Morgan to sit down. "Welcome to Arlington, Mr. Tremayne. I'm so pleased that you came today. Edward was telling me that you sold those two excellent mares to him for Frannie and Deb."

"Yes, ma'am, it was my distinct pleasure to be able to provide the Misses Fitzhughs with what I believe to be superb saddle horses," Morgan said enthusiastically. "And I was just telling Colonel Lee that it always gives me great pleasure to sell my horses to someone I know will be a good, caring owner."

Mary nodded. "Yes, Edward was telling me that you flatly refused to sell any of your horses to one of the planters in your area. It seemed you found the care they would receive was not up to your standards."

Awkwardly Morgan said, "Um—er—I apologize, Mrs. Lee, but you caught me quite off guard. I wasn't aware that the details of that little incident were generally known."

Her mouth curled upward in a small smile. "All of northern Virginia is like a small town, Mr. Tremayne. Generally everyone knows everyone else's business. I understand that you are from Fredericksburg?"

"No, ma'am, I have a horse farm outside of Fredericksburg, about ten miles west on the Rapidan River. My family is originally from Staunton, in the Valley."

"And how did you come to these parts, sir?" Mary asked politely.

"My mother inherited a townhouse in Richmond, and the family travels there quite often, because we have many old friends there. Actually, I inherited my farm from a great-uncle on my mother's side. She was a Carter, and my property was in the Carter family for almost fifty years."

Mary's face lit up. "Oh, is she one of the Richmond Carters?"

"Yes, ma'am."

"Why, then you're family, Mr. Tremayne! Please, you must tell me all about your mother's family. And your father's, too, for since you are surely my cousin I must hear all about this new connection."

Her delight and interest was obviously genuine, and Morgan readily began to explain his mother's genealogy. They had not been talking for very long when Morgan saw out of the corner of his eye that the Misses Fitzhughs had come up to them and made their curtsies to Mrs. Lee.

As it was unheard of for children to interrupt their elders, she kept talking while the girls stood patiently waiting. ". . .and later I shall determine if you and my husband are actually third cousins or third cousins once removed," she finished thoughtfully then turned to the girls. "Good afternoon, Frannie, Deb. You both look lovely. Are the riding habits new?"

"Oh yes, ma'am," Frannie gushed. "Father bought us horses, saddles, tack, spurs, and riding habits. Which do you prefer, Mrs. Lee, my blue one or Deb's green one?"

But Mary ostensibly knew these two girls too well to fall into that trap. "In my opinion, that deep shade of blue particularly complements your complexion, Fran, and that dark green flatters yours, Deborah."

"Thank you, ma'am," they said in unison, though they obviously were dissatisfied with Mrs. Lee's diplomacy.

"Anyway, Mrs. Lee, we wondered if we might steal Mr. Tremayne," Deborah said mischievously. "Everyone wants to know all about Serafina and Delilah, and also we were hoping that he would get Vulcan to do his tricks."

"Just who, pray tell, are Serafina and Delilah?" Mrs. Lee demanded, her brow lowering.

"That's what I named the mares, ma'am," Morgan said hastily. To the girls he asked, "You aren't going to name them? They're very intelligent, you know. They would catch on quickly."

"No, no," Fran replied. "We like their names. So, Mr. Tremayne? Will you come meet everyone and tell them about Serafina and Delilah? And then will you and Vulcan please perform?"

"I'll be glad to talk horses with anyone anytime, ladies. But I doubt very much that Mrs. Lee wants a circus starting up at her nice party."

"I gather that Vulcan is that great black horse you ride, Mr. Tremayne? And he does tricks?" she asked curiously.

Morgan grimaced. "Well, I would say that he shows off when he wants to. If he doesn't want to, then he just balks and sulks."

Mrs. Lee laughed.

Morgan thought that she had a very youthful laugh for her age. He couldn't quite tell how old she was, because he could see that she was sickly. He only thought that she looked older than Colonel Lee.

Mrs. Lee said, "As a matter of fact, Mr. Tremayne, I was telling Colonel Lee just awhile ago how much I wished to see a circus. So please, if Vulcan agrees, I would love to see you perform. I assume that the drive will do?"

"Yes, ma'am," Morgan said resignedly. "We don't require three rings."

"Hurrah!" Deborah cried. "Please go ahead, Mr. Tremayne, and get Vulcan. We'll introduce you to everyone after."

Morgan went to the barn and untied Vulcan, who showed his annoyance at being crowded into a lean-to with other lesser horses by irritably chewing on his bit. Morgan checked the saddle, the cinch strap, and the bridle, to make sure they were secure. Then he led Vulcan out onto the plantation drive.

To his bemusement, most everyone at the party lined the wide gravel road. He saw Colonel Lee standing behind Mrs. Lee, and realized with a start that she was in a wheelchair and had evidently wanted to come have a ringside seat.

He stopped in the middle of the drive and stepped in front of the prancing horse. He put his hands on both sides of Vulcan's head, just under his ears, and stepped very close to him. "Listen, Vulcan. I know you've never performed for a crowd before, but there's no reason to be nervous. Just do what I've taught you, okay? Okay?"

To Morgan's relief, he bobbed his head enthusiastically, as if he were saying, "Yes." It meant that Vulcan was in a good mood. He hoped.

He swung up into the saddle easily and sat motionless, the reins slack, for a few seconds. Vulcan shifted, bobbed his head again, then stood perfectly still.

Morgan steadily pulled the reins back tight. Under him the horse rose until he was in a picture-perfect rearing stance. Morgan heard "Ooohs" from the crowd. Vulcan pawed the air once, twice, then came back down in a collected stand. Then he began his gaited trot.

It had taken Morgan many, many hours to teach Vulcan this tightly choreographed gait, and this time Vulcan did it perfectly. He lifted his right hoof, brought it up until it almost clapped against his chest, then kicked it out smartly. It was a proud gait, and Vulcan arched his neck while holding his head perfectly straight. Morgan reflected that he had never done so well. Perhaps he ought to have an adoring crowd all the time.

Morgan reached the crossroad then pulled on the right rein. Vulcan made a sharp about-face and landed, still in his gaited trot, heading back up the drive smoothly. When he reached their starting point, Morgan pulled on the left rein then pulled on both simultaneously. Vulcan turned, reared again, then came back to a show horse stance.

The crowd applauded and shouted. Mrs. Lee was smiling with delight.

Morgan dismounted, said another word to Vulcan, then led him to stand in front of Mrs. Lee. "He does one more trick sometimes, Mrs. Lee," Morgan said. "I hope he shows you the proper respect now." Morgan bowed, and after a second, Vulcan tossed his head, bent his left leg back, and bowed.

Mary Lee said, "Thank you so much, Mr. Tremayne. I will never forget this day."

❧

Morgan did meet everyone, all fifty-seven of them.

Soon after Fran and Deborah Fitzhugh started introducing him, they got sidetracked and disappeared when he was dancing with Miss Mary Custis Lee. He thought the Lees' eldest daughter was charming and vivacious, and he soon found out that all their children were warm and gracious, much like Mrs. Lee.

Colonel Lee was certainly a courteous, gallant gentleman, but in many ways he stood apart. Part of it was that Robert E. Lee had an innate reserve, and part of it was that he inspired such a great deal of respect that it bordered on awe. At least that was the way Morgan saw him, but he could see that Lee laughed much more when he was talking to his family, so he could tell that he was much more approachable to his wife and children.

Morgan had danced with Mary Custis, Agnes, and Anne and had just finished a vigorous Virginia reel with Milly when he begged a chance to have a cup of tea.

As he was heading to the tea tent, Colonel Lee fell into step beside him. "I find tea to be so much more refreshing than coffee in warm weather," he remarked pleasantly.

"I agree, sir." A jolly-faced black woman served them tea in fine china cups.

Lee took an appreciative sip then said, "Mr. Tremayne, will you sit with me for a minute? I'd like to talk to you."

"Of course, sir."

They went to two lounge chairs that were set apart from the ladies and settled into them. "That was quite a performance you and your horse put on, Mr. Tremayne," Lee said, his eyes lit with amusement.

"Thank you, sir, but it is Vulcan that does the performing," Morgan said. "He just allows me to sit on his back while he shows off."

Lee nodded. "He is spirited, I can see. A fine stallion. And really, Mr. Tremayne, that is what I wanted to talk to you about, your horse farm and your horses. You see, I am considering buying a horse, maybe two."

Morgan blanched. "Oh, sir—Colonel Lee—please don't think that I put on that show just as a. . .a. . .vulgar sales pitch! I assure you—"

Lee held up one hand, shaking his head. "No, Mr. Tremayne, that is not what I think at all. If it were, I certainly shouldn't be interested in buying anything from you. No, I have been talking to Mr. Fitzhugh, and he gives you the highest recommendations. Truthfully I have been thinking of buying a good saddle horse for the girls, and now that Rob is sixteen, I think he's ready for his own horse. So I would like for you to consider if you have any three- or four-year-olds that would suit."

With vast relief, Morgan said, "Sir, I have eight three-year-olds that would suit."

"Good," Lee said, settling back in the comfortable chair. "And I will tell you, Mr. Tremayne, that Mrs. Lee would never allow me to buy a horse from a stranger. But she has assured me that you are either our third cousin or third cousin once removed, so she has given me permission to purchase two horses from you. In fact, I think that if she were still riding, she would try to buy Vulcan from you."

Morgan grinned boyishly. "Colonel Lee, I will never sell Vulcan. But I would give him to Mrs. Lee."

A small smile lit up Lee's face. "Don't tell her that, please, Mr. Tremayne. It's better for all of us if she doesn't know."

PART TWO

PART TWO

CHAPTER SIX

Morgan Tremayne pulled Vulcan to a stop to look up at his house. He had named his property Rapidan Run Horse Farm, for the house was plain and functional and not nearly grand enough to warrant a fancy name like so many of the large plantation homes in Virginia. Still, he felt a sense of deep pride when he surveyed the house, prettily situated on a rise above the Rapidan River, the manicured grounds cool and green under sheltering oak trees. The house rose above, a two-story rectangular box set on its end. The windows were exactly spaced above and below, and a modest gabled pediment was above the front door. The only nod to any whimsy was that the clapboard house was painted red.

Morgan had inherited the farm four years ago, on his twenty-first birthday, and he had been surprised and somehow pleased to see the faded red paint on the house. In the next two years he had enlarged the barn, added stables with fifty boxes, a carriage house, and two servant's cottages. He had painted them all red.

"Let's go, boy," he said to his horse and rode up the small hill by the path that led to the back door.

On this glorious spring morning in June 1859, the double doors to the detached kitchen were propped open, and even before Morgan rode into the yard he could smell pies baking. He had a keen sense of smell—in fact, all his senses were sharp—and he guessed a peach pie and a cherry pie.

His servant Amon hurried out of the paddock as he dismounted, and at the same time Amon's wife, Evetta, came out of the kitchen, drying her hands on her apron. Both of them started talking at once as they neared him.

Amon said, "That there little filly outta Dandy is just as sweet as she kin be, Mr. Morgan. Not like her daddy—"

Evetta said, "You been wandering out in that Wilderness again like some wild man in Borneo, I guess, and without breakfast, too—"

"—'cause I see he's been running you, that Vulcan devil, 'stead of you ridin' him—"

"—which you need breakfast, Mr. Morgan. Haven't I told you ten thousand times to eat something—"

"—Even Ketura could break her, she's so nice and polite—"

"—my peach pie and cherry—"

"I knew it!" Morgan said, grinning as he handed Vulcan's reins to Amon. "I could smell those pies all the way in the Wilderness. You say the little filly—is it that pretty dappled gray one you mean?"

"Yes, sir," Amon said.

Morgan nodded. "I want to come see her work out. Go on and tend to Vulcan, Amon, and I'll come out to the paddock as soon as I've had some coffee. Er—can I have some coffee, Evetta?"

"I suppose so," she said ominously. "Since I made a big ol' pot of it for *breakfast.*"

Over his shoulder Morgan said, "Just coffee right now, Evetta. I'll make up for it at dinner. I'll have a peach pie."

He went into the house and upstairs to his bedroom, shrugging off his black frock coat. It had been chilly in the predawn when he had left for his morning ride. He quickly washed his hands and face and combed his thick auburn hair. He was by nature a neat and tidy man, though he was neither a fop nor was he finicky.

His bedroom reflected this. It was spare, with a plain oak bedstead and bed precisely made, a sturdy armoire, and washstand with toilet articles meticulously arranged.

Hurrying back downstairs, he went out to the kitchen, where Evetta was standing at the worktable, kneading dough. Evetta was a black woman of thirty-five, small and sturdy. She looked up when he came in, and he saw that she had apparently swiped her forehead, for a white flour streak lay across it. One eyebrow was white.

She started to say something, but Morgan, hiding a smile, told her, "I'm just going to get a mug and go watch Rosh and Santo working the two-year-olds." He got an oversize white stoneware mug and poured a steaming cup of strong black coffee.

"I don't s'pose you're planning on eating today, then?" she said sarcastically, pounding the dough with vengeance. "Tomorrow, mebbe? Week from Thursday?"

"Aw, Evetta, you fuss like a mama goose. I'll eat at dinnertime. I'm fine until then."

"Not no 'just peach pie,' neither," she grumbled.

"Okay, not just peach pie. And I'm going over to Mr. Deforge's later on this afternoon. For tea, he says, about four o'clock. So I'll have a late supper, okay?"

She nodded. "Glad you told me, Mr. Morgan. We need to send them a couple of chickens. I'll have Amon take care of that."

"Why am I always taking dead chickens to Deforge's?" Morgan complained.

Evetta's mouth drew into a straight line. "Cleo says that Miss Jolie don't like chicken."

"She doesn't? Mr. DeForge doesn't either?"

"I wouldn't presume to know nothing about that," Evetta answered primly.

"But if they don't eat chicken, then why am I always taking them chicken? But wait—they have chickens of their own. I've seen them! Or are those just for the eggs?"

Evetta gave a careless half shrug.

Morgan rasped, "This is very confusing. But if Miss Cleo wants chickens, I'll take them to her." He went to the door and turned. "You know, Evetta, I think I'd better get a mirror to put in here."

"Wha—?"

He went out to the enclosed paddock and stood up on the bottom railing to see over the high fence. Sipping his coffee thoughtfully, he watched Amon and Evetta's two sons, Rosh and Santo, as they worked two mares. Though they were only eighteen and sixteen years old, both of them were very good horsemen, like their father. That was the main reason Morgan had asked Amon and Evetta to come to Rapidan Run to help him.

They had been servants at Tremayne House, Morgan's family's farm in the Shenandoah Valley. Amon and his sons had worked in the livery stables there, and Morgan had seen how expert they were at handling horses. They had agreed to come work for him, and they were one of the main factors contributing to the success of Rapidan Run Horse Farm. That and the fact that Morgan had chosen to breed American Saddlebreds, a relatively new equine strain.

The Tremaynes had cousins in Kentucky who had begun breeding them in the 1840s, when the superiority of the bloodline was just beginning to be recognized. Morgan had gotten all his breeding stock from his Tremayne cousins at a very reasonable price. Without exception he had found them to be wonderful horses. As saddle horses, they had comfortable, ground-covering gaits and were sure-footed, but still they were stylish, flashy horses that were beautiful for harness, strong enough for farm work, and fast enough to win races.

After four years, Morgan now had eleven brood mares and three stallions, eight three-year-olds ready for sale, ten two-year-olds, six yearlings, and nine foals less than a year old. All the two-year-olds were good horses, trainable, and generally all of them had good temperaments. Vulcan's progeny had a tendency to be high-strung, though generally not to the degree that he was. With Morgan's and Amon's expert care, they molded these nervy tendencies into high-spirited, lively horses.

Ketura, Amon and Evetta's daughter, suddenly popped up beside him. "Can I watch, too, Mr. Morgan?"

"Sure."

She was thirteen years old and was in that awkward stage between being a child and being a young woman. She was skinny, with long legs and arms, and had a tendency to be clumsy. But she was a comely girl with a dazzling smile and enormous dark eyes. Supposedly she was training with her mother to become a housemaid and cook, but for the last year or so Morgan had noticed that she liked to spend much more time with the horses than in the house or kitchen. Evetta continually fretted about it, even though technically Ketura was Morgan's servant, and he didn't care. Even as he was reflecting on this, Ketura cast a cautious look behind her toward the kitchen. Morgan decided to talk to Evetta. If Ketura would rather help with the horses, that was fine with him.

After a while she asked, "Mr. Morgan, did you go riding in that Wilderness again this morning?"

"Sure did. I didn't go too far inside, though. I mostly rambled along the river."

"Ain't you scared?"

"No, of course not, Ketura. What's the matter? Have you heard tales about the Wilderness?" He had heard that people thought it was haunted.

The Wilderness was aptly named. It was seventy square miles of second-growth forest, which meant that many of the trees were stunted and covered with parasitic vines, and the ground was a snarled undergrowth of weeds and brambles. The north side of the Wilderness was bordered by the Rapidan River, and the land along the riverbank was low and clear. But the ground in the Wilderness itself was treacherously uneven, with rock outcroppings, low craggy hills, and ravines, and it was crisscrossed by dozens of streams and brooks. When the area had heavy rain, in several places it became a pestilential dead marsh.

"Yes, sir, people say there's ghosts and monsters in there," Ketura answered, hugging herself.

"I've ridden all over it in the last four years, and I haven't seen one ghost or one monster," Morgan said gently.

"But it is spooky."

"Maybe. But I like it."

"Mama says that's 'cause you like being alone," she said casually. "Is that right?"

Perplexed, Morgan thought over the girl's innocent question. His first impulse was to answer, *Yes, I like being alone. I prefer living alone, riding alone, staying up late at night to read alone.* But if that were true, why did he want to get married so badly?

Six months ago he had started "courting" a girl from Fredericksburg, Leona Rose Bledsoe. He was beginning to think that she was the woman he wanted to marry. Morgan was a rather bookish, commonsensical, levelheaded man, and he had never put much stock in "being in love." He believed that a man and a woman should marry if they suited each other, amused each other, and were approximately equal in intelligence, and Leona Rose Bledsoe fit all these requirements. He could easily imagine being married to her, so he assumed he must "be in love" with her. At least, that's what one part of his mind insisted. Another part of him knew that he was a solitary man, and that it was by his own choice.

Ketura was watching him curiously, so he finally replied, "I do enjoy exploring the Wilderness by myself, Ketura. So sometimes I do like to be alone."

She opened her mouth, and Morgan could see that more questions were coming.

But he was saved by Evetta shouting at Ketura at the top of her lungs. "You there perched up on the paddock railing like a crow-bird! Yes, miss, I'm talking to you. I'm going in the house this here minute, and let me tell you something, if that downstairs dusting and polishing ain't done, I'm gonna pinch your head clean off!"

Ketura jumped down and scampered to her.

Morgan turned back, searching beyond the paddock to his pastures, four of them, planted with Bermuda grass for summer and ryegrass for winter. In the near pasture he could see several newly-weaned foals running and hopping and playing on their still-spindly legs. Morgan thought that that sight, this day, this home gave him feelings of peace and contentment he had never known. Even though he was alone.

Rosh, the older boy, was working with the filly Amon had spoken of. She was out of Vulcan by Bettina, Morgan's favorite mare. The filly was a pretty silver gray, with highlights of darker gray in her coat so that she was the color called "dappled." Rosh had her on a long tether, walking her around in tight circles, and Morgan could see that she was going to be naturally gaited. The distinctive, showy trot was more pronounced in some horses, and this filly would be one of those, he could see.

He decided to name her Evie. He couldn't remember each of the foals until he named them, and then he could always remember their sire and dam. It was a double-edged sword, though. Once he named them he was loath to sell them. At heart he loved them all.

Dismissing his meandering thoughts, he called out, "Amon, would you turn all the two-year-olds out to pasture and then bring in the three-year-olds two at a time?"

"Sure and certain, Mr. Morgan," he replied.

In a few minutes, Rosh and Santo brought out two colts and walked them around the paddock, first in file and then abreast. Amon joined Morgan on the fence as he studied the horses. They were both chestnuts, one with black points and one with a white face and socks on his front feet.

"Here's what we need, Amon," Morgan said thoughtfully. "Colonel Lee has four daughters, from twenty-four years old to thirteen years old. They all like to ride, and from what I saw they are fairly accomplished. Two of the daughters are somewhat frail, though, so I don't want them to have anything too high-spirited. Now the son, Rob, is sixteen, and he's a handful, I can see, but he can ride. He even rode Vulcan."

Amon's brows shot up. "He did? And howsomever did that go?"

Morgan shrugged. "For some reason Vulcan was on his best behavior at the Lees'. I don't know why, but he's made up for it since we got home yesterday. Tried to nip me this morning. Anyway, he was just as cool as a breeze when Rob Jr. mounted him. Plodded around in a circle like he was the pony ride at the fair."

"Can't never tell about that horse, though, Mr. Morgan," Amon said darkly. "He was jist as likely to toss him as he was to carry him."

"I know, but I couldn't very well tell Colonel Lee that my own horse is unridable, could I?" Morgan said.

At one time or another, Vulcan had bucked off Morgan, Amon, Rosh, and Santo during his early training. Now he didn't throw them, but he was an excitable horse. The entire time Rob Jr. had been riding Vulcan, Morgan's heart had been in his throat.

"Anyway, I'm already thinking about Diamond Jack for Rob," Morgan continued. "But I haven't made my mind up about the ladies' mounts. I want them to have the very best I've got."

Amon thought for a few minutes then said, "What about Roebuck, suh? I know you were thinking about keeping him, but all together I'd have to say he's the best of the three-year-olds. Did they want a mare in perticklar?"

"No, Colonel Lee left it completely up to me," Morgan answered. "But Roebuck, it would be hard to part with him."

Roebuck was a three-year-old out of Vulcan and Bettina, and he was that very unusual color, a palomino. He was a creamy-golden color, with white tail and mane. He hadn't inherited Vulcan's temperament, though he was a big horse like his sire, almost fifteen hands. Instead he was sweet tempered, patient, and calm like his dam. Morgan had been considering keeping him strictly because of his unusual coloring, but suddenly he knew that the Lee daughters would take just as much care of him as he himself would.

"Right," Morgan finally said, "you're right, Amon. Get Rosh and Santo to saddle up Roebuck and Diamond Jack. Let me see them do a workout."

The boys brought out the two geldings, the graceful and collected Roebuck and Diamond Jack, another gelding out of Vulcan by a spirited bay mare named Lalla. Diamond Jack was solid glossy black except for a blaze on his face that was in the exact shape of a diamond, hence his name. He was showy like Vulcan, prancing and preening and proudly tossing his head.

Morgan got his portfolio and took notes as he watched the boys work the horses, and then he rode both of them himself, a short ride up his dirt drive to the woodline where he got them both into a gallop. Both of them were magically smooth runners.

Rejoining Amon, he told him to come into the house, and they went into Morgan's study. The floor plan of the house was timeworn and simple: a hall down the middle with a parlor on one side and dining room on the other, and on the second floor four square bedrooms, each exactly the same size. Downstairs, Morgan had converted what was supposed to be the parlor into a study/library with a comfortable seating area in front of the windows. He took his seat in one well-worn overstuffed leather armchair and motioned for Amon to sit down on the other side of the small cherry tea table between the chairs.

"You know, Amon, I haven't told you yet how much I appreciate your advice about the Fitzhugh girls. Even though I had met them, I didn't realize how important it would be to them to have different horses. I just thought—sisters—close in age—same horses."

Amon grinned, a wide, delighted smile that lit up his entire ebony face. "Back at home, you 'member, Mr. Morgan, Evetta had three sisters. I knows how they fight and argue and try to top each other. I figgered them two highfalutin Fitzhugh girls were much the same. Seems like women everywhere are kinda like that."

"Are they?" Morgan asked with honest surprise. He had very

little experience with women. Growing up he had one younger brother, Clay, and he had twin sisters now, but they were only five years old. Morgan barely knew them. "Guess I'll have to take your word for it. I could sure see when I delivered Serafina and Delilah that it would never have done to have given them the two chestnuts. They each started right in about how much prettier their horse was than the other. So thank you, Amon. I appreciate the advice. I'm going to give you a small bonus on that sale—five dollars."

"Thank you, Mr. Morgan," he said with dignity.

"You're welcome. That kind of brings me around to what I wanted to talk to you about. Now that Rapidan Run is making some money, I'm going to do what's called profit sharing with you, Amon. Beginning today, you and your family are going to make one percent of my profit on each sale and each stud fee. I know you realize this, because you've learned every aspect of the business, but I do want you to make clear to your family that one percent of the profit is not one percent of the sale price. Even though I sell the horses for two hundred fifty or three hundred dollars, what I'm actually making on them is about half that."

"Yes, sir, I knows that. And I knows you wouldn't be making near that much if you didn't farm your own forage," he said shrewdly. "That's right kind of you, Mr. Morgan. I can promise you me and my family will work all the harder, knowing that we got us a share."

"I don't see how you could work any harder than you do, all of you," Morgan said warmly. "And it's not any charitable virtue on my part, Amon. It's only right and fair."

"Maybe, but it ain't what you'd call commonly done, profit sharing with servants," Amon said. "Me and Evetta, we haven't met any other servants here, only slaves."

Many years ago, when Morgan's great-great-great-grandfather had settled in the Shenandoah Valley, he had been Amish, and he had abhorred slavery. Though it was his forebear who had eventually married a girl outside of the Amish faith and had become an

Episcopalian, he kept his Amish sensibilities. None of the Tremaynes had ever had slaves. Morgan himself hated the institution, and so naturally Amon and Evetta, along with the other black servants at Tremayne House, were employees.

"Yes, I know, Amon, but you know you and yours will never have to worry about that," Morgan said firmly. "So, since you're getting a percentage now, I have to tell you that I lowered the price of two horses when I quoted to Colonel Lee. I'm only charging him two hundred apiece for them."

"For our two best geldings?" Amon said doubtfully. Normally Morgan charged three hundred for geldings, two hundred fifty for mares.

"Yes, Mr. Fitzhugh told me something of the family problems the Lees are having. I'm glad he did, for I certainly would never have known it from talking to Mrs. Lee or Colonel Lee. Apparently, Mrs. Lee's father, who owned Arlington and several other properties, left his affairs in something of a mess, and Colonel Lee is the executor. Mr. Fitzhugh said that Colonel Lee has been using his own money to try and fulfill all the bequests in Mr. Custis's will. When I saw what kind of people they are, I decided to give them the best price I could."

"Fine with me," Amon said. "I b'lieve the good Lord's gonna bless us, and this place, Mr. Morgan, with whatever you decide to do. So when are you taking the geldings to Arlington?"

"I'm going to leave on Friday," Morgan said. "Taking Vulcan on the train left me, Serafina, Delilah, Rosh, and Calliope all to bits and pieces. That horse would drive a saint insane. I figure we'll stop at Alexandria on Sunday and spend the night to recover before I take Diamond Jack and Roebuck to Arlington."

Amon grimaced. "So you're a-going to take that Vulcan on the train again."

"Going to try," Morgan said. "He's got to learn."

"Mebbe so, mebbe not," Amon said darkly. "Why don't you just ride Laird, Mr. Morgan? He's one fine-looking gelding and got a lot sweeter temperament than that Vulcan."

"Because Vulcan is good advertising. You know that, Amon. So far this summer I've got him booked out for four studs. People see him, they want a foal from him."

"That is true," Amon admitted. "He's a big showoff, prancing about and preening and tossing his head. Anyways, if you're set on it, I'll give him a bath tomorrow and use that mane and tail cream and shine him up."

"No, I'll do it," Morgan said. "I need to take every opportunity to show that horse who's boss."

Amon's face worked.

Finally Morgan laughed. "All right. I know, I know. So I need to take every opportunity to show that horse who *wishes* he were boss."

"Yes, sir," Amon said with amusement. "If you're set on it— and if that Vulcan will let you. Good Lord watch over you an' keep you, sir."

CHAPTER SEVEN

The brilliant sunshine of June caught Jolie DeForge full in the face as she stepped out of the house and then crossed the porch. Though she was thirteen years old now, the face that the golden sun lit up was more like a ten-year-old's, for with her wide-spaced dark eyes and tiny nose, mouth, and chin, she looked very much like a little kitten.

No one would ever suspect that she had black blood. Her skin was of an unusual shade, a very light olive, and her complexion was pure and smooth. Her hair was black and shiny, but instead of coarse curls, it was satiny, as her mother's had been. Since she was so young, she still wore it down, flowing around her shoulders, with the top and sides pulled away from her face with a sky-blue ribbon. She wore the dress of a young lady of good family, a fine-quality muslin of blue and green stripes, with a satin sash that matched her hair ribbon.

Jolie went to the enclosure around the chicken house and scooped out some feed into a five-gallon bucket and started lightly spreading it around. The chickens came running and at once began pecking at the feed. Jolie watched them with a smile. "Ophelia, don't be so greedy. Let Juliet have some of that seed."

She had named the hens after characters in Shakespeare, which Cleo, the housekeeper, had long ago warned her not to do. "If you name them, you'll get to thinking they're pets, Jolie. Just don't do it, chile."

Jolie had found that to be true, and finally, after many broad hints to Mr. DeForge, DeForge House no longer had chicken for supper. They had loads of eggs, but that was because no chickens were ever killed and Box and Cleo kept them "broody" so they wouldn't have little chicks.

After she'd fed the chickens, calling each one of them by name, she went back to the summer kitchen, which was in back of the main house, connected by a bricked, covered walkway. DeForge House, a majestic Greek Revival home looming above the banks of the Rapidan River, had an enormous kitchen in the cellar that was used in the winter, because it gave the big house additional heat.

As Jolie thought of this, she wondered for perhaps the thousandth time about her benefactor, Henry DeForge. He was 59 years old now—Jolie could always recall his age because he was born in 1800, and so the math was easy—and he obviously had a lot of money, because he had bought this plantation, and only he and Jolie lived in the fifteen-room house. He wore nice clothes, she knew, and she always had nice clothes, but that seemed to be the extent of Mr. DeForge's extravagance. He had a business in Baltimore; he had been teaching Jolie some of the basics of bookkeeping, and so she knew that his company, DeForge Brothers Import & Export, Ltd., made quite a bit of money. But Mr. DeForge had no horses and no carriage, he never entertained, and he never bought new furnishings or accessories for grand DeForge House. Besides the necessities, the only other thing Jolie had seen him purchase was books.

Jolie entered the stifling kitchen. Cleo had an enormous bowl underneath her left arm and was whipping the batter so vigorously she could have powered a boat. "Sponge cake for[...] as she put on a stained and worn canvas bib apro[...] will be so happy. Do you want me to help you, Cleo.[...]

"No! No'm, it's fine. I kin do it," Cleo blurted out.

Jolie had tried three times before to make sponge cakes, Henry DeForge's favorite food. All three times she had neglected to beat the eggs and sugar enough to give the cake its airy texture, and twice she had yanked the cake out of the oven to test its doneness, which made it promptly fall into a gummy mess.

"You go ahead and work out in the garden, Jolie. Box weeded them tomato plants just three days ago, but I swear it looks like they're gettin' took over again."

"I'll put a stop to that," Jolie said briskly, forgetting all about the sponge cake or helping Cleo in the kitchen. She would much rather be outdoors. She liked working in the gardens, for DeForge House had a rich and plentiful, varied kitchen garden, and the flower gardens around the house were gorgeous.

Humming softly to herself, she knelt down by the first staked tomato plant in the row and started working out the weeds with a claw. Two of the field slaves were working the kitchen garden today, two boys in their teens. Jolie talked to them as they worked, desultory things like the weather, how tall the corn was growing, what vegetables they would take to the farmer's market on Saturday in Fredericksburg. The boys mostly just mumbled yes'm and no'm, but Jolie knew them by name and knew their families, and she talked to them as if they were school friends.

By one o'clock, her back was aching, her fingers were sore, and she was very hungry. She went back to the kitchen to beg something from Cleo.

"I'm a-makin' this mayonnaise for tea," Cleo said impatiently. "You can help yourself to whatever you want, Jolie, but I don't have time to stop right now to fix you something."

"That's all right," Jolie said hastily. "I see you've got some of that ham left. I'll just have a couple of slices of that with some cheese."

"Good thing we don't have no hogs what you named, or we'd never have the likes of bacon nor ham," Cleo muttered.

Ignoring her, Jolie put a slice of ham and a chuck of cheese on a stoneware plate, poured herself a mug of apple cider, and went outside to sit on the bench by the door. She ate slowly, staring into space.

She was reflecting upon her age. She had turned thirteen two months previously, and for some reason she had thought that she would be very, very different once she was in her teen years. But she didn't feel any different, and she sure didn't look any different. She was still thin and gangly with no hint of a womanly shape.

Her life was exactly the same as it had always been. Mr. DeForge taught her lessons five days a week in the mornings. In the afternoons she went outside to work in the gardens or take long walks or go down to sit on the riverbank and read and nap. Sometimes, when Mr. DeForge felt well enough, he would go with her, and they would have a picnic at teatime. Either she would read aloud to him, or he would read to her. These times were treasured by Jolie.

She ate very slowly, and she wasn't yet finished when Cleo appeared at the door, hands on hips. "You know you look like a field hand, Jolie. Ain't you going to have tea with Mr. DeForge and Mr. Tremayne?"

Jolie jumped up, scattering plate, ham, cheese, and cider. "Mr. Tremayne's coming for tea? Why didn't you tell me?" Turning, she started running toward the house, skirts flapping.

❧

As Morgan rode to the DeForge place, he wondered about two things: the chickens and Jolie.

When Morgan had inherited his farm in the winter of 1855, he had immediately traveled here and surveyed the property, assessed the state of the house and the outbuildings, and checked on the one-hundred-twelve acres of fields that went with the property.

Also, as soon as he could, he had called on all his neighbors. Henry DeForge was his nearest neighbor, as it was only about five miles along the river to DeForge House. Mr. DeForge had received him most cordially, and in the four years since then they had become fast friends.

Mr. DeForge had, in the course of time, told Morgan that he and his brother had a successful import/export business in Baltimore, Maryland. In 1840, Henry DeForge had been diagnosed with consumption, and that was when he semiretired from the business, bought this property in Virginia, and moved down here. He was very much a recluse. He never traveled; he didn't even own a horse and buggy. He had made arrangements with various shopkeepers in Fredericksburg to have his supplies shipped to him by boat on the Rapidan.

As far as Morgan knew, he was the only visitor to DeForge House, and that was strictly by invitation only. Though he knew that DeForge was a good friend, he was a rather formal, insular man, and each time Morgan visited, Mr. DeForge would make an appointment with him to visit the next time.

In four years of long visits, Morgan and DeForge had talked about their lives, their families, their plans for the future, politics, religion, books, and public figures, but Henry DeForge had never spoken once about Jolie. On his first visit, Morgan had been introduced to the nine-year-old child with Old World gallantry. Mr. DeForge had said, "Mr. Tremayne, it is my honor to make known to you Jolie. Jolie, may I introduce you to Mr. Morgan Tremayne." The child had curtsied prettily but had not said a word, and DeForge had gone on visiting with Morgan. Since then Morgan guessed he might have heard her speak a dozen times.

Morgan Tremayne was not inherently a curious man. He firmly believed that the world would be a much better place if people minded their own business, and he set about doing that very thing. But sometimes he did, in passing, wonder about Jolie. It seemed she had no last name, but only slaves had one given name. Jolie wasn't a slave, that much was obvious, but apparently neither was she a DeForge relative.

"None of my affair anyway," Morgan grunted to himself. Still, he couldn't help but wonder about the chickens.

He let Vulcan have his head, and instantly the horse started galloping wildly, an all-out run. Vulcan did love to run. Morgan wore spurs, but he never *ever* used them on Vulcan. He might have to touch his sides with his boots to get him to turn, but Morgan fancifully believed that if he actually spurred Vulcan to a gallop, the horse would probably jump six feet straight into the air, buck him off, and streak away like a red-hot railroad engine. Very soon Morgan was at the bottom of the hill at DeForge's.

The plantation house was built like most on the river: the drive came up to the back door, with an unspoiled lawn in the front sloping gently down to the riverbank. On Morgan's left were DeForge's farm fields, where he raised cash crops only: corn, peanuts, sweet potatoes, tomatoes, beets, and turnips. Bordering the house on the left were two orchards, cherry and pecan. Directly behind were all the outbuildings, the barn, a storehouse, the creamery, the smokehouse, and the slave cottages. Henry DeForge only had the old couple, Box and Cleo, as house slaves. He had about twenty working field slaves, and Morgan guessed there might be around thirty slaves on the property counting the women and children.

There was a hitching post and watering trough in the yard, and Morgan dismounted and began to tie up Vulcan when a young boy came running up. Morgan remembered his name. "Hello, Howie. You going to take care of Vulcan for me?"

"Yes, suh, if'n he'll let me," the boy said, but he took the reins, and Vulcan meekly allowed him to lead him into the barn.

Morgan was amused; he knew that Vulcan liked visiting here because the slaves gave him lumps of sugar and sweet cherries, no matter how many times Morgan warned them not to do it. Every time he visited DeForge's, he was always afraid Vulcan would be sick the next day.

He walked up the gravel path to the back door, raising his head to catch the scents. Anywhere on DeForge's grounds it seemed one could smell jasmine and roses. It amused Morgan to see the kitchen garden, which grew exactly the same crops that were grown on the farm. But in time he had come to learn that Mr. DeForge was a generous man and apparently didn't need money, because he allowed his slaves to take most of the cash crops to market and sell them. The kitchen garden supplied the home produce. Morgan noted the herb garden and saw that it was thriving. Someone on the place was a good gardener.

Box, a tall, angular black man, met him at the back door, bowing. "Good afternoon, Mr. Tremayne."

"Good afternoon, Box." Morgan gave him his hat and gloves and said, "I've got two chickens in that canvas sack on my saddle. I forgot to tell Howie to bring them up here. Evetta says they're for Cleo."

"Yes, suh. No, suh. It's all right, suh. I'll fetch 'em, and I know Cleo will want to thank you personal. Mr. DeForge is out on the veranda, Mr. Tremayne."

"Thank you, Box. I can find my own way." Morgan went to the front door, passing the butler's pantry, the storage pantry, the formal dining room, the parlor, the music room, and the sitting room, and finally went out onto the veranda.

DeForge and Jolie were seated around a white wrought-iron table, sipping lemonade. Henry DeForge was a tall, distinguished-looking man with thin silver hair and thick side whiskers and sharp blue eyes. However he was ill, and he had good days and bad days. Morgan could see this was a good day. He wasn't nearly as pale as he had been on Morgan's visit two weeks ago, and his shoulders weren't weakly slumped. Jolie looked fresh and pretty in a mint-green dress with a green ribbon in her hair.

He shook hands with DeForge, and Jolie offered hers, dropping her eyes shyly. Morgan bent over it, remembering a couple of years ago, when she had jumped to her feet and curtsied when he had come into the room. DeForge had gently told her, "Jolie, you are a lady, and Mr. Tremayne is a gentleman. Ladies do not rise to greet gentlemen. In fact, it is supposed to be the other way around. Gentlemen are supposed to rise when you enter or leave a room. I know that I don't do that, but that's because I'm old and tending to laziness."

Morgan seated himself and accepted a glass of lemonade from Jolie. "Thank you, ma'am," he said. "Mm, I see you still have ice, Mr. DeForge. Delicious, I got rather heated riding Vulcan, and it made me thirsty."

"How is that devil of a horse?" DeForge asked.

"Devilish," Morgan said lightly and told DeForge about how he had shown off at Arlington. "But it was a good visit, I think. Colonel Lee is going to buy two horses from me."

"Excellent," DeForge said briskly. "Business is good, eh? What about your spring plantings?"

Henry DeForge had three hundred acres that had lain fallow for almost twenty years. After he had gotten to know Morgan, DeForge had leased the acreage to him to raise forage crops for the horses, and with three hundred acres, there was plenty to sell. Morgan had also hired ten DeForge slaves to work the fields, paying them by the day. Unlike other slaveholders who leased out their slaves, Henry DeForge wanted no money for himself.

"The oats and alfalfa already look strong and healthy," Morgan told him. "That's some good soil in your fields, Mr. DeForge. My winter rye and barley was a bumper crop, and the soil shows no sign of weakening. Next year, of course, I'll rotate to legumes and corn, but I think I'll go ahead and do another winter rye and barley."

They talked about crops and weather for a while; though Henry DeForge was not a farmer in the proper sense of the word, he was interested in agriculture, as he was interested in many things.

"Mr. Ballard says that we are to have a blue moon this season," DeForge said, his eyes alight, "and that Widow Tapp's cow gave birth to a white calf. These are, I understand, very good omens for farmers."

"Hope so," Morgan said. "But speaking of livestock, may I ask you a question, sir? Every time I come to visit, Evetta makes me bring Cleo a chicken or two. Is there something wrong with your chickens?"

DeForge chuckled and glanced at Jolie. Her cheeks flamed, and she dropped her head. DeForge said, "Jolie has named all of the chickens, and so they have become her personal pets. Naturally I can't execute a pet. I don't really mind one way or another, because chicken is not my favorite meat, but I understand that Cleo takes great exception to it."

"It's the stock," Jolie said in a small voice. "She says you must use chicken stock in lots of dishes."

"Mm, true. It's unfortunate that you still have to kill them to get the stock," Morgan said lightly. "Don't worry, Jolie. I'll tell Evetta to make sure Cleo has plenty of anonymous dead chickens."

"Thank you, Mr. Tremayne," she said, her face still downcast.

"Jolie, would you please go check on Cleo?" DeForge asked. "I'm about ready for my tea." Jolie rose and went through the front door.

Morgan didn't rise when she left the table. To him she was very much a child, and gentlemen weren't constrained to show the same politeness to children as they were to adults.

DeForge said, "Speaking of omens, have you kept up with the news out of Washington, Mr. Tremayne?"

"Somewhat, sir. I admit I've been so very busy that sometimes I let the newspapers pile up for days."

DeForge frowned. "I see some very bad signs for the future of this country. Arrogant hotheads, who normally would never be paid any attention by sane persons, seem to be the dominant forces on both sides of the Mason–Dixon Line. And it's not just Washington and New York in the North, you know. From Maine to Minnesota they're all getting up in arms."

"But surely you don't think we'll go to war, do you?" Morgan asked, shocked. He knew Mr. DeForge, though he never traveled, kept up with national news every day. He took newspapers from Fredericksburg and Richmond and also Washington, New York, Chicago, Indianapolis, New Orleans, and Austin, and once a month he was delivered papers from California. He was a very sharp, intelligent man.

"Last year at this time I didn't think so," he said quietly. "This spring I do think so. I don't believe it will be next spring, because next year is election year. But I'm afraid spring of 1861 will not be nearly this peaceful and sweet."

Morgan sat and stared into space, stunned. Of course he was aware of the growing tensions between the slave states and the free states. He knew that in many ways, "bleeding Kansas" was symbolic of the entire nation, with "free staters" battling proslavery "border ruffians" in a series of ugly violent incidents that had begun five years ago. But to actually believe that the United States of America would be dissolved and any state would ever consider secession had not entered the darkest recesses of Morgan's mind.

He wondered now if DeForge was suffering from some worry that had ballooned into a big fear. Morgan thought that sometimes happened to older people. But quickly he pushed the thought away. Henry DeForge was not a man to suffer from baseless fear, nor was he given to exaggeration.

Morgan frowned. Perhaps it was he who was blind, refusing to see the disaster looming so clearly in the forefront of his friend's mind. "What would you do, sir, if there was a war?" he asked.

DeForge shrugged. "I know that Maryland is considered a border state, but I'll never believe she would secede. Personally, I have great sympathy for the South. I've lived here for almost twenty years, and I love it here. I've been happier living here than any place I've ever been. If Virginia seceded, I would stay here and face the consequences."

Jolie rejoined them and slipped back into her seat. "Cleo will be here in a few minutes with tea, Mr. DeForge."

"That's fine, child," he said absently. Then he continued

speaking to Morgan. "But are you asking what I would do, in the practical sense, if we were at war?"

"I suppose so," Morgan said. "I'm still trying to imagine such a terrible thing."

"Yes, you may think I'm just an old worrywart," DeForge said with a smile. "But for a few moments let's talk as if I'm in my right mind. If I knew that I was going to be caught in a war, I would start hoarding. I would hoard gold, first of all, because it is truly a universal currency. Then I would hoard all of the necessaries I could gather. Foodstuffs, wood, coal, tools, nails, fabrics such as wool and cotton, soap, candles—anything and everything I could think of that I would need to run my homestead."

Morgan frowned. "But surely we will always be able to buy such things as food and clothing. I mean, those are the absolute necessities of life. Surely we wouldn't end up back in the Dark Ages!"

"Before I became ill, I traveled all over," DeForge said calmly. "I've been to the Far West, to Maine, to Florida, all over the Midwest. Let me explain something to you, Mr. Tremayne. The Southern slave states will never be able to win a war against the industrialized North. I have an import/export business. In the North and the Midwest they import and export everything. They have thriving industries, they have disposable incomes, they are not land-poor like so many planters are. The South exports cotton, period. And they have to import everything else." He shook his head. "I could be wrong about the coming war, certainly. It may not come in a couple of years. It may not come to that at all. But one thing I do know, Mr. Tremayne. If it does come, the South will end up desolately poor and naked. It's simple economics."

Jolie's gaze had been darting back and forth between Morgan and DeForge as they spoke. Her eyes were huge and luminous, her expression one of deep distress. DeForge focused on her, then took her hand in his. "I apologize, Jolie. Children shouldn't have to listen to such things, especially just an old man's ranting."

"You're not old," she said. "And you never rant."

"Exactly," Morgan said in a low voice. He was all too afraid that Henry DeForge knew exactly what he was talking about. He quickly pushed the unwelcome thoughts aside and forgot them.

But later, with deep regret, he was to recall every word that Henry DeForge had said.

~

Jolie was curled up and seemed almost boneless with her legs tucked under her and her body bent. She was sitting on one side of the enormous fireplace in the parlor, while Henry DeForge sat on the other side.

In spite of the fact that it was a warm night, DeForge had ordered a big fire built, and he wore a wool shawl. Occasionally he coughed, a painful racking sound that made Jolie wince. Still, she kept reading aloud:

> "'We are friends,' said I, rising and bending over her,
> as she rose from the bench.
> 'And will continue friends apart,' said Estella.
> I took her hand in mine, and we went out of the ruined
> place; and as the morning mist had risen long ago when I
> first left the forge, so, the evening mists were rising now,
> and in all the broad expanse of tranquil light they showed
> to me, I saw no shadow of another parting from her."

With a sigh, Jolie closed the volume. "I just love *Great Expectations.*"

"It's always been my favorite of Dickens's novels. Oh Jolie, you're not crying!"

Quickly Jolie wiped the tears from her cheeks. "But it's sad. Pip had such a hard life and then lost the girl he loved."

"Why, he didn't lose her, child," DeForge said. "Look at that last sentence. 'I saw no shadow of another parting from her.' They didn't part from each other. The two shadows stayed together, so it's a happy ending."

Jolie managed a weak smile. "Why, it's so, isn't it? I'm so glad. I think it's awful to lose someone that you love."

"Yes, it is," DeForge said quietly, staring into the flames. "It is truly awful."

After a few moments, Jolie said hesitantly, "Mr. DeForge? May I ask you a question?"

"Of course, Jolie."

"Well, you see, I am thirteen now. Do you—would you be able to tell me about my parents?"

"That's right," DeForge said with surprise. "I forgot. You did turn thirteen in April, didn't you, Jolie?"

"Yes, sir. And you've always said I needed to be older before you told me about my parents. I just thought that maybe thirteen is old enough."

"I see. You may be right, Jolie. Maybe thirteen is old enough." He shifted in his chair, which brought on a coughing spell.

Jolie wanted to run to him and hold him, but she knew he didn't like gestures of tenderness such as that.

Finally the coughing subsided, and he went on in a weak voice, "I will tell you about your mother. She was a quadroon. Do you know what a quadroon is?"

"No, sir."

"It means she was one-quarter black and three-quarters white."

"So I'm black?" Jolie asked with no visible surprise.

"You are one-eighth black, yes. But you are not, and never will be, a slave," DeForge said firmly.

Jolie digested this for a while then asked, "My mother, what was she like? Was she nice?"

"She was a very beautiful woman, inside and outside. She was sweet and kind, and she was very religious, although I know that doesn't mean much to you, since I haven't brought you up that way." A curious half smile touched his lips. "She would be very angry with me if she knew I had neglected that part of your education."

"She would?" Jolie asked, astonished. "But she was a slave, wasn't she? If she was black, she had to be a slave. Surely she couldn't get angry with you!"

"Yes, she was a slave. But still she was angry with me at times."

"Do you—is there a picture of her, Mr. DeForge?" Jolie pleaded. "I would love a picture of her more than anything."

DeForge hesitated for a long time. Finally he turned to stare back, unseeing, into the fire. "No, there is no picture of her."

"Oh. No, I guess there wouldn't be, not if she was a slave," Jolie said sadly. "But Mr. DeForge, what about my father? Did you know my father?"

In a curiously dead tone he said, "Yes, I knew your father. He was not a good man. He was not good to your mother. She died in childbirth, having you, Jolie, and he was bitter and angry because of that for a long time."

"You're saying 'was,'" Jolie said. "Is he dead?"

"I hope so," DeForge said angrily. "I truly hope so. I don't want to talk about him any more, Jolie. In fact, I'm very tired. I'd like to go to bed now."

"Of course, sir. I'll get Box," she said, jumping up.

Later, as Jolie lay sleepless in her bed, she figured out what had been wrong with the conversation she'd had with Mr. DeForge. It had had a false ring to it, and now she knew why.

It was the first time he had ever lied to her.

CHAPTER EIGHT

The next year was very good for Morgan. Rapidan Farm thrived and prospered. Morgan had at last been accepted in Fredericksburg, which was an insular, proud little town.

He visited the DeForge place regularly, as he was invited, and even though there was such a difference in their ages, he thought of Henry DeForge as his closest friend.

Somewhat to his surprise, he also kept in close touch with Mrs. Robert E. Lee at Arlington. She wrote him regularly, and every time he had business in the northern part of the state, he stopped by to see her. Colonel Lee had returned to active duty in Texas in February of 1860, and it seemed to Morgan that she was always particularly glad to see him then, because she was alone at Arlington. The girls traveled a lot, and when Millie turned fourteen, they had sent her to boarding school in Winchester. Morgan always stayed long hours with Mrs. Lee, talking about family and also about business things concerning the plantation, for Mrs. Lee was now running Arlington by herself, as she had done for so many years as her father grew older.

the SURRENDER

November 7, 1860, was a fine, icily clear day. Morgan and Vulcan made their way along the worn path between the two farms to DeForge House. The week before, Henry DeForge had purposely asked Morgan to come to tea on the day after the election. Morgan was troubled. Abraham Lincoln, an ardent abolitionist, had been elected. For the most part he had ignored politics, as his own life seemed so settled, so safe and secure. Even now he didn't much want to think or talk about slavery or secession or the Union. He hoped that Mr. DeForge didn't want to talk about it either, but he thought very likely that would be the topic his friend wanted to discuss.

When he reached DeForge House, he saw the black buggy in the backyard and immediately recognized it. It was Dr. Travers's buggy. The doctor had a little homestead just downriver from DeForge House. Morgan sprang out of the saddle, threw the reins around the hitching post, and ran into the house.

Cleo met him at the door. "He had a bad spell. It's the first time he's tole us to call the doctor," she said, troubled.

"Is the doctor with him right now?"

"Yes, sir. If'n you'd like to wait in the parlor, Box has got a good fire in there."

"Thanks, Cleo. I'll wait. I'd like to see him if I could."

"Yes, sir. He 'specially said he wants to talk to you, Mr. Tremayne."

Morgan nodded and went into the parlor. He walked up to the fireplace and stripped off his gloves to warm his hands. Silently he stared down into the flames, wondering just how ill DeForge was. Morgan had seen that he had grown visibly weaker in the past year, and the coughing fits he suffered seemed to come more often. But he still had been alert, interested in all of Morgan's news of the farm, knowledgeable and articulate about current events. He never complained.

Morgan became aware that someone was watching him, and only then did he see Jolie sitting in a chair up at the front of the room by the window. She was sitting bolt upright, her hands restless in her lap. She looked terrified. "Hello, Mr. Tremayne. I'm sorry I didn't let you know I was here, but I just couldn't get the words out somehow."

"It's okay, Jolie," he said soothingly. "How is he? Tell me what happened."

"He was fine, just fine this morning," she said, obviously bewildered. "He ate a good breakfast, and we played chess. He asked Cleo for sponge cake for tea. But then he started coughing, and it seemed like he couldn't stop. He got out of breath, and we got scared. Finally he told Box to go for the doctor."

"I know Dr. Travers. He's a good man. Maybe this is just a touch of catarrh."

She shook her head. "His handkerchief. . .there was blood."

Morgan didn't know what to say. He himself was extremely healthy, as was his entire family. It was true, he did know Dr. Travers because he had made it his business to know all his neighbors. But he had never had to call him for medical reasons.

They waited in silence for what seemed a long time. Finally they heard footsteps on the marble stairs, and Dr. Travers came in. He was a young man, in his early thirties, with sandy brown hair and kind brown eyes. He had two children, a boy and a girl, and another one on the way, Morgan knew. He also knew that Dr. Travers was poor, for although he was the only doctor for miles around, the small farmers couldn't afford to pay him much in cash. Instead, they paid him in chickens or tomatoes or canned jam or sides of bacon. Morgan himself had recommended him to Mr. DeForge when the slaves had gotten influenza that spring.

Jolie jumped up when he came into the room then stood, her hands curled into tight bloodless fists at her side. "How is he?" she asked in a strangled voice.

"He's sleeping quietly," Dr. Travers answered, stepping up to warm himself at the fire. "I gave him a sleeping draught. He didn't want to take it, but. . ." He made a helpless little motion with his hand. "Hello, Mr. Tremayne," he said. "One reason Mr. DeForge didn't want to take the medicine was because he insisted that he had to talk to you. But—I'm sorry, Jolie, but I guess you probably already know this. Mr. DeForge has consumption, and that, unfortunately, is an incurable disease. The best thing I can do for him is give him something to stop the coughing and help him sleep."

Morgan asked, "But how is Mr. DeForge. I mean, where is he in the course of the disease?" Morgan didn't want to ask if he was dying in front of Jolie.

Dr. Travers seemed to understand the question very well. "We don't know much about why the disease progresses at different rates in different people. But I feel optimistic about Mr. DeForge for several reasons. One is that he's had this disease for many years, and so it's obviously progressing very slowly in his case. I personally think that moving here, away from Baltimore or any other large industrial city, has likely helped him. Most big cities have a noxious atmosphere. Here the air is clean and pure. Another thing that encourages me is that Cleo tells me that his appetite is good," he said, glancing questioningly at Jolie.

"Oh yes, sir," she said eagerly. "He eats well and eats regularly. I make sure of that."

"That's good, Jolie. One of the first signs of a terminal stage is a loss of appetite and refusal to eat. If he still wants to eat and eats good, nourishing food, then I would say that we have nothing to worry about just yet," he finished warmly.

Jolie took a deep breath and sat back down, obviously relieved.

Morgan was still worried. "Dr. Travers, I was planning on going back to my home in the Shenandoah Valley tomorrow for Christmas, so I plan to be away for at least a month. Does Mr. DeForge. . .that is, do you think he'll be all right?"

Cautiously the doctor replied, "No man knows his appointed time, Mr. Tremayne. But based solely on what I've seen and heard here today, I see no reason why Mr. DeForge shouldn't recover quickly. Barring any complications, that is."

"You're going away for a month?" Jolie exclaimed. "But that's such a long time!"

"Yes, I know," Morgan said thoughtfully. "It's the first time since I've moved here that I've felt able to take a long holiday."

"Oh, I see," Jolie said slowly. "You would want to be with your parents and your brother and sisters for Christmas."

For a moment it jarred Morgan, thinking of Jolie and Henry DeForge here alone during the holiday season. But it wasn't really his concern, was it? His primary responsibility was with his own family. "I'll give you my address, Jolie," he said with a reassuring smile. "I'd like it if you and Mr. DeForge would write to me."

"Of course," she said stiffly.

"You say Mr. DeForge is asleep? How long will he sleep, do you think?" Morgan asked Dr. Travers.

"I hope through the afternoon and all night," he answered. "I'm leaving more laudanum with Cleo just in case he needs another dose. I think if he rests quietly for the next twenty-four hours he'll be much better."

Morgan nodded. "Jolie, please tell Mr. DeForge I'm sorry we didn't get to talk today, but as soon as I get back, I'll come by and get caught up on all the news. Good-bye for now, Jolie, and God bless you and Mr. DeForge."

"Thank you, Mr. Tremayne," she said.

Morgan smiled at her as he left. He thought of how small and defenseless she seemed in that big armchair. When the cold brisk air touched his face and he heard Vulcan's welcome nicker, he felt the burden of worry for his friend lift. He said a quick prayer for Mr. DeForge and Jolie and then turned his thoughts to his trip home.

Morgan lifted the brass lion's-head door knocker and rapped sharply twice.

The Bledsoes' maid, Nance, answered the door and made a quick, awkward curtsy.

"Hello, Nance. Is she in the parlor?" Morgan asked as he handed her his hat and gloves.

"Um, yes sir, but, um. . . ," she stammered.

Morgan ignored her and went into the parlor with the ease of a longtime caller. He had been seeing Leona for almost two years now. He went into the small but elegantly furnished sitting room and stopped in surprise.

Leona was there, seated on one end of the long camelback sofa. On the other end of the sofa sat Wade Kimbrel.

Leona looked up, and Morgan thought for a moment that she looked angry, but then her expression smoothed out, and she rose, coming to him with her hands outstretched. "Well hello, Morgan. This is a surprise. I thought you were leaving for the Valley."

"Yes, I am. I'm taking the 5:00 train," he said, eyeing Wade Kimbrel, who remained seated. He made a quick bow over her hands, and she motioned him to an armchair by the fireplace.

Leona Rose Bledsoe was now twenty-one years old. Morgan had actually met her back in 1855, when he had moved to Rapidan Run. Although his family had connections in Richmond, Morgan had wanted to be a part of nearby Fredericksburg, and so he had formed all his business associations there, including getting his own lawyer. He had decided to go with the largest firm in the wealthy little town, Mercer & Bledsoe, and Leona's father, Benjamin Bledsoe, had been his lawyer for the last five years. He had started attending St. Andrew's Episcopal Church upon Benjamin Bledsoe's recommendation. At church Morgan had gotten to know the family: Mrs. Eileen Bledsoe; Gibbs Bledsoe, Leona's brother, who was one year younger than Morgan; and their daughter, Leona. But she had been only sixteen at the time, and he had dismissed her as a child.

In January of 1859, Morgan had turned twenty-five, and though he didn't really consciously know it, he began to feel that he should settle down. He knew several pleasant girls in Fredericksburg, and he knew even more in Richmond. But it was then that he noticed that Leona Rose Bledsoe had become a striking, vibrant young woman. She was not pretty, in the conventional sense. Tall, with strong features and flashing dark eyes, she had a rather imperious manner. But she was extremely intelligent, and she was an interesting woman. In the previous year, to Morgan's amusement, she had begun to hold what would be called a "salon" on the Continent. She had many callers, men and women both. Every Friday evening she had a musicale, when she would play the piano and sing, and others would perform, too. All of her friends were from the oldest, finest families of Fredericksburg.

Except for Morgan. He had persistently courted her for a year before she would allow him to see her alone, without her mother in attendance. Yet here she was, with Wade Kimbrel, and Eileen Bledsoe was obviously not in the parlor.

Kimbrel remained insolently seated, one leg crossed over the other, his arm laid comfortably along the back of the sofa. When Morgan sat down, he merely nodded and said, "Tremayne."

"Kimbrel," Morgan said shortly. To Leona he said, "I wasn't aware that you were such close friends with Mr. Kimbrel."

"Morgan, I'm surprised at you," she said dismissively. "It's rude to speak in the third person when that person is present."

"Got a burr in your saddle, Tremayne?" Kimbrel drawled. "Mr. Bledsoe has been my family's attorney for twenty years now. Of course I'm friends with Leona. I've known her all her life."

Morgan frowned. Leona had given him permission to use her given name only four months ago, and she had agreed to call him Morgan. Still, when he was speaking of her, he called her Miss Bledsoe out of respect.

But Kimbrel's intimate use of her name wasn't the only thing that bothered Morgan. Wade Kimbrel was his nearest neighbor, aside from Henry DeForge. Just across the river from both of their farms was Wolvesey, an eight-thousand-acre cotton plantation that John

Edward Kimbrel had established in 1780. The Kimbrels had had slaves ever since then, and now Wade Kimbrel had over seventy slaves.

Wade had inherited the property from his father, who had died when Wade was only twenty. He was now thirty-two and had never married. He was a fine-looking man—tall, burly, with jet-black hair and a ferocious mustache. The talk around town was that he had courted several women, but it seemed they could never quite bring him to the point of marriage. He was considered to be something of a rake.

And Morgan knew, because he had seen firsthand, that Kimbrel mistreated his slaves. He had called on Kimbrel not long after he had moved to Rapidan Run, and as he had passed through the miles of cotton fields, he had seen Kimbrel's overseer beating a slave until he passed out. Morgan had not questioned Kimbrel about it, feeling that it was none of his business, but when Wade Kimbrel had wanted to buy a horse from him, Morgan had flatly refused. "You mistreat your slaves, you'll mistreat your horses," he had told him. He and Kimbrel had been enemies ever since then.

Now Morgan made himself calm down. He didn't often lose his temper, and he disliked it when he did. He felt it showed a lack of self-control. "I apologize, Kimbrel. Of course I know you're friends with the Bledsoes. I was just a little surprised, that's all."

Kimbrel shrugged carelessly.

After an awkward silence, Leona said brightly, "I was surprised, too, I admit. I had no idea you were still in town, Morgan." Morgan had told her on Sunday as he was walking her home after church that he would be going to Staunton on Wednesday.

"I wouldn't have thought of leaving without saying good-bye," he said somewhat stiffly.

"Good-bye, then," Kimbrel said.

"Oh! Wade, you are wicked. I thought you were leaving anyway," Leona said with amusement.

"I've decided to stay for a while. Why don't you invite me for supper?"

"I suppose I might as well. Father will be home any minute, and I know he will anyway," she said.

Morgan felt confused, embarrassed, and apprehensive. It was as if he weren't even there. Somehow he had taken for granted that he and Leona had an unspoken agreement between them, and that their relationship was special. Even as he thought it, he realized how vague this supposition was, and obviously he was very much mistaken about Leona. He was so perturbed that he wanted to get away, get some fresh air, and think. He shot out of the chair, and both Leona and Kimbrel looked up at him in surprise. "I have to go," he said hurriedly.

Leona rose gracefully and took his arm. "I'll see you out," she said. She walked him to the door, then turned and rested her hands on his shoulders. "You must come see me as soon as you get back," she said. "I will miss you."

"I'll miss you, too, Leona," he said unhappily.

She kissed him lightly on the cheek and said, "Good-bye, then, Morgan. God be with you."

❧

Morgan returned on the first Saturday of the new year. As the train neared the station in Fredericksburg, Morgan looked out the window at the so-familiar landscape and smiled to himself.

In the month that he had been gone, he had completely cleared his mind of the confusion he'd felt at his last meeting with Leona. He had made some crucial decisions, and now he felt that his course was set. He would ask Leona to marry him after a short engagement. Perhaps they could be married in the spring, he thought. That would give him time to fix up the house, buy some new furnishings. Leona was good at that kind of thing, and he was sure that she would be excited to furnish and decorate her new home.

Idly he reflected, as the train hurtled on, on the surprise he had felt when he had realized that he was actually homesick for Rapidan

Run. He had always regarded Tremayne House as his home. But he supposed it was a sign that he was a man, and that it was time to start his own family apart from his parents. His spirits grew even more buoyant.

Leona will make an excellent wife, he thought with satisfaction. *Mother and Father will love her. Mother, especially. They have so much in common.*

Again he smiled as he thought of the surprise he had for Leona. He was bringing home a carriage, a fine four-seater landau with a folding top. True, it was secondhand. His father had just bought his mother a new barouche box, and originally Mr. Tremayne had intended to sell the old landau. But Morgan grabbed it up—though he did pay his father for it—because he knew that Leona would need it. It was fine for him to travel into Fredericksburg on horseback, but a lady needed a carriage.

He had telegraphed ahead and instructed Amon to bring Ace, a big brown gelding that served as their work horse, when he came to meet him. Ace pulled the farm wagon, and Morgan thought, considering Ace's placid temperament, that it wouldn't spook him or make him nervous in the new experience of pulling a carriage.

The long shrill whistle sounded, and the conductor began his chant: "Fredericksburg! Coming into Fredericksburg!"

Out his window Morgan saw Amon and Rosh waiting. Amon waved then bent to speak to a slight man standing with him and pointed to Morgan. The stranger looked up at Morgan searchingly.

Morgan stepped off the train steps and hurried to the three men waiting for him. "Hello, Amon, Rosh. I can't tell you how good it is to be home."

"Yes, sir," Amon said gravely. "Mr. Tremayne, this gentleman is Mr. Silas Cage. Mr. Cage, this here is Mr. Morgan Tremayne."

Cage, a short, thin, earnest-looking young man with spectacles, shook Morgan's hand. "I'm very glad to meet you, sir. I know this is unorthodox, but it is extremely important that I speak with you."

"Right now?" Morgan said with astonishment. He had just had a fifteen-hour train ride, and he had some complicated arrangements to make to get himself, his luggage, and the carriage home.

"Yes, sir. I am an attorney, and I have an extremely urgent matter that requires your immediate attention, Mr. Tremayne."

"Is something wrong at home?" he demanded of Amon.

"No, sir, everything is fine. We's all fine, and all the horses is fine," Amon reassured him.

"Thank heavens," Morgan said with relief. "All right, Mr. Cage, I'll be glad to speak to you as soon as I've made some arrangements."

"Would you come to my office?" he asked. "It's right on Dalrymple Street, just off Main. The one-story red brick with the wrought-iron gate."

"I'll be there as soon as possible, sir," Morgan assured him.

Cage hurried off.

As they walked to the yard to collect the carriage, Morgan asked Amon, "Do you know what that's all about?"

"No, sir," Amon said uneasily. "What I mean is, he come to the house two days ago, looking for you. He told me he needed to see you right quick, but he didn't tell me why."

"But you know something about it, Amon, I can tell," Morgan insisted.

"Not for sure, Mr. Tremayne. Alls I know is that old Mr. DeForge, he died three days ago."

"What!" Morgan said, halting abruptly. "He died! But no one wrote me, no one telegraphed me!"

"I think that Mr. Cage did think to send you a telegram, but it appears you ain't got it, huh?"

"No, I didn't," Morgan said thoughtfully. Tremayne House and farm were about eight miles outside of Staunton. It was conceivable that a telegram had come there and it might not have been delivered to the farm until after he left.

Morgan resumed walking, his head bowed. His friend had died, and he hadn't been there. He did not think that Henry DeForge was actually a lonely man; his reclusive tendencies seemed to be voluntary. But now Morgan heartily wished that he had been here the last month. He would miss Henry Deforge terribly.

Numbly he instructed Amon about taking the carriage home. He and Rosh had brought Vulcan, so Morgan said, "You two go on home. After I speak to Mr. Cage, I'll be along."

It was a short distance to Cage's office, so Morgan didn't ride. He took Vulcan's reins and walked slowly. Even though it was just after noon, it grew dark and started to snow, a wet, heavy snow. Morgan was so beset by grief that he barely noticed.

He knocked on the door of the small house, for when Morgan found the place he realized that Mr. Cage must have his office at his home.

A young sweet-faced woman answered the door. "Mr. Tremayne, please come in. I am Mrs. Cage. My husband is in his office, if you'll follow me." She ushered him down the hall to a tiny room with every wall filled with books.

Cage sat behind a work-scarred desk. He rose to shake Morgan's hand again. "Please, sit down, Mr. Tremayne. I know you must be very tired after your journey, and again I apologize for intruding upon you in this manner. My wife will bring us tea shortly."

"That would be very welcome," Morgan said. "I've gotten into the habit of having afternoon tea. In fact, it's because of my friendship with Henry DeForge that I formed the habit. He always had what he called high tea."

"Yes, I know," Mr. Cage said sadly. "I was not as close a friend as you obviously were. I was his attorney. But I will miss him, too." He took a deep breath, leaned forward, and clasped his hands together on the desk. "I assume that your servant told you of Mr. DeForge's death."

"Yes, I didn't know of it until just now," Morgan said. "He didn't write me while I was gone, but I didn't think that too unusual. He was ill when I left, and I thought that perhaps he simply didn't feel like corresponding. But his death is a shock. I understood from Dr. Travers that his condition at that time wasn't critical."

"Dr. Travers was right," Cage said. "He did recover nicely from that downturn he took in November. For the rest of that month and until the last two weeks in December, he was as well as I've ever known him to be. But just before Christmas the consumption worsened again, and Dr. Travers attended him, with the same instructions, to get plenty of rest and take laudanum to ease the pain and coughing. The problem was that he developed pneumonia. That's actually what killed him, not the consumption. And it was fast. Dr. Travers diagnosed pneumonia four days after Christmas, and he quickly grew worse and died on January 3rd. It was a great shock."

"How I wish I'd been here," Morgan said quietly. "I considered Mr. DeForge my closest friend, almost like a father to me, though I'm not sure he returned my regard in the same manner."

"Did he think of you almost as a son? Yes, he most certainly did," Cage said, to Morgan's surprise. "I'm sure you realize by now that I need to speak to you because of Mr. DeForge's will. He has left you some—bequests."

At that moment a soft knock sounded on the door, and Mrs. Cage entered with a tea tray. Morgan thought that Cage looked relieved, and he wondered why. Mrs. Cage efficiently served them tea and then slipped out of the room.

With clear reluctance Cage continued, "First of all, Mr. DeForge willed you the three hundred acres that you've been leasing from him."

"He split that out from the estate?" Morgan said with surprise. "Well, that was very generous of him."

"Er—yes." Cage took a sip of tea. "Mr. Tremayne, Mr. DeForge's will is a bit complicated. I was there two days before he died, and I was with him for several hours, finishing up the details of his final wishes. He dictated a letter to me, and it is to you." Slowly he took a long envelope from a drawer and handed it to Morgan.

My dear Morgan,

I know that I have little time left, and so this letter must necessarily be short and to the point.

When I bought my property, which was then known as the Strickland place, the slaves were included in the purchase price. I fell in love with a beautiful quadroon girl named Jeanetta, who was one of my maids. She was my mistress for five years, and we were carefree. But in the sixth year, she became pregnant, and in April of 1846, she died giving birth to Jolie. I never gave Jolie my name, just as I never gave Jeannetta my name, and now I am bitterly ashamed of it.

I know that it is too late for me to regain my honor and make things right for Jolie. So now, in my last days, I am asking you to help me make amends.

I have been setting money aside for Jolie and have accumulated ten thousand dollars. For this reason I have appointed you as Jolie's guardian. Use whatever is necessary to educate her until she is eighteen and then give her what's left.

But Morgan, I'm afraid I must ask you to do even more. It is my dying wish that Jolie would be protected and nurtured, and yes, even loved. Can you find it in your heart to do that? I can't demand that you do so or make it a provision of my will. I can only hope that the generous and kind heart that I've seen in you will dictate what is right. I know you to be a man of honor, and I beg you to make a vow to God to be faithful to my daughter.

The letter was simply signed, "Henry DeForge."

For a long time Morgan couldn't speak, he was so stunned. He simply sat there, staring blankly into space.

Cage, with compassion written on every feature, sat quiet and still.

Morgan had no idea how long he sat there, speechless, but finally he roused a bit. "This is a great shock," he said gutturally. "I had no idea. Tell me, Mr. Cage, was this decision about me being Jolie's guardian something that he decided just before he died?"

"No, it wasn't. I made up this will four years ago. I understand that he had known you for about a year, and he designated you as Jolie's guardian then. Of course," he said, taking off his glasses and polishing them with his handkerchief, "at that time he was only thinking of you being a trustee for the money. He always intended to speak to you about taking Jolie into your home. He's told me through the years that he felt so well, and he didn't feel that his time was near, and so he didn't think it was the right time to burden you with it. Who knows? He might have lived well past Jolie's eighteenth birthday, if he hadn't come down with pneumonia."

"Maybe that was what he wanted to talk to me about in November," Morgan said wearily. "Maybe he had some idea even then."

"It's true, he did. He told me at the last. He so regretted that he'd never talked with you about it, found out how you feel about it," Cage said, eyeing Morgan shrewdly. "So how do you feel about it, Mr. Tremayne?"

Morgan shifted uncomfortably in the hard chair. "Shocked. Bewildered. And—yes, angry. This is a terrible burden to ask a man to bear."

"It is. And Mr. DeForge knew it. He did make provisions just in case you felt you couldn't act as Jolie's guardian. He knew full well that you might refuse. In fact, he said that you should," Cage finished with an odd look on his face. "I think that might have been the last joke he ever made."

Morgan ignored this; he didn't feel any lightness in this conversation at all. "What alternate arrangements did he make for Jolie?"

"He asked me if I would be a trustee for her inheritance. He instructed me where to send her to school, to purchase a house for her, and to finance her if she thought she may be able to open some sort of shop," he said. "Jolie is clever, you know. Mr. DeForge thought that she might very well be able to find her own way, when she's older."

"But he didn't ask you to take her in," Morgan said bluntly, with some bitterness.

"No, he didn't. You see, Mr. Tremayne, my wife is only eighteen. It's awkward. My wife is still very young herself to take over any responsibility for a fourteen-year-old girl."

"Jolie is fourteen?" Morgan said, astounded. "I had no idea. Somehow I still think of her as a child. She still looks like a child."

"She will be fifteen in April. And yes, she is petite and still childlike," Cage agreed.

Morgan threw the letter down on Cage's desk and began to pace. "Fourteen! That's even worse! I'm single, you know. How am I supposed to have a fourteen-year-old girl living with me alone? And I hope to be married soon. How can I ask my fiancée to take Jolie into our home? It's impossible! The whole thing is just impossible. It can't be done!"

"It can be done, sir," Cage said mildly. "The question is whether you are willing to do it."

Morgan's head snapped toward the attorney, and he saw the kindness and understanding on his face. Resignedly Morgan sat back down. "I don't suppose I have much time to consider it, do I?"

"It would be hard for Jolie. Mr. DeForge is to be sent to Baltimore tomorrow, and Box and Cleo are returning with him. He brought them from Baltimore when he moved, you know, and to them it's still home because they have family there. So Jolie would be at DeForge House alone."

"Tomorrow?" Morgan passed his hand across his forehead. "Of course, he died three days ago. It's just all happened so fast, to me. Yes, I see what you mean, Mr. Cage. I'll go get Jolie tomorrow. First thing in the morning. I apologize, sir, but I'm extremely tired now, and I'd like to go home. May I make an appointment with you later to discuss the details?"

"Certainly, Mr. Tremayne. I'll be happy to see you at any time," he said courteously. They rose, and Morgan started toward the door, but Cage said, "Mr. Tremayne? There is one more thing I should tell you now."

"Yes? What is that?"

"In my last conversation with Mr. DeForge, he told me to tell you this: that he knew he had never been able to show it, and he could certainly never say it, but he loved you. He loved you as if you were his own son."

❧

The next day was a dreary, depressing day indeed. It had snowed throughout the night, and Morgan had slept very little. He was awake for most of the night worrying. A darkened dawn brought more lowering gray clouds, a portent of more snow to come.

He called Amon and the family together after he picked at his breakfast. "I don't know how to say this, except just to say it. When Mr. DeForge died, he named me as Jolie's guardian. She's coming to live here. Today."

None of them were surprised. Evetta nodded and said, "Lawyers might be tight-mouthed, but servants ain't. Cleo and Box knew, and they told us."

"Guess I must have been the last to know then," Morgan said dryly. "So I'm sure you see that it's put me in a bad position. I didn't even realize until yesterday that Jolie is almost fifteen. To me she's just a little girl. Anyway, I can't possibly have her living here with me alone. Evetta, Amon, would it be all right with you if Ketura moves in, and she can serve as our maid? I guess it might seem silly to you, since you just live right out the back door, but to me it makes a difference who's under my roof."

"We allus knew something like that, Mr. Tremayne," Amon said. "Ketura, here, she's already volunteered to be Miss Jolie's maid. It ain't silly, neither. It might only look more proper, but there you are. It looks more proper."

"Good," Morgan said with relief. "That's one problem overcome.

Now for the big thing. How are we going to get Jolie and her things moved here? You know I'll have to bring her bedroom furniture. None of the three spare bedrooms have anything. Oh—Ketura, do you have a bed?"

"Sure I do, Mr. Tremayne," she said, smiling. "My daddy made me a nice bed and my very own chiffarobe. It even has a long mirror on the door. Don't you 'member? You bought the mirror for me, a long time ago when I was little."

Vaguely Morgan recalled helping Amon, Rosh, and little Santo build furniture to furnish their two cottages, though he couldn't recall about the mirror. "Okay, Amon, can you and the boys go ahead and quick-quick get Ketura's things moved in here? I'm going to put Jolie in the bedroom just across from me, and Ketura's will be next to hers. The reason I'm hurrying you is because I'm afraid it's going to start snowing again," he said, casting a cautious look out the window. "I can't figure out how to get Jolie and her things moved here." He closed his eyes and rubbed his forehead. "It's hard for me to think straight."

"Mr. Tremayne, we'll git that little girl here today. Don't you worry. And her furnishings and stuff. Me and the boys'll get Ketura moved in, and then we'll bring the wagon over to DeForge's and load her up."

"How? There's already six inches of snow on the ground. You know, Amon, that the only path over there is a bridle path. How can we get the wagon over there and back with a heavy load of furniture?"

"Muscle it through," Amon said. "Me and Rosh know that we can double-team Ace and Calliope, and they can do it."

"I hadn't thought of that," Morgan admitted. "Yes, you're probably right. But still, what about Jolie? She can't ride, and it might take us hours to get the wagon through."

"It might. You're just going to have to go fetch her," Amon said. "She can ride back with you. But you better take Philemon, sir. You know that Vulcan devil ain't gonna allow no two human bein's on his back."

Morgan managed a small smile. "I'm glad you're thinking, Amon, because I'm sure not. I worried all night about this and just couldn't reason it out. Never been so muddle-headed in my life," he added in an undertone. Rising, he said, "Then I'm going right over to get Jolie. Seems like all of you are ready, even if I'm not."

Evetta said, "Me and Ketura are cooking up some good solid food for dinner, Mr. Tremayne. You bring that child straight on home. She don't need to be rattling around in that dead house by herself not one minute longer than she has to."

Morgan got his heavy overcoat and wool slouch hat. When he went out the back door, he saw that Amon apparently had already saddled Philemon, which was his own horse, a big gentle chestnut gelding. Morgan marveled again at how much his servants knew and how clear-headed they were thinking, while he felt like he was wandering around in a stupor. "Thanks, Amon. See you shortly."

Morgan was much preoccupied during the short ride. The Wilderness bordered both his and DeForge's properties, and the ride between the farms skirted the northern edge of the forest. Normally he would be enchanted by the snow scene, but on this day he barely looked around.

When he reached DeForge House, he noted that there was not one slave out anywhere. All of the slave cabins' chimneys had threads of smoke coming out of them, so Morgan figured they must all still be there. No one came to take his horse.

He made his way to the house and knocked hesitantly. Immediately the door flew open, and Jolie stood there. "Oh, you've come," she cried. "I–I've been afraid—afraid."

Morgan came in and shed his overcoat, hat, and gloves.

Jolie took them and carried them as they went into the parlor. Absently she sat down on the sofa, still holding them.

Morgan went to the fireplace, glad to see a healthy, glowing fire built. "I'm so sorry, Jolie. Sorry about Mr. DeForge, sorry that I wasn't here, and I'm sorry you've been afraid. Don't be. You do know about the arrangements Mr. DeForge made for you?"

She nodded, but her eyes were filled with uncertainty. "Mr. Cage told me that you are going to take care of me now. Is—is that true?"

"Yes, that's true. You're going to come live at my house, at Rapidan Run. Ketura is going to be your maid."

"My maid? Ketura? But she's my friend, the only friend I have that's my own age. I don't need a maid, anyway," she said fretfully.

"Oh, but you do," Morgan said with an attempt at lightness. "You're a very wealthy young lady now, you know. Mr. Cage told you about the money Mr. DeForge left you, didn't he? Of course he did. And wealthy young ladies must have a lady's maid."

"Oh. Then I suppose I will, if that's what you want."

"It's not what I—oh, never mind. We can talk all about everything later. Right now I think I'd better go ahead and take you to my house, Jolie. I'm afraid it's going to start snowing any minute, and I don't want you to have to ride in a freezing snowstorm."

"I'm ready," she said eagerly. "Just let me get my cloak. I already have my winter boots on." She practically ran out of the room.

It struck Morgan that Jolie might have been sitting there for days, in her winter boots, waiting for him or someone, anyone, to come help her. He determined he would be more welcoming, warmer toward her. He was still in a state of disbelief that his life had been turned upside down in this way, and he realized that he had a distracted air.

She came running back in, practically breathless, pulling on a long, luxurious wool mantle in a deep shade of pine green. It had a hood lined with dark gold satin, and when she pulled it up, it framed her face perfectly. Looking up at him, she seemed very young and innocent, with her wide tragic eyes and cupid's bow of a mouth. "I didn't take too long, did I?"

On impulse, Morgan bent and gently hugged her. He noted that she grew stiff, and so it was a very brief light caress, and then Morgan stepped back again. "Here I am, having to apologize again, Jolie. I'm hurrying you, and it's not really necessary. We'll make it home just fine. Amon and the boys are on their way with the wagon, and I'd like it very much if you would show me your bedroom and whatever else in the house you would like to take."

Vast relief washed over her face, and she slowly pushed back her hood and took off her cloak. "Thank you, Mr. Tremayne. I did wonder about my things, but I didn't like to ask."

Morgan ventured to touch her again. He reached out, and with his forefinger gently pushed Jolie's chin so that she would look up at him. "Jolie, I want to tell you right now, you never have to be afraid to ask me anything at all. I made a promise to Mr. DeForge that I would take very good care of you, and I will. I want you to know that."

Her eyes filled with tears as she stared up at him. It made her enormous, dramatically dark eyes positively luminous. "Oh, Mr. Tremayne, I'm so glad you've come. Now I know I won't have to be afraid."

"Never again," Morgan said firmly.

"Never again."

CHAPTER NINE

On December 20, 1860, South Carolina had seceded from the United States of America. Morgan had given it very little thought, because he was at home in the peaceful, quiet Shenandoah Valley. The heated politics of northern Virginia and Washington, DC seemed far away.

On January 9, 1861, Mississippi seceded from the union. Morgan didn't notice. On that day, Jolie had been at his home for exactly three days.

Early that morning Evetta had told him in a most accusatory manner that Jolie had no clothes. About halfway through the diatribe, Morgan managed to grasp that it wasn't that Jolie actually had no clothes, but that the clothes she had were unsuitable. Apparently Henry DeForge could see Jolie no better than Morgan could, for she was still wearing little-girl outfits—one-piece dresses that came about halfway down her shin, with lacy pantalettes underneath.

According to Evetta, this was outrageous. "There she is, that poor chile's got no idea that she's walking around a-showing her ankles!

And there's her hair, all down with baby ribbons in it! She shoulda started putting her hair up already! Shame on you, Mr. Tremayne!"

On January 10, 1861, Florida seceded from the United States. Morgan didn't notice because he spent the entire day in Fredericksburg, frantically searching for a dressmaker that could make Jolie some new clothes. Quickly.

On January 11, 1861, Alabama seceded from the union. It escaped Morgan's attention because that was the day that he found out that Wade Kimbrel had bought Henry DeForge's property. Wade Kimbrel came by Rapidan Run early in the morning to crow over Morgan.

Just after noon, two of DeForge's field slaves, the boy Howie and his brother Eli, came running up to the farmhouse. They pleaded for Morgan to buy them.

He was still trying to explain to them that he couldn't do such a thing when Kimbrel's overseer rode up. He was an ugly great brute named Gus Ramsey. He told the boys they were going to be beaten within an inch of their lives, and if they ran again, he'd kill them. When Morgan protested, the man threatened to have him arrested for harboring runaway slaves. He could do it, too. It was the law of the land. Morgan was depressed all day long.

On January 19, 1861, Georgia seceded; on January 26th, Louisiana seceded; and on February 1st, Texas seceded. Morgan did at last begin to take note of what was happening outside the borders of Rapidan Run.

But it wasn't until February 4th that he fully realized how deeply he was involved in these events. On that day, the Confederate States of America was formed. Jefferson Davis was elected president by the representatives of the states that had seceded, and Montgomery, Alabama, was named its capital.

The following morning, February 5, 1861, Morgan was sitting in his study after breakfast reading the newspaper, poring over the details of the events from the day before. The joining together of the seceded states, naming the association, electing a president, all of these things made it become jarringly real to Morgan. He realized that war was surely coming.

No, Virginia had not seceded—yet—but he knew she would. And like thousands of other men throughout all the states, he wrestled with making the choice of what he would do. Fight? Fight against the United States, his homeland? It was unthinkable. But the alternative was also inconceivable. Fight against Virginia? To Morgan, as to others, Virginia was more of a home to him than the rather intangible union of states that had been formed almost a hundred years ago. Virginia was much more than the simple geographic location of his house. Virginia was his motherland.

Abruptly Henry DeForge's voice invaded his thoughts. *"If I knew that I was going to be caught in a war, I would start hoarding. I would hoard gold, first of all, because it is truly a universal currency. Then I would hoard all of the necessaries I could gather. Foodstuffs, wood, coal, tools, nails, fabrics such as wool and cotton, soap, candles, anything and everything I could think of that I would need to run my homestead."*

With another jolt, Morgan realized that he had responsibilities now. He was no longer a single man who could make any decision he wanted and it would not affect anyone else. Everything he did now would deeply affect another person, besides his family. He was solely responsible for Jolie DeForge.

Whatever I do, I have to make sure she's safe, that she's secure. I promised. . .

The promise was made posthumously, of course. Once Morgan decided to take Jolie, he swore a solemn oath in his heart to God, and to the memory of Henry DeForge, that he would take care of her to his utmost for as long as he lived. Morgan was that kind of man. Once he gave his loyalty to someone or something, he would brave any evil to defend that bond.

And that's exactly how I feel about Virginia, about my home, he realized with sinking heart, for then he knew that he would, he must, fight for his home. Then he thought, *But I need time. . .time to make sure Jolie is well provided for, that her future is secure. Do I have enough time? Please, God, grant me the time. . . .*

Just then Jolie came in, interrupting his dark reverie. He looked up and managed a smile. "Hello, Mouse. Had breakfast yet?" "Mouse" was a joke between them. After Jolie had been with them a couple of weeks, Morgan had told her that she looked like a kitten, but she was as quiet as a mouse. Sometimes he called her "Kitten" and sometimes, as when she came unexpectedly into the room, he called her "Mouse."

Morgan realized she was wearing one of the new dresses he had bought her, a simple brown wool dress trimmed with coral-colored satin ribbon. The dress had puffed sleeves and wide skirts. Ketura had dressed her hair. It was parted modestly down the middle and made into a simple bun at the nape of her neck. But to Morgan these things didn't make her look any more mature. He thought they just made her look like a little girl playing dress-up.

"Yes, sir," she answered. "Are you ready to help me with my geometry?" Morgan had continued teaching her in the mornings, as Henry DeForge had done since Jolie was five years old. Morgan had been pleasantly surprised at how educated Jolie was. She knew American history, English history, European history, she was conversant in French, she read many novels and nonfiction such as biographies, letters of note, and prominent men's journals that were very much beyond the normal comprehension of a fourteen-year-old. She was skilled in arithmetic, and DeForge had even taught her the basics of bookkeeping.

But she was weak in geometry, because Henry DeForge had been weak in the higher mathematics, and he had no interest in trying to school himself. Also, Jolie was not at all "accomplished" in the sense that was usually meant to describe young ladies. She had no musical talent at all, aside from a clear, sweet soprano voice, and she couldn't draw. Also, she couldn't seem to learn the very basics of cooking. She was a passable seamstress and seemed to be determined to better her skills. Much to Morgan's surprise, he had found that she was a formidable chess opponent. It took all his concentration to keep her from beating him.

Now he said vaguely, "Sorry? Oh yes, you said geometry." He folded the paper and slid it across his desk to her. "I think that today we'll put off geometry. There are some serious things I need to talk to you about, Jolie."

She scanned the banner headline: CONFEDERATE STATES OF AMERICA IS BORN! PRESIDENT ELECTED—VICE PRESIDENT ELECTED—MEMBER STATES DESIGNATE MONTGOMERY, ALABAMA, AS THE CAPITAL.

She sighed deeply. "This means there will be a war, doesn't it?"

"I guess so," Morgan said quietly. "I've tried to ignore the whole thing, but it's just not going away like I want. So there are some things we need to settle."

She bit her lower lip, and Morgan hurriedly added, "No, Jolie, don't be afraid. We just have to talk about your future, that's all. Remember, I promised you that you'll never have to be afraid again. And that's what I need to make sure of now. How best to take care of you."

"But I can stay here, can't I?" she pleaded. "You aren't going to try to send me away again, are you?"

When she first moved in, Morgan had suggested that she might like to go to boarding school. After all, she could afford the very best. But the thought had so obviously terrified her that Morgan had told her to forget it and had never mentioned it again. It had taken him a while to see it from her point of view. Of course she would be frightened out of her wits, to be sent to a strange place, with strange people, when her entire life had been spent with a loving, indulgent father. No wonder she had been terrified.

"No, no, Jolie," he said soothingly. "I know now that is not feasible. No, the problem is that I need to make sure you are safe here. That Rapidan Run is safe, and that Amon and his family are safe. I need to make plans. I need to do some things to prepare."

He found himself groping for the words to explain, when to his surprise Jolie said, "It's because of what Mr. DeForge said, isn't it? On that day you were talking about if a war came."

"You were there?" he said blankly. Though he recalled every detail of Henry DeForge's worn face and all his words, he had no picture in his mind of Jolie being there that pleasant spring day on the veranda. A pained look came over her face then vanished.

Evenly she said, "I was there, and I remember what he said. About hoarding gold and food and other things. That's what you're worrying about, isn't it? Making sure that Rapidan Run has food for us and the horses stored up in case the war makes it hard for us to buy things?"

"That's it exactly, Jolie. You're a smart little mouse, you know." He shifted in his seat and rested his chin on one hand, studying her face. "Do you remember about Mr. DeForge's will, Jolie? Not about your money or me taking care of you. Do you remember me telling you that you have a personal line of credit at Mr. DeForge's company for life?"

"Yes, I remember."

"Do you know what it means?"

"Yes, because Mr. DeForge taught me a lot of things about business," she said confidently. "A line of credit means you can buy things and pay for them later."

Morgan nodded. "I thought it was kind of odd at the time. But now I'm beginning to think that maybe Mr. DeForge could foresee a lot of things that others, certainly including myself, could not. I would like your permission to use your line of credit at DeForge Imports & Exports, Ltd. Though the debt will be in your name, of course I will repay it all."

"That's okay, Mr. Tremayne. I know what you're going to buy with the credit line. But let me ask you something. I have so much money, Mr. Tremayne, why don't you use that instead? I don't mind you using my credit line, but you don't have to run up a debt."

It amused Morgan that she was talking in such a grown-up manner, while to him she still looked very much like a tiny little kitten. "No, I'm not going to use any of your money at all, Jolie. That is your legacy, and it's meant to last you all of your life if it has to. Besides, it's all in gold, which is another thing that I thought was odd of Mr. DeForge to do, and once again he's proved to be much smarter than I. Do you remember what he said that day?"

"About gold? Yes, I do. He said he would hoard it first of all, because it's the universal currency." Her smooth brow wrinkled a bit. "I don't really understand what that part means."

"It means that the actual value of paper money may rise and fall, and sometimes in emergencies, like a war, it can lose its value. In other words, what you can buy with it can change, and change quickly. One day you may be able to buy a pair of shoes for a dollar, and the next day that same pair of shoes might cost you five dollars. That means that the dollar has lost much of its value."

"I see," she said slowly. "But that doesn't happen to gold?"

"No, never. Gold is precious. Any man, woman, business, state, king, or government will take gold in payment for goods."

"Then we'd better hoard my gold," she said soberly. "One day we may need it."

"I hope not," he said emphatically, "and I pray not. But I'm going to prepare as if that day is coming, Jolie. Like I've promised, I never want you to be afraid again."

She smiled sweetly. "With you, I'm not afraid, Mr. Tremayne. Now that I know you've promised to take care of me, I don't worry any more. My—father"—she still stumbled over it—"always said that you were an honorable man, and I know that means you keep your promises. So I know I'll never have to be afraid again."

CHAPTER TEN

Colonel Robert E. Lee stood in the twilight, still and unmoving. His eyes were focused across the lazy river below him on the city only three miles distant. As he watched, the lights began to glow, thousands of streetlamps and thousands of lamps in the windows of homes and offices. Washington was lit up as if there were a celebration.

But there was no celebration. In spite of the festive appearance, the city buzzed with dark and dangerous business. Men who represented the United States of America were making life-and-death decisions about their rebellious brothers, joined together into the Confederate States of America. And Robert E. Lee was enmeshed in his own momentous struggle.

It was March 1, 1861. Lee had been recalled to Washington from his post in Texas, and he had reached Arlington on this day. He and Mary had talked for hours. As always, he could confide fully in her, and only to her. It helped him to see the way clearly.

Earlier in February he had written to a friend:

The country seems to be in a lamentable condition and

*may have been plunged into civil war. May God rescue us
from the folly of our own acts, save us from selfishness, and
teach us to love our neighbors as ourselves.*

But no matter how closely Robert E. Lee adhered to these
principles, other men did not. He knew now that war was certain.

Wearily he told Mary, "In the event of Virginia's secession, duty
will compel me to follow. We are loyal Americans, Mary, but we
are Virginians first. To raise my hand against my home, and my
family, would be dishonorable. My heart, my hand, and now to my
sorrow, my sword is with Virginia."

❧

On April 12, 1861, shells burst on Fort Sumter far away in South
Carolina. Two days later, the federal fort surrendered to P. G. T.
Beauregard, brigadier general of the Confederate States Army. On
the following day, Lincoln issued his proclamation to a nation
gone mad. He called for seventy-five thousand troops of volunteer
militia to "suppress treasonable combinations" and to "cause the
laws to be duly executed."

Lee was still waiting in trepidation, hoping against all hope that
Virginia might not secede. He was a simple man with an innocent
heart, and he couldn't see that it was impossible that Virginia would
remain neutral. The North and the South were at war. She must
choose.

On April 17, he received word from Richmond that the
convention had gone into secret session, and he then knew his fate.
On that same day he received a letter and a message. The letter was
from General Winfield Scott, the general commanding the Federal
Army, requesting Lee to call at his office as soon as possible. The
message was delivered by one of Lee's cousins, the young John Lee.
Francis P. Blair asked him to call the next day. Blair had been the
editor of *The Congressional Globe* for many years, and now he was a
"kingmaker" in Washington.

On the morning of April 18, 1861, Colonel Robert E. Lee called on Francis Blair at his son's home on Pennsylvania Avenue. Blair received him personally and wasted no time. "Colonel Lee, a large army is soon to be called into the field to enforce the federal law; the president has authorized me to ask if you would accept command."

For over an hour Blair used all his considerable skills to try to persuade Lee to stay with the Union. Lee remained firm; his course was set.

Of the conversation, he later said, "I declined the offer he made me to take command of the army that was to be brought into the field, stating as candidly and as courteously as I could, that though opposed to secession and deprecating war, I could take no part in an invasion of the Southern States."

After his interview with Blair, Lee went to General Scott's office. He had known General Scott for many years, having served under him in the Mexican War. He had always been the old general's favorite. Without delay Lee told him about Blair's interview and his answer.

"Lee," said Scott sadly, "you have made the greatest mistake of your life, but I feared it would be so."

Lee returned to Arlington and to Mary's always-comforting presence. He was disheartened and said little except that he had been offered the command and had refused it.

The next day, on April 19th, he learned that Virginia had seceded from the Union. He spent many hours that day pacing in his and Mary's upstairs bedroom and kneeling before his Father, fervently praying aloud. Finally he came downstairs.

Mary was waiting patiently for him.

"Well, Mary," he said calmly, "the question is settled. Here is my letter of resignation and a letter I have written General Scott."

She nodded. "Robert, I know that you have wept tears of blood over this terrible course that the country is set on. But you have made the right decision. As a man of honor and a Virginian, you must follow the destiny of your state. Only I know what this has cost you. Aside from loving you as my own dear husband, I esteem you as an honorable, courageous man. You always have been, and I know that you always will be the best man I've ever had the privilege of knowing."

By April 25th, Robert E. Lee was a brigadier general in the Confederate States Army.

～

Morgan lifted the now-familiar lion's head knocker, and as usual Nance opened the door. He greeted her then handed her his hat and gloves.

"Mr. Tremayne, Mr. Bledsoe's waiting to see you in the parlor."

"He is?" Morgan said with surprise. Leona had sent him a note asking him to call.

"Yes, sir." The maid offered no more information, so Morgan followed her into the parlor and waited for her to introduce him. "Mr. Bledsoe, Mr. Tremayne's here, sir."

"Come in, Tremayne," Benjamin Bledsoe called out.

Morgan walked inside, feeling awkward at the unaccustomed formality. Normally Leona was waiting for him when he called, alone in the parlor. But he admitted to himself things between them had been very strained since he had taken Jolie as his ward. Somehow he hadn't been able to tell Leona about her, even though four months had gone by. In fact, he hadn't seen Leona much at all in those months. And when he did, he knew there was a growing distance between them. He had felt helpless, not knowing how to get close to her again. Morgan was feeling buffeted by many things these days.

Benjamin Bledsoe was standing with his back to a small but warm fire when Morgan entered. He was a tall man with a commanding presence. He had thick silver hair, carefully styled, and a sweeping silver mustache. His eyes flashed sharply at times. Leona was much like him.

"Come in, Tremayne. Sit down, sit down," he said, waving toward an armchair.

When Morgan sat down, Bledsoe loomed over him in a most intimidating manner. Morgan was sure it was on purpose.

"I need to talk to you, Tremayne. You've been scarce around here lately. Leona's wondered at it. What are you up to these days?" he demanded. It was not a rhetorical question.

"I've had some changes in circumstance you might say, sir," Morgan said with difficulty.

"Not with your business, I hope," Bledsoe said sharply.

"No, sir. That is. . .Rapidan Run is doing very well."

"That's good, Tremayne. After all, I know that you're very keen on my daughter, and I would never allow her to waste her time on a pauper."

"No, sir. I am not a pauper."

Bledsoe clasped his hands behind his back and stared down at Morgan with narrowed eyes. "Are you aware that Gibbs joined the army last week? He went to Camp Lee in Richmond and volunteered for Jeb Stuart's cavalry."

"No, sir, I wasn't aware. I have heard of Jeb Stuart, though. My brother—"

But impatiently Bledsoe interrupted him. "I would like to know what your intentions are concerning this war, Tremayne. Surely you aren't still wavering like some of the insipid weaklings I know. Virginia needs all her loyal sons to defend her now. Don't you believe that?"

"Yes, sir, I do. But there are some things I must do, some affairs I must settle before I can think about joining the army."

"What can possibly be more important than fighting this war? It's all going to be over in no time, anyway. Southern men, particularly Virginia men, have more dash and courage than ten Yankees. If they dare to cross the Potomac River, we'll send them back running like whipped pups!"

Morgan had heard this, and other declarations like it, countless times in the last year or so. *"One Southern man can beat three Yankees, five Yankees, ten Yankees. We're dashing and courageous and brave and valiant, and they are nothing but whelps with no honor. Hurry up and join up, or the war will be over."* Morgan was heartily sick of it.

Now he struggled to keep the distaste out of his voice. "Sir, I'm afraid I can't completely agree with you there. I believe that it is going to be a long, terrible war, and I believe that people on both sides are going to suffer. Victory is not inevitable, as so many people seem to think, and a quick victory is highly unlikely."

Bledsoe's mouth tightened. "So that's your opinion, eh? And you have more important things to do right now? That makes you look like a coward, Tremayne. I never thought I'd say that. I've always regarded you as a sensible, forthright gentleman. But now I'm not so sure."

"But sir, if I could just explain—" This time Morgan cut off his own words. How could he explain? How could he explain the terrible burden he felt for Jolie, and how bitterly he regretted not heeding DeForge's warning and preparing himself for war? Since that momentous day of February 5th, Morgan had worked himself half to death trying to make Rapidan Run into a fortress, a self-sustaining stronghold, a place that he could be sure would withstand the desolation of war. Suddenly now he was feeling the weariness that plagued him each day. He finished dully, "It's just that I have so many responsibilities now. There are some things that I simply must do before I can join the army."

"Sounds like lame excuses to me," Bledsoe said. "You're a single man with a profitable business, and there's sure no reason it couldn't continue to be profitable. I know your man Amon has been practically running it for a couple of years now. There are thousands of men, men with wives and families, who haven't hesitated to join up to fight for their land and homes." He stopped talking, watching Morgan carefully.

But Morgan could think of nothing to say.

"Well, I know Leona has invited you for supper, Tremayne. I suppose I can forget this unfortunate state of affairs—just this once. But after this, I don't think you need to see my daughter anymore. You're not the man that I thought you were."

"Don't you think that it's up to Leona who she sees?" Morgan argued heatedly. "She's a grown woman, and she makes her own decisions."

"That she does," Bledsoe said with grim amusement. "Don't be surprised if she makes a decision that you won't like, Tremayne. I know her better than you do."

$\sim$

The meal was pleasant enough.

Morgan could not take his eyes off of Leona Rose. She wore a rose-colored dress, her favorite color, and the pale alabaster of her shoulders and the rich coloring of her cheeks caused him to stare at her. She rebuked him once saying, "You're just staring at me, Morgan."

"Well, a mummy would sit up and stare at you, Leona."

"Oh, you foolish boy!"

Gibbs Bledsoe said very little during supper. He was wearing the uniform of a cavalryman and proud of it. He was a fine-looking young man with blond hair and blue eyes, slim and handsome. He was an imaginative fellow, full of dreams and often practical jokes. As a matter of fact, Morgan had always been fond of Gibbs.

When they had finished supper and retired to the parlor for after-dinner coffee, however, Gibbs said, "You'll notice that I joined Jeb Stuart's cavalry."

"Yes, I know. My brother Clay tells me he's probably the finest horseman in Virginia except, perhaps, for General Lee."

"Yes, he is, and he's a fighting man, too."

Gibbs had been drinking wine steadily, and now he said rather rudely, "I've always thought you were a good man, Morgan, but I hear talk that you're not going to support this war."

SURRENDER

Morgan sighed. "As a conscientious man, I do find it hard to support war."

"Well, man, what's holding you back? We're being attacked. The Yankees are going to send their armies down here. Wouldn't you defend your native state?"

"It may come to that."

"It's slavery, isn't it?" Benjamin Bledsoe spoke up. "I know you and your family have never had slaves, and that you actually pay your free blacks like employees."

"That's true, and yes I'm opposed to slavery. I think it's a foolish economic system."

"What do you mean by that?" Gibbs lashed back. "We've done very well in the South using slaves."

"I'm not sure we've done all that well, but we could have done better using free labor. Look at it, Gibbs. A good field hand costs as much as three thousand dollars, and he might drop dead the day after you buy him. At the most you might get a few years out of him, and then you've lost your capital."

"There's no other way to raise cotton."

"Well, as for that, I think we're making a mistake."

"What do you mean? A mistake about what?" Gibbs demanded.

"We're a one-crop country. Look at the North. I don't admire many of their manners, but they are inventive. They have shipyards, foundries, factories manufacturing everything from tinned peaches to cannon. We can't fight those cannons with cotton. And now, with the blockade, I doubt if we can even sell it."

"We'll sell it to England."

Morgan had thought this out a great deal. "Maybe. But how are we going to get anything in? We can't eat cotton, our horses can't eat cotton, and we can't build our houses with it. In two years, we're going to be hungry, Gibbs."

Now Gibbs brought up the ancient argument. "This war will never last for two years. We'll send them packing, probably within six months. Our men are more outdoorsmen than the Northerners.

They don't know anything about hunting, and that's all it is, really. It's just that we're hunting Yanks instead of deer."

Morgan gave up. "Gibbs, I really don't think it's that simple. I guess we'll just have to agree to disagree."

Finally Leona spoke up. "Morgan, it's just hard for me to understand you. Don't you see that this war is going to be our moment? It will be in the history books forever, how the Confederate States of America declared their states' rights and the rights of all the people in those states to live as they please. Our children, and all of our descendants, will see that we are heroes! We fought and died for the Glorious Cause!"

Morgan was astounded. Never in his life had he thought that Leona Bledsoe would be so blind. It was alien to him that she would have such romantically shallow sentiments. Numbly he shook his head. "Leona, I don't think you've actually thought this through. No war can be glorious. Especially civil war, brother against brother. 'A house divided against itself cannot stand.'"

"Great heavens, Morgan, I've never known you to be so dreary!" she said heatedly. "You, who can claim a friendship with General Robert E. Lee himself. I'm sure he would give you a commission, and you could be an officer, maybe even on his staff! But here you sit, mouthing self-righteous platitudes. Is it possible that my father is right? Morgan, are you a coward?"

That question began to haunt him, and he knew he must find the answer soon.

CHAPTER ELEVEN

When President Lincoln had issued his call on April 15th, for a seventy-five-thousand-man militia to subdue the treasonous Southern states, he had given the Southern forces twenty days in which to "disperse and return peaceably to their respective abodes." Morgan, along with the Confederate government and military, took this to mean that President Lincoln would wait until May 5th to begin active military operations against the South. Morgan knew this meant that after that fateful day, he would no longer be able to buy supplies—or at least have them delivered. He was sure that the Northern blockade would become effective, deadly effective then.

Since February, Morgan had traveled to Baltimore twice, to place complicated orders with DeForge Brothers Imports & Exports. Henry DeForge's brother was older than he was and had long retired, but the general manager of the firm was a professional, helpful man named Paul McCray. When Morgan explained his connection to the firm and his guardianship of Jolie DeForge, Mr. McCray then personally helped Morgan with all his needs. Morgan ordered foodstuffs, household supplies, farm supplies, tools, leather, textiles, and hardwood lumber from all over New England and the Midwest. McCray obligingly made the arrangements to have them shipped to Richmond, and Morgan knew rivermen who could deliver to Rapidan Run. Mr. McCray even helped Morgan with purchasing the things that he needed that could be found in the South, such as smoked hams, coal from western Virginia, beef from Texas, and fruit from Florida. Morgan, of course, had always simply purchased such things from a general store; he had never bought in bulk. Mr. McCray's help was invaluable. Morgan had to build a storehouse and a smokehouse, and by the end of April every single building, including the house, was stocked full of everything he could think of that Jolie might need. . .in case something happened to him.

Morgan's winter crop of barley and rye did very well, but at harvesttime in March he was discouraged. He had three hundred acres of crops, and only four men to bring it in. He knew there would be no affable leasing of slaves, with daily payment to them, from Wade Kimbrel as he had with Henry DeForge. Kimbrel would charge Morgan, certainly, and he would never let a slave of his have one penny. Furthermore, Morgan knew that any former DeForge slaves would run the minute they set foot outside of Wolvesey property, so he was sure that Kimbrel would stipulate that they could only work under his cruel overseer's supervision. It was just an impossible situation.

But again, as he had done so many times before, Amon saved the day. "Mr. Tremayne, I know about a dozen free men and boys livin' in shacks in that ol' Wilderness. I'll git 'em to work, whether they want to or not." Sure enough, Morgan was able to employ fourteen sturdy field hands to bring in the crops. And this year, instead of selling what he wouldn't need, he stored it all in dozens of metal-lined barrels, another item that Mr. McCray had known where and how to order.

On the first day of May, Morgan received something of a shock.

SURRENDER

A letter arrived from Mary Lee, from her home at Arlington. The tone of the letter was light and rather careless. One part read:

> *The rose garden here is perfectly lovely this spring. I've been able to paint it on these warm sunny days. Twice I have had good results, I think. Perhaps the next time you visit, Cousin Tremayne, you may give me your opinion of them.*

Morgan was horrified that Mrs. Lee would still be sitting placidly at Arlington. After May 5th, he thoroughly believed the property would be behind enemy lines. The very next day he headed out to Arlington, with Amon driving the carriage and Rosh and Santo driving the wagon. By May 14th, he had moved her, with some of the family belongings, to her Aunt Fitzhugh's home in Ravensworth.

General Lee was in Richmond during this time, and he had sent her many letters trying to get her to leave her beloved home. He could not go to her, of course.

Morgan didn't even try to consult with General Lee. He just went to Arlington and took charge of Mrs. Lee and then returned home. He did send a brief note to the general explaining what he had done and reassuring him that Mrs. Lee was well and safe for now.

General Lee sent a courteous note of thanks back to him.

Morgan continued working hard at Rapidan Run. As always, running a horse farm was a tremendous amount of labor. And once the harvest was over, it was time to plow and ready the fields for spring planting. To Morgan, May, June, and the first two weeks of July, 1861, seemed to flash past him in a blur.

But on Tuesday, July 16th, Morgan rejoined the world, his world that was at war. Over thirty thousand men in gray were coming together and marching north.

❧

On June 20, 1861, a great comet appeared in the sky. It lit up the night; the stars paled in comparison. Many thought this was an ill omen, a foreshadowing of war and blood and desolation.

It was rumored that an elderly slave named Oola, who belonged to some close friends of Mary Todd Lincoln and her husband, Abraham, could conjure spells. She was a tall, large woman with eyes like gimlets and gray-black skin drawn tight over her grim face. She said of the great comet, "You see dat great fire sword blaze in the sky? There's a great war coming, and the handle's toward the North, and the point's toward the South. And the North's gonna take that sword and cut the South's hide out. But that Lincoln, man, chilluns, if he takes that sword, he's gonna perish by it."

Lincoln had already taken up that sword, as had hundreds of thousands of men, North and South. The young men of the North flocked to enlist. Lincoln had called for seventy-five thousand, but he could have tripled that number and not been disappointed.

At the time the whole thing looked like a big picnic—to men who were not soldiers and knew no better. One young private in the Union Army wrote home about

the happy golden days of camp life where our only worry
was that the war might end before our regiment had a chance
to prove itself under fire. The shrill notes of the fifes, and
the beat and roll of the drums. That's the sweetest music
in the world to me.

It was true, the sound of jaunty military marches sounded everywhere. Boys whose recruit roster was not full rode about the country in wagons with drummers and fifers seeking recruits. They rode into the towns with all hands yelling, "Fourth of July every day of the year!"

The training these recruits received was very sketchy indeed. Almost all of them, including most of the officers, were amateurs, and it was not uncommon to see a captain on a parade ground consulting a book as he drilled his company. Most of the privates had been recruited by one of their acquaintances, and the volunteer companies elected their officers. Naturally they had been on a first-name basis with their lieutenants and captains all their lives, and these men could see no point whatever in military formation, drill, and particularly discipline.

For many long frustrating months, General Lee, the consummate soldier engineer, fought to overcome the prejudice by Southern men that digging earthworks was beneath them.

President Lincoln was a man bowed down with care. The government offices were packed with office seekers, as they always were with a new president. Abraham Lincoln was not a brilliant military strategist, and he knew it. He chose his war cabinet with care, but it was hard for him to discern exactly the right course to take, the voice to listen to, the man to trust with so much at stake.

In a meeting with the war cabinet, General Scott, the brilliant soldier who had won the Mexican War, became angry at those who said the war would be easy. He almost shouted, "You think the Confederates are paper men? No, sir! They are men who will fight, and we are not ready to engage the enemy at this time."

Edwin Stanton, secretary of war, stared across the room with hostility in his cold, blue eyes. "General, we've been over this time and time again. I concede that we are not as well prepared as we would like to be, but neither are the rebels. And I must insist that we have here more than a military problem. Surely we all realize that our people must have a victory now. If you do not know how transit and changeable men are, I do! If we do not act at once, the issue will grow stale. Already the antiwar party is shouting for peace, and many are listening. We must strike while the iron is hot!"

The argument raged back and forth until finally President Lincoln stood up, his action cutting all talk short. Every man in the room was alert waiting for his word. He said firmly, "Gentlemen, I have listened to you all, and I have prayed for wisdom. I presume that Jefferson Davis is praying for that same quality. We have little choice. I feel that from the military point of view, General Scott is absolutely correct, but as Mr. Stanton has pointed out there is the matter of the people. They must agree to this war, and they must have something immediately. Therefore, the army will move at once. General McDowell will be in command, and he will be ordered to march as soon as possible and engage the enemy. Some of you disagree with this decision. I can only ask you to put aside your objections and join with me in prayer for our union."

Thus it was that the first great battle of the Civil War was set in motion. The objective of McDowell's army was Manassas Junction. If this could be taken by the North, the railway system of the South would, for all intents and purposes, be wrecked. So the army marched out of Washington, led by General McDowell, who was the President's choice. Practically no one else thought him at all a capable soldier, much less a capable commanding general.

Still, the Union forces invaded the South. Young men in blue faced young men in gray across a little creek in northern Virginia called Bull Run. That night many of them still felt great bravado; the Yankees had sightseers coming to observe the festivities, and the Rebels believed that they would each and every one of them beat three or four Yanks.

Shortly after dawn, even the most naive of them knew that this was to be a day of fire and blood. Sheets of flame lit up the bright spring air as the cannons exploded and the muskets blasted. As for General McDowell, he had been in only one battle in his military career, in the Mexican War, and he had not particularly distinguished himself. Mostly he was famous for his Homeric appetite. Once he ate an entire watermelon which he pronounced "monstrous fine."

But on the morning of July 21st, the General did not find the situation at Bull Run Creek monstrous fine. First he tried throwing his men directly across the creek and meeting the enemy head-on. But to his shock, he found that the Rebels were a murderous and implacable enemy. He tried to flank them, and he found that the Confederate commander, General P. G. T. Beauregard, hero of Fort

Sumter, had moved his men to again face the now-ragged blue line dead-on.

All of that endless day, the two armies maneuvered and struck, maneuvered and struck. The Union Army, who had believed that this would be little more than a military drill and an opportunity to show off, began to disintegrate. A few men began to run, and the inevitable happened in the mob mentality.

The panic spread. First squads threw down their muskets and ran, and then companies, and finally almost the entire rabble, were fleeing back toward Washington. The seasoned officers could not stop them, and they themselves tried to retreat in good order, but it was impossible. An artillery caisson was turned over on the Bull Run Bridge, blocking the way to safety, and it only fueled the madness. With a few exceptions, the entire Union Army was in full flight. The spectators in their fine carriages turned and ran for the safety of Washington, too.

And so the boys in blue were soundly beaten and had, as so many had predicted, turned tail and run away in disgrace. In a way it was unfortunate that the Confederates had won First Bull Run. It only served to reinforce the strongly-held belief that it would be a short war and an easy victory.

But to Abraham Lincoln, it meant something altogether different. He had no need of any military adviser to tell him that old General Scott had been right. The Confederate Army was by no means a paper tiger. It was going to be a long, tragic, costly war.

❧

The line of ambulance wagons, the walking wounded among them, seemed endless.

Morgan, on the side of the road south to Richmond, watched with horror. In his head he had known this would happen. But having a mental certainty and seeing the reality were two very different things.

Then a sight galvanized him. He saw two of his friends,

brothers, walking down the road. The older brother, Blair Southall, had a bloody bandage around his head, and his left arm was in a crude sling. He was supporting his brother, Nash, who was barely able to limp along. His right pants leg was bloody from the thigh all the way down to his shoes.

Morgan jumped off Vulcan and pulled him over to the two men. "Blair? Nash? Here, get up on my horse. I'm taking you home."

Blair looked up, blinking because of the blood smeared in his eyes. "Morgan? That you, my friend? What did you say? You think I can ride that devil of a horse?"

Beside him, Nash gave an odd half sigh, half moan and crumpled to the ground, his face bloodless and sickly white.

"Mount up, Blair," Morgan ordered and helped the injured man step into the stirrup then pushed him up into the saddle. He picked up Nash Southall with newfound strength and lifted him up. Between them, he and Blair managed to get him mounted behind Blair, completely collapsed against his back. Morgan took Vulcan's reins and whispered to him, "You know what's going on, boy. Be easy; go easy." The slow ride back to Rapidan Run was probably the lightest, smoothest walk Vulcan had ever done.

Amon, Rosh, Santo, Evetta, Jolie, and Ketura all came running down the drive to meet them.

Tightly Morgan said, "These are friends of mine, Blair and Nash Southall."

Evetta said, "Git 'em in the house. Jolie, Ketura, you come on right now and help me."

"There are more," Morgan said. "Many more. I'm going to take the wagon back and bring home as many as I can. Understand?"

"Well, don't just stand there. Hurry up," Evetta said, throwing her arm around Nash Southall, who had come to, and helping him as he stumbled toward the house.

Quickly Amon said, "Mr. Tremayne, I'll drive the wagon. You, Rosh, and Santo ride. We can double up two men again like you just did. Evetta's got good sense. She'll have them girls getting the barn ready so's we can take as many as we can."

"You're a good man, Amon," Morgan said, remounting Vulcan. "I thank God for you and your family." He turned and sped off toward the Richmond road.

By nightfall there were eight wounded men in the house and eighteen in the barn. Morgan paused for a moment to watch Jolie as she went to each man's pallet and knelt down. She was checking bandages, giving them water, promising hot soup and fresh bread, smiling at them, reassuring them. She looked up and saw him and got to her feet to come over to him.

Morgan said, "You're a fine young woman, Jolie. Not many young ladies would do this. Not many of them could."

"I just want to help them, sir." She sighed. "I wish we could have taken them all."

CHAPTER TWELVE

E vetta's made a treat for us all today," Jolie said, bringing an enormous steaming platter into the dining room and setting it in the center of the table. "Roast beef with carrots and potatoes and turnips. I love turnips," she added, so childlike that the men at the table exchanged amused glances.

Unaware, Jolie took her seat at the foot of the table and said, "Mr. Southall? Would you take Mr. Tremayne's seat at the head of the table, please?"

Morgan had gone to Mrs. Mary Lee's rescue again. She had written him that her rheumatism was bothering her some, and Morgan had known that meant she was hurting a lot. He had left this morning to take her to the Hot Springs, in Bath County. She had been there before and swore by the healing properties of the waters.

Blair Southall now took Morgan's seat, and the other six men, including his brother, sat down. Blair said a short blessing, and the men began to dig in. Seated by Jolie, Nash Southall rolled his eyes. "Gentlemen! Bunch of rooting hogs, that's what you look like. Get your big paws off that platter and pass it down here to me so I can serve Miss Jolie."

Shamefaced, Blair started the platter down the table. But he and the others then started helping themselves to the bread, the cornbread, the stewed apples, the celery sticks, the sliced tomatoes and cucumbers, and the corn relish.

Jolie marveled at them. Henry DeForge and Morgan were finicky eaters. It wasn't that they disliked certain foods; they both liked a wide variety of meats and vegetables and fruits. It was just that they ate sparingly. Jolie had never seen a robust, hungry man eat before. She herself could hardly eat for watching them.

These seven men were all that was left of the original twenty-six men they had taken in. Over the last two weeks the others had recovered, probably much quicker than they would have in the overcrowded hospitals in Richmond. Evetta, Ketura, and Jolie were all excellent nurses, and thanks to Morgan's hoarding, they had good food and plenty of it.

This was the first time they had all sat down to eat in the dining room, however. Until this morning they had been fifteen, but today Dr. Travers, who had joined the army and was now a captain, had pronounced eight men fit for duty, and they had returned to Richmond to join their units.

Jolie watched Blair Southall, a big bear of a man six feet tall with a barrel chest. He was Morgan's age and handsome, she supposed, though he was tough looking, with thick black hair and a full mustache. Nash was only eighteen and was built more like Morgan, though he wasn't as tall. He was slender, with sandy blond hair and expressive brown eyes. Both of the Southall brothers were keen outdoorsmen, and Morgan had many times taken them hunting in the Wilderness and fishing on the Rapidan. If they had been surprised to see Jolie living in his home, neither of them showed it. They were well-brought-up, gallant young men.

During the next week, Dr. Travers came by twice and finally certified all the men fit for duty.

On the morning the Southall brothers were leaving, Jolie was surprised to see Nash Southall come find her in Morgan's study. Since the wounded men had been recovering, she had resumed her lessons, whether Morgan was there or not. She looked up as Nash came in and said, "You aren't leaving yet, are you? I was coming to tell you good-bye."

"Blair's still polishing up his brass," Nash said, coming to perch up on the corner of Morgan's desk by her. "He thinks since he's a lieutenant that he should look like a peacock on parade all the time."

Jolie giggled. "Nash, you're one to talk. You're the natty one in the family. You can't fool me, you know. I'm the one who had to mend your uniform, not once but twice."

"Guess you're right," he admitted. "I can't help it. I don't like to get dirty. I can see I'm going to have a little trouble with that in this man's army. Anyway, Jolie, I want to ask you something. How old are you?"

"I'm fifteen," she answered, mystified.

He nodded. "I thought so, but when you were nursing all of us, you seemed so much older, so much more mature. But you sure don't look older. Morgan said he's your guardian. Is that right?"

"Yes, my father died a year and a half ago, and Mr. Tremayne was kind enough to take me in."

"I see. So that's all there is to it, then?"

"What do you mean? Oh wait, I think I see. Between me and Mr. Tremayne, you mean? He's my guardian, Nash," she repeated with some vehemence and some bitterness.

Nash asked quietly, "Then do you have a sweetheart, Jolie?"

Jolie's cheeks turned a delicate shade of peach. "No, I don't have a sweetheart, Nash."

He grinned. "Good. Then I'll be back, Jolie. I'll be back to see you just as soon as I can. Er—that's all right with you, isn't it? I mean, you don't think I'm an ugly toad or a dead bore or anything, do you?"

Jolie smiled. "No, I happen to think that you're handsome and interesting. Yes, I'd like for you to come visit me, Nash. Whenever you can."

❧

Morgan returned on the last day of August. He rode in late that afternoon, tired and dusty and world-weary. Everywhere he had looked he had seen the machinery of war, whether it was men in uniform or cannon or overflowing hospitals or women rolling bandages.

I'm not even a part of it. I haven't even joined the army, he reflected grimly. *How can I be so sick of it all? And after only one major battle? What am I going to do? What is the right thing to do, Lord?*

He caught sight of his neat red house up on the hill, and his spirits lifted. He would talk to Jolie about it. She never said much, but Morgan had found her to be a good listener. When she did say anything or offer her opinion, it was always thoughtful and intelligent. He spurred Vulcan to a fast canter.

When he got onto the grounds, he saw Jolie in the training paddock, mounted on Calliope, Rosh's dependable mare.

Leading the mare around in circles and laughing up at Jolie was Nash Southall.

Morgan leaped out of the saddle and stamped up to the paddock. "What's going on? Jolie, what are you doing, perched up there sidesaddle, without a sidesaddle? You're going to fall off and break your silly head!"

Jolie and Nash turned, both of them with looks of surprise. Jolie called, "Hello, Mr. Tremayne! Welcome home! And I won't break my silly head. This is the fourth time Nash has helped me ride this way."

Nash led the mare to the fence where Morgan was standing. "Hello, Morgan. Why are you so upset? Miss Jolie's doing very well. If she had a lady's saddle, she'd be galloping along before you know it. Besides, I'd never let her fall." He smiled up at Jolie.

"I'm not upset," Morgan snapped. "I'm just surprised. I've been teaching Jolie to ride, and I didn't think she was ready to try sidesaddle yet."

Nash stepped back and held his hands up. Jolie jumped into them, and gently he set her on the ground.

She came to Morgan and said, "But sir, you know I can't ride astride, bareback, all my life. And you're much too busy to teach me the proper way. I just thought I could try sitting sidesaddle, and if I could do it, maybe you could order me a lady's saddle."

"I can do that, certainly," Morgan said in a calmer tone. "When I'm sure you're ready. Nash, how is it that you're not back with your unit yet? You look all healed up and fine to me."

"Sure I am, Morgan. Blair and I went back last week. I just came by to see Miss Jolie."

"You did? Oh. Oh, I see. I guess," Morgan said uncertainly.

"He can't stay for supper. He has to be back in camp tonight," Jolie said. "Do you mind if I ride just a little more, Mr. Tremayne? Nash has to leave soon."

"I guess that'll be all right," Morgan said. "Nash, it's good to see you. I'm glad you and Blair are all fixed up. But I'm really tired. I think I'm going on in and getting a nice, long, hot bath."

"Go ahead, Morgan. I won't keep Miss Jolie long," he said easily. "See you next week."

Morgan went back into the house and had an hour-long soak. Jolie came in for supper and told him all about the men and how they had recovered so well in that last week they'd been there. Morgan let her chatter on.

When they were finished, he said, "Jolie, would you mind coming into the study with me? I need to talk to you."

"Of course."

Carrying his coffee cup, Morgan went and seated himself behind his desk, instead of sitting in the chairs by the windows.

Jolie sat across the desk from him.

"Jolie, I have to admit I was shocked when I saw you and Nash this afternoon," he said evenly. "Do I understand that he is court-ing you?"

"I think so," Jolie answered with some difficulty. "I'm not too educated about these things, Mr. Tremayne. He asked me if I had a sweetheart, and when I said no, he asked if he could visit me. That's courting, isn't it?"

"Yes. But Jolie, it's not fitting. You are much too young to have men courting you."

"But I'm fifteen! Evetta says that lots of girls get married at fifteen, or even fourteen."

"Married! Good gracious, Jolie, you can't be thinking of marriage!"

"Of course I am," she replied with a tiny smile. "I'm a fifteen-year-old girl. But I'm not thinking of marrying Nash Southall, nor is he thinking of marrying me. We just like each other, that's all. He's sweet and fun, and he makes me laugh. What's wrong with that?"

Morgan frowned, and it was some time before he answered. "There's nothing wrong with that, of course. It's just that you've led a very sheltered life, and you're very innocent. I don't think you're ready for beaus yet, Jolie."

"Mr. Tremayne, most girls are innocent at my age, aren't they? I mean, they should be. Am I so odd, so bizarre, because I'm an octoroon and because my father wouldn't dare claim me while he was alive?" She spoke passionately, and her eyes filled with tears.

"No, no, Jolie, that's not it at all," Morgan said quickly. "Please don't cry. I don't know what to do when ladies cry. My mother never cried in front of me. It makes me very nervous."

Suddenly Jolie smiled through her tears. "You called me a lady. Even you know deep down that I'm not a child anymore, Mr. Tremayne. I am a young lady, and having Nash Southall visit me shouldn't scare you at all."

"No, it shouldn't," Morgan said, almost to himself. "All right, I guess I won't kick Nash off the property when he comes to see you.

But you just watch yourself, Jolie. I don't want to see you get hurt."

"I won't," she assured him.

❧

Summer passed quickly; fall lingered sweetly, it seemed to Morgan. It didn't get really cold until the last of October, when the first snowfall, a light, pretty one, blanketed northern Virginia.

The two vast armies were huddled in their winter camps. Abraham Lincoln and his war cabinet were planning their spring campaign. Jefferson Davis and his generals were trying to figure out what Lincoln was planning, and General Lee was working hard to push for an offensive campaign beginning in March of 1862.

Morgan felt as if he had suddenly come to a halt and had breathing space. He felt no anguish over whether to join the Confederate Army or not, for he knew that there would be no great battles during wintertime. He had winter crops to plant and horses to train. In the spring, he would make his decision. He must make his decision. . . .

PART THREE

CHAPTER THIRTEEN

Jolie heard the sound of a bird outside her window and slowly opened her eyes. March had just come and, as always, the spring was a delight to her. Slowly she got up, stretched, and then swung her feet out of bed and moved over toward the window.

She stared at the bird nibbling at the sunflower seed that she had put out. It was a medium-sized bird with a ladderback design and a red head. "I thought I knew all the birds," she murmured, "but you don't look like a woodpecker to me." She watched the bird until he evidently had eaten his fill then leaped into the air and flew away.

Jolie went to her armoire and for a moment could not decide what to wear. She finally selected a well-worn blue cotton dress. Sighing, she put it on. She had to struggle to pull it down. Close to turning sixteen, it seemed as if her figure had developed overnight. Every dress and blouse she owned was too tight across her chest, the sleeves were too short, and most of her skirts were too short.

Leaving her room, she walked through the house and went out to the kitchen where Evetta was rolling out dough, preparing to make biscuits.

"You can't wear that dress, Jolie. It ain't modest." Displeasure was in Evetta's face, and she added, "Go put on something decent."

"All my dresses are too tight. I don't know what I'm going to do."

"Well, you're going to have to have new dresses. That's what you're gonna do. You tell Mr. Morgan that you got to have some new clothes."

"I don't like to ask for things."

"You're just too proud. That's what's the matter with you, child. Now, you do like I says."

Amon came in, moved behind Evetta, then put his arms around her and lifted her off the floor. "My, it's fine to have a good-looking wife."

"You put me down!" Evetta protested, even though she really liked the attention.

Amon set her down but gave her an extra squeeze. "My next wife, she's going to be more loving than you."

"Never mind your next wife. I'm all the wife you needs."

The outside door opened, and Morgan came in. "Good morning," he said cheerfully. "Do I smell bacon and eggs?"

"You sit down there, Mr. Tremayne," Jolie said, "and I'll get your coffee."

Morgan sat down. Amon, Rosh, and Santo joined him, and they talked, as always, about horses. Ketura came in, and she and Jolie helped Evetta finish and serve the men. Finally breakfast was on the table.

They all bowed their heads, and Morgan asked a quick blessing; then he filled his plate and began eating hungrily. "Good cooking, Evetta, as always. Thank you." Morgan was always courteous, showing his appreciation to Amon and his family.

"You're welcome, Mr. Tremayne. You know, sir, she don't like to say, but Jolie really needs some new clothes. She's outgrown just about everything you got her last year."

Morgan looked thoughtful. "All right, Jolie. We can go into

town to Sally Selden's and order you some things. Would you like to do that?"

Jolie eagerly said, "Oh yes, sir, please. And may Ketura come, too?"

"Of course. In fact, I'll bet Ketura could use a new dress or two. We'll make it a shopping day for the ladies. Be ready to go in about an hour."

❧

Morgan drove the wagon into Fredericksburg, and Jolie thought he seemed carefree and confident, not weighted down and burdened as he had so often been since the war started. He made jokes and teased Jolie and Ketura unmercifully. "So I guess I'm taking you two ladies to the mill, to buy you some flour sacks for new dresses, isn't that right?"

They giggled and cried, "Oh no! No, sir, Mr. Tremayne! Please, please!" Their high youthful voices on the gentle spring air seemed to please him.

Despite all his teasing, he stopped the wagon on Main Street, just in front of a small, neat brick shop. Over the door was a sign that read: SALLY SELDEN, DRESSMAKER AND MILLINER. Morgan jumped out of the wagon and came to gallantly help Jolie and Ketura down.

Instantly they went to look in the shop window. In it was displayed a cambric dress, white with a print of tiny yellow daffodils. The mannequin had a straw hat with a wide graceful brim. It had a yellow ribbon around the crown, tying underneath the chin. The hat was trimmed with real daffodils and white baby's breath.

"Oooh, that's just beautiful," Ketura breathed. "That would look so, so pretty on you, Jolie."

"It would on you, too, Ketura," Jolie said wistfully.

Standing behind them, Morgan said, "Tell you what. Both of you order yourselves that dress and hat. You pick out the material you want. I don't guess you'd want the same thing. Seems like ladies don't like it when that happens for some reason. Anyway, go ahead and order a couple of nice dresses each, and let's see, maybe three dresses for everyday. How does that sound?"

"Really?" Ketura said, her big brown eyes as round as saucers. "Even me, Mr. Tremayne?"

"Even you, Ketura. And by the way, you'd better order a nice new hat for your mother, too, or we'll all be in big trouble."

Jolie went up on tiptoe and kissed Morgan's cheek. "Thank you, Mr. Tremayne. Being able to get something for Ketura makes me almost as happy as getting new clothes myself."

"I know," he said lightly. "That's one thing that makes you a very unusual girl, Jolie. Now I've got a couple of errands to run, and I'm going to stop by the Club Coffee Shop to get the papers and the latest news. You two don't go wandering around, do you hear me? When you get finished, you come straight to the coffee shop. Jolie, do you remember where it is?"

"Yes, sir." She pointed down the street. "It's just down there, across the street. I can see the sign from here. We promise we'll only go there."

"Okay. Have fun. And take your time. I know girls like to do this stuff for hours and hours." Morgan climbed back up into the wagon.

Jolie called out, "Mr. Tremayne?"

"Yes?"

"Um—maybe—perhaps—two hats, sir? Each?"

"Minx," he said affectionately. "Two hats. And don't forget Evetta."

Morgan went first to the wheelwrights, because he thought that one of the wagon wheels was jinking a little. He left the wagon there and walked to the bank and made a deposit. Vulcan had already gone out to stud and ruefully Morgan sighed as he handed over the Confederate money to the teller. Already fifty dollars in Confederate money was equal to about ten dollars gold. As he had predicted, the blockade was working all too well. Coffee was a dollar a pound, tea five dollars, a pair of shoes were anywhere from ten to fifteen dollars a pair. Morgan knew that it was only going to get worse.

From there he stopped by Silas Cage's office and gave the attorney an update. He had made friends with Cage in the time since Henry DeForge had died. Pretty, young Mrs. Cage had given birth to a little girl just before Christmas, and Morgan duly admired the new baby. After they finished discussing his new daughter and Jolie, Cage took off his glasses and polished them with his handkerchief. By now this was a familiar sign to Morgan. He knew Cage was going to tell him something important.

"Morgan, I've decided to join the army," he said quietly.

"I see," Morgan said. "That's going to be real hard on Mrs. Cage, isn't it?"

He put his glasses back on. "Yes. But it's something I have to do. I love this country. I mean Virginia. I have to fight for her. It's just that simple. Maybe I'm presuming on our friendship, but I would like to know. Are you planning on joining the army, Morgan?"

"Yes," he said instantly. His quick definite answer was something of a surprise, even to Morgan himself. Now he realized that all winter he had, in the deepest recesses of his mind, firmly decided to join. "But I'm not sure when I'm going to join up, Silas," he temporized. "You know that I've spent the last year making preparations, planning, stocking up, so that Rapidan Run, and Jolie, will be safe if something happens to me. Oh, I'll just say it. In the back of my mind I've always known that I was doing all of those things in case I was killed in battle. So right now I've got just a couple more things to do. I've got spring planting, and I've got ten three-year-olds that are just about ready to be sold. And of course I'm selling them to the Confederate Army. I did just want to make sure they're trained and ready before I do."

Silas nodded. "I understand. I think you've been very wise, Morgan. I know it's been hard, because I know all too well how people think you're a coward if you don't join. But I determined I was going to wait until after my daughter was born before I left her and my wife. It was the right thing for me to do, and I'm sure you've done the right thing for you, too."

The men parted on good terms, and Morgan went on to the coffee shop. It was a gathering place for the men of the town, some of whom came first thing in the morning and stayed until dinnertime. All the newspapers were sold there, and the men gathered and talked and discussed the latest news for hours at a time. Morgan joined three men sitting at a table, all acquaintances of his: young Asa Cooke, whose father was a railroad engineer; Bert Patrick, who owned the largest general store in town; and Will Green, who was Morgan's favorite saddler.

Bert said as Morgan sat down, "Hello, Morgan, good to see you again. It's been a couple of weeks since you've been in town, hasn't it?"

"Three weeks, in fact. Guess the war's put a hitch in river deliveries, because I haven't seen Dirk Jameson or his boys for the last week." Jameson had a sturdy twelve-foot boat, and for years he had delivered the newspapers and other supplies to Henry DeForge and Morgan.

"They all joined up, even Old Jameson himself," Asa said eagerly. He was a bright boy with red hair, freckles, and a toothy smile. "I'm joining up, Morgan, this very day!"

"You're too young," Morgan said shortly. "You need to stay at home and take care of your pretty mama and your sisters, Asa." Morgan knew the family. Asa was the only son, and he had five sisters.

"Nope, my papa told me I could join up when I was seventeen, and today is my seventeenth birthday. My mama and my sisters are all real proud of me, Morgan. They want me to fight for the Glorious Cause. I'm glad I'm seventeen now. I was getting worried I might miss the whole thing!"

"You're not going to have to worry about that, boy," Will Green said. He was an older man, in his fifties, and he was one man who was in complete agreement with Morgan about the war. He had no illusions of glory, and he knew that the South was going to be fighting against almost impossible odds in the long run. He and Morgan had agreed that it was likely to be a long run, indeed. "You're going to have plenty of time, and chances, to get your fool self killed."

"Pshaw," Asa said disdainfully. "I gotta hurry up and get my five Yanks, Mr. Green, before they all scoot back to Washington for good, like they did at Bull Run."

Bert Patrick said, "The news hasn't been that good since then, has it? Morgan, you know about Fort Henry and Fort Donelson, don't you?"

"No, the last paper I got was around February 12th."

Bert shook his head. "Fort Henry in Tennessee was captured by federal gunboats. And then a new young whippersnapper they got, name of Ulysses S. Grant, of all the outlandish things, took Fort Donelson. Word is that he demanded, and got, an unconditional surrender. Made those Tennessee boys look pretty bad, except for a hotshot cavalryman we got out there in the West, General Nathan Bedford Forrest. He refused to surrender, and somehow he snuck out of Fort Donelson right under Grant's nose. Him and about two hundred of his men. But that's two pieces of real bad news right there. We lost control of the Tennessee and Cumberland Rivers"— he snapped his fingers—"right there, just like that. Not to mention fourteen thousand fighting men at Fort Donelson."

"Only good news I've heard tell lately is that President Davis has recalled General Lee to Richmond," Will Green said soberly. "I know he's an experienced engineer, and he's needed to shore up the coastal defenses in the Carolinas and Georgia, but he's a Virginia man. We need him here."

Morgan knew that Mrs. Lee hadn't seen her husband for over a year now. She had written him in February, telling him that she was going to go to the White House, one of George Custis's holdings on the Pamunkey River that he had given to his son Rooney in his will. Morgan hadn't been needed to move her this time, as

Rooney had managed to get a leave to pick her up from the Hot Springs, where she had wintered, and take her to his plantation. The White House was just west of Richmond, and Morgan thought that he would be able to take the carriage and bring her to Richmond if the general wanted him to. "When is he due back?" Morgan asked eagerly.

"Any day now," Will answered. "And a good day it'll be, I'll say. Joe Johnston is a good man, but in my opinion, His Excellency would do well to look to Robert E. Lee to command this army."

The table agreed, for Lee was a famous man in Virginia, a favorite son. Even Asa said, "I hope he comes today. I'd sure like to know I was going to be one of Robert E. Lee's boys. That would just be the icing on the cake."

Privately, Morgan thought, *I have to agree with the boy there. When I join, I'd like to know that General Lee is my general. Maybe it's time. . . .*

❧

As Morgan had foreseen, it took Jolie and Ketura two hours to pick out fabrics, decide on the dress patterns, try on hats, and for Mrs. Selden to get their measurements. "I'm so glad Mr. Tremayne brought you into town, Jolie. Every time he orders something for you, sight unseen, I just shudder, thinking it can't possibly fit you. You're not a little girl like you were when you were with Mr. DeForge. You're turning into a young woman now. And a very pretty one, too."

"Thank you," Jolie said. "But Mr. Tremayne thinks I'm still twelve years old, I guess. I wonder that he's not still ordering me pantalettes."

Mrs. Selden laughed. "No, I think I would put a stop to that." Sally Selden had been making Jolie's clothes ever since Jolie was born. When Jolie turned two, Henry DeForge brought her in, and once a year, every year, after that. Naturally Morgan had had to confide in Mrs. Selden when he took Jolie after Mr. DeForge died, and he kept ordering clothes from her.

Morgan had still not made it public knowledge that he had taken guardianship of Jolie, but Fredericksburg was, after all, a small town. Mrs. Selden had always kept her friends and neighbors updated about the exotic octoroon child that Morgan Tremayne had taken in. Morgan hadn't even found a way to tell his own family about Jolie. And he had never mentioned her to Leona Bledsoe.

And so it was rather a cruel trick of fate that Gibbs Bledsoe was walking down Main Street and was right in front of Mrs. Selden's shop when Jolie and Ketura came out, arm in arm. Gallantly he stopped and lifted his hat and let them pass, thinking, *What a lovely girl she is, and her maid's a pretty sight, too.*

Then he heard Jolie say, "Oh dear, Ketura, we've been here for two hours! Hurry, hurry! I hope Mr. Tremayne isn't getting impatient with us."

Bledsoe's mind clicked! And he knew who she was. Taking two long strides, he caught up with them and fell into step beside Jolie. She looked up at him with surprise. "Well, well, well," he drawled. "So this is the big secret that Morgan's been keeping from my sister. Pardon my rudeness, Miss Jolie DeForge. My name is Gibbs Bledsoe, and my sister's name is Leona Rose Bledsoe. Do you know that name, by any chance?"

"Yes, sir," she said stiffly, looking straight ahead. But Gibbs saw that she clutched Ketura even closer with nervousness.

It amused him. "You are one fine, handsome young woman, Jolie. My sister's not going to be happy to hear that. I think she had more of a picture of a little black girl in her mind."

"I am part black, sir. But I don't think you should be talking to me like this. It's not very respectful," Jolie managed to say. She hurried hers and Ketura's step, but Gibbs easily kept up.

"Morgan should know better than to let a pretty girl like you wander around with just your maid to accompany you. Here, take my arm. I'll escort you, and you, girl, you can walk behind like a proper maid does."

"You don't have to do that," Jolie said desperately, trying to pull away from him.

But he insistently took her hand and tucked it around his arm. "No, I want to. We should get to know each other, Jolie. In fact, maybe I should come out to Rapidan Run and visit you sometime. Maybe you could accompany me to the town hall for the next dance."

"No, sir. Mr. Tremayne would never permit that."

"He wouldn't? Stodgy old Morgan. Keeps you hidden and won't let you loose."

"No! It's not like that!" she said desperately. She tried again to pull away from him. "Please, Mr. Bledsoe, let me go. Mr. Tremayne is right over there in the coffee shop. Ketura and I can cross the street by ourselves."

"Nonsense," he said then pulled her out into the busy street, dodging carts and buggies and riders.

Jolie looked back to make sure that Ketura was following them, which she was, a dogged look on her face.

They got onto the plank boardwalk, and Morgan came storming out of the coffeeshop. "Gibbs, stop hauling on her like she's a side of beef! What are you doing anyway? You shouldn't impose yourself on young ladies you haven't met. Mind your manners, boy."

Gibbs Bledsoe had a fiery temper and growled, "Don't you ever call me 'boy' again. And it's your fault that I haven't met Jolie, Morgan. You know very well you should have told me, and particularly Leona, about her a long time ago."

"Maybe I should have, but I'm not going to stand out here on the street and argue with you. In spite of what you think, or whatever vicious gossip you've heard, Jolie and Ketura are ladies who deserve respect, and I intend to make sure they get it."

Gibbs glared at him. "Maybe you'd better make sure you're really the gentleman here, Morgan. At least I acknowledged that I know Jolie." With that parting shot, he turned on his heel and hurried off.

Morgan turned to the two girls. "I'm sorry," he said helplessly. "I'm so sorry, Jolie."

She answered spiritedly, "You have nothing to apologize to me for, Mr. Tremayne. I just want to forget this whole thing. And please, sir, don't ever tell me you're sorry for anything ever again. It's just not right."

Morgan gave in. "All right, Jolie. For now at least. So, are you ladies ready to go back home?"

"Yes, please," Jolie said, brightening. "But we have some—things we need to pick up at Mrs. Selden's."

"What things? She didn't have any ready-to-wears, did she?"

"No. At least not dresses," Jolie said, taking Ketura's arm again as they walked down the street to the wheelwright's. "It's—um—hatboxes. Six hatboxes."

"Six?" Morgan repeated.

Jolie said, "Remember, you said we could get two hats. Each. And of course we couldn't forget Evetta."

"Ah yes, it's all coming back to me now. I do recall getting ambushed just as I was leaving, and something about lots of hats," Morgan teased her. "Six hatboxes, you say. Guess Calliope can handle that."

When they were on their way out of town, they passed the town square.

About twenty young men and boys were there, drilling in new gray uniforms. At least they would march two steps then hoist their rifles to their shoulders and pretend to shoot. "Got one Billy Yank!" one of them cried. "Got four more to go for my quota!" The men laughed, and one of them shouted, "How 'bout we all decide to get ten? No graybelly is any match for a Virginia fighting man!"

Morgan sighed deeply as they passed.

Jolie looked up at him curiously. "Mr. Tremayne?"

"Hm?"

"You're going to join the army, aren't you." Though it was in the form of a question, the tone of it was not. And she sounded sad.

"Not today, Jolie. That's all I can tell you. Not today."

❧

The next day Morgan came back to town and called on Leona. She was having tea with her father and mother in the parlor, and Leona cordially asked him to join them.

Morgan had been unsure of her reception. He knew that Gibbs had surely told the family about meeting Jolie.

But as soon as Leona had served him tea, Benjamin Bledsoe started in. "Morgan, Gibbs told me about meeting your girl yesterday. We've heard about her, of course. I was wondering if you were ever going to own up to it," he said disdainfully.

"It?" Morgan repeated sharply. "Sir, Jolie is not an 'it.' She's a young woman, a well-brought-up, respectable young woman, I might add. It is true I haven't discussed her with you, or with anyone else for that matter. I had no idea that everyone was so interested in my private affairs."

"Perhaps you may truly be that naive, Morgan. But surely you see that you should have told Leona about her a long time ago."

"Maybe," Morgan said doubtfully. "Then again, as I said, this is a private matter. In fact, it's a private *family* matter. I am Jolie DeForge's legal guardian, and in my view that makes me her family. I, for one, wouldn't be interested in knowing all of your family business, Mr. Bledsoe. I wouldn't think I had the right."

Benjamin Bledsoe took the mild rebuke with surprising equanimity. "Maybe you're right, Morgan. Adopting a child is a very personal thing. How old is the girl?"

"She's sixteen."

"She is part black, isn't she?"

"She's an octoroon."

Leona Rose had been listening carefully with a neutral expression. But now she said, "You sound very high and noble, Morgan, but most people aren't. They talk, and the fact is that you have a young girl—a very pretty young girl, Gibbs tells me—living with you. Looking at it objectively, it's pretty scandalous."

Stung, Morgan retorted, "That is nowhere near an objective view, Leona. It's a malicious and skewed version of a situation that is perfectly innocent. This, in fact, is exactly why I don't talk about Jolie very much. I don't want to hear it." He had never spoken so sharply to Leona, and she looked thoroughly taken aback.

Gibbs came in and looked around. "You all look as solemn as a bunch of owls. Hi, Morgan. I'm still angry with you, in case you didn't notice."

Morgan said, "Gibbs, I'm sorry we had that altercation, but let me ask you this. Suppose a man had taken the liberties with your sister that you did with Jolie. What would you think of that?"

Gibbs Bledsoe had a hot temper, but really he was a fair-minded young man. He shook his head ruefully and answered, "I'd do exactly what you did. I'm too touchy." He winked at Leona. "Like my sister."

"Let's put it all behind us then," Morgan said with relief.

But Leona Rose Bledsoe was far from relieved and far from amused. She rose to her feet and snapped her fan shut angrily. "Men! The things you get away with! Well, you're not going to just pat me on the head and brush me off, Morgan. You're so worried about your responsibilities to that little black girl, and you never seem to think about your responsibilities to me!" Majestically she sailed out of the room.

Nervously her mother followed her.

Morgan, Gibbs, and even Benjamin Bledsoe looked guiltily at each other.

Gibbs gave a low whistle. "You fell into it this time, Morgan. Glad I'm not in your shoes."

"You could help me out here, Gibbs," Morgan said helplessly. "Can't you go talk to her, tell her not to be mad at me?"

"Not me, brother. I'm no coward, but I'm not squaring off against my sister."

Benjamin Bledsoe cleared his throat. "Er, Morgan, Leona is a little upset just now. Usually it's best to leave her alone until she gets in a better—I mean, until she feels better. Maybe you'd better go and come back tomorrow. Or even the next day."

"Right," Gibbs said forcefully. "You better stick your head in first, Morgan, to make sure you're not still in the bull's-eye."

"Maybe I'll come back on Monday," he said uncertainly.

"Maybe that's best," Mr. Bledsoe said with relief.

Morgan went toward the door then turned around when Benjamin Bledsoe said, "Morgan?"

"Sir?"

"I called you a coward once. I'm sorry for that. Any man that's determined to hold his own with my daughter is no coward."

"No, sir," Morgan heartily agreed and hurried away.

CHAPTER FOURTEEN

Throughout the Civil War, the major problem of the South was that the North could quickly forge an arsenal of weapons. The industrial power that had been built up in the Northern states was immense. Unlike the wealthy elite of the South, who were only interested in growing cotton, businessmen in the North were interested in capital investment, in utilization of natural resources, of machines and equipment and factories. Quickly the North was able to turn their industrialized cities into factories that could turn out the implements of war. Ironclad ships, muskets, cannons, and ammunition all came like a flood once the North geared up. The South had nothing to compare with this. Many of their weapons were those captured from the North, of necessity.

The North outnumbered the South tremendously. The North was thickly populated, whereas the South had many fewer citizens and many blacks, who were not permitted to fight. This was starting to become a factor, but at the beginning, on both sides of the Mason–Dixon Line, young men, and older men as well, rushed to join the respective armies of the Union and the Confederacy.

SURRENDER

But it was not a matter of armament or soldiers that made the difference in the two foes, at least not until the end. The real problem the North faced was finding generals who had the courage, the nerve, and the quality of bold leadership of all great military men. Though the rhetoric of the South was high and overblown, the fact remained that many Southern generals and colonels were exactly that kind of man. It was not so in the Union Army. Throughout the history of the Civil War, generals such as Pope, Burnside, McDowell, Hooker, and others knew how to build armies but lacked the killer instinct of sending these armies into the fierce cauldron of bloody battle.

One such man who arose was General George Brinton McClellan. He was thrust into a difficult position. After the Bull Run disaster, the armies of the North, as well as the citizens and the government itself, felt that trying to subdue the Southern states was well-nigh impossible. There was a peace party, well populated by those who clamored for peace at any cost. The newspapers that had once been screaming, ON TO RICHMOND, were now begging the government to turn to peace.

General McClellan, who before the war had been the president of a railroad, was summoned to Washington and rode sixty miles on horseback to the nearest railway station. When he arrived in Washington, he found the city almost in a condition unable to defend itself. To his shock, McClellan found himself looked up to from all sides as a deliverer.

He wrote to his wife that evening:

I find myself in a new and strange position here. President, cabinet, and General Scott are all deferring to me. By some strange operation of magic I seem to have become the power of the land.

When asked if he could help rescue the cause, McClellan replied proudly, "I can do it all."

He set out at once to reconstruct the Army of the Potomac.

Rigid discipline was the order of the day, and something new came into being. Little Mac, as the soldiers called this man, transformed the army from a whipped mob into a hot-blooded army that seemed to have never known the taste of defeat.

He was a young man, only thirty-four, his eyes were blue, his hair was dark auburn, parted on the left, and he was clean-shaven as a rule, except for a rather straggly mustache. He was of average height, robust and stockily built with a massive chest. The newspapers began to write about him, and the name "The Young Napoleon" became his journalistic title. And, indeed, he did have a Napoleonic touch. The soldiers liked him. They understood that he was firm, a strict disciplinarian, but he was fair.

Within ten days of his arrival in Washington, he could say proudly, "I have restored order completely." The army seemed to be reborn. Reviews were staged, with massed columns swinging past reviewing stands. Equipment was polished new and gleaming, and there was a camaraderie in the Army of the Potomac that had been lacking from the beginning.

Yet in the small hours of the night, it seemed, McClellan had grave doubts. "I am here in a terrible place," he wrote. "The enemy has from three to four times my force." This was not guesswork. These numbers came from Allen Pinkerton, the railroad detective, who was supposedly a master spy. Later it would seem that he had invented numbers in his mind rather than sent spies.

In addition to feeling he was being overwhelmed with Southern forces, McClellan had to fight his way in Washington against Lieutenant General Winfield Scott, who had been a great man in his day. McClellan saw him merely as an old man who had not the strength nor the wisdom to fight a war. "He understands nothing, appreciates nothing." McClellan spoke of General Scott. "I have to fight my way against him." Later on he said, "General Scott is the most dangerous antagonist I have."

Lincoln, desperate in the hope of finding a fighting general, did everything that McClellan requested. Finally General Scott retired, and McClellan was appointed to fill his place in command of the army. He spoke so positively that Lincoln wondered if McClellan was as aware of the the monstrous burden of responsibility as he himself was. "The vast labor weighs upon you, General," he said, half chiding.

"I can do it all," McClellan said confidently. Indeed, he had made a prediction: "I shall crush the Rebels in one campaign." Still, his constant bickering with politicians bothered him.

He wrote to his wife:

> *The people think me all powerful. . . . I can't tell you how disgusted I'm becoming with these wretched politicians.*

He did not include Abraham Lincoln, who showed a great deal of deference to General McClellan. But Lincoln, who had been boning up on the science of war, was chafing for action, and McClellan kept putting him off and putting the country off. When someone said that McClellan did not show him the proper respect, Lincoln responded, "I will hold McClellan's horse if he will only bring us success."

Little Mac finally made a decision. He had never enjoyed the concept of a full frontal battle on the plains, as McDowell had done at Bull Run. He came up with another plan of campaign. He would load his soldiers aboard transports, steam down the Potomac in the Chesapeake Bay, then south along the coast to the mouth of the Rappahannock. There he would be less than fifty miles from Richmond, his objective. Without loss of a man, he would have cut his marching distance in half and would be in the rear of the enemy, who would be forced to retreat and fight on grounds of McClellan's choosing.

Unfortunately, he ignored the details, including the assembling of transports for the 150,000 men he planned to invade with. Then the rains came in the middle of his campaign, and the fields were turned to quagmires, and the roads were axle-deep in the mud.

This gave him another excuse for not attacking.

Now Lincoln saw that he was looking at a general who was not the man to lead the Army of the Potomac. But what was done was done. No matter how Little Mac delayed, surely battle would come.

❧

"I wish you didn't have to go, Robert. I know that in many ways this is your dream, but I still wish you could just stay here with me." Mary reached up and put her hand on her husband's cheek. Anxiety was in her expression, and when he leaned forward and kissed her, she held on to him tightly. "I'm so afraid for you," she whispered.

Mary Lee had finally wended her way to Richmond and was living in a rented house on East Franklin Street. Lee had come to bid farewell to her. McClellan was approaching at a rapid speed, and everyone knew that there was going to be a life-and-death struggle over the city of Richmond.

"I have to go, dearest," Lee said, "but I won't be the commanding general. I'll be way back in the lines, so you needn't worry. Just pray for me."

"Of course I will. I always do that."

"Then, Mary, you know that all will be well, no matter what happens. The Lord will protect you and me, always."

❧

Lee left the house, mounted Traveler, and rode to the outskirts of town. There he met with Joe Johnston, who was an old friend of Lee's and was the commanding general of the Confederate forces in the east.

With him was President Jefferson Davis. Davis's thin aristocratic features were tense. "You're sadly outnumbered, General Johnston."

"I think you are correct, but there is nothing we can do about that. We must all fight as best we can."

SURRENDER

Lee said nothing, but he stayed close to Jefferson Davis. In truth, he had been kept from a higher position in the army because he was the only man who could get along with Jeff Davis. Other generals were short with him or were egotistical, and since Davis fancied himself a fighting man, as he had been in the War of Mexico, instead of a political figure, the clash was inevitable.

Although he was not outwardly resentful toward his president or his old friend from both West Point and Mexico, Joe Johnston was rather arrogant, and he kept his council and plans much to himself. He only gave Davis and Lee the bare outlines of his strategy. Eventually Johnston politely suggested that General Lee ride out on the field and said that he hoped he could soon send some much-needed reinforcements. Of course, Jeff Davis could not bear to stay away from a battle, and so both he and Lee witnessed the Battle of Seven Pines.

The battle itself proved to be the worst-conducted large-scale conflict of the entire war. What it finally came to was a military nightmare. The Southern troops had little contact with each other, and therefore Johnston could not get them to move as he ordered. He was never able to position his divisions properly. Casualties were high, and the gain was small. But the most significant casualty was General Johnston himself. He was hit in the right shoulder by a bullet. As he reeled in the saddle, he was wounded a second time when a shell fragment struck him in the chest and unhorsed him.

They were trying to get the wounded general back behind the lines to an ambulance when he bade them stop. Weakly he said, "Would someone go back and see if they can find my sword? I would not lose it for ten thousand dollars."

A courier went back under fire, found the sword and his pistol, and returned. Finally the ambulance drove away toward Richmond. A courier hurried to President Davis and General Lee with the news that General Johnston had been wounded, perhaps fatally.

That night Davis and Lee rode around the field of battle, surveying it and talking to the senior officer on the field, General Gustavus W. Smith. He had been ill, and he was showing great battle strain.

They rode on in the darkness. The only account of their conversation was Jefferson Davis's: "When riding from the field of battle with General Robert E. Lee. . .I informed him that he would be assigned to command of the army. . .and that he could make his preparations as soon as he reached his quarters, as I should send the order to him as soon as I arrived at mine."

Lee tackled his monumental task. After he took charge, he immediately organized an offensive. It came to be called the Seven Days' Battle, but it was really a series of battles: Gaines' Mill, Savage's Station, Frayser's Farm, and Malvern Hill.

Lee did his best, but his troops were untrained, and he himself had not had an opportunity to teach his officers how to maneuver quickly and effectively and how to keep constant lines of communication open to the commanding general.

The last battle took place on Malvern Hill. The Union troops under McClellan were up at the crest of the hill, and Lee felt he had the Army of the Potomac on the run. He then made one of the most serious mistakes of his career. He ordered a charge, and as his troops swarmed up the hill, they were mowed down by the artillery and musketry entrenched there.

Thus, the Seven Days' Battle ended, and McClellan's grand Peninsular campaign was ended. It was, however, a great victory for Robert E. Lee. He had broken up the Union army, cowed them with his masterful offensive, and once again, the Northern troops fled back to Washington in defeat.

McClellan was promptly relieved of command. Lincoln simply could not understand how a man who had vast superiority in both troops and artillery could lose against a smaller, less well-armed force. Once again, he started searching for a capable commander.

But he did not have General Robert E. Lee.

"I have a present for you, Jolie."

Jolie looked up from her book and saw Morgan beckoning her. Obediently she followed him out the back door. There she saw a new gleaming sidesaddle on the hitching post. "Oh, Mr. Tremayne! Thank you, thank you!" she said excitedly, running to it to feel the soft leather and studying the leg hook and single stirrup.

"That's not all the present," Morgan said, grinning. He gave a short sharp whistle, and Rosh came out of the stables, leading a three-year-old mare.

She was a beautiful horse, a deep chestnut that was almost a mahogany red, with black points. She was small but was the perfect size for a small lady like Jolie. Her head was neat, her eyes were soft and sweet, and she was proud and alert in her stance.

Jolie had seen the mare, but it had never occurred to her that Morgan would give her such a valuable gift. "You mean she's mine?" Jolie whispered.

"All yours. One of the finest mares I've ever bred."

Jolie threw her arms around Morgan crying, "How can I thank you, Mr. Tremayne? Oh, I can't believe it!" She became aware then that he was slightly pushing her away, and Jolie realized that he was becoming more aware of her developing figure. She stepped back hurriedly and asked, "Can I go for a ride?"

"Of course you can. She's your horse. You can go any time you want. Just be sure that somebody at the house knows."

"I'll saddle her all by myself. I know how," Jolie said excitedly. She saddled the mare quickly. In a fast, agile motion she mounted, positioned her right leg in the leg hook, and caught the stirrup securely with her left foot. Primly she arranged her skirts.

"You look like you've done that a hundred times," Morgan said admiringly. "When you first came, I didn't think you'd ever be a rider. Especially such a good one."

"That just shows that you don't know everything," Jolie said sassily.

"Guess I don't," Morgan said mildly. He had already saddled Vulcan, so now he mounted him, and the two cantered down the drive.

❧

When they reached the river path, Morgan laughed when he saw Jolie gamely kick the mare into a gallop. Vulcan kept up with them easily, and Morgan watched her ride with a critical eye. He knew horses, and he knew riders. Some people had a natural affinity for riding, and Jolie was one of those. She kept a beautiful erect seat and instinctively knew just how to control the spirited mare.

After a good long run, they slowed down and walked along the path, skirting the river on one side and the Wilderness on the other. It was a delightful time for both of them.

Only the setting sun made Jolie want to return home. "I don't want to be in the Wilderness after dark," she said, casting a dire look at the thick forest. "I would be so afraid."

"You promised me once that you'd never be afraid again," Morgan said quietly. "And I promised you that you would never have any reason to be. Do you remember?"

"Oh yes, I'll never forget that day, Mr. Tremayne," she said in a low voice. "That was the day you came for me and brought me here. You brought me home."

"I'm very glad I did, Jolie."

"So am I, sir. So am I."

When they returned, Morgan waved away Rosh and Santo. "We'll see to the horses. Jolie needs to get used to taking care of her mare." They unsaddled then started brushing down the horses. "You know we've just always called her Little Chestnut. What are you going to name her, Jolie?"

"I'm going to call her Rowena, after the beautiful princess."

"Pretty name for a pretty horse."

They finished up and took the horses into the stables. "I know you're tired, Jolie. Your first ride is always the hardest. Let Rosh and

Santo grain them. Let's go on inside."

"First, I want to thank you again, Mr. Tremayne," she said, holding her hand out. "It's the most wonderful present anyone has ever given me. You're very, very good to me, and I'm grateful."

Morgan caressed her hand, savoring the softness of her skin. He stared down at her, searching her face, her wide, clear forehead, her warm eyes, her tiny straight nose and perfect mouth. She really had grown up, he saw clearly for the first time. Still, she was very young.

Morgan knew when he was an old man he would still have this picture in his mind. The young girl with glossy black hair and enormous dark eyes, staring up at him, filled with gratitude. He knew that he had done the right thing. Not just in giving her the horse, but in everything. For the first time since that cold January day, he knew in his heart that he had done a good thing, a righteous, unselfish thing, and it was good.

For the first time in a long time, Morgan was at peace.

CHAPTER FIFTEEN

After the Seven Days' Battle, the Army of Northern Virginia took the next six weeks to refit and reorganize.

Jolie received letters from Nash Southall when he had time to write. He wrote proudly how he had served with distinction during the constant battles and skirmishes of June and July and had received a promotion to second lieutenant. He said as soon as they returned to Richmond, he would get an extended leave and would return to his home outside of Fredericksburg. The first thing he promised her he would do was go to Rapidan Run to see her and show off his dashing new uniform.

Jolie was thrilled for Nash and his promotion. She was also excited about seeing him again, but when she tried to decide if she was excited to see a good friend or a charming suitor, she had no answers. She hoped seeing him would reveal her true feelings for Nash Southall.

❧

When Nash rode up on a hot morning in the middle of July, Jolie met him at the door, smiling. "You're getting earlier and earlier, Nash. I'm a lady of leisure, you know. You come much earlier, and I might not even be up yet."

"I know that's not true, especially since you got Rowena. You know, Jolie, you don't have to muck out her stall every day," he said as she led him into the study/sitting room. "That's what servants are for."

"I want to do it," Jolie said with emphasis. "She's my responsibility now, and I want to take care of her."

"So many heavy burdens for one so young," he teased.

"You don't make fun of me, Nash Southall," she said, sitting on the sofa beside him. "It wouldn't hurt you to get those manicured hands dirty doing some real work for a change."

"Nah, a gentleman of my station does not do manual labor," he said lazily. "At least, that's what my father's always told me. Say, Jolie, do you think Evetta's got any coffee? I have to admit that I'm still kinda groggy. I was in such a hurry to see you I got up at dawn's crack and galloped off without breakfast."

"I'm sure we can find something for you, you poor, starving, sleepy boy. C'mon. We've all had breakfast hours ago, but Evetta's usually got some biscuits left over. Maybe you can get her to take pity on you and fry you some eggs."

They went out to the kitchen, and although it was with much grumbling, Evetta fixed Nash a full breakfast and a fresh pot of coffee.

After he finished, he asked Jolie, "Would you go for a walk with me? Down to the river?"

"Of course, I know the breeze is much cooler down there." Jolie got her pretty straw hat, and soon she and Nash were walking down the little hill that the farmhouse was perched on to the small landing on the Rapidan. She sat down, took her shoes off, and let her feet dangle in the cool water.

Nash threw himself down beside her, lying on his side and propping one arm on his bent knee.

Jolie said, "Tell me about the battles, Nash. It must be terrible."

A frown marred his smooth features. "Yes, it is terrible. Much worse than I had imagined. It's kinda hard to talk about. You can't explain it. I think only people that have been in a battle really understand what it's like."

"Oh," she said in a small voice. "I apologize, Nash, I didn't mean to make you uncomfortable."

"You couldn't do that if you were trying to," he said warmly. "I'm always comfortable with you, Jolie. You're smart and fun and sweet, and I like being with you very much. Jolie, I wanted to ask you something today. Would you come to my home this weekend and meet my mother? My father, you know, is a major, and he's at camp in Richmond. But I've told my mother and my sister all about you, and they want to meet you."

Instantly Jolie became alert. This sort of thing, she had learned, was serious business. A Southern gentleman didn't invite a young woman to meet his family unless the lady was considered marriageable. And as to her queries of her true feelings for Nash, seeing him had not defined them as she had hoped. "I–I'm not sure, Nash. You've sort of taken me by surprise."

"Please come," he urged her. "You'll like my family, I'm sure. We've got a big house, plenty of servants, and a bridle path in the woods nearby. You can bring Rowena," he said slyly.

"I'll have to ask Mr. Tremayne. I don't know if he'll give me permission."

"Sure he will. Morgan knows my family. It's all perfectly nice and proper. How about if I bring the carriage Friday morning? I'll bring a groom to ride Rowena. And you can stay the night, and I'll bring you back Saturday morning. You'll enjoy it, Jolie. You'll see. My mother's kind of stuffy, like old Morgan, but my sister is lots of fun. And of course, I am superbly entertaining," he finished loftily.

She punched him lightly on the arm. "Silly thing. All right, Nash. If Mr. Tremayne gives me permission, I'll come."

They went back into the house, talking a mile a minute. Morgan had several maps in his study, and Nash showed Jolie where his family's plantation was.

After another half hour, Morgan came in from his morning ride. "Morning, Nash. What are you two cooking up?"

"Nash has asked me to come meet his family this Friday and Saturday," Jolie said excitedly. "May I have permission to go?"

Morgan stared at Nash, considering. "So you want to take Jolie to meet your mother and sister. I assume Major Southall and Blair are still in camp."

Nash nodded. "But it's perfectly proper. You know that, Morgan. My mother's anxious to meet Jolie."

For a moment Jolie thought that Morgan intended to say no. She had learned to read his expressions so easily, and now she saw that he was opposed to the idea of her going.

He looked at Jolie and asked abruptly, "Is this what you want to do, Jolie?"

"I think it would be nice. . .if it's all right with you."

Morgan hesitated, studying them thoughtfully. Finally he shrugged and said, "All right then, you may go. Nash, I'm warning you—"

Nash held up one slim hand and said, "I know, I know. If anything happens to Jolie, you'll kill me in some awful way. She'll be fine, Morgan. I'll take good care of her."

"You'd better," Morgan rasped. "I mean it."

"I know," Nash said, now soberly. "I mean it, too. I'll take good care of her. After all, she's my girl."

❧

The grand five-glassed barouche pulled up in front of Maiden's Way, the Southall mansion, and Jolie was impressed. It was a beautiful home with tall white columns along the wide portico of the main hall, which was two stories. Two long, low graceful wings were on each side.

A dignified woman with snowy-white hair and a young blond

woman with an hourglass figure came out to meet them.

Nash helped Jolie down and performed the proper, intricate introductions.

Mrs. Southall immediately took Jolie's arm, and his sister, Leila, took the other. "I'm so looking forward to finally getting to know you, Miss DeForge. I've heard so much about you from both of my boys. They tell me that you are an excellent nurse. And you're the first young woman that Nash has ever brought home," Mrs. Southall said.

Leila said, "Yes, we were very surprised. Nash has had several lady friends, as young as he is. But this is the first time he's shown much interest."

Jolie thought this was said in a somewhat snobbish manner, but she didn't want to judge Leila Southall after ten seconds of acquaintance. "Nash is a fine young man. I know you must be very proud of him, and Blair, too."

A shadow crossed Mrs. Southall's face, and she replied automatically, "Of course we are proud of our sons. Major Southall knew they would make fine soldiers."

Too late, Jolie remembered that it wasn't considered ladylike to call young gentlemen by their given names. She was beginning to think that this might not be as much fun as she had thought it would be.

They entered the grand foyer. A flying staircase with an ornate black wrought-iron banister soared up to the second floor. A maid in a black dress, white apron, and white cap curtsied as Mrs. Southall led Jolie to the foot of the staircase.

"Lindy will show you to your room, where you can freshen up, my dear. I've had a light luncheon prepared, so we'll expect you back down in about half an hour."

"Yes, Mrs. Southall," Jolie said and followed the maid upstairs. Her room had an enormous grand tester bed, an armoire that would hold a year's wardrobe, and a dressing table with a triple mirror mounted on it. Jolie took off her bonnet and jacket, splashed her face with the cool scented water in the washbowl, and patted her hair. Nervously she wondered how many minutes had gone by, and she decided to venture back downstairs right away.

Lindy was waiting for her and silently conducted her to a grand dining room.

The table seated eighteen, and Jolie saw with a sinking heart that she was stranded in the middle, across from Leila, while Mrs. Southall was at the head and Nash at the foot. He seemed miles away. But he smiled reassuringly to her then said a blessing.

As soon as he finished, Mrs. Southall began questioning Jolie. "I've only met Mr. Tremayne once, when he came to a large party here at Maiden's Way. I'm afraid I wasn't able to talk to him extensively. Tell me, dear, are you in fact a blood relative of his?"

"No, ma'am. My mother died in childbirth, and my father, Henry DeForge, died three years ago. At that time, Mr. Tremayne became my guardian."

"I see," Mrs. Southall said, although it was plain that she didn't. "And was your father able to leave you any kind of legacy?"

Jolie thought that this was positively rude, so she merely said politely, "Yes, ma'am."

The silence after this was very awkward for a few moments, but Jolie didn't care.

Finally Nash spoke up. "You know, I brought Jolie's mare. We're planning on going riding after luncheon. Leila, would you like to go with us?"

"Good heavens, no. It's much too warm for such physical activity. I'm going to take a nap," Leila answered in a bored tone.

Mrs. Southall said thoughtfully, "I think I'll just pop over and visit Amelia Blankenship this afternoon. If you don't feel I'm neglecting our guest, Nash."

"She's my guest, Mother," Nash said with a touch of impatience. "Don't worry. We've got a busy afternoon planned."

"Do you," she said evenly. "That's fine. Just please don't be late for dinner, Nash. Eight o'clock sharp."

"Just like it's been my whole life," he said, grinning crookedly. "I think I've got it now, Mother. Eight o'clock sharp."

Finally they finished the sandwiches and slices of tart apples with cheese, and Jolie and Nash were able to go riding. They rode around some of the cotton fields. Already they were beginning to bloom. Everywhere Jolie looked, she saw orderly rows of the dark shrubs with their virginal white flowers. It amused Nash that she thought cotton fields were pretty.

The woods that were part of the plantation were carefully manicured, and Nash and Jolie dismounted and walked for a long time. Jolie picked long vines of the wild jasmine and trimmed her hat with them. The sweet scent filled the air wherever she went.

At about six o'clock, they started back toward the house. When they came up the long drive, Nash said, "I don't see a servant in sight. Oh, well. You go on in, Jolie, and I'll take the horses around to the stables."

As Jolie went inside, she could hear Mrs. Southall and Leila talking in the parlor.

"I tell you, Leila," Mrs. Southall was saying, "it's the same girl."

"It can't be, Mother!"

"I tell you it is! Mrs. Blankenship told me, and you know she knows about everybody and everything in the county."

"And she said what about this girl?"

"Her mother was black."

"I can't believe it! She looks as white as we are."

"But she's not. She's an octoroon, Amelia said. In fact, she says that she told me all about Henry DeForge and Jolie when he died, and that Morgan Tremayne had taken her in. But somehow I suppose I didn't connect the story with the girl Nash has been telling us about, until this afternoon when she named Mr. DeForge as her father. Good heavens, Nash can't possibly know the girl has black blood in her!"

Jolie heard all she needed to hear and went at once to her room. That night at supper she could barely speak. She suffered through the evening and went to bed, and the next morning she insisted that Nash take her home, very early before his mother and sister had even gotten up.

Nash noticed that Jolie was disturbed, and he asked, "What's wrong, Jolie?"

"I don't want you to come and see me anymore, Nash."

"What have I done?" he asked with amazement. "I haven't hurt your feelings somehow, have I?"

Jolie knew that he would have to know the truth. "I'm an octoroon. You didn't know that, did you?"

Nash swallowed hard. "You–you're part black?"

"One-eighth black, and your mother found out about it yesterday. I'm not welcome here, Nash. I would never be welcome here."

"I don't care if you're an octoroon," Nash insisted. "That doesn't make one bit of difference to me."

"That's very sweet of you, but you have to consider your family. So, find you a nice young woman who has no black blood and court her. Like I said, I don't think I want you to come visit me again, Nash. It's just not meant to be."

CHAPTER SIXTEEN

"Why, it's you—Miss Jolie, isn't it?"

Jolie had come into Fredericksburg without Morgan for the first time. She was determined to buy a gift for Morgan, since he had given her Rowena and her saddle. She was peering into the window of a tailor's shop when she heard her name called.

She turned and saw a Confederate officer coming toward her. "Why, Colonel Seaforth, it's good to see you."

At Bull Run, Colonel Seaforth's two boys, Edward and Billy, had been wounded, and they were two of the men that Amon had loaded up into the wagon and brought to Rapidan Run. Colonel Seaforth had come by to thank them all for taking such good care of his sons. "It's good to see you, too, Miss Jolie."

Jolie saw that the colonel's face was marked with strain, and she knew at once that something was wrong. "Is something troubling you, colonel?" she asked quietly.

"I'm afraid it is. My youngest boy, Billy. He was wounded in action three days ago."

"Not seriously I hope."

Seaforth dropped his eyes and stared at the ground as if he was trying to find exactly the right words, and finally when he raised his head, misery was in his eyes. "It's very serious, Miss Jolie. He's here, at the hospital."

"Where is he wounded?"

"It's a stomach wound."

Jolie did not answer for a moment for an alarm sounded in her spirit. She had heard enough talk about wounds to know that a stomach wound was almost always fatal. "I'm so sorry," she said. "I'd like to go see him. Do you think that would be all right?"

"Oh, yes. He needs somebody to cheer him up. His mother is here, and we take turns, but my wife isn't too well, and this has just almost killed her."

"What about Edward?"

"Oh, he's fine. He's off at Chattanooga right now with his unit, so he can't be here. Could you come now, do you think?"

"Why, of course I could, Colonel. My friend Amon is just down the street, waiting for me with the wagon. Let me go talk to him." She went and told Amon, "I'm going to go to the hospital to visit Billy Seaforth. You remember him? He's wounded again, and it sounds serious this time."

Amon nodded. "I know where the hospital is, Miss Jolie. I'll take you and wait."

Jolie climbed up into the wagon, and Colonel Seaforth paced his horse alongside. He was silent, and Jolie knew that this was indeed likely to be a trying visit.

Colonel Seaforth pulled his horse up in front of the hospital. "If you'll go on in, Miss Jolie, I'll go hitch up my horse and show your man where to park the wagon."

Jolie went inside and was shocked by the odor. The place was a beehive of activity, with doctors and nurses scurrying from one patient to the other. Colonel Seaforth joined her, and Jolie said, "Why, there are some patients out in the hall, Colonel."

"It's that way in every hospital in Virginia," he said sadly. "I wish we could have gotten Billy a room, but there's no such thing anymore."

They made their way through the hospital until finally they arrived at a corridor divided off into wards. "Right in here, Miss Jolie," Seaforth said. They went inside, and Colonel Seaforth led her through the maze of beds. He stopped and said to the woman sitting beside a soldier, "Amy, this is Miss Jolie DeForge. You remember, she took care of Billy and Edward when they were wounded. This is my wife, Amy."

"I'm so sorry about Billy, Mrs. Seaforth," Jolie said. Her eyes went to the figure of the young man on the bed. She was shocked at the pallor of his face. He had a sheet over him, but she could see that the blood had seeped out from under the bandages and stained the sheets underneath him.

Amy Seaforth looked up, her eyes filled with tears. She was a frail woman with silvery hair, and she looked thin and gaunt.

"You look absolutely exhausted, Mrs. Seaforth. Why don't you go and get some rest, and you, too, Colonel. I'll stay right here with Billy."

Colonel Seaforth said with relief, "I've been trying to get her to do that. Come along, dear. Miss DeForge is a wonderful nurse."

"All right. I do think I could rest a little," she said.

"You take as long as you want," Jolie said firmly. "I'll be right here."

The two left, and Jolie sat down beside Billy. His face was flushed, and she put her hand on his forehead. *He's got a fever. I need to bring that down if I can.*

She'd had this problem when she'd taken care of the the wounded men. She knew that the only cure for fever was to take cool, wet cloths and bathe the body. She waited until an orderly went by and said, "I need to get some clean water and some cloths to try to bring this man's fever down."

"Yes, ma'am," the orderly said. He had a harried look on his face and was carrying a filthy mop and a bucket. "You'll have to see

Mrs. Franklin for that."

"Where will I find her?"

"That's her right over there. See? The little woman." He added with a grimace, "With the fussy look on her face."

Jolie did not know the woman, but she found out that Mrs. Beverly Franklin had gone straight to Jefferson Davis and gotten a letter from him that said, "Mrs. Beverly Franklin will be in charge of Unit B. Medical personnel will give her full cooperation." The physicians in charge resented her. The orderlies hated her. But she had given good service and had collected a group of women from town who helped her.

"Mrs. Franklin?"

"Yes, what is it?"

"My name is Jolie DeForge. I would like to try to bring Billy Seaforth's fever down if I could. All I need would be some water and some cloths."

Mrs. Franklin stared at her. "Are you a nurse?"

"No, not really, but I took care of Billy and his brother Edward when they were wounded before."

"At the hospital?"

"No, ma'am, we took them home."

Beverly Franklin's voice was strained, and she was pale with exhaustion. "If you really want to take care of him and you have a place, then I suggest that you take him there."

"Out of the hospital?"

"Look around you. You see how little personal care each man gets. We have to go from one to the other." She hesitated and then added, "He's gravely wounded. The doctors don't offer much hope."

Instantly Jolie made up her mind. "Yes, ma'am. I'll bring my driver in, and if you can get some help, we'll load him in the wagon. We'll take good care of him at our house."

"That would be best. I wish we had a place like that for all the seriously wounded. If you like, I'll send a messenger to Colonel Seaforth to let him know that you've taken Billy to your home."

"Thank you, ma'am."

Thirty minutes later Jolie was in the wagon. She had made a bed for Billy in the back, and instead of riding in the seat next to Amon, she sat down in the wagon bed and put his head in her lap. As they left the hospital, she leaned over and whispered, "Billy, you're going home with us."

"Who is this?" Billy muttered.

"It's Jolie."

"Jolie? You're going to take care of me?"

"Yes, I am, Billy. Now you just lie still and rest. We'll be at Rapidan Run soon."

❧

The sun was low in the sky when Amon pulled up in front of the ranch house.

Morgan came out at once and took one look at Jolie in the back holding the soldier's head in her lap. "What's this, Jolie?"

"It's Billy, Billy Seaforth. He's been badly wounded, Morgan. He wasn't getting any care in the hospital, so I brought him home."

"You did the right thing. Amon, we'll put him in the spare room. Bed's all made up. Will that be all right, Jolie?"

"Yes, if you'll bring him in, I'll get some cool water and some cloths. I need to bring his fever down." She moved inside and told Evetta what she had done.

"That poor young man," Evetta said. "You say he ain't got much chance?"

"That's what the doctors say, but I'm going to pray that he'll be all right." She got the cool water out of the well and several clean cloths. When she got to the room, she found that Amon and Morgan had put the young man in bed. She said, "I'll take care of him now."

"You let me know if you need any help, Miss Jolie," Amon said and left the room.

Morgan stayed and looked down at the pale face. "Well, Billy," he said, "are you awake?"

"Yes. . .yes, sir."

"I'm sorry to see you like this, but we'll do the best we can for you. You know what a good nurse Miss Jolie is."

"Yes, sir, I know that."

"I sent a message to your parents, Billy. They'll be out as soon as your mother is rested up," Jolie said.

"You're too good to me, Miss Jolie."

"Not a bit of it. Now, we're going to get that fever down."

❧

Jolie arched her back for she was tired. Billy had grown worse in the two days he had been there. His parents had moved in to the house. She had grown to love Mrs. Seaforth, and it hurt her to see how the parents were suffering.

She looked out the window and saw that the moon was high in the sky, a silver ball that casts its beam down on the earth. She went over to look out the window and tried to pray, but it seemed she had prayed herself out. The whole household seemed to be quiet in a strange sort of way, as if the wound of the young man had infected them all.

It was half an hour later when she heard Billy crying out in a feeble tone. Quickly she went to him and said, "What is it, Billy?"

"I don't know. I feel. . ." He could not say any more.

Jolie felt his pulse. It was rapid and irregular, and this frightened her. Several times she called his name softly, but he did not respond. Quickly she left the room and went to knock on the door where his parents were. "Colonel Seaforth, Miss Amy, you'd better come."

The colonel opened the door, pulling on a dressing gown. Behind him, Amy said fearfully, "Is it Billy? Is he worse?"

"I think so. I didn't know what to do, but I think you should be there."

They hurried down the hall to Billy's room.

Morgan stepped out of his bedroom and asked, "Is Billy worse?"

"I think he's dying."

Morgan bit his lower lip. "Poor boy. I wish we could do more for him, but you've done all you could, Jolie. If he passes on, you won't have a thing to reproach yourself for."

Jolie said, "Maybe so, but I still feel so helpless."

"So do I. This is the worst of war. So many young boys rode out with high hopes and excited about being in a war, being soldiers, and so many of them have died."

Finally they crept inside Billy's room and hovered just inside the door.

Amy was weeping already, and Colonel Seaforth was standing straight, as if he were before a firing squad.

The minutes passed slowly, and then Billy opened his eyes. He cried out, "Mother, is it you?"

"It's me, Billy."

"I'm glad you got here." He turned to face his father and said, "Sir, I hope I've been a good son."

"The best son in the world, Billy. The very best." Colonel Seaforth's voice was husky, and it broke at the last.

"Thank you, Father. Tell Edward I love him and. . .tell him. . . good-bye. . . ." His voice faded. He took a deep breath, but he did not seem to expel it.

Colonel Seaforth moved around the bed, leaned forward, and kissed his son's forehead. "Good-bye, Billy," he whispered.

Amy Seaforth fell on her son and held him as best she could.

Morgan turned to leave the room, and Jolie followed, knowing she couldn't possibly help the Seaforths in the depths of their grief. When she and Morgan were in the hall, Jolie said, "I can't help crying."

Morgan said, "I could cry myself. Maybe I will." But he didn't.

Jolie knew he was trying to be strong for her.

The rest of the saga was simple. The Seaforths arranged to take the body of their son away, and as they were leaving, they told Jolie and Morgan when the service would be.

Jolie watched the family leave, and sadness gripped her heart.

Morgan did not speak except to say, "We'd better get some rest."

Jolie nodded and retired to her room. She had learned to love Billy Seaforth, as if he were her brother. It was a completely new feeling, and it overwhelmed her.

Jolie finally went to bed and cried herself to sleep.

❧

It had been a week since Billy's funeral, and Jolie had been very aware that Morgan was brooding. His morning rides were getting longer and longer, and when he returned he was unusually silent.

He came back from one of those rides and found her in the stables, currying Rowena. He dismounted and walked over to her.

She saw that there was determination on his face. "What is it, Morgan? You've been so troubled, I know it."

"Jolie, I can't let other men fight for me and for my land. It's time. I have to join the army."

Fear came to Jolie then. "I was so hoping that this day would never come," she said miserably. "I wish you never had to leave me."

"You're a sweet girl, Jolie." He put his arms around her and held her. She knew that it was the action of a man not with romantic overtones but simply with the desire to comfort her.

Desperately she clung to him and thought, *I love him so much, and he doesn't know it and probably never will.*

He released her.

She reluctantly stepped back and asked, "When will you go?"

"Going to leave tomorrow. I've got to get this thing done."

"We'll wait for you to come back, and we'll believe that you will."

Morgan smiled at her. "You're strong, Jolie. I'm proud of you. I always will be."

CHAPTER SEVENTEEN

The following morning, Morgan packed his things, left his room, and found Jolie waiting for him.

"Do you have to go now?"

"Yes, I do, Jolie." He saw that she looked troubled and felt a moment's guilt. "I hate to leave you like this."

"I don't understand. I thought you were against the war."

Morgan shrugged his shoulders. "It's hard to explain, Jolie. I expect there are lots of men like me who hate slavery but have to defend their native states. As I told you yesterday, I just can't let other men do my fighting for me." He saw that she was afraid and said, "You remember now, if I don't come back, you know where your money is. Amon and Evetta will take good care of you and help you."

"All right." She hesitated and then asked, "Have you told Leona about signing up?"

"No, I'm going to do that right now."

"When will the army be leaving?"

He smiled briefly and shook his head. "I don't have any idea,

Kitten. To tell you the truth, I'm probably going to be stuck in Richmond since I'm volunteering for the quartermaster division. So don't worry too much."

"I can't help it. You've already said that the whole Army of Northern Virginia will be going out to meet the Yankees."

"I guess we will. They've got a new general named Pope. Nobody knows much about him, but he can't whip Bobby Lee, as all of our men call the general." He leaned down and kissed her cheek. "I know I don't have to tell you to pray for me."

She threw her arms around his neck and gave him a desperate hug. "No, you don't. I'll pray for you, Morgan. Always."

❧

Jolie watched Morgan ride away and felt a tremendous sense of emptiness. She had felt loss before, when her father died and when Billy died. But now there was anger mixed in with her grief, and she knew it was directed toward Leona Bledsoe.

He loves that woman, and she's nothing but a flirt! She likes to play with men just like a child plays with dolls, and Morgan can't see it. He's a fool where that woman is concerned!

She reveled in her anger for a few minutes. But then she remembered what Morgan had said, and she said a prayer for him instead. Her anger dissipated like dandelion fluff on a strong summer wind.

❧

"Morgan, I'm so glad to see you."

Morgan had arrived at the Bledsoe residence and had been greeted by Leona, who had answered the front door.

"I was watching out the window, and I saw you ride up. Can you stay long?"

"No, I've got some news, Leona."

"What sort of news?" Her eyes grew larger. She looked beautiful, her complexion glowing, her eyes luminous. Her wine-colored dress set off her figure admirably.

"I'm joining the army, Leona. Today."

Instantly Morgan saw that the news struck Leona as being something absolutely wonderful. She hugged him then pulled him by the hand toward the parlor. "I'm so proud of you! Come on, we have to tell my family."

Morgan allowed himself to be pulled inside, and soon he was in the drawing room with Mr. and Mrs. Bledsoe.

"We've got news!" Leona said excitedly. She paused for dramatic effect and said, "Morgan's joining the army."

"Wonderful!" Mr. Bledsoe exclaimed. He came forward with a huge smile to shake Morgan's hand. "I'm pleased to hear it, my boy. Very pleased indeed!"

Leona said, "Sit down, Morgan, and tell us all about it. Have you spoken to General Lee yet?" She patted the sofa for him to sit close beside her.

Morgan sat down and said slowly, "No, I have no intention of talking to General Lee. I'm just going into Richmond and volunteering for the quartermaster's division. It's hard to explain, but in the last year I've had lots of purchasing experience. I figure I'll make a pretty good scrounger."

All of the bright smiles around him faded. Leona repeated, "Scrounger?" as if it was in a language she had never heard. "But— Morgan, what will be your rank?"

"Private, I'm sure," he said as lightly as he could. "I'm no military man, and I'm sure no officer."

Benjamin Bledsoe was now frowning darkly. "Let me get this straight. You're telling us that you know General Lee and Mrs. Lee personally, and he might even be said to be in your debt for the times you helped Mrs. Lee move around, and you aren't even going to go to him and ask him to give you a commission? He could do it so easily, and he should do it!" When he finished, he was almost shouting.

Morgan said stiffly, "Mr. Bledsoe, I don't mean to correct you, but you're just wrong with that whole speech. General Lee owes me nothing. I helped Mrs. Lee because I'm her friend. And—and—you're just wrong, sir. Wrong about him, and wrong about me."

Leona said indignantly, "What are you talking about, Morgan? You're not making any sense. Of course you deserve a commission. There's nothing at all wrong with seeking that. It's done all the time, by all kinds of honorable men! It shows courage and ambition."

"No, it doesn't, Leona," he retorted. "How can I explain it to you? I can't even believe that we're arguing about this."

"I can't either," Leona said, her dark eyes flashing dangerously. "Morgan, it's really very simple. If you insist on joining the army as a private and your highest aspiration is to be a scrounger, I really have nothing more to say to you."

He stared at her in disbelief. "You mean, we've been together all this time, and suddenly you're telling me that I'm not good enough for you?"

"That's what she's telling you," Benjamin Bledsoe interjected. "I've had my doubts about you for a while now, Morgan, and I was right to have them."

Morgan never took his eyes off Leona.

She met his gaze defiantly. "I'm sorry, Morgan, but I don't think we should see each other anymore. You're just not the man that I thought you were."

He stood slowly. "If you think I'm the kind of man to smugly ask for political favors of a man that I respect more than any man I've ever known, then I'm happy to tell you that you're right. I'm definitely not that man." He left the Bledsoe home without another word.

He mounted Vulcan and rode south toward Richmond. After about a mile, his anger faded and was replaced with depression. *I've lost Leona, and now, of all times! When I'm going to war!* He felt sorry for himself for a while, but then he reflected, *It's not that I just lost Leona. I don't think I ever really had her. I don't even think I ever really knew her even.* This comforted him somewhat.

But lingering in his mind all the way to Richmond was the wish that he could talk to Jolie. She would comfort him; she always did. But now it was too late. He had an appointment to keep.

CHAPTER EIGHTEEN

Morgan went into Richmond, signed up, and requested the quartermaster division. When he told the recruiting officer of his background, the man had immediately assigned him to it. He'd been given a desk in crowded headquarters and told to find horses, horses, and more horses.

Three days later, he got word from his amazed lieutenant that he was to report to General Lee's office. Morgan had to wait for three hours in an anteroom that was like an anthill, but finally a young corporal called him into Lee's office.

Lee stood up and came around his desk to shake Morgan's hand. "Private Tremayne, it's good to see you. Please sit down."

Morgan sat on a plain straight chair in front of Lee's desk, which had many papers on it, but they were all arranged neatly.

Lee sat down and said, his dark eyes alight, "I had to hear from my wife that you had enlisted. Then I had a time chasing you down. I was a little surprised to hear you were crammed into a corner somewhere shuffling papers."

"Important papers, sir," Morgan said. "You see, I know where to find horses that no other man can find. In this army, that's real job security."

"Yes, sir, it surely is," he agreed. He regarded Morgan steadily for long moments. "As I said, I was a little surprised to hear that you had enlisted, Private Tremayne. I've certainly had many other men, to whom I owed a much lesser debt of gratitude, come to consult with me when they joined the army."

"You don't owe me any kind of debt at all, sir. It was a pleasure for me to help Mrs. Lee. I enjoy her company very much."

"Yes, so do I," he said drily. "I understand that you specifically requested the quartermaster division. You feel that is where you can best serve?"

"Sir, I would really rather be taking care of horses, as I obviously love to do. But under the circumstances, I thought I would be most useful in procurement and forage."

Lee nodded. "That's thoughtful of you, Private Tremayne. Many men never seem to be able to understand exactly where they fit in. However, I would like to make a request of you."

Surprised, Morgan said, "Anything, sir."

"I would like for you to consider volunteering as my aide-de-camp. I can think of no other man better suited to take care of my horses and those of my staff. Also, I know that you know this country, and you're probably a very good scrounger. That may not be an oft-used title, but it's certainly an important one."

"Sir, I think I'd be an expert scrounger. It's an honor to serve you, General Lee, and I accept your offer, with thanks," Morgan said happily.

"Good. Now, I suppose you'd better have a rank. The general commanding's staff usually does," Lee said reluctantly.

"Oh no, sir, no. I can't possibly accept that," Morgan said and saw the relief flood Lee's face. "I don't want to pretend to be an officer. I don't have the training or the knowledge. And it seems to me, sir, that the general commanding can have anyone on his staff that he likes."

Lee gave him his wintry smile. "Come to think of it, you're correct, Private Tremayne. Very well. Please report to my chief of staff, and he'll outline your responsibilities."

"Thank you, General Lee, for your faith in me," Morgan said simply and then took his leave.

❧

Watching the battle unfold, Morgan had been amazed at the daring of General Robert E. Lee. He had known the man as a person of infinite tact and patience and of great calmness and serenity of purpose. But Morgan hadn't realized that Robert E. Lee was daring, too.

Early in August, Lee had sent Stonewall Jackson on a mission that had defeated part of Pope's army. Pope had lost that skirmish but had assumed that Lee would remain near Richmond. After all, Pope had forty-five thousand men against Jackson's twenty-four thousand.

By shifting their troops around, Lee and Jackson had an army that outnumbered Pope five to four. Unfortunately, a copy of Lee's attack orders was carelessly lost by one of Lee's officers.

When General Pope saw the order that was brought to him, he exclaimed, "With this paper, if I can't beat Bobby Lee, I'll retire."

In two days, Lee realized that Pope would have seventy thousand men, and shortly after that, when he was joined by other Union forces, he would have over a hundred thousand. In the face of this emergency, Morgan was shocked, as was the entire army, when Lee divided his army into two forces. He sent Jackson on a large march completely around the Union right flank, and on August 26th, Jackson struck with all his force. The Union troops had no idea that Jackson was near, and they were fragmented.

By August 30th, Pope had made every wrong move that a general could make. Well-placed, massed Confederate artillery broke the Union assault. When Longstreet hit the Union forces, the battle was lost completely, and Union forces retreated into the defenses of Washington yet again.

In the North, they called it Second Manassas. In the South, they called it Second Bull Run. Everyone called it a solid Confederate victory.

∾

The troops returned to Richmond once more. As it was after every battle, the hospitals overflowed with wounded men. Again they were quartered in private homes and warehouses and barns. There were funerals every day, which were a taxation on the spirits of Richmond citizens.

General Lee gave Morgan a two-day leave of absence, and Morgan spurred Vulcan to an all-out gallop all the way to Rapidan Run.

Jolie must have been watching for him, because as he neared the stables, she flew out of the back door. He barely had time to get off his horse before she threw herself at him.

He caught her up and smelled the freshness of her hair and was shocked at the firm roundness of her figure. He had to remind himself again and again that she was a woman now and not the little girl he had first known. "Aw, Jolie, don't make so much of this," he said.

"I will if I want to!" Jolie cried. He saw there were tears in her eyes. She tugged at his arm. "Come on into the kitchen. I know you're starved."

"I could use some of Evetta's good cooking, that's for sure."

Soon everyone was in the kitchen, and Morgan was eating and, between bites, telling of the battle and what it was like being on General Lee's staff. After lunch he said, "Come on, Jolie. Come walk with me. I want to go see my horses."

The two went out and walked along the fenced-in pastures. It was a pleasant day. Summer was dying slowly and reluctantly, and the air was heavy like old wine.

For Morgan it was a time of joyful relaxation. On the way to battle and in the midst and fury of it, his nerves had been pressed to the limit. Now he soaked in the sight of his horses, the mares contentedly grazing, the new foals playing, the geldings running just for the fun of it. All thoughts and images of war and battle faded away. "It's good to be home," he said quietly.

"It's good to have you home."

Jolie stayed close to him all afternoon, as he talked to Amon and went through the stables, looking over every horse and checking the tack and the feed. Finally she said, "Let's go in, Morgan. You probably need to take a nap before supper."

"Sleeping in my own bed sounds really good. I think I will."

Morgan slept until supper, got up, and ate like a starved wolf. "I had forgotten what a fine cook you are, Evetta. This is delicious."

"Nothing but barbequed ribs."

"Always my favorite, you do them so well."

Evetta smiled and, in a rare show of affection, came and brushed Morgan's hair back from his eyes. "We done miss you around here, Mr. Tremayne. We surely have."

"I've missed all of you, Evetta. You've done a good job, Amon, you and the boys. The place looks great."

After supper, Evetta and Amon left, and Ketura went up to her bedroom.

Morgan and Jolie went into his study and sat quietly for a long time, watching the small cheerful fire that Morgan had built. Morgan felt a sense of peace soaking in.

❧

After about an hour Morgan said, "You know, I'd like to have some popcorn. You have any?"

"Yes, I'll make it." Jolie got up quickly and found the corn and the long-handled covered pan they popped it in. Soon the homey sound of corn popping filled the room. She poured it into two bowls then sat down and started munching.

Morgan looked down in his bowl and said, "I wonder why

some corn pops and some doesn't. We always called these that didn't pop 'old maids.'"

"Why do you call them that?"

"I don't know. Because they didn't do any good, I guess."

"Not very fair to women. Some women can't be wives. Nobody asks them."

He grinned at her and said, "And old bachelors just get to be crusty old complainers. Like me."

"Not like you," Jolie said firmly. "Oh, I just remembered, I have a letter you'll want to read." She went to the desk and got it. "It's from Colonel Seaforth."

Jolie watched his face as Morgan read it. When he had finished, Jolie saw that he was grieved.

"They miss that boy of theirs, don't they?" Morgan said quietly.

"Of course they do. He was such a sweet boy. Such a loss!"

They munched for a while in companionable silence.

Jolie finally asked, "Are you sorry you joined the army?"

"I can't say I'm sorry, no. I know it was the right thing to do. But it's hard, Jolie. It's the hardest thing I've ever done."

She considered him. The lamplight fell across the surface of his cheek, darkening and sharpening the angles of it. She saw in him those things his friends and the people who knew him loved—the tenacity, the faithfulness that never wavered, the fierce loyalty, the determination to always do the right thing. He was a man to stay by his friends, for good or bad, to the end of time. These were qualities that people admired in Morgan, and Jolie admired them, too. It had nothing to do with the feelings she had for him. She just recognized him for what he was, an honest, honorable man.

"I wish you didn't have to go back. I wish this war was over, and you could stay home," she said. Her voice was so low it was almost inaudible.

"I wish that, too. But you do understand, don't you, Jolie, that this is something I have to do?"

"I do understand. I know that's just the kind of man you are."

"Sometimes I wonder what kind of man I am," he said regretfully. "But one thing I do know, it was time for me to join the army and fight. Fight for this place, for Amon and Evetta and their children, for my family, and for you. I'm just glad that you know that, Jolie."

"There's something else I have to ask you, Morgan. Are you going to marry Leona Bledsoe?"

Ruefully, he answered, "No, I'm not. Or rather, Leona Bledsoe isn't going to marry *me*."

"What?"

Morgan shrugged. "She decided that she didn't want to have anything to do with a lowly private."

"But you love her, don't you? Did you—are you terribly hurt, Morgan?" Jolie asked anxiously.

"I was, but somehow now it doesn't seem to matter quite so much. I haven't forgotten her, but no, it doesn't hurt anymore."

Jolie felt a rush of overwhelming relief wash over her. Then she had a thought that shocked her. *I could make him want me. I could lean against him and kiss him and make him forget Leona Bledsoe once and for all!* Jolie immediately chastised herself, angry that she would even think of using such wicked feminine wiles to trap Morgan.

She was distracted for the remainder of their conversation, and when Morgan said good night, she hurried upstairs before he kissed her on the cheek. She definitely didn't trust herself.

As she lay in bed, wide awake, she thought, *I have to be better than that. Morgan is too good a man to have me use cheap tricks on him like Leona did. But oh, how I wish he would love me! I know I'll never love another man in my whole life.*

Please, God, keep him safe. Keep him safe. . . .

She finally fell asleep, still praying for the man she loved.

PART FOUR

CHAPTER NINETEEN

Private Tremayne stuck his head inside the brightly lit tent.

Captain John M. Allen, assistant quartermaster forage, did not look up from his camp desk. He was scribbling furiously. "Yes?" he said absently.

"Sir, I'm reporting back from leave and ready for duty," Morgan said, stepping inside the tent and saluting.

"Hm?" He finished a sentence with a flourish and a final period then looked up. He was a young man, only twenty-nine years old, but he was balding and wore thick spectacles that glinted oddly in the light. And his demeanor was that of a much older man. He was grave and always seemed distracted, as if his mind was racing ahead of the moment to the next order, the next column of numbers, the next inventory report. "Oh, it's you, Tremayne. Yes, yes, go on. You know what you should be doing better than I." He went back to his scritch-scratching.

Morgan ducked back out of the tent and headed behind the line of officers' tents that surrounded General Lee's modest tent headquarters. The horses were picketed there in neat rows underneath a stand of oak trees.

Morgan frowned as he passed them. He saw that someone had put a nervous, flighty gelding right next to Traveler. He would have to remedy that right away.

A good-size tent was pitched nearby, and Morgan went there first. It was not lit, and as he neared, he could see in the darkness that two figures sat on camp stools just outside the tent flap. "Hello, Meredith, Perry. I'm back, as I guess you can see."

Both men murmured, "Good evenin', Private Tremayne."

Perry was General Lee's body servant. A tall, solemn black man, he had all the dignity such an exalted position should bestow upon a man.

Meredith was Lee's cook. He was average sized, of average height, but his wide grin was like a summer sunburst. He was much more jovial than Perry, but then he wasn't actually in General Lee's presence very often. Morgan suspected that when Meredith talked with the general, he was like everyone else was, pretty much: on his best, most dignified, most polished behavior. General Lee brought these finer qualities out in a man. Meredith said, "I wanted to burn your camp stool for kindling 'cause you didn't scrounge me enough rich pine to get a hot quick fire going this morning. But Perry wouldn't let me."

"You rascal," Morgan said as he popped into the tent, retrieved his stool from underneath his bunk, and popped back out again. "Right over there, on the west side of this field, is a pine forest. You should have gone out there and found your own rich pine for the general's breakfast."

"Was too late by the time I knowed I was short on it," Meredith said lazily. " 'Sides, that's your job."

"Yes, guess it is," Morgan admitted. "That's my title these days. Aide-de-Camp, Scrounging. And Private Tremayne-my-horse-needs-blank. Make up any ending you choose."

It was true, but Morgan was not displeased with his duties. Far from it, he was doing exactly what he wanted to do. He helped

Captain Allen find forage for the horses all over the South. He knew every farm, every barn, every storage shed and storehouse in northern Virginia, and he could always find chickens, beef, eggs, bacon, flour, cornmeal, and sugar for General Lee and his staff. But mostly he took care of Traveler, General Lee's beloved horse, and all of the staff officers' horses.

These staff officers had deeply resented Morgan at first. Word had gotten around that he was the only person General Lee had personally requested as an aide-de-camp. But Robert E. Lee would never in his life show favoritism to any man under his command, and his staff came to see that he treated Morgan with the same courtesy and respect that he treated everyone else, whether a general or a servant.

Morgan made an effort to show Lee's officers that he had no ambitions for promotion or recognition. From his very first day in the field, he wordlessly groomed every officer's horse, checked each animal regularly to make sure it was in sound health, paid endless attention to each horse's preferred diet, checked the shoes of each, and even brushed each horse's teeth. Without being asked, he took care of all the tack, keeping the saddles clean and well-shined, the stirrups set just right, even the saddlebags and rifle sheaths polished.

Soon it was true. Everyone, from young couriers to assistant adjutant generals, was coming to him and saying, "Private Tremayne, my horse needs. . ." Anything from shoeing to liniment to a tooth check to a hoarded apple filled in the blank.

In those first few hard and lonely days, as they marched to engage the enemy, Morgan had also started helping Perry and Meredith with the general's supply wagon. In spite of the fact that General Lee's camp tent was not very large and his furnishings were simple and few, both men were constantly anxious that they should have everything perfect for him. A clean tent, clean sheets for his cot, clean uniforms, polished boots, adequate lamplight, plenty of wood for his camp stove, a good stock of food staples, seasonings, coffee, tea, and fresh fruit when they could find it.

Morgan helped them with his expert scrounging, and he helped them to organize everything in the wagon so they could quickly load up and move or unload and camp. He had his own little tent, of course, but Meredith and Perry's was actually a four-man tent, and eventually he just sort of moved in on them. They had the room, and it seemed so much trouble to pitch his own tent. It suited Morgan just fine, though it caused some whispers among the officers, particularly the ones who were slaveowners. Morgan didn't care.

Now, as the three men sat on the little stools looking out at the sweet Virginia night, Morgan said, "I brought us two tins of tea and some coffee and sugar. How's the general's stock holding out?"

"Jest fine since you been with us, Mr. Morgan," Meredith answered.

"Good. In a couple of weeks, I'm going to have three hundred acres of rye and barley ready to harvest, so the horses will be fixed up, too. Maybe Captain Allen will give me and about ten stout fellows leave to go harvest it."

Perry pursed his lips. "We'll have to see 'bout that. 'Cause we're heading up North, you know. To Maryland."

"We are?" Morgan said with astonishment. "When?"

"Day or two, I gather," Perry answered. He didn't purposely eavesdrop on Lee's councils of war, but like most people who were accustomed to having servants, General Lee rarely took note of their presence.

Morgan jumped up. "I better get to seeing to those horses right now. I've been gone two days. I'll bet they're in an unholy mess. Did you know that some idiot picketed Colonel Corley's fidgety gelding right next to Traveler?"

Perry and Meredith exchanged amused glances. "No, sir, Mr. Morgan, I sure didn't know that," Meredith said solemnly. "You'd better get to tendin' to that right now."

"I sure better," he grumbled, heading off toward the horses. But he heard his two friends talking as he walked.

"I ain't never seen the like of a man that loves horses so much," Perry observed.

"Oh, yes you have, Perry," Meredith said. "His name is Marse Robert E. Lee."

Morgan couldn't help but grin as he continued toward his favorite task.

❧

The only way in which Morgan had insisted on insinuating himself near to General Lee was because he was determined from the beginning to follow the general when he was in the saddle. It was Lee's habit, as the army marched, for him to ride with them, passing through the ranks of cheering men to encourage them. And he constantly rode around the battlefields, surveying the ground with his field glasses, watching the masses of men and artillery as they maneuvered. Normally when General Lee was on the move, only two or three of his most senior staff and a few ready couriers accompanied him.

On August 15th, when General Lee left Richmond to face General Pope, Morgan saddled up Vulcan and moved up behind the three couriers who were following General Lee and his officers. The first time Lee stopped for a short rest, Morgan dismounted quickly and pushed his way rudely up to Lee and took Traveler's reins without a word as Lee dismounted.

"Good afternoon, Private Tremayne," Lee said, the first words he had said to him since that day two weeks previously in his office.

"Good afternoon, sir," Morgan replied.

General Lee walked to the side of the road and stretched a bit, slapping his gauntlets into one palm, a habit that he had.

Morgan gently led Traveler and Vulcan to the side of the road and stood, waiting.

Colonel Robert H. Chilton, Lee's chief of staff, stalked up to Morgan and said in a severe undertone, "General Lee did not request that you accompany him personally, Private Tremayne."

"No, sir, he didn't," Morgan said. "But it seems to me that you and the other officers would appreciate someone just to see to the horses while you're conferring with the general."

"Oh," he said, his severe expression lightening just a bit. "I see. Perhaps you're right, Private. But be sure you remain quiet and unobtrusive. General Lee does not appreciate any fussing and flapping in his presence."

"No, sir," Morgan said respectfully. "I will be quiet, sir, and I'll keep the horses calm."

"See that you do," he snapped then thrust the reins of his horse into Morgan's hand.

Soon Morgan was holding the reins of five horses: Traveler, Vulcan, two belonging to colonels, and one belonging to a major. Quickly Morgan improvised. He tucked Vulcan's reins into his belt, casting a cautious glance back at his temperamental horse. Vulcan seemed to stare back at him with disdain and tossed his head, but he didn't attempt to pull away. Morgan then gently pushed Traveler to his right side, followed by a colonel's horse. Morgan looped Traveler's reins around his thumb and forefinger and the other set of reins around his ring and pinky fingers. He did the same thing with the horses on his left side and jockeyed the reins around the same way. This way, two horses were on one side of him, two on the other, and Vulcan behind. Morgan kept up a soft, reassuring nonsense conversation to keep the horses still and calm, hoping that it wouldn't be in the same class as fussing and flapping.

When General Lee and the three officers returned to retrieve their horses, General Lee merely said, "Thank you, Private Tremayne." But Morgan saw a quick gleam of amusement in his eyes, and he knew that General Lee had overheard Colonel Chilton and was amused, probably about the fussing and flapping. Of course, Lee could never single Morgan out by having a light conversation with him; there were about a hundred thousand men who would love his doing just that with them, and it would cause untold jealousies if one man was that lucky. Still, Morgan knew that he and General Robert E. Lee had just shared a private joke. Morgan knew it would be a treasured memory to him all of his days.

Morgan saw the reality of Meredith's comments about Lee's love for horses as they neared that all-important boundary, the Potomac River.

It had been raining steadily for three days and two nights, and the roads were like mucky bogs. In some places the artillery caissons sank to the wheel hubs.

Morgan was following Lee and his officers, having pulled up closer behind than usual because the general was riding right through the marching men. They always pressed him, the boldest reaching out to simply touch Traveler, who always bore such adulation with great dignity. Many times the men would fall into step behind General Lee, and Morgan had been obliged to push through them so that he wouldn't fall far behind.

They passed the marching infantry and began to ride alongside the road because the artillery wagons were strung out in a long line. The second caisson they approached was stuck, its left wheel canted down into a deep rut, the cannon muzzle pointed crazily up toward the nearby hills.

Morgan heard shouting and cursing, and as he came around the caisson, he saw a man beating a horse. Instantly he spurred Vulcan and flew to a stop just beside the man. Morgan opened his mouth to shout at him, but behind his left ear he heard, "You, sir! Stop beating that horse this instant!"

Morgan saw the man freeze, stick in midair, staring in horror, his mouth open.

Morgan turned to see General Robert E. Lee, his eyes flashing dark fire, his mouth set in a thin grim line. Righteous indignation seemed to form a red aura around him. It grew strangely quiet.

General Lee spoke again, and his voice was quieter, but his face was still flushed with anger. "You are doing no good to your horse, your men, or your army, Sergeant." Sharply he turned Traveler and rode past the caisson.

After a moment, Morgan recovered himself and followed him. He looked back at the man, whose face was such a tragic mask that he looked more like he'd been gut-shot than reprimanded. Morgan knew exactly how he felt but had little sympathy for him. Mostly he was happy that the man had suffered such shame. Personally Morgan thought all men who beat horses should be beaten themselves.

All that long march, Morgan reflected upon the incident. It was a side of Robert E. Lee that he had never seen, never even imagined. To him, Lee had always been the perfect picture of a gentleman, unfailingly courteous, diplomatic, tactful, gallant to women, patient and kind to children, and longsuffering with the burdens of being a leader of men.

Finally Morgan came to realize that, yes, Lee had all those virtues, but he must also feel the heat of strong emotions, because he would not be a whole man if he did not. He just kept his temper tightly controlled, because that was the kind of man that he was. It was very rare for Lee to allow that temper to show, and Morgan was convinced that when he did, it was because he chose to do so. Morgan valiantly swore to himself that he would never *ever* do anything to deserve that kind of treatment from Lee. He had seen that there were worse things than beatings after all.

❧

The Army of Northern Virginia marched into Maryland, fifty thousand strong. General George McClellan, back in command, marched south with ninety thousand men. They met at a little town called Sharpsburg. By it ran a lazy stream, Antietam Creek. After three days in September of 1862, Sharpsburg in the South and Antietam in the North automatically conjured up visions of piles of dead bodies. September 17th came to be known as the Bloodiest Day.

General McClellan, true to form, could not bring himself to

order his troops to fight the fast-maneuvering Confederates in a large-scale attack. He threw in his men piecemeal. He sent Joe Hooker in here, and Stonewall Jackson furiously beat him back. McClellan ordered Burnside to cross Antietam by that bridge, and his troops were mercilessly slaughtered. Two fresh divisions arrived over there, but McClellan said they should not engage until they had received "rest and refreshment."

No one could ever figure out why McClellan simply would not order his army to fight the kind of all-out battles that were crucial for victory in the field. It was not that he was personally a coward. He had served with distinction in the Mexican War. He had even served briefly with Robert E. Lee, surveying Tolucca. For his service he was twice brevetted.

Little Mac did have a tendency to procrastinate and dawdle, but this still did not explain why, when he finally did have a superb army fielded, he would not fight the enemy. Some suggested that he was simply intimidated by Robert E. Lee, and this may have very well been true. But particularly at Sharpsburg, where he had the advantage in numbers of almost two to one, it would seem that he could have rock-solid confidence enough to simply overrun the ragtag horde of screaming rebels.

But he did not, and after three days of fighting, Lee was withdrawing back across the Potomac, his walking wounded and ambulances and slow supply train completely unmolested.

General Lee's plan of invading the North had failed. Though the Army of Northern Virginia had a tactical victory over the Union Army, they could not hold the ground, and so in reality the outcome was inconclusive. The North had won a strategic victory because the rebels had to withdraw.

And so General Lee led his men back to blessed Virginia, to the fertile and peaceful Shenandoah Valley to rest and refit. It was fall when they came back home, and it was beautiful. For this, and for many other things, General Robert E. Lee gave simple thanks to God.

SURRÊNDER

∾

Morgan Tremayne found himself in a singular position in the Army of Northern Virginia. He was certain that no other private was as fortunate. As they readied to march, he reflected that the thousands of lowly privates, corporals, and sergeants couldn't possibly be as well-informed as he was. He knew exactly where they were going—Fredericksburg—and exactly what they were facing—125,000 Yankees. He knew that again General Robert E. Lee was outnumbered, because Morgan understood that once the two corps of the thinly-stretched army gathered together to face this new threat, there would barely be seventy-eight thousand Rebels.

The average man in the field never had such information until he was looking across some creek or pasture at another average man in blue. In fact, Stonewall Jackson was so secretive that even his brigade commanders sometimes did not know where they were going. Stonewall had a habit of going around, loudly asking if anyone had good maps of the roads to X when their destination was actually Y.

"Hit don't fool nobody no more," Meredith had told Morgan with amusement. "Wherever Ol' Blue Light's axing for maps, they knows that's the place where they can't be found."

"True, but I guess they still don't know the place where they can be found," Morgan had said, chuckling.

Meredith and Perry were half of the reason Morgan was so well-informed. Most of the officers had their own cooks, and cooks talk. Morgan reflected wryly that if a spy was smart, he'd forget trying to infiltrate the upper echelon of officers and just become a cook. They heard everything, and they told each other everything.

Perry, on the other hand, was stubbornly closemouthed. He heard practically every meeting that General Lee had at his headquarters. For months he wouldn't tell Morgan anything, and it frustrated Morgan to no end, but he finally gave up trying to weasel information out of the silent, somber man.

However, Morgan was as fully dedicated as Perry in ensuring that General Lee never had to worry about his clothing, personal equipment, and supplies. Morgan made sure that Perry had chalk for white gauntlets, boot polish, leather soap and conditioner, valet brushes, laundry soap, plenty of needles and thread, and brass and silver polish. Whenever Morgan had time after caring for the horses, he would help Perry mend or launder General Lee's clothing, linens, and blankets.

It was during these quiet nights in winter camp that Perry began to talk to Morgan about the events of the day. Morgan determined to keep Perry's confidences and never spoke to anyone else about things Perry had told him, not even Meredith.

And, too, Morgan himself became party to many of General Lee's talks with his officers. Lee rode Traveler every day, and often his commanders and staff accompanied him. Over time they began to regard Morgan much as they did Meredith and Perry, as a useful servant tending the horses but not as a person that would have any interest in matters above their station. They talked freely while he stood, mutely holding the horses or riding just behind General Lee and overhearing every word.

When he wrote to Jolie, Morgan was always extremely careful never to reference exactly where the army was, and particularly any future plans that he learned of. He knew all too well that this, not enemy spying, was the way word got around the country about the army's movements. The mail was running faithfully, and practically every home, plantation, or shack in Virginia had someone's mother, father, sister, or brother there. Men who would rather die a torturous death than betray the Confederacy unwittingly mailed out all kinds of information every day. Morgan made certain that he was never guilty of this.

On October 6th, General Lee got word that the Yankees had crossed the Potomac and were heading south. That day Morgan wrote a long letter to Jolie, telling her all about the beautiful fall hardwoods in the mountains and about all the horses he cared for.

But on November 6th, when Perry told Morgan that the Army of the Potomac was at full strength and heading for Fredericksburg, Morgan agonized over the letter he wrote to Jolie that day. He ached to warn her that apparently a big battle was going to be fought just ten miles from Rapidan Run. At the end of the day, his letter was all about the gallons of maple syrup he'd found at a nearby farm and the kind farmer who had happily sold it to him for practically worthless Confederate money.

On November 9th, it was reported to headquarters that for some reason the Union army had come to an abrupt stop in their march to the Rappahannock River. The next day—within twenty-four hours after the Army of the Potomac itself had found out—Lee knew the reason for the halt. Little Mac had been replaced by General Ambrose E. Burnside, and the transfer of command had taken place on that day.

As they washed General Lee's dishes that night, Perry told Morgan, "Gen'ral Longstreet had supper with Marse Robert tonight, you know."

"Yes, I saw him ride up," Morgan said. "How is Old Pete these days?"

Perry appeared to be considering a very complex question, for he sucked on his lower lip for a time then said, "D' ye know, Marse Robert calls him 'My Old War Horse.'"

"No, I didn't know that," Morgan said with interest. Such were priceless tidbits that he often gleaned from Perry.

"Yassuh, he does," Perry asserted. "Marse Robert, he can talk to Gen'ral Longstreet easier than some of them younger, flightier officers. They say Gen'ral Longstreet is slow, but I'm of a mind that he's careful. Anyways, Marse Robert tole him tonight at supper what he thought of this new man Mr. Linkum is a-throwin' at him now."

Perry had very complex unwritten and unspoken rules for his conversations, and Morgan knew them now. If he showed too much eagerness to hear this conversation repeated, Perry would stubbornly clam up. If, however, Morgan showed only mild interest, Perry would repeat the conversation or the comment, sometimes word for word. So Morgan kept vigorously scrubbing a pillowcase on the scrubboard and said carelessly, "Is that right."

"Dat's right. Gen'ral Longstreet tole Marse Robert that this man named Burnside is the Yankee gen'ral now, and he was glad 'bout it. Said this Burnside weren't near as good as Gen'ral McClellan. But seems like Marse Robert was sorry to hear him go. 'We always understood each other so well. I fear they may continue to make these changes till they find someone whom I don't understand,' said Marse Robert."

Morgan almost smiled. It was a typically genteel comment Robert E. Lee would make about a deadly enemy. It was funny, too, because whenever Perry quoted Lee, his speech became flawless, as Lee's was. Morgan liked the old servant and had come to enjoy his company greatly, whether he was telling Morgan crucially sensitive information or just discussing which kind of laundry soap he had found most effective.

Somewhat to Morgan's surprise, he realized that he thought of Perry and Meredith not as servants or as two more of hundreds of black men he had known but as valued friends.

The Army of Northern Virginia left the pastoral hills around Culpeper and marched east. On the storm-swept afternoon of November 20, 1862, General Lee handed Traveler's reins to Morgan and took half a dozen steps up to the crest of a hill. He took out his field glasses and studied the ground.

Below him lay the old picturesque hamlet of Fredericksburg, nestled in neat squares along the flat west bank of the Rappahannock River. The east bank rose up into a range of hills called Stafford Heights, and this was where the enemy was encamped. But behind Fredericksburg, the land sloped up gently to this long wooded ridge that was about the same elevation as Stafford Heights. Lee knew that Union artillery could not reach his army, but they could rain down mortars on the town below. Lee wondered if this could possibly be a feint, but the numbers arrayed on the hills across the river convinced him that it was not. Still he was puzzled. What could this new general be thinking?

❧

Even Morgan, who knew nothing of military strategy or tactics, wondered the same thing. It was simple, really. The Yanks were on the offensive, so they were going to make the first move; they would attack. But that meant that somehow Burnside would have to throw tens of thousands of men across the river, and then they would be down in a valley with Robert E. Lee holding the priceless high ground above them.

Morgan reflected that perhaps the generals might know something that he did not, and he stopped wondering about it to turn and look longingly to the north. *If I were a bird, and I flew straight north, I would fly over the plains and the Wilderness until I got to the Rapidan River, and then I would see Rapidan Run and Jolie.* Even though he was so close to home, naturally Morgan wouldn't ask for a leave. Battle was coming.

❧

General Lee's headquarters tent was pitched underneath a stand of Virginia pine trees that soared forty feet, forming a lush green bower. The staff tents sprang up like mushrooms around him.

Morgan was glad to find that about thirty feet behind the tent line was a long row of smaller trees, perfect for picketing the horses. He, Meredith, and Perry pitched their tent close by.

It was about midnight when they were awakened by a persistent hissing from the tent flap opening. "*SSSSTTT! SSSSTTT!* Is dis you, Mr. Tremayne?"

Meredith and Perry looked up quizzically, but Morgan jumped out of his cot and ran to the opening. "Rosh! I thought that was you!" He hugged the boy hard. "What are you doing here? How'd you find me?"

"I almost didn't," Rosh said mournfully. "I've had about fifty people yellin', 'Halt! Who goes there!' at me in the last two hours. Took me longer to get to this tent than it did to get to the camp."

"I'm surprised they let you through," Morgan said, throwing his arms around Rosh's shoulders and pulling him into the tent. "General Lee's headquarters are just up there, on top of the ridge. Here, give me that oilskin and your hat. Come over here and stand by the stove."

It was still raining, a cold, cutting November storm, and Rosh's cape and hat were dripping. Morgan shook them, scattering icy drops, and hung them up on the clothesline they always kept up behind the stove. Meredith and Perry were already asleep again, with Meredith snoring softly.

Morgan said anxiously, "How's Jolie?"

"She's doing real good, Mr. Tremayne, considering. We all worry 'bout you all the time, of course." He pointed to the east. "All them fires over there on the other side of the river. That's Yankees, isn't it?"

"Yes, it is," Morgan said soberly. "I don't know when they're going to cross that river, but for sure they are."

Rosh nodded. "Figured that. Daddy came to town this morning and saw 'em over there like a big ol' anthill. He rushed back home, and we loaded up the wagon to bring you some things."

"That's good of you, Rosh, but there's going to be a big battle here any time now," Morgan said worriedly. "I want you to go back home and help take care of the farm."

Rosh's face wrinkled with worry. "You—you don't think them Yankees is going to get to Rapidan Run, do you?"

"No," Morgan said vehemently. "I think General Lee is going to stop them right here. But still, with over a hundred thousand bluebellies wandering around, I want you to be at home to take care of everything just in case."

"Yes, sir," Rosh said, sighing. "Do you want me to go ahead and unload the wagon and go on back tonight?"

Morgan saw that he was exhausted and said, "No, no. Is Calliope pulling the wagon? She still hitched up?"

"Yes, sir, I still wasn't sure which of these hunnerd tents you was in," Rosh answered with annoyance.

Morgan nodded. "C'mon, we'll go rub her down and get her with the other horses. They stay warmer that way. Unloading the wagon can wait until morning. When we get Calliope settled, we'll get a cot for you, and you can sleep for whatever's left of the night."

They got Calliope bedded down, and then Rosh bedded down. Morgan went back to sleep instantly as soon as he lay down. He had found that, like any good soldier, he slept hard when he could.

In the morning, he was delighted to find that Amon had mixed up twelve buckets of hot mash for the horses. Morgan and Rosh heated water on the camp stove and fed the horses first thing. Meredith fussed at them and made them sit down and eat breakfast, for Rosh had also brought four dozen eggs, a side of bacon, grits, a wheel of sharp cheese, and two smoked hams.

"Best breakfast I've had for a while," Morgan said with appreciation. "How are the stores at the farm holding out, Rosh?"

"Still seems to me like we got as much as we ever started out with," he said with a big grin. "Daddy says we're livin' in the Land o' Goshen."

Morgan had intended to send Rosh back as soon as the wagon was unloaded, but Rosh said, "You know, Mr. Tremayne, now I can see my hand in front of my face, they's lots of big branches that got blowed down in the storm. It wouldn't take me and you but a coupla hours to build a brush shelter for them horses, with the wagon to haul and all."

"That's a great idea, Rosh," Morgan said gladly. "I hate having to picket horses out in the open. Let's get to it."

It took them more that two hours, but as they started working, they found themselves constructing an arbor that was almost as weatherproof as a snug log cabin.

They were still poking small evergreen branches in the cracks and holes when Meredith came out, nervously drying his hands on his dirty apron. "Mr. Morgan, you said you was from around these parts, didn't you?"

"Yes, my farm is just about fifteen miles from here, due north. That town down there, Fredericksburg, is the nearest, so it's sort of like my hometown," Morgan replied. "Why?"

"Marse Robert had a bunch of officers to dinner, and Perry heard 'em talking. Seems like one of them heathern Yankee gen'rals over there tole the mayor of Fredericksburg that he was mad at 'em, 'cause some boys was snipin' at 'em acrost the river, there. And 'cause they been millin' flour and grain and manufacturing clothes and the like to give to bodies in rebellion 'gainst the US gov'ment. He demands they surrender the town, yes, suh."

"Did he say what he was going to do if they didn't? This Yankee general?" Morgan demanded.

"He said he was gonna blow up the town to pieces," Meredith answered with disdain. "Shame on him is what I say. Ain't no soldiers left in no town in Virginia. Bound to be a bunch of old folks and slaves and women and children down there. Anyways, Marse Robert says he's not going to be able to take the town, 'cause something about the ground down there. But he's not going to let the Yankees just dance in there and take it, neither. So he told the mayor that there was going to be fightin' there, one way or t'other, and that they better 'vacuate."

Morgan exclaimed, "Evacuate!" With distress Morgan stared toward the river, though he couldn't see the town because they were on the far side of the hill. After long moments he said, "Thank you, Meredith, and thank Perry for letting me know."

"Yes, sir, Mr. Morgan, sure 'nough." He turned and hurried back up the hill.

Morgan dropped his head and paced back and forth.

Quietly Rosh went down the row of horses, stroking their noses, murmuring endearments. As usual, Vulcan wouldn't let Rosh touch him. He temperamentally shook his mane and backed up a step.

It was a full ten minutes before Morgan stopped pacing. He stared at the wagon, then at Calliope, the faithful sturdy mare that did most of the hard work around the farm. His face changed, hardened. He had come to a decision. "Rosh, listen to me," he said. "I want you to go back to the farm just as fast as you can. Calliope's going to have to rest, so double-team the wagon with Lalla and Esmerelda. Hitch up Antoinette and Bettina to the carriage. I know there are only four brood mares left, and they all four have foals, but the situation is getting desperate."

He continued, "Get Amon to drive the carriage into town, to Mr. Benjamin Bledsoe's house. Have him tell Mr. Bledsoe that they can come stay at the farm tonight, and then we can take them somewhere else farther behind the lines if they want, or they can stay at Rapidan Run.

"Then I want you and Santo to take the wagon into town. Go to Sally Selden's, you know she's a widow and has those two kids. Then go to Silas Cage's house, you know where that is, don't you? Good. His wife is there with their child, and I think her mother may be there, too. Then go by the general store and see if Bert and Maisie Patrick need somewhere to go, and then go to the saddler's. I know Will Green probably still has his old mare, but I don't know if he has anywhere to go. That's—that's all I can think of right now. But Rosh, if you've got room left, take any woman and her children. Now listen to me. You're only going to have time to make one trip. Don't come back to Fredericksburg. It's going to be a war zone."

CHAPTER TWENTY

It was already three o'clock in the afternoon when Amon drove the carriage into Fredericksburg. Throngs of people were in the streets, but they were orderly. There was no panic, no shouting, no pushing or shoving. In fact, an unearthly quiet lay like an oppressive fog over the town. Everyone cast anxious glances to the thousands of fires across the river. Almost all the refugees were women with children and older people. They carried little bundles, usually a blanket tied up and containing clothing and more blankets and perhaps some prized possessions such as silver and jewelry. Sadly Amon thought that the thin women wouldn't be able to carry the family silver very far. It was surprising how quickly two pounds could get unbearably heavy.

Amon had come in on the east–west River Road, and he had not met a single soul. It appeared that everyone was going north, perhaps to Falmouth, or south, toward Richmond. They were walking. He saw several single riders on horses, but not one cart or wagon or carriage. He supposed the ones who were fortunate enough to have those were long gone. As he passed, people looked up at him and inside the empty carriage, but no one said a word. They seemed to be numbed into silence. They were all white people. To Amon they looked hollow-eyed and haunted.

He went down Main Street, for the Bledsoes' home was only one block over. He was passing the Club Coffee Shop when he heard a churlish shout that seemed to echo abrasively in the silence.

"Hey, you, boy! Here, boy!" He turned and saw the tall figure of Benjamin Bledsoe come running out of the coffee shop into the street and grab the horses' harness. Antoinette and Esmerelda took great exception to this. They were cosseted mares who had never heard an angry shout in their lives, and they weren't used to strangers. Both of them started violently, and Antoinette reared and knocked Bledsoe down into the filthy, stinking, freezing mud of the street.

I'm in for it now, Amon thought with dread. He jumped down, grabbed the crosspiece of the harness, and started talking soothingly to the nervous mares.

"What's the matter with you? Help me up!" Bledsoe said, slipping as he tried to rise. Of course, Amon couldn't attend to him for a few moments or the horses would have bolted. Bledsoe obviously knew this, but it didn't help his temper any.

Finally Amon got the horses quieted, and he helped Bledsoe to rise. Immediately he said, "That's Morgan Tremayne's carriage. Are you stealing it, boy? Because I'll have you hanged if you are!"

"No, sir," Amon said patiently. He had known this was going to happen. "Mr. Tremayne sent word for me to come to town to get you and your family, Mr. Bledsoe."

"Huh? He did? Oh. Quite right, too. What took you so long, you simpleton? It's going to be dark soon," he growled. "Help me up, up onto the seat. I'm not sitting in the carriage. I'm filthy. Hurry up, boy."

Amon got him situated, climbed up, and they started down the street. Bledsoe neither looked at him nor said a word as they drove. He was occupied with trying to wipe off his shoes with his handkerchief.

When they arrived at the Bledsoe house, he jumped down himself and hurried into the house. Amon sat for a moment, stifling his anger. He had met the Bledsoe family before, when he had driven Morgan into town to take them on rides and picnics. Amon loved Morgan Tremayne and believed that he was the best man he had ever known except for his father, Caleb Tremayne, but he had never been able to understand how Morgan could be so blind about the Bledsoe family. As far as he was concerned, the Bledsoes and other people like them were perfect examples of why the phrase "white trash" had been invented.

Guess he's so crazy 'bout Miss Leona that he's done blinded his own self about these people. I thought he was through with that woman, but it 'pears now he's not. Rosh said he thought about her first.

He climbed down and went to soothe Antoinette and Esmerelda some more. Esmerelda was a good-natured horse, normally very mannerly, but Antoinette was saucy and snobbish. She was still snorting and stamping impatiently.

Leona Bledsoe came out of the house and stamped down the brick walk. "Amon, where's the wagon?" she demanded.

"Rosh and Santo are bringing it into town, to get some of Mr. Tremayne's friends."

"What? Nonsense! Morgan cannot possibly have meant for us to leave town in just the carriage. What are we supposed to do with all of our furnishings, our paintings, our china and silver, our linens?" she snapped.

Obviously Amon could not answer that, so finally she said, "Oh, very well. Come with me and get our trunks now, when we see Rosh and Santo we'll just tell them to come fetch our things."

Amon said politely, "No, ma'am, I'm 'fraid the boys can't do that. They got strict orders from Mr. Tremayne 'bout picking up some folks and taking them out to the farm."

"Fine. Then they can just turn right back around and come back here," she argued.

"No, ma'am. Mr. Tremayne said once we got everyone to the

farm, on no 'count was we to come back to town."

"Mr. Tremayne said this and that! What if I *order* you to come back and pack up this house!" she said, her dark eyes flashing.

Amon merely regarded her gravely. He was not a slave, and Leona Bledsoe knew it.

She looked at him with such rage that he thought she might strike him. But then the moment passed, she took a deep breath, and when she spoke again it was in a normal, if rather stiff, tone. "Very well. Come into the house and fetch the trunks. As soon as my father changes clothes and I can get my mother to stop screeching, we'll leave."

It was somewhat of an exaggeration. Mrs. Bledsoe was not exactly screeching, but her voice was so shrill that it made Amon grit his teeth with every word as he followed Leona up the stairs to the bedrooms. "Benjamin! What about Mama's tapestry? I am not leaving this house until that tapestry is safely wrapped in oilcloth and put in the wagon!"

Mr. Bledsoe growled loudly, "Then I guess you are not leaving this house, Eileen!"

"Oh! OHHH! How can you say such a thing to me! I notice you're taking your portrait. That was the first thing you packed! I'm not—"

Leona opened the door of her parents' bedroom, stuck her head in, and said, "There is no wagon. Just the carriage. Are your trunks ready?" She turned to Amon and said, "Two trunks in here, and mine is in the bedroom just down the hall."

Two fine brassbound trunks lay in the bedroom, both large and bulky—and heavy. Amon picked up one and headed downstairs, thinking wearily, *Now she is a-screechin'*, as behind him Mrs. Bledsoe started arguing with her husband and Leona about the wagon. It was stupid, of course, but Amon was just glad that she wasn't arguing with him. At least Leona wasn't stupid. When she was beaten she knew it, and she just cut her losses and moved on.

Amon returned and got Mrs. Bledsoe's trunk and stacked it

on top of Mr. Bledsoe's on the back carriage rack and lashed them down. There wasn't room for another trunk on the slender wooden board, so Amon was going to have to put the trunk inside.

He went back inside and found the family in the parlor, putting on their capes and gloves and hats. "Miss Leona, there's no more room for your trunk on the back. I can put it inside, but it's going to crowd you a bit."

"What! Why can't you lash it to the top?" she asked.

"It's a cloth top, with light wood bows so's you can fold it down," he answered.

"But what about our big trunk, with the linens and silver?" Eileen wailed. "Benjamin, we cannot possibly leave that here! The Yankees, with the Bledsoe silver? No, no—"

"Be silent, woman!" he said with gritted teeth. "I would try to explain to you again, but it wouldn't do a whit of good. Amon, go get Leona's trunk and let's go! It's dark already. It looks like the rain is turning to sleet, and *the Yankees are coming*! So everyone just shut up and get in that carriage!"

❧

Amon passed Rosh and Santo on the north side of town. He cringed a little as the boys called out to him, hoping the Bledsoes would not hear. "You got 'em Daddy? The Bledsoes? Who's that up there with you?"

Amon gave up and pulled the carriage to a stop alongside the wagon. "I got the Bledsoes, and these is some ladies and two chilluns that's half froze to death. I'll introduce everyone proper when we all get home. Now you boys don't argy-barge around. You fill up this here wagon and git on home." The raindrops that were falling now were large and made slushy plops on Amon's hat. The rain was beginning to freeze.

"Yes, sir," they said in unison and moved the wagon along.

Out of the corner of his eye, Amon had seen Mr. Bledsoe pop his head out of the carriage window, but he said nothing and almost instantly pulled his head inside again and closed the shutter.

Amon sighed with relief. He'd had just about enough of listening to Mr. Bledsoe call him boy, and Mrs. Bledsoe's shrieks, and Miss Leona's complaints. The volume on all three of them had gone up considerably when he had stopped to pick up the Archers.

When they left Fredericksburg, it was full dark, so Amon lit the carriage lanterns. Even though the rain was so steady they couldn't light the way for him, somehow he found the yellow globes of light on each side comforting. He passed many people, still walking slowly out of town. Each time he did he felt a little stab of guilt, but he knew he couldn't take all of them. How could he choose to take this lady or that limping old man and not the next one?

Then he came upon an old lady who was standing up very straight but was walking with a noticeable limp. She used a walking stick with her right. A young woman had her arm entwined with hers and was holding the hand of a young boy, who was holding the hand of a very small girl. None of them, even the children, looked behind as the carriage neared. But as he drew up with them, the little girl looked up at the lanterns, pointed, and smiled. The young woman saw her and smiled back at the child.

It was the only smile Amon had seen on that dark day, and his heart melted. He jerked the reins, shouted, "Hup," to the horses, and brought them to a sudden stop. Jumping down, he came to stand in front of the two ladies. Doffing his hat, he bowed as if they were in a drawing room. "How d'ye do, ma'am, miss. My name is Amon, and this here is Mr. Morgan Tremayne's carriage. I'm taking some folks out to our farm. Would you ladies need me to take you someplace? Or if you've a mind, we'd welcome you at Rapidan Run."

The older woman, whose face was drawn in pain, and the pretty younger woman just stared at him. The boy was looking up at him in bewilderment, and the little girl's mouth was a round *O*.

Behind him, he heard the shutter crash, and the Bledsoes all started talking at once. Loudly. Rolling his eyes, he said, "Please don't pay no mind to these folks. They're just upset with the 'vacuation and all. I'm afraid there won't be room in the carriage, but if you do need a ride or would like to visit us for a while, I b'lieve I can make room for you up on the driver's seat."

The two women exchanged glances, and the older lady said with great dignity, "God bless you, sir. We have nowhere to go, and if you could take us in for a day or two, we would be most grateful."

The younger woman asked doubtfully, "Are you sure we can all get on that seat?"

"Yes, ma'am, I'm sure," Amon said firmly. "Your boy can squeeze up right next to me, and if you can hold the little girl in your lap, we'll make it just fine."

Behind him he heard Bledsoe roar, "Boy, you don't even know what kind of people they are! And I strongly protest. My wife and daughter are getting chilled while you stand there and chat with strangers!"

In a low voice, Amon said, "I'm sorry, ma'am, miss."

The younger woman smiled at him. He thought that she had the purest, sweetest smile he had ever seen, except for maybe the little girl's. "I don't know what you mean, Amon. I didn't hear anything at all. Now, if you would be so kind as to help my mother-in-law up, we'll be on our way."

It took them over three hours to reach Rapidan Run. Along the river, a single rider could make it to Fredericksburg in an hour. But the River Road ran south, looping around the Wilderness and then east, so it was about five miles farther. Amon had to go very slowly, because the night was as black as a coal mine, and the road was muddy and slippery.

The young lady introduced everyone. The older lady was her mother-in-law, Mrs. Archer. She was Connie Archer, and her ten-year-old son's name was Sully. The little girl was Georgie. Amon liked Connie Archer immediately, because she spoke to him like Morgan Tremayne did, as equals with no hint of the strain that white people showed even when they were kind. Mrs. Archer said very little, but Amon thought that may be because she was obviously in pain. Every time the carriage went over even the slightest bump, she pressed her lips together and closed her eyes tightly.

Finally they drove up the path to Rapidan Run and then the drive that led straight to the back door. Every window in the house was lit, the kitchen windows were bright, and Amon could smell fresh bread baking. He thought that perhaps a homecoming had never been so welcoming.

Jolie stood at the back door waiting.

Amon helped the Archers down first, which enraged Benjamin Bledsoe, but Amon was long past caring. In just a little while, he could go into his own house, have a cup of hot cider, sit at his own fire, and forget about the Bledsoes.

Poor Jolie, he thought as he handed down Mrs. Bledsoe and Leona. *Wouldn't be surprised if she and Ketura don't come to my house looking for shelter themselves.*

∿

Jolie didn't waste any time with social convention. She immediately took Mrs. Archer's arm and called, "Please, everyone just come in. Follow me."

The Archers went in first, and behind them Mrs. Bledsoe harrumphed, "Dreadful manners that child has."

They went into the house and down the hall, but as they came to the foot of the stairs, Leona said, "Jolie? That is who you are, isn't it? I would prefer to be shown to my room immediately, and I'm sure my parents would, too. We've had quite a trying day."

"Of course, Miss Bledsoe," Jolie said politely. "It's upstairs, the second room on the left. Mr. and Mrs. Bledsoe, your room is right across the hall from Miss Bledsoe's." Jolie turned and led the Archers into the parlor.

"Just a moment, Jolie," Leona said curtly. "We are going to need some hot water and brandy. And my mother and I will need your assistance with unpacking and attending us."

Jolie said evenly, "Soon we'll have supper. Evetta and Ketura are cooking right now. After supper I'll be glad to take you out to the kitchen, so that you will know where the pots for heating water and the cookstove are. Mr. Tremayne does keep brandy in the house, but it is strictly for medicinal purposes. However, warm mulled wine will be served at supper. Perhaps that will do. And Miss Bledsoe, I plan on doing everything I can to help all of our guests here at Rapidan Run. But I am not your maidservant. I'm afraid you and your mother will be obliged to look after yourselves while you are here."

As Jolie spoke, Leona's face grew stormier with each word. When Jolie finished, she said in an ominous tone, "We will talk about this later, Jolie."

"Yes, Miss Bledsoe," she said and turned again.

Mrs. Bledsoe was aghast. "What did I just say? What did I just say! That child is not fit for polite company! The impudence! I would say to her—"

"Mother," Leona said between gritted teeth, "shut up."

Jolie worked hard getting the Archers warmed up and their little bundles of clothing sorted out. She sat Mrs. Archer in a rocking chair right next to the fire and fetched hot bricks wrapped in flannel for her feet. "I would like for you to take one of the other bedrooms," she told Connie Archer. "One has a generous double bed, and we could fix comfortable pallets for the children."

Mischievously Connie looked upward to the second floor, where they could hear a muffled high-pitched constant drone coming from the bedroom upstairs. "Thank you, Jolie, that's very generous, but I think we'll be much more comfortable down here."

"I can't possibly walk up the stairs anyway," Mrs. Archer said with ill-disguised relief. "I never thought I'd be glad of that, but there you are. The Lord can turn even the rheumatism into a blessing in disguise."

It was after nine o'clock when Rosh and Santo got back with

the wagon. They brought six adults and six children with them. Will Green, the saddler, rode his mule. All told, there were twenty-six people that found Rapidan Run a blessed haven on that terrible night.

❧

Jolie was surprised, but she found the next few days enjoyable. She had never been around a group of women, and she had never been around children. She immediately found that she loved children, and she hoped that she might have four or even six children herself. It was also a revelation that the company of genteel, kind women was pleasant and an education in itself. Jolie, of course, had never had a mother or sister. Cleo and Evetta had been mother substitutes, but they weren't the real thing. Ketura had become much like a sister, but she was exactly the same age as Jolie, and so she didn't know the benefits that an older sister might bring.

The refugees at Rapidan Run were a varied group. There was Bert Patrick of Patrick's General Store, and his cheerful, garrulous wife, Maisie. The Patricks had never had children, and it had come about that they had virtually adopted a neighbor's son, Howie Coggins. Howie was twenty-eight now, and he had been in the army and lost a leg at First Bull Run. He had a wife, Greta, and three children. Bert and Maisie's wagon had been stolen the previous night, and they had gotten stranded in the city.

Jolie's dressmaker, widowed Sally Selden, had come with her four-year-old son, Matthew, and six-year-old daughter, Deirdre. Silas Cage's wife, nineteen-year-old Ellie, whose daughter was now eight months old, had wept with relief when Rosh and Santo came to get her. Old Will Green, the saddler, had decided to stay in Fredericksburg and tough it out, but then he decided that he didn't want the bluebellies to get his mule, Geneva, and he had saddled her up and plodded along with the wagon.

Jolie especially enjoyed Connie Archer, an average, rather plain woman with mousy brown hair and weak eyes. But she had a smile that positively made her face glow, and she was gentle and kind. She cared for her mother-in-law with the utmost tenderness, though Mrs. Archer was a rather stiff, formal woman who complained when her arthritis was especially painful. However, Mrs. Archer melted and became positively jolly with her grandchildren, Sully and Georgie. She seemed a different woman when she was with them.

Within three days they had established a routine. Everyone except the Bledsoes got up early. The women helped Evetta with breakfast, Mrs. Cage and Mrs. Archer kept all the children, the men helped Amon and Rosh and Santo with their chores.

Jolie managed to keep the dawn for herself. She still went out and mucked out Rowena's stall and exercised her and then groomed her. Her cooking skills had not improved much, and Evetta was happy to excuse Jolie from it. Jolie got back at breakfast time.

The women ate in the farmhouse, and the men ate in the kitchen. After the washing up, Maisie and Sally Selden helped with the baking and roasting meat and other cooking for dinner and supper, while Jolie, Ketura, and Connie Archer cleaned the house and did the laundry. After dinner in the afternoon, they all sat at the dining room table and sewed.

Jolie would have been very happy during this time if it were not for two things: the constant worry over the war and the Bledsoes. Basically the family would have nothing to do with any of them. They came down to eat, heat water for washing up, and to get tea or coffee. That was all. All three of them stayed in their bedrooms all day. The only exception to this was that Leona sought out Jolie once or twice a day to make demands on her.

"Jolie, it's ridiculous for my parents to have to come down to simply get a cup of tea. I assume Morgan has a tea service. Where is it?" she said the day after they arrived.

"It's in use, Miss Bledsoe. We keep tea available to everyone in the afternoons. You will find the teapot and cups on the sideboard in the dining room."

"Jolie, I need these petticoats ironed."

"Jolie, my mother says that her sheets are scratchy. Don't you have any finer-quality linens?"

"Jolie, it is simply impossible for us to carry enough hot water for baths. I insist that Amon and those two boys provide us with hot water for baths every other night."

"Jolie, Mrs. Cage's baby kept us up half the night last night. Why doesn't she stay in one of the servants' cottages? There are two cottages, and only five in that family. Why are we all stacked up in here like tinned sardines?"

And on and on. Jolie always politely refused her demands, and she was puzzled that Leona never argued. She simply turned on her heel and stalked back upstairs. She was relieved, however. Regardless of how much she told herself that Leona was a hateful snob and that she didn't have to cater to her or her caterwauling mother, Leona still intimidated her frightfully. Jolie was only sixteen years old and had no sophistication or cleverness about people. And Leona was a very striking woman.

Two years ago, after she had gotten to know Amon and his family well, she had asked Amon about her.

"Is she very beautiful?" Jolie had asked wistfully.

Amon shook his head. "Nah, she's the kind of woman that white men calls handsome. Don't ask me why. That's just white folks for you, I guess. Mebbe it's cause she's tall and proud and has those kinda eyes that spark. And she dresses like the Queen o' Sheba, too."

Jolie had to agree with all of that. Leona was five feet ten inches tall and slim. She stood with her head held high, her neck long and graceful. She had rich, abundant hair and always wore jeweled combs and hair ornaments. Her clothes were all of the finest fabrics, her tailoring exquisite.

She made Jolie feel like a little ragpicker, for once again Jolie had blossomed out since the previous winter, and all of her blouses were too tight. Her work shoes were worn, and her nice shoes were too small. Most of her skirts were thin from hard wear and constant washing. Jolie had four nice wool ensembles, but they couldn't compare with Leona's clothing. And Jolie never would have worn them on the farm anyway. It wasn't practical. She determined that she would keep out of Leona's way if possible, though she wasn't about to hide on her own farm.

But on the fourth day, Leona sought her out for the "talk" she had promised on the night of their arrival. Though the Bledsoes never came downstairs until breakfast was on the table, Leona must have been awake to see that Jolie went to the stables early in the morning. It was, in fact, the only time she was alone.

She had just started clearing the soiled hay out of Rowena's stall when Leona came into the stables, wearing a gorgeous chocolate-brown hooded mantle with black grosgrain trim. Throwing back the hood, she said with apparent gaiety, "So here's where you get off to every morning, little girl. Mm, such hard work. Your hands are going to be as rough as Amon's. Come here, Jolie, I want to talk to you." She looked around, up and down the long row of boxes. "Isn't there anywhere to sit in this place?"

Resigned, Jolie said, "In the tack room there are some stools." She threw her shawl back around her shoulders and led Leona to the far end of the stables. The stove was next to the tack room, and it was warm and smelled of leather and horse. Jolie liked it, and she was sure that Leona hated it.

Leona bent and dusted off the stool with one gloved hand, then sat and regarded Jolie for long moments.

Jolie became very uncomfortable under such scrutiny. Nervously she clutched her shawl tighter and hooked her boots on the stool's rungs and smoothed her skirt over and over.

She looks amused. . . . She's laughing at me, Jolie thought bleakly.

Finally Leona cleared her throat with a tiny, delicate sound. "First, Jolie, I must apologize for my and my parents' behavior the last few days. I assure you, we are normally polite, well-spoken people. It's just that we were in such shock, with the Yankees threatening to bombard us, and then having to leave all of our possessions. In particular, my mother is suffering, which explains why she's been so impatient and cross."

An apology, no matter how insincere and incomplete, threw Jolie completely off guard. She swallowed hard. "I—it's fine, Miss Bledsoe. You don't have to apologize."

"Perhaps not, but I do, anyway. Now. I have come to see in the last few days that I don't quite understand your role here, Jolie. Please explain it to me," she said peremptorily.

"I—I beg your pardon? My role?" Jolie repeated, bewildered.

"Yes. You don't know that word? I mean, your position in Mr. Tremayne's household."

Jolie knew what the word *role* meant perfectly well, but it seemed silly to bluster about it now. "I don't know about a position," she said slowly. "He's my guardian."

"Has he formally adopted you? Legally?"

"No, that is, I don't think so," Jolie said with difficulty.

"So basically he took in a penniless orphan, as an act of charity," Leona said with a condescending smile.

Stung, Jolie started to fling her inheritance in Leona's face. She was far, *far* from penniless. But a tiny little voice in her head suggested that it was none of Leona Bledsoe's business, and she shouldn't try to fight Leona on her own ground. She was sure to lose. It startled Jolie to realize that she was, somehow, in a fight with Leona. Though Leona was speaking pleasantly, even warmly, she was definitely attacking Jolie. What did she want? What was she trying to win? Jolie had no idea.

She was quiet for so long that Leona continued, "That is so like Morgan. He's a generous, charitable man. But I must admit that I'm rather surprised he chose to take in an octoroon. Heaven knows there are many poor white children who desperately need a benefactor."

"It's—not like that," Jolie said in confusion. "Mr. Tremayne was very good friends with my father, and he—helped me because of him."

"Ah, I see," Leona said. "Yes, Mr. DeForge, I remember him. I believe that he didn't actually tell you that he was your father? Yes, now I recall Morgan telling me that Mr. DeForge was quite embarrassed to have a black child on the wrong side of the blanket, as it's said."

Jolie stared incredulously at Leona. Then her eyes filled with scalding tears. She dropped her head, buried her face in her shawl, and sobbed.

Leona stood and patted her lightly on the shoulder. "Don't cry, dear. I'm sure Morgan has made up for all of that. I know he must be a wonderful father to you."

"He is not!" Jolie cried. "He's—he's not old enough to be my father!"

"Yes, of course," Leona said soothingly. "Calm yourself, Jolie. There's really no need for such dramatics. I can see that you have had a good life here. Why should you be crying when so many people are suffering so much more than you are?"

"Yes, that's true," Jolie said woefully, making a valiant effort to stop the helpless flow of tears. "Mr. Tremayne has taken very good care of me. And I am grateful and happy. Usually."

"Yes, Morgan has taken care of you, but he's a single man, and he has no idea how to raise a little girl," Leona said, smoothly taking her seat again. "You see, Jolie, Morgan has obviously indulged you, and it's made you proud and rather smug. Such unattractive qualities in children. I mean, you seem to think that you are fit to be a hostess for Morgan's household! It's preposterous to see you, a little black girl, lording it over me and my parents. No, no, Jolie. I'm sure that Mr. Tremayne would be extremely upset if he knew of your behavior since we arrived here."

Jolie was horribly confused. She had tried to do her best to make everyone feel welcome and to make sure that they were comfortable and well fed. True, she had refused to be Leona's house slave, but surely Morgan never meant for her to be that! Did he? She had thought she knew exactly what Morgan would expect from her, but now she wasn't sure.

Leona was watching her coolly.

Jolie said, "Maybe what you say is true, Miss Bledsoe. I'm just not sure. I need time to think. But anyway, I have some questions, too."

"Yes, I'm sure you do, but I'm certainly not going to be interrogated by you," Leona said, rising and pulling up her hood. "As you said, you do need to take some time and think this through. I would hate to have to tell Morgan that you insulted me and my family while we were guests in his home." She started toward the door but then turned back, and now Jolie saw the touch of malice in her. "I will answer one of your questions, Jolie, because you apparently have a very mistaken idea of my relationship with Morgan. He is in love with me. He has been for years. That's why I have much more right than you do to say what happens in this house."

"No, you don't," Jolie said, too loudly, she knew. In a less panicky tone she said, "Besides, Mr. Tre—Morgan told me that you and he weren't together anymore. That you told him you didn't want to be with a private. You wanted him to be an officer, and you got mad at him when he wouldn't, and you told him you didn't want to see him anymore."

"Lover's squabbles," Leona said, waving her hand. "You can't possibly understand the complex relationships of adults, particularly since you're black. Besides, just think, Jolie, who did he think of first when the whole city was in danger? Me. Do you doubt me? Ask Rosh. And know that this is the last time I'll make any explanations to the likes of you." She whirled around, her mantle billowing, and walked out.

CHAPTER TWENTY-ONE

Jolie," Ketura whispered, laying her hand on Jolie's shoulder gently, "are you crying?"

The two girls were sleeping under the dining room table. Jolie had worked out the sleeping arrangements. Ellie Cage, with her eight-month-old daughter, Janie, had the spare bedroom upstairs, and Bert and Maisie Patrick, who were in their sixties, had taken Ketura's bedroom. The Bledsoes were in Morgan's room, while Leona was in Jolie's. Will Green and Howie Coggins slept in the barn. The other women and children were all sleeping in Morgan's study/sitting room.

Although there had been room in the study for Jolie and Ketura—it was the largest room in the house, taking up over half of the first floor—they had decided to sleep in the dining room, finding that under the table, right by the fireplace, was a cocoon of warmth.

Now Jolie turned over, and by the golden flicker of the flames Jolie could see her friend's concerned face.

"You are crying," Ketura said. "I've never seen you cry, Jolie, not even with everything you've been through. Whatever is wrong?"

"I don't think I can talk about it," Jolie said helplessly. "Every time I think about it I just cry. I hate to cry. It gives me a such a headache."

Ketura sat up and crossed her long legs. "Sounds like you better talk about it. Maybe if you can tell someone, you won't cry anymore. You can tell me anything, Jolie. You know that."

Slowly Jolie pulled herself up into a sitting position, hugging her knees close under her chin. "I know. I'll try, but it's all kind of like this big red blur." Jolie did cry as she told Ketura about her conversation with Leona Bledsoe, but by the time she was finished, she had stopped weeping. Her headache had even lessened.

Ketura's big round eyes grew more and more distressed as Jolie talked. "Oh Jolie, what are you going to do?" she asked anxiously.

"Do? I don't know what to do! You've got to help me, Ketura! I'm—I'm afraid!" Jolie said, grabbing the girl to her and hugging her close.

Ketura clung to her, then pulled back and wiped the remnants of tears from Jolie's face. "I don't know what to do, Jolie. That lady scares me, too. Maybe we should go talk to one of the ladies, tell her what Miss Bledsoe said and did to you. I know, what about Miss Connie? She's the nicest, sweetest lady I've ever met, and she's smart. She'd know what to do."

"She is nice and she's so kind, but I barely know her. I had a hard enough time telling you, Ketura. I couldn't possibly tell a stranger all this. Besides, she doesn't know Morgan, she—she couldn't help me decide what he wants and what he means for me to do. Why don't we go talk to your mother? She's smart, too, and she knows Morgan. Evetta could help."

"I don't know," Ketura said slowly. "Mama's smart, but she doesn't have much use for mean white ladies. I think she'd just tell you to ignore Miss Bledsoe and get on about your business."

"Maybe," Jolie said, "but even just that might help. I'm so awfully confused."

The girls got up and put on heavy dressing gowns and went outside. They had thought that they would go to Amon and Evetta's cottage and wake her up. But they saw that the kitchen lamps were blazing, so they went to find Evetta there.

When they went in, they were surprised to see Connie Archer standing over a big pot on the stove, stirring the boiling syrup that gave off the sticky sweet aroma of hot peaches. Two more pots were on the range. Six piecrusts were lined up along the wooden counter on the back wall. Evetta was just shaping up the last one. They looked up as the girls came in.

"Oh. Hello, Evetta. Hello, Miss Connie," Jolie said awkwardly. "We didn't know you were here."

"Guess you musta, since you come in," Evetta said crisply. "Now Jolie, I don't need you in here twitchin' around and making me forget every one thing I'm doing. Besides, you girls need your rest. Go back to bed."

"But I wanted to talk to you, Evetta," Jolie said nervously. "Please?"

"Then talk."

Jolie's eyes slid to Connie Archer, and she fidgeted. A knowing look passed over Connie's thin face, and she said, "Girls, why don't you sit down? I was just going to make myself some cocoa. Why don't I make three cups, and we'll share? Evetta, would you like some cocoa?"

"No, thank you, Miss Connie, but you go right ahead and take you a little break," Evetta said in the warmest tone Jolie had ever heard her use. "Everything's ready. All's I got to do is pour up these pies and pop 'em in the oven, and I can do that by myself, thank you."

When Connie had poured up three mugs of the warm, creamy chocolate, she brought them over to the worktable and sat down on the stool next to Jolie. "What a great luxury to have chocolate for Christmas! Do you know that the Patricks haven't even been able to get it for the last couple of months. We all owe Mr. Tremayne a very great debt of thanks."

"Yes, we do," Jolie said dully. "He worked very hard in the last two years to make sure that we didn't want for anything here at Rapidan Run."

"I don't know him, but I feel as if I already do," Connie said quietly. "I know that he is a courageous man, because he's gone to fight in this terrible war. He's a kind man, because I can see the love you all have for him. He's a charitable man because we're all here, all of us. And I know that he's a generous man because I, a perfect stranger, am sitting here drinking his valuable cocoa."

"He's all of that and so much more," Jolie said.

Connie nodded. "I'm sure he is, and I so look forward to the time that I might get to know such a man. But for right now, Jolie, I'd like to get to know you. You see, I'm thirty-two years old now, but I can remember when I was sixteen. It was very difficult. I didn't understand my place in the world. I didn't understand what people wanted of me. It seemed I never knew the right thing to do. I had lost my parents, you see, and I felt I had no one in the world to help me. But the Lord sent me someone, a teacher, a lovely woman who didn't do a thing except listen to me. And that helped me more than anything in this world. So, Jolie, may I be your teacher? It might only be for this one night, I don't know. But I do think now that the Lord sent me and my family here for a purpose. I think He sent me here for you, Jolie."

A moment of profound silence came when Connie's soft voice faded on the air. Then Ketura breathed, "Oh Jolie, you've got to talk to this lady. If you don't, I will."

"No, I–I'll try," Jolie said. "I believe you, Miss Connie. But I'm so confused, so upset. I don't even know if I'm making any sense or not. Somehow I just want to cry, and whine, I guess, and just go on and on about how Miss Leona Bledsoe was so mean to me. But I know that's childish, and feeling sorry for myself won't solve anything."

"That already shows a great deal of maturity on your part," Connie said. "Especially for a sixteen-year-old girl. But I'm not at all surprised, Jolie. I've only known you for four days, and I've already seen that though you may look like a young girl, you have a love in your heart that makes you wise and good much beyond your years. Now, why don't you just try to set aside all the emotions you feel and tell me what Miss Bledsoe said to you?"

Jolie was able to do just that. Her account of the conversation was much more coherent than when she had told Ketura. She hadn't been able to say much more than that Leona had been horrible to her and had made her feel like she was childish and selfish and arrogant.

But after that cleansing outburst, and particularly after Connie Archer's soothing, restful assurances, Jolie felt calm and clear headed. She was able to remember the conversation practically word for word and could articulate Leona Bledsoe's attitude that had made it so much worse than the actual words she had said.

"We were in the stables, you see, and when she left I thought that she'd made me feel as if I was like the horse droppings she was so careful not to step in. That's how low I felt," Jolie finished painfully.

As Jolie had talked, Connie Archer had kept her eyes fixed on Jolie's face, and she hadn't said a word.

Ketura had murmured, "Oh, no," a couple of times, hearing the story again.

Behind them, Evetta was busily making pies and putting them in the oven, but she let her feelings be known several times by derisive grunts. Now she said, "Huh! I'm surprised that hussy knows what horse droppings even is, 'cause she don't know the upside of a horse from the backside. She's so scared of 'em she won't even look at 'em."

"She is?" Jolie said with surprise. "I didn't know that."

"No, you didn't," Connie said firmly. "But that's the thing about Leona, you see, that most people don't realize. She's frightened. She is frightened out of her wits. And I don't mean just of horses, either."

Ketura said with disbelief, "Miss Bledsoe, scared? I didn't think she was frightened of anything. She's so scary herself."

"She sure is," Jolie agreed forcefully.

Connie studied them. "You really think she is scary? So, you're actually frightened of her? Like you're frightened of snakes, or of being in a strange dark place, or of fire?"

After long moments, Jolie said, "No. . .no, not like that."

Evetta muttered, "Mebbe like the snakes."

Connie said, "No, you're not frightened of her. What you are is intimidated. That's a very different thing. It's much easier to overcome feelings of intimidation than it is to overcome true, real fear."

"Maybe," Jolie agreed halfheartedly. "But I don't know how to keep from feeling like—like—"

"Like she's better than you?" Connie supplied quickly. "Like she's prettier than you, like she's smarter than you, like she knows Mr. Tremayne better than you, like she deserves more respect, more love than you? That's what intimidation is. And you can get out from under that easily, Jolie, and you, too, Ketura, just by recognizing what she's doing. She's deliberately making you feel that way, because it's her weapon, and a very weak and pathetic one it is, too. Attacking people where they are most vulnerable is a coward's tool. And she is a coward, because she is so afraid, and instead of facing her fears and overcoming them, she belittles other people to make herself feel powerful."

"But what is she afraid of?" Jolie demanded. "I don't understand. She *is* beautiful, she *is* smart, she *is* rich, and it seems like men just fall in love with her so easily! What can she possibly be scared of?"

"All right, let's consider everything you just said, Jolie," Connie said, "which is pretty much exactly what you see when you don't know Leona like I do. Beautiful? Maybe, although I'm not so sure that exactly describes Leona's looks. She's exotic and striking, yes—"

Loudly, Evetta interrupted, "I think that her face is hard enough to dent an ax handle."

A quick look of amusement passed over Connie's face, and she continued, "And she is extremely intelligent. She's smart enough to realize that a woman's looks don't last forever. She's only twenty-five now, but for years she's been using expensive lotions and exotic ointments and bathing perfumes and herbal preparations for her hair and skin.

"And that brings me to your next point. Leona is not rich. As a matter of fact, she is poor. The Bledsoes have been broke for a long time, and Benjamin Bledsoe was in debt up to the ceiling of their expensive two-story house before the war even started. After that, of course, there was no one he could borrow from. Leona's had to do without her expensive creams and milk baths for a long time now. Believe me, she's scared to death. Scared of losing her looks, scared of being poor, scared of having to do without, but mostly scared because now there's no one to coddle her, adore her, fulfill her every wish. All those men who fell in love with her so easily are gone now."

After long moments, Jolie said in a low voice, "I see what you're saying, Miss Connie, and I guess you must be right about Miss Bledsoe being scared about her looks and being poor and all. But you're wrong about one thing. All those men aren't gone. Morgan Tremayne hasn't deserted her."

"No, I know he hasn't. And I'm not surprised. He strikes me as the sort of man who is very loyal to his friends."

"But do you think that's all it is?" Jolie asked desperately. "He thought about her first, Rosh told me! Morgan sent the carriage just for her! Don't you think he must still be in love with her?"

"I don't know," Connie said calmly. "He may be. Men can be so blind, so terribly ignorant, when it comes to women like Leona. But even if he is, it shouldn't make any difference to you, Jolie."

"But it does! It's—it's everything. It's what frightens me most of all!" Jolie cried passionately.

A sudden look of recognition came over Connie's face, and she reached over to take Jolie's hand. "I see," she said quietly. "I will pray about that, Jolie. But I meant what I said. When Mr. Tremayne left, he entrusted you and Ketura and Amon and Rosh and Santo with this place, with his home. He obviously believed you would be faithful stewards. And you have been. You have taken in strangers and cared for us, shared all of your worldly goods with us, sheltered us when we had no home. You have all demonstrated true godly love, for you knew that we could give you nothing in return."

"That is what Morgan intended all along," Jolie said slowly. "I know him."

Evetta shoved the last pie in the oven, slammed the door shut, and came to stand in front of them, flour-covered hands firmly planted on her hips. "Well, you don't know all about him. You didn't know he made out a new will afore he left to go help Gen'ral Lee. Yes, sir, he did. He left this place to us, to all of us, to my family and to you. He left us equal shares in the farm, but he left the big house to you, Jolie. So the way I sees it, this place is ours, no matter where Mr. Tremayne is, 'cause that's what he wanted us to know by doin' that."

Jolie absorbed this then said, "So Miss Bledsoe was wrong, after all. I really do have much more right than she does to decide what happens in this house."

Evetta sniffed. "Thass right. So you need to quit stewin' your frilly little britches about whatever bugs crazy white ladies got in their addled brains, 'scuse me Miss Connie, and git back to goin' about your business."

Ketura sighed, "Told you so."

Jolie managed a smile. "And it did make me feel better. But it was mostly you, Miss Connie. Thank you so much for helping me," she said simply.

"You're welcome."

"But there's something I'd like to ask you, Miss Connie," Jolie said, puzzled. "You seem to know Miss Bledsoe really well. But I know she hasn't spoken one word to you since you all came here."

"No, she wouldn't," Connie said quietly. "The reason I know her so well is that she—she—" For the first time she faltered and searched Jolie's and Ketura's faces as if she were trying to read their minds. Then, with a regretful sigh, she continued, "I suppose I can tell you. It's a shame, but in these times children have had to grow up much too fast and know terrible things that no child should have to face. Leona Bledsoe had an affair with my husband. That's the reason why I know her so well."

Even Evetta paused in her work and stared.

Connie continued, "It was in the spring, three years ago, just when we were all realizing that war was coming. My husband was Mr. Lucien Lewis's personal secretary. Mr. Lewis was president of Merchant's and Planter's Bank. I say that Martin and Leona had an affair, but really it—they were only together twice. Leona seduced him, you see, because she wanted him to persuade Mr. Lewis to loan her father money. Martin told her that it was impossible, as he had no such influence over Mr. Lewis. Then Leona tried to persuade him to embezzle money for her."

"What's 'bezzle?" Evetta demanded, still frozen with a spoon in her hand.

"Steal it," Connie answered shortly. "It's funny, I guess, in a way. A man can be seduced by a woman, and it's as if he sort of gets sucked into that sin slowly, like sliding into a bath that's almost too hot. But stealing, particularly when you know you would get caught, is quite jarring. Apparently it can bring even the most deluded of men to their senses. Martin knew then what kind of woman she was, and he realized what a terrible thing he had done."

Evetta banged the spoon against a pot and then stirred it with repeated dull clangs. "A flyswatter can swat spiders as good as they swat flies." Somehow they all knew what Evetta meant.

Jolie asked, "And so Mr. Archer told you? He confessed to you?"

"No, he didn't have the chance, really," Connie answered, and the pain of the memories showed in her face. "Leona told me. I mean, she sent me a note. Hand-delivered, so that she could be sure that Martin was at work so he wouldn't intercept it. It was a terrible shock, and things were very bad for us for about a year."

"That is horrible!" Jolie said compassionately. "So much worse than those stupid things she said to me! Oh, how did you bear it, Miss Connie?"

"I didn't bear it at all for a long time. I made Martin pay for it. Every day, all day, I punished him. But finally I realized that I was hurting myself as much as I was hurting him. I forgave him then. It took much longer to trust him again, but finally I did. And I thank the Lord Jesus for giving me that spirit of forgiveness," she said, tears springing to her eyes.

"When I told Martin good-bye when he was leaving to march into Maryland, it was the last time I ever saw him. He died at Sharpsburg, and he's buried there. But we parted with love and sweetness, and I'm so thankful to God. Because that's what gives me joy, and strength, to this very day."

❧

On the night of November 25th, as Jolie poured out her heart to Connie Archer, Morgan Tremayne walked through a hard, cold rain to the top of what was beginning to be called Lee's Hill. It was not the highest point of the ridge of hills that ran behind Fredericksburg, but it gave the best vantage point for the battle that was coming.

The Yankees were concentrated directly behind Fredericksburg, to the south for about three miles, just along the Rappahanock River. Lee's Hill was prominent, as it was a slightly lower prominence and was almost directly in the center of the Union dispositions. Morgan knew that Longstreet's corps ranged out to his left and two of Jackson's divisions to his right. He suspected that as soon as General Lee was sure that the battle was to be here, he would call on his most trusted general, Stonewall Jackson, to fortify the line.

Two days later, Lee became certain that Burnside's attack was here, no matter how unlikely it seemed to him. He sent for Jackson, who marched his men 175 miles in twelve days. He arrived on December 1st.

By then General Lee, and indeed the entire army, was puzzled. Why did Burnside not attack? His men had been on the field for over two weeks. What was he doing?

The answer could not have been made known to General Lee by even the best of spies, because even the Union Army did not know why Burnside tarried. He had ordered pontoon boats to build bridges across the river, and somehow the orders had been misunderstood, or not communicated correctly, and then due to the heavy rains and the swollen creeks and rivers the delivery of them had been delayed. Then Burnside had decided to change his attack to a crossing eighteen miles downstream, called Skinker's Neck. But Lee had anticipated this possibility, and all others, too. Burnside hesitated when he found out that thousands of Confederates waited for him downstream.

The next few days he seesawed in an agony of indecision. Finally he decided to go with his original plan, to build five bridges across the river and to pour his men into Fredericksburg. He envisioned tens of thousands of men in blue sweeping through the little empty town, across the plains beyond, up the gentle little hills, and overrunning the Confederates with ease.

But that was not the vision that General Robert E. Lee had, at all. Finally, on December 11th, at 2:00 a.m., the engineers began building their pontoon bridges. They learned, first of all, of the plans Robert E. Lee had for the battle. It was to slaughter every man who tried to cross that river. General Longstreet had posted Brigadier General William Barksdale's tough Mississippians, including some of the best sharpshooters in the army, in Fredericksburg to delay the Union advance as long as possible. They waited all along the waterfront, behind walls, in rifle pits, in basements, on roofs. When dawn came, the slaughter began. Engineers, using tools to build bridges, were unarmed. The sharpshooters sent them back time and time again, all that morning and into the afternoon. Finally the

The SURRENDER

Yankees brought their artillery down and began shelling the town. That worked until about 2:30 that afternoon. When the Yankees ceased firing the artillery, the sharpshooters came out of hiding and began picking off the engineers again. Eventually Burnside ordered that infantry be rowed across the river in the pontoons. They finally managed to get a foothold on the waterfront and began moving through the town. The Mississippians fought them fiercely; for every foot of ground that they gained, men died. But finally the Confederates were safely ensconced on Marye's Heights, and the Union Army occupied Fredericksburg.

It was about 4:30 p.m. On Lee's hill, General Lee advised couriers to send the word to commanders to be ready for an attack.

But when night fell, he was still watching the river, where more and more men were pouring across. But the frozen night was not dark, for the entire scene was lit with a lurid orange glow. Fredericksburg was burning.

General Lee finally retired to get some rest, telling his aides to awaken him at once if it looked as if General Burnside was making a move. But General Lee could have slept late on the morning of December 12th, if he had chosen to. On that day he stood on Lee's Hill and watched through his field glasses as thousands of Union soldiers vandalized and looted the little town.

Appalled, Morgan tied up the horses and came to the crest of the hill to use his own field glasses. The looting was vicious. Every house still standing was broken into, and everything of value was stolen.

But it was the vandalism that was so needless and cruel that it became almost bizarre. Soldiers dragged furniture out into the streets and built huge bonfires. Pianos were danced on until they fell apart, and some were filled with water to use as horse troughs. Paintings were dragged out and slashed with bayonets and then stamped on. Large alabaster vases were smashed to bits. Even picket fences surrounding little gardens were yanked up and set on fire.

Morgan was so angry that he made an inarticulate growling

sound in his throat then quickly looked guiltily at General Lee, who was standing only a few feet from him.

Lee's face showed no anger. Instead he looked disgusted, as if someone had said an obscene word to a group of ladies.

The looting went on all day, because it took all day for General Burnside to get his eighty thousand men across the Rappahannock, and it became evident that that was the only plan for December 12th.

The next day dawned, a cold, foggy morning. About 10:00 a.m. the fog lifted and the Union assault began. All day long, at every point along the battle line, waves of Union soldiers tried to advance the heights, and they died. Again and again they came, long lines of them bravely marching into the face of artillery and thousands of muskets. They fought as they had been commanded: to walk toward the enemy, and when within range, to fire their rifles, then reload and march forward again. Thousands of them never got within firing range. More thousands of them never got the chance to reload.

Far to the right it seemed as if at last Union forces had found a weak spot, a heavily wooded shallow valley, part of Stonewall Jackson's line. The atmosphere on Lee's Hill was tense, as they all strained to see any indication of the men in blue streaming back away from Jackson's line. But no such welcome sight met their eyes. They couldn't hear because of the throaty continuous roar of the cannon.

But then, distinguished only as a soprano note to the artillery's bass, they heard the high, quavering Rebel yell. One Union chaplain reported that it was an "unearthly, fiendish yell, such as no other troops or civilized beings ever uttered." Even as their hearts rose at the eerie cries that were so welcome to them, they saw Union troops running out of the woods, throwing down their rifles, and staring behind them in terror. Then behind them ran ragged men in gray, screaming their banshee song, insanely joyous in pursuit.

Morgan felt a thrill of triumph as he watched. He had not

fought in a battle. He had never even fired his rifle. But at this moment, for the first time, he understood men of war.

General Lee turned to General Longstreet and said, his dark eyes flashing, "It is well that war is so terrible—we should grow too fond of it!"

On and on they came, dashing themselves to pieces against the entrenched might of the Army of Northern Virginia. They fought until a dense gray twilight fell. It was bitterly cold, and the Northern Lights, which were rarely seen this far south, colored the air with a surreal display. Over nine thousand men had been wounded on this day. Many of them died of their wounds, lying on that bloody field, and many of them froze to death.

General Lee fully expected Burnside to renew his attack in the morning, but it did not come. In the morning, sharpshooters picked off some men on the field below and scattered Yankees who were collecting their dead and wounded close to their lines. Those were the only shots fired that day.

On the next, Burnside asked for a truce for the burial of the dead and the relief of the wounded. Lee agreed. All day long, surgeons, ambulances, and burial details were busy on the body-littered fields. There was no blue or gray now. Surgeons attended wounded men, no matter their uniform, and burial details interred Billy Yanks and Johnny Rebs side by side. No shots by the men of war were fired on this day.

On the next morning, December 16th, Burnside was nowhere to be seen. The Army of the Potomac had melted away in the night.

CHAPTER TWENTY-TWO

Jolie, Ketura, Evetta, Rosh, Santo, and Amon waited as long as they could. As the days turned into weeks, and still no tidings, no newspapers, no mail, and above all no sound of distant battle came to Rapidan Run, Jolie finally said to Amon, "I cannot stand this one more day. We must have some news! What has happened? Did we dream it? Did they decide not to fight, and everyone just packed up and went somewhere else?"

"That ain't it," Evetta assured her. "Them armies is still there, all right. I guess they's just making scary faces to each other 'crost the river. But she's right, Amon. We got to know something. I know Mr. Tremayne didn't want you to get caught in the battle, but maybe if you could get some idea of when that might be, we'd know to stay away."

"I've had it up to here, too, sitting around and waiting," Amon admitted. "I'll go as close as I can, but not till tonight."

"Then you gotta take me, Daddy," Rosh said. "I know exactly where Mr. Tremayne is, just in case it seems like we can go on in."

So Amon and Rosh set out for the battlefield at twilight. As far as they knew, all the Yankees were on the other side of the Rappa-hannock, but they were still cautious. They decided not to take the River Road. Rosh knew the way across country that would take them to the southernmost point of the line of hills above Fredericksburg. "Can you find your way at night?" Amon asked hesitantly.

"Yes, sir. Mr. Tremayne taught me," Rosh answered confidently. "He could find his way around this country blindfolded. One of those nights we were out camping he showed me this way."

But they didn't need to know the way. When they had traveled about a mile south of Rapidan Run, they began to understand the glow in the sky they were seeing ahead. Fredericksburg was on fire. Sadly, they returned to the farm.

∾

Everyone, even the Bledsoes, were waiting in the house for Amon and Rosh. When they finally returned, Jolie could tell from their demeanors that the news was not good.

"I'm sorry, folks, but it looks like there's a real big fire in the town," Amon told them quietly.

"What? What's on fire?" Leona demanded.

With compassion, Amon repeated, "It's a real big fire, ma'am."

"You mean you don't know? Are you telling me that you didn't go into town and see what was burning? And try to help?" Mrs. Bledsoe cried in outrage.

"Ma'am, when we left, they wasn't anybody left in that town," Amon explained patiently. "And that means that there's prob'ly just Yankees there now. I don't hardly think I'm gonna go help 'em put out the fires they started anyways."

"How dare you speak to me like that!" Mrs. Bledsoe shouted, her voice shrill with hysteria.

Jolie wanted to rail at the woman, but she didn't. She couldn't. Regardless of how Mrs. Bledsoe was acting and how outrageous her behavior was, she was Jolie's elder, and Jolie wasn't about to show her any disrespect.

But she wasn't Maisie Patrick's elder, and Maisie's view at that moment was that Mrs. Bledsoe didn't deserve an iota of respect. She stepped in front of Mrs. Bledsoe defiantly and said, "Eileen, everyone here is sick to death of your shrieking and wailing and the way you're treating all of us respectable people. Calm down. If you can't calm down and act like a civilized person, then go to your room. Benjamin, I'm surprised at you. How can you let her embarrass herself in this way?"

He looked disconcerted. He had lost his bluster, which was practically the only way he knew to deal with people. In the last two weeks, he had become a parody of himself, a mumbling, indecisive, fumbling old man.

Leona, her head held high, stepped up and took her mother's arm. "You have no right to speak to my mother that way, Maisie. Just leave us alone."

"I'll be glad to," Maisie retorted, "if you'll go away."

Leona whirled around and, practically dragging her protesting mother, flew up the stairs. Benjamin, after one shamefaced look at the others, hurried after them.

Maisie turned to them and said defiantly, "There are probably a hundred thousand men out there who are going to try their best to kill each other in the next day or so. Half of them are our families, our sons, our husbands, our brothers. For anyone to be hysterical over their parlor or their china or their Grandma's portrait right now is just shameful. I don't regret what I said one little bit."

❧

It wasn't the next day. On that day, eighty thousand Union soldiers crossed the Rappahannock, while the ones already landed destroyed Fredericksburg.

Everyone at Rapidan Run was so anxious with anticipation and dread that each avoided in-depth conversations with any other. Evetta burned a pudding and volubly called her own self a variety of colorful names.

SURRENDER

So it was a kind of release when the sound of artillery came to them late the next morning. All day long they heard it, like a constant rolling roar of far-off thunder. After dinner they all gave up any pretense at working. Wherever they were in the house, or out on the grounds, they constantly searched toward the south. Of course they couldn't see Fredericksburg, ten miles away. But they could see the death-gray smudge rising and growing in the southern sky. It was smoke from Confederate cannons and a hundred thousand muskets. The distant din didn't stop until nightfall, and then the sky was lit with the strange aurora.

Jolie stood for hours out on the tiny front porch, staring up, wondering if it was an evil omen. If that's what it was, she was sure Morgan must be dead.

The next day and the next were eerily quiet. Again they were utterly mystified. Amon didn't wait for Evetta to prod him this time. On December 17th, he said, "I'm going. It's so quiet I'm wonderin' if they ain't every last one of 'em dead. That's how crazy I'm a-gittin'."

"It ain't just you, Amon," Evetta said. "Not knowin' will make a body a lot crazier than knowin'."

Amon and Rosh again set out early that evening. It was two o'clock in the morning before they returned. Again, all of them were sitting up waiting. Mrs. Bledsoe was truly ill now. She had been shocked out of her hysteria by Maisie's sharp words and had finally mentally rejoined the real world—the one where her only son was fighting in a war. She had been suffering heart palpitations and near-fainting spells, and Jolie had finally given her a bottle of brandy. She suspected that Benjamin Bledsoe and Leona had partaken, too, from the high, hectic color on Leona's sharp cheekbones to Mr. Bledsoe's bleary eyes. She didn't care. She didn't even care who had won the battle. All she could think about was Morgan Tremayne.

When Amon and Rosh came in, she didn't have to ask or say a word. She could tell from their faces that Morgan Tremayne must be alive and well. Before they had even said a word, Jolie sat back in the straight chair, put her head back, closed her eyes, and took a deep, trembling breath.

The others crowded around them, firing questions at Amon and Rosh both. Finally Maisie raised her voice above the insistent cries of the women and the hoarse, rapid-fire interrogation by the men. "I'm telling my own self to shut up now," she said loudly. "And I suggest you all do the same. Let the men tell us what they know, and maybe then they can answer our questions." Finally it was quiet.

"Mr. Tremayne's alive and fine, jist fine," Amon said with a broad smile. "He says to tell you all that he's so glad you're all here together, with me and my family and Jolie. Friends need to stick together real close in these dark ol' days." The smile faded, and the big man looked distressed. "We won, all right. Yes, sir, we did. I couldn't see those lowlands 'tween Marye's Heights and town, but Mr. Tremayne says there must be a thousand men buried down there, most all of 'em Yankees. He says it looked like ten thousand of 'em got wounded. And now they're gone. Not a Yank in sight on either side of the river from Falmouth down to Massaponax."

"Have they sent out the lists of wounded and killed yet?" Ellie Cage asked with anguish.

"No, ma'am. Mr. Tremayne says that's gonna take some days, always does."

"What about Gibbs? My son, Gibbs Bledsoe?" Mrs. Bledsoe asked in a weak, fearful voice. "Morgan is friends with him. Surely he knows whether—surely Morgan knows how he is."

"Mr. Tremayne sends his 'pologies to you, ma'am, 'cause he knows you must be worried to death about your son. But Mr. Tremayne says he only knows that General Stuart was far, far down the river, guarding the army's right flank. He said he'd seen General Stuart at headquarters, but he didn't know about any of his men."

"Did he send me a message?" Leona demanded, her eyes brilliant and her mouth tense.

"Uh—not personal, no, ma'am. He just ask who all was here, and like I said, to tell everyone how welcome they was, from him. He didn't hardly have time to send word to everyone," Amon said in a very gentle voice. "The battle might be over, but they was still all scurryin' around, busy as beetles. And Mr. Tremayne hurried us off, like he wanted us to get word back to everyone."

Leona seemed mollified with Amon's diplomacy and tact and said nothing more.

Connie Archer said softly, "And so the Yankees are gone. Does that mean that we can go home now?"

"Yes, ma'am," Amon answered. "Mr. Tremayne said that he don't know much about the town, 'cause he ain't been down there yet. All he knows is that there's no Yankees there. So whoever wants to go home, me and Rosh and Amon will be glad to take you."

❦

On Christmas morning of 1862, Mary Custis Lee sat in her rolling chair at the front windows and watched the snow fall. It was a pretty sight, but as soon as the feather-flakes hit the earth, the scene became grimy and dreary. East Franklin Street in Richmond was always busy, as were all the streets in the heart of the capital city. The humble rented house had a generous covered front porch, but no garden or yard, so it loomed right up over the street.

Soldiers dashed up and down, some on foot, some on horseback, always hurrying. Even in the dry heat of summer, the street was always a mire of mud and horse droppings.

Still, in good weather, Mary sat on the porch hour after hour, day after day, knitting socks of Confederate gray. But in the cruel winters, she was in so much pain she could barely sit up at all, and when she did, she huddled close to a hot fire.

Today, however, she had decided to brave the icy drafts around the window to watch the charming snowfall as she opened her special Christmas presents. They were Robert's letters.

Mary Custis Lee was not a sentimental woman. She was

intelligent, clever, forceful, plain-spoken, and pragmatic. She had saved Robert's letters through the years, because they documented so well the times and events in his life, but she rarely visited them. It had only been in April of 1861, when her husband had become General Robert E. Lee of the Confederate States of America, that she began to treasure them. Last Christmas she had started her tradition of giving herself the best Christmas present: rereading Robert's letters.

Opening one letter that crackled with age, she began to read and was transported back to those heady days of their youth, when he was a lonely second lieutenant at Fort Monroe and she had wintered at Arlington. She saw again the wonderful years there when Robert was working in Washington. She relived the terrible two years of the Mexican War and the joy of his homecoming. Then there were the blessed peaceful years, at Baltimore and West Point. The death of her father was still sorrowful to her, though it was muted now, and she remembered how her grief had been mixed with joy that Robert had been at Arlington with her for two years. Then he had gone back to Texas, but only for a short time. The events after March 1, 1861, when Robert had returned to Arlington, seemed fast and frantic.

Grimacing with pain both physical and in her soul, she opened Robert's letter of October 20, 1862, only three months ago:

> *I cannot express the anguish I feel at the death of my sweet Annie. To know that I shall never see her again on earth, that her place in our circle, which I always hoped one day to enjoy, is forever vacant, is agonizing in the extreme. But God in this, as in all things, has mingled mercy with the blow, in selecting that one best prepared to leave us. May you be able to join me in saying, "His will be done."*

Mary looked up, now sightless with hot tears stinging her eyes. No, she had not been able to join Robert in his acceptance of God's will. She did not think it was merciful that Annie, their sweet Little

Raspberry, had died. She was angry, and she was bitter. Hers and Robert's only grandchildren were dead. Robert E. Lee III, Rooney and Charlotte's son, had died the previous June. He was only two years old. Charlotte had given birth to a little girl in November, and the child had died on December 2nd, only twenty-three days previously.

No, Mary thought savagely, *I am not him. I am not like him! No one could be so humble, so forgiving, so ready to accept such grievances and call them merciful! I cannot say, "Your will be done!"* All that was within her raged for a long time.

But Mary Lee had known the Lord for many, many years. He had been her love, her companion, her most faithful friend long before Robert E. Lee was. And she realized this, and she knew her love for the Lord Jesus was stronger than her anger, stronger than her bitterness, stronger even than her love for Robert and her children. Her heart broke, and she surrendered.

After a time of tears, she dried her eyes and opened her last, most treasured letter, though it was not the last one in time. It was dated June 22, 1862, when Robert had just named the Confederate army in the east "The Army of Northern Virginia."

> *I have the same handsome hat which surmounts my gray head. . .and shields my ugly face, which is masked by a white beard as stiff and wiry as the teeth of a card. In fact, an uglier person you have never seen, and so unattractive is it to our enemies that they shoot at it whenever visible to them.*

Mary looked up again, but instead of seeing a galling darkness, she saw her husband's face. He had always been the most handsome man she had ever seen, and this was not the rosy imagination of an adoring wife. Men and women alike remarked on Robert's fine and noble countenance. Even one of the newspapers had crowned him "the handsomest man in the army." But she knew that Robert's lines, in his mind, were simple unvarnished truth. There was not a shred of vanity in him.

And then she read her favorite lines Robert had ever written:

> *But though age with its snow has whitened my head, and its frosts have stiffened my limbs, my heart, you well know, is not frozen to you, and summer returns when I see you.*

She looked up again, a dreamy smile transforming her pain-wracked, drawn face into the vivacious Mary Custis of Arlington. It really was a beautiful snow.

❧

It snowed on Christmas morning, a pretty, light snow of big flakes. After dinner Jolie sat in the rocking chair, looking out the study windows on the grounds that sloped down to the river. All the sharp edges of nature were softened. The world beyond the borders of Rapidan Run may rage in fire and blood and death, but here all was clean and silent and tranquil.

"Hello, Mouse."

Jolie's eyes widened. Then she jumped out of the chair and leaped into Morgan's arms. For long moments they hugged, holding each other tightly.

Then Morgan lifted her up and swung her around in circles, laughing. "I'm glad to see you! I've missed you!" he said.

Breathlessly, Jolie said, "Put me down, Morgan! I'm so dizzy I can't see straight!"

He set her down, and she smoothed her skirt then felt her hair. "Is it standing on end? Feels like it. I've missed you, too, Morgan. Very much. Welcome home. And Merry Christmas! How long can you stay?"

"Let me at least take off my hat and coat and sit down. Hm, a real chair. Not sure I remember. . ."

Jolie took his snow-soaked slouch hat and heavy overcoat.

"Silly moose," she said. Once when she had been little, her father had called her a silly goose. The next time she used the phrase herself, she had transformed it into 'silly moose,' and that's what she had said ever since then. "Sit down. What do you want, tea, coffee, cocoa?"

"How about if you sit down with me for a minute and stop fast-firing questions," he said good-naturedly.

Jolie went and hung up his hat and coat, then returned and obediently sat on the sofa across from his old armchair.

He cocked his head to the side and studied her. "You look different. You're growing up. And it seems like every time I don't see you for a while, I'm always surprised by how pretty you are. And you're filling out. You don't look so much like a gawky little girl anymore."

"I was going to thank you for the compliment," Jolie said with mock wrath, "but now I think I'll pinch you instead. But I don't want to talk about me, Morgan. I want to know everything, everything about you, and General Lee, and the horses, and the Yankees—"

A shadow crossed his face, and now Jolie saw that when he wasn't smiling weariness and sorrow marred his smooth features. "Jolie, I wish I could give you everything that you want right now," he said with an attempt at lightness, "but I can't talk about me right now. All I want to think about, and talk about, is home. Please?"

"Of course, Morgan," she said quickly. "I'm sorry. I didn't think. Why don't we go to the kitchen and get mugs of hot coffee, as we used to do, and then go to the stables?" She smiled slyly. "I know you're going to pretend you came home to see us, but we all know you too well. You only came home to see the horses."

"I did not!" he said with indignation. "I missed you all so much, and I'm dying to see everyone. Right after I check on the horses, of course."

They spent the entire afternoon seeing the horses, the stables, riding around the pastures, inspecting the barn and the storeroom and the root cellar and pantry. "Looks like we've still got plenty of stores," Morgan said with relief. "For both the humans and the horses."

"I'm glad horses can't eat meat and vegetables," Jolie said mockingly, "or the humans would be eating oats and barley."

Morgan requested that Amon and the entire family join him at supper at the dining table in the farmhouse. "And that means you, too, Evetta," he said sternly. "No hopping up and down and serving us. I want you to sit down and eat with us like a Christian woman."

"I'll do that, but I s'pect only till they's something you want out in the kitchen," she said suspiciously.

"If there is, I'll get it myself," he said. "If there's one thing Perry and Meredith have taught me, it's that I am most definitely not Marse Robert, so I can wait on my own self along with all of the other lesser beings in the world."

They had supper late, and true to her word, Evetta sat down like a Christian woman. Morgan said a heartfelt prayer of thanks for their family and for the great bounty of their meal. Everyone else had, without being told, understood Morgan's need for a time free from dealing with worries with life-and-death consequences, and they kept the conversation airy and cheerful.

As they were finishing up with pecan pie and coffee, Morgan said, "Now tell me all about everyone from Fredericksburg who stayed here after the evacuation. I'm not even sure who was here."

Everyone turned to Jolie, and she swallowed hard. But she managed to say blithely, "You know about the Bledsoes, of course, and Ellie Cage and Mr. and Mrs. Patrick and Will Green. But you didn't know the Cogginses, did you? Or the Archers. First, let me tell you all about Connie Archer. She's just a wonderful woman. . . ."

Jolie went on telling Morgan about the good things, the funny things, the odd little quirky things that one didn't know about people until living with them. She said very little about the Bledsoes, and what she did say was kind.

Jolie noticed that Amon and Evetta were listening to her with approval written all over their honest faces. Evetta even smiled at her.

They all sat at the table laughing and talking for over two hours. Even when Evetta finally rose to clear the table, everyone, even the men, helped her. They all trooped out to the kitchen, and Evetta made a fresh pot of coffee.

At ten o'clock, Morgan suddenly yawned hugely. He looked vaguely surprised, as if he'd been ambushed by a practical joker.

Jolie and Ketura giggled.

"I must be getting old. Next thing you know I'll be dribbling soup down my chin and forgetting where I put my teeth," Morgan grumbled. Then he grew sober. "But before I go to bed, there's something I have to tell you all."

They all grew very still.

Morgan went on, "I have to go back, first thing in the morning."

"Oh, no," Jolie whispered, but it sounded loud in the quiet kitchen.

"I have to, Jolie," he repeated firmly. "And this may be the last leave I'll have for—well, I can't know for how long, because I'm not requesting leave anymore. You see, I thought about it the whole time I was riding here. It's not fair. In fact, I feel guilty, almost dishonorable, taking a leave right now. There are thousands and thousands of men who are far away from home. They can't just saddle up and ride to their farms in an afternoon. Some of them haven't been home in two years. In good conscience, I can't come home and then go back and face them."

"But they would do the same thing if they were only ten miles from home!" Jolie cried. "And I'm sure General Lee would give them a leave, just as I know he must have given one to you, or you wouldn't be here!"

"He probably would, if in fact we all asked him for leaves, which of course we don't," Morgan said, taking the sting out of his words by speaking very gently. "But in any case, General Lee himself won't even take a leave to go home. I know that President Davis urged him to visit Mrs. Lee in Richmond, but he refused, and I know why he did. It's because he believes that he must set an example for his men and also because he very consciously shares the hardships of his men. It's the same thing when people send him food or ask him to stay at their homes. He sends the food to the hospitals and eats our rations. Unless he's so ill he has to stay in bed, he lives in his tent. Even that is plain and simple and without any luxuries. The only frill he has, if you can call it that, is a little brown hen named Abigail. She lives under his cot and lays him an egg every morning," Morgan finished with an oddly sad smile.

"But I still don't understand," Jolie said stubbornly. "That's all very admirable of General Lee, but like you said, Morgan, you're not Marse Robert. You're not responsible for setting an example for tens of thousands of men."

"But I am," he said slowly. "We all are."

Jolie decided to leave Morgan in peace for the night, but she knew that she simply must ask him about Leona Bledsoe before he left in the morning. She tossed and flailed around, turning her bed into a mare's nest trying to think of how to ask him about Leona without upsetting him or worrying him. Finally she thought, *If he's not in love with her, then nothing I say will upset him, and if he is in love with her, then nothing I say will worry him. Now I'm the silly moose.* Finally she slept soundly.

She must have awakened as soon as Morgan did, in a glowing dawn. Quickly she dressed then ran downstairs to wait for him.

He came down about five minutes later.

She met him at the bottom of the stairs, saying, "I knew you'd try to sneak out, but you're not going to get away with it, mister."

"I wouldn't try to sneak anything past you, Jolie," he said, grinning. "You're too smart for me. In fact, I'm finding out that most ladies are." He took her arm and started toward the back door.

Jolie plucked at his sleeve and asked, "Now that you've

mentioned it, could I talk to you for a minute before we go get breakfast?"

"Sure," he said, doing a quick turn and leading her into the study. "Mentioned what?"

"Ladies," Jolie said as carelessly as she could. "I wanted to ask you about one."

"Ah, I bet I know who. Leona Bledsoe, right?" he said playfully as he handed Jolie onto the sofa, and he settled into his old shabby chair. "I forgot to tell you yesterday. Well, I guess I forgot to tell you because there's nothing to tell you."

"Morgan," Jolie said, summoning all her patience, "make sense."

"That's just it. I can't even really tell you why I got so weird about Leona," he said, obviously perplexed. "Just minutes after I had sent Rosh off that night, I started wondering about my silly self. I kept thinking, why send the carriage after the Bledsoes? They're a wealthy, prominent family with loads of friends and resources. Why not send the carriage for Ellie Cage and the baby? Or the Patricks?" He shrugged. "I guess it was just some throwback gut reaction. 'Send the carriage for the Bledsoes.' Kind of pathetic of me, I feel like now."

Jolie was so enormously relieved she almost felt dizzy. She felt silly and rather pathetic herself, letting Leona Bledsoe make her so miserable. She knew Morgan Tremayne as well as she knew herself. In fact, she probably understood Morgan better than she did herself. Morgan could never love and honor the woman she had seen here, in those difficult weeks. Jolie didn't know what Leona had been like before, and she didn't care. Now Morgan was here, and now Jolie knew that he loved her deeply. He may not love her in the way that she loved him—with a deep, desperate longing and passion—but he certainly did not love Leona Bledsoe in that way, either.

Morgan was watching her curiously, and finally he asked, "Jolie? Leona didn't insult you, did she? Amon was telling me that she was the worst harridan that ever lived while she was here. I can't imagine Leona acting like a snarling fishwife, but apparently she did. So, did she say something ugly to you, Jolie?"

Jolie smiled radiantly. "I hope never to lie to you, Morgan, so I will tell you that yes, she did. But I also will tell you that I don't care about that now, not in the least."

"Good," he said with relief. "Because after what Amon told me, I realized that Leona is far beneath your notice. You're a nobler, more honorable person than she has ever been. She's not the grand lady, Jolie. You are."

In an hour Jolie stood holding Vulcan's bridle, looking up at Morgan. *Do not cry*, she told herself sternly, *until after he leaves*. "I'll miss you, Morgan," she said softly, her dark eyes like rich velvet. "I'll pray for you always. Good-bye." She let go of Vulcan's bridle.

"Good-bye, Mouse," he said.

She watched him until he disappeared into the snowy woods.

CHAPTER TWENTY-THREE

Although the Battle of Fredericksburg had been a ghastly defeat for the North, and the Army of the Potomac had crept away in the middle of the night as they had done before, this time they didn't retreat all the way back to the safety of Washington. They stayed on the far side of the Rappahannock River, ranging up and down in their thousands, looking for another way to get at the apparently unbeatable team of Robert E. Lee, Stonewall Jackson, and James Longstreet. And so, General Lee and his army settled into winter quarters in his old tent on the hills behind Fredericksburg.

When Private Morgan Tremayne reported back for duty on December 26, 1862, that is where he went. In the coming months, although his gaze and his mind often went fifteen miles to the northeast, he was determined not to ask for leave until Robert E. Lee did.

On January 20th of the new year, General Ambrose Burnside, who had been devastated both personally and publicly by his ignominious defeat, again marshaled his army to cross the Rappahannock River to attack the Rebels. It rained for four days and four nights. The army became so mired down in Virginia sludge that they had to give up and retreat. It was dubbed Burnside's Mud March, and this debacle finished off Burnside. He was replaced on January 26th by General Joseph Hooker as commander of the Army of the Potomac.

By the end of January, Morgan was beginning to see that being in the army did not mean going from glory to glory in a series of battles. What it meant was weeks and months in camp, resting and refitting from the last battle and preparing for the next one. Morgan was lucky, he knew. He was never bored because he had his horses. He could, and did, spend all day feeding them, grooming them, exercising them, shoeing them, diagnosing and doctoring them.

He was riding Vulcan one bright morning when he came upon some troops from Georgia and Texas who whooped and hollered as they played in the snow. It was obvious that they had never seen such a phenomenon. As delighted children invariably do in a good sticky snow, a snowball fight started. Morgan walked Vulcan around for hours, because by early afternoon he estimated there must have been at least five thousand men, spread out for miles around, in snowball fights. He grinned so much that his face hurt that night.

Morgan had told Amon that he could come to camp twice a month as long as the Yankees stayed on the other side of the Rappahannock. Each time he came, he brought food for Morgan and hot mash for the horses. Morgan shared the food with Meredith and Perry and all the other officers' lowly privates and servants. But he jealously gave the hot mash only to Traveler and Vulcan and the staff officers' horses.

Amon also brought good news from Jolie and from Rapidan Run. The horses and foals were doing very well, and the army had sent two dozen men to harvest the winter forage crop. At the end of February, Morgan asked hesitantly, "Does Jolie ever ask to come with you?"

"No, sir," Amon replied. "I think she knows that'd prob'ly worry you too much."

Morgan was relieved. He hadn't forbidden Jolie to come to camp, because he wanted no shadows of war to dim that perfect Christmas day. But he had hoped that she would comprehend that it would be a hardship for him. He began to realize how very mature and wise she had grown to understand that.

At the end of March, General Lee grew ill, and for the first time he agreed to be moved to a private house near Fredericksburg. He wrote to Mary:

> *I am suffering with a bad cold as I told you, and was threatened, the doctors thought, with some malady which must be dreadful if it resembles its name, but which I have forgot.*

The doctors called it an inflammation of the heart sac. It was a very serious condition.

April came; spring came; warm weather came; and with it came the Army of the Potomac. They crossed the Rappahannock above Fredericksburg, over 138,000 strong, and marched west then south. They came to the Rapidan River and began their crossing at Germanna Ford and Ely's Ford. The roads from the fords led into the Wilderness, and by May 1st, they were concentrated in the largest clearing in that blighted wood. The only three roads in the Wilderness intersected there, and because of that the clearing with the one old house was called Chancellorsville.

❧

Morgan felt as if every single nerve ending in his body were raw when he found out that the Yankees had crossed the Rapidan and were invested along the south banks all the way to where it flowed into the Rappahannock. That meant that Rapidan Run was now behind enemy lines. Dread and fear overcame him, but only for a few moments. The reality was that he could not help Jolie and Amon's family by going to them, even if it had been possible. The best thing he could do was pray for victory and deliverance. After a short wordless prayer to that effect, he turned his mind to those things that he could do: he took care of the horses and followed General Lee.

Morgan had never put himself forward to General Lee, but he did so the night of May 1st. General Lee had come to the edge of the forest south of Chancellorsville to consult with General Jackson. Before Jackson arrived, General Lee pored over a crude map with several of his officers. Morgan stood nearby holding the horses, as usual, but in the close woods he was nearer to the conference than usual. He heard one colonel say, "Perhaps we can find a local who knows the country, General Lee."

Without thinking, Morgan sprang forward and said, "General Lee, sir? I know these woods. This is very near my home."

General Lee turned to look at him quizzically then recognition dawned on his face. "That's right," he said quietly. "I remember, Rapidan Run Horse Farm. Tell me, Private Tremayne, can you tell me if we are looking at this map upside down or right side up?"

In fifteen minutes Morgan had improved their map greatly, and then Stonewall Jackson arrived. Morgan withdrew back to the horses, and the two men moved away from their officers to lay out the map on the ground and study it. This meeting was memorialized by the humble name of the "Crackerbox Meeting," because that's what Lee and Jackson sat on as they decided the disposition of the entire army. The conversation ended with three simple words so typical of General Lee. "Well," he told Stonewall, "go on."

The next morning Hooker's Union forces advanced. . .and successfully. But once again, the fey fear that seemed to strike Union generals who faced Robert E. Lee assaulted the swaggering "Fighting Joe" Hooker, and he ordered all to fall back to Chancellorsville and hold a defensive position. This, of course, gave Robert E. Lee what he loved most: the initiative.

The fighting was fierce on May 2nd and 3rd, and on that day, they broke the Union line, and Hooker withdrew a mile. By May 6th, the vast army had fled back across the Rappahannock. Lee had beaten them with only sixty-two thousand men, and those split up into three forces.

When he heard that the Yankees had withdrawn from the Rapidan, Morgan was so relieved he felt weak. But even though he was only about seven miles from his home, he didn't see Rapidan Run. General Lee quickly gathered the wounded and the men in the field, and the march back to the heights above Fredericksburg began.

Morgan had heard on May 3rd that Stonewall Jackson had been wounded somewhere in the Wilderness, shot by his own men because of the overlying spirit of unease and confusion that seemed to rule in that place. He was anxious and disheartened when he heard the news.

On Sunday, May 10th, General Jackson crossed his last river to rest under the shade of the trees. Morgan was deeply saddened, and he saw many battle-hardened veterans weep unashamedly at the news. The entire South mourned.

General Lee, however, had little time to weep, even for his most beloved comrade in arms. In June, the Army of Northern Virginia would invade the North for the second time.

❧

Morgan was always acutely aware that his view of the war was vastly different from that of other soldiers. As he wrote Jolie, "I hold the horses while the real soldiers fight the war."

He had never been in battle. He had always observed it from afar, standing behind General Lee and talking softly to Vulcan and Traveler. Sometimes it was not so "afar" that Morgan didn't feel the hot rush from artillery shells screaming over his head or the sharp whistle of a rifle round close to his ear. Robert E. Lee liked to get as close to the battle line as possible and still retain a coherent view of the field. Sometimes that was close to people shooting at each other, indeed.

Of course Morgan saw the aftermath, the grisly bodies, the little creeks and streams running crimson, the horror of wounds of war. But though these images were the most vivid and graphic, they were but a small fraction of his memories. Most of the pictures that loomed large in his mind were very different, of quiet evenings with Meredith and Perry, of the few times that General Lee had groomed Traveler while Morgan groomed Vulcan, and they talked of little inconsequential things, of the strange predatory exultation he had felt on Lee's Hill above Fredericksburg.

Two little incidents that happened on their march north imprinted on Morgan's mind, and he knew for the remainder of his life they would become part of his most vivid recollections of Robert E. Lee.

On June 25th, General Lee, riding his beloved Traveler, crossed the Potomac River into Maryland. On the Yankee side of the river, a group of ladies holding umbrellas in the drizzly rain were waiting for him. They stepped in front of him, and General Lee courteously dismounted to doff his hat and bow. As always, Morgan slipped forward to take Traveler's reins.

The ladies were on a mission. They had an enormous wreath of white roses for Traveler to wear as a garland. General Lee was silent for a fraction of a second, and behind him Morgan thought, *He's horrified. I can almost hear him thinking. . .things like that are all fine and good for General Stuart, but. . .* Morgan had difficulty keeping a straight face.

At a stand, the general balked. But the ladies were very insistent. Still General Lee declined the honor. Finally Morgan stepped forward slightly, doffed his hat to the ladies, and said, "General Lee, perhaps I may have the honor of carrying this magnificent garland and walking beside you and Traveler."

Though reluctantly, the ladies assented. Morgan walked into

Maryland by General Lee's side, holding a rose garland in his arms, Vulcan's reins tied to his belt. As soon as they were out of sight of the ladies, General Lee said, "I believe you may mount up again, Private Tremayne."

The next day, in the afternoon, they crossed into Pennsylvania. At the head of the column rode General Lee, his uniform immaculate, his seat on Traveler perfect, as nobly handsome as when he was the Marble Model.

As the army marched through a small town, a group of well-dressed women stood on the walk in front of a large house to watch the invaders. A young girl stood in front of the women, defiantly waving an American flag. When she saw General Lee, she lowered the flag and said loudly enough for a hundred men following the general to hear, "Oh! I wish he was ours!"

Lee's plan was to draw the Yankees into battle at Harrisburg, which would enable him to cut their east–west communications. On their way out of Chambersburg, General Heth heard of a supply of shoes in nearby Cashtown, and he sent a brigade for them, since many men in the army were barefoot. They found themselves engaged by Union cavalry. Within the next two days, following the capricious tangents of war, the two armies found themselves in the little sleepy town of Gettysburg.

People remembered the fields of battle at Gettysburg. Soon everyone in the South and in the North knew the Peach Orchard, the Wheat Field, Devil's Den, Round Top, Little Round Top. But the one that Southern people always recalled with anguish was Cemetery Ridge. Here was where they charged when Major General George Pickett led his division of thirteen thousand Rebels and seven thousand of them fell.

On that hot, dusty afternoon, General Lee took his hat off and rode with the remnant as they streamed back to the safety of Confederate lines. "This was all my fault," he said. "It is I who have lost this fight, and you must help me out of it the best you can."

On July 4, 1863, the defeated Army of Northern Virginia

retreated back toward the Potomac River and the safety of Virginia soil. The train of wounded stretched more than fourteen miles.

～

After Gettysburg, the army quartered south of the Rapidan, about twenty-five miles west of Fredericksburg. General Lee established his field headquarters at Orange Court House. Morgan wished valiantly for the old quarters on the hills above Fredericksburg. One reason was that the brush shelter he and Rosh had built for the horses had proved to be as sturdy and almost as weatherproof as a log cabin. The other reason was that he was too far away from Rapidan Run for Amon to be able to come to camp.

For the first time since he had joined the army, he was homesick. He missed Jolie, and he missed Rapidan Run. His homesickness always took that form in his mind, in that order, and it interested him when he realized it. He missed Jolie terribly, perhaps even more than he missed his home. Why was that? How had that happened? In his disheartened state, he honestly didn't know. All he knew was that it was true, and this revelation only made him more forlorn.

In August, when they finally settled down in the fields and pastures around Orange Court House, bleak news from the western theater greeted them. In May and June, a rising star Union general named Ulysses S. Grant had besieged the vital city of Vicksburg, Mississippi. On July 4th, the day the Army of Northern Virginia had begun their retreat from Gettysburg, Vicksburg had surrendered. Longstreet was sent west, to help in the defense of Chattanooga.

In September, they were elated when they heard of a resounding victory by Confederate General Braxton Bragg at Chickamauga. In November, they were utterly downcast when the news of Chattanooga's surrender reached them.

Even though life in camp could be monotonous, Morgan was glad that the army fought no great battles in the winter of 1863–1864. They could not recover so readily from the defeat at

Gettysburg, the first they had known. And they were hungry, they were short of blankets, they were threadbare, and they were ill-shod. Morgan spent much of the time helping the quartermasters as they implored Richmond for supplies and searched desperately for new sources.

But as surely as the dawn follows the darkest night, renewed hope and strength come in springtime. By March of 1864, the army was still poorly fed and many were still barefoot, but the days were warm and the air was scented with jasmine. Men found renewed vigor in their hearts and minds and renewed strength in their reverential loyalty to Robert E. Lee.

Darwin's theory of evolution was hotly argued in some quarters of the camp. But one carefree spring day, an earthy veteran told the debating scholars, "Well, boys, the rest of us may have developed from monkeys, but I tell you none less than God could have made such a man as Marse Robert."

❧

In May, the Army of the Potomac crossed the Rappahannock again. This time they didn't poke along as they had under General McClellan, they didn't procrastinate for days as they had under General Burnside, and they didn't swagger in a parade as they had under General Hooker. They marched fast and relentlessly now, for they had a new commander, Ulysses S. Grant, and he was a true man of war.

Grant's orders were identical to Hooker's in one area alone. He ordered the army to cross at Germanna Ford and Ely's Ford and to march into the Wilderness. On May 3rd, Morgan stood by the side of the Plank Road, holding the horses while General Lee conferred with General Longstreet, thinking grimly that it had been exactly a year since he had looked at that dark forest. Again sickening dread assailed him when he thought about Rapidan Run, in danger of being overrun by the Union Army.

He deliberately eavesdropped on General Lee's conversation

this time. Lee knew of the Union crossings at the fords on the Rapidan, but he did not yet know the exact disposition of the Union Army. "I believe he will make a feint around on my left," he told Longstreet, "but I believe the main attack will come on our right. I wish that we had a clearer picture of their concentrations, but the dispatches come fast and furiously, and they are often hazy and confused."

Morgan stepped up to the two men, saluted, and said, "General Lee, I would like to volunteer to scout out the Federal concentration on your right."

Lee studied him. "I believe that you would be an excellent scout, Private Tremayne, for I've seen before how well you know this country. However, you are not a trained soldier, and through no fault or reluctance of your own, you have no experience in battle."

"That's true, sir. But I assure you that I can find the easternmost Yankee pickets, and I will take great pains to assure that they do not find me," Morgan said forcefully. "If they do find me, though, I will strive to do my duty, sir."

Lee nodded as if that were obvious, but he argued in his gentle manner. "In the morning I will send my two best observers, who have performed this same sort of covert task for me many times. I believe that would be the better course."

But Morgan was determined. "Sir, there is just one more thing I would like for you to consider before making that your final decision."

"And what is that, Private?"

"I can find them in the dark."

❧

Just as twilight descended, Morgan mounted Vulcan, said a quiet good-bye to Perry and Meredith, and headed across the plains toward the southern border of the Wilderness. He was challenged several times, because Confederates were camped all over the roads and fields and pastures, waiting to be told exactly where to march to engage the enemy.

Each time he was challenged, Morgan replied, "Scout from headquarters" and started to retrieve his orders from General Lee. But not one man looked at it. After seeing him clearly they waved him on. Morgan didn't realize it, but he was a well-known figure because he rode with General Lee. They called him Marse Robert's horsemaster.

He went to a southeast point on the border of the woods and without hesitation plunged into the dim gray shadows of the Wilderness. After Vulcan had trotted forward a few steps, Morgan pulled him to a stop. He knew that if he waited and made himself relax for a few minutes, his eyes would adjust to what seemed like impenetrable blackness. Slowly the darker shapes began to form themselves into recognizable things—trees and boulders and an earth mound and a tangle of vines. Morgan could see. He gave Vulcan the lightest of kicks, and the horse walked slowly forward.

Morgan reflected that his mission would seem like the worst of folly to anyone else, and rightly so. Men got lost in the Wilderness in glaring daylight, and finding one's way at night seemed impossible. But to Morgan it was not. He had good night vision and sharp instincts for place and direction, but that was not what gave Morgan confidence at night in the Wilderness. It was because he knew this place so well, because he had taught himself. In the years that he had been at Rapidan Run, he had ridden into some part of the forest bordering his land almost every day. He had regarded it as a self-imposed challenge, to learn of this place. He had spent nights traveling through the woods, constantly mapping the place in his head, until he found a good place to camp. He wasn't afraid of the Wilderness, because he knew it.

But other men would fear it, because even courageous men feel vulnerable and apprehensive in a thick forest at night. Morgan was pretty sure he knew where the small squads of outlying pickets would be. About midway on the east side of the Wilderness were three little clearings, all roughly in a line from east to west, separated by the uneven ground of ridges and ravines, some of the dozens of small streams that traced all through the woods, and piles of sharp boulders and rocks. Morgan knew that three or four men alone at night in this place would want any open space they could find, instead of trying to sleep in a hostile jungle of stunted scrub pine, thorny tangles of vines, and tall misshapen oaks looming over them.

He sensed, rather than calculated, that he was nearing the first clearing, and he dismounted. "Be very, very quiet," he whispered to Vulcan. He began to creep forward. It was eerily quiet. The only noise was the occasional *shreep, shreep* of a cricket, its cheerful call odd and jangling in the portentous silence. Morgan was careful to gently pull any branches and vines away so that he and Vulcan could pass quietly.

Ahead and on his left was a group of white boulders, the biggest of them almost six feet tall. They gleamed dimly in the scant starlight, and Morgan was glad to see this landmark. About a hundred feet past the boulders in a straight line was the first clearing. Confidently now, Morgan made his way to the large boulder. At exactly the same moment he stepped around it, he heard a hoarse whisper.

"We aren't ever going to find—"

He came face-to-face with two Yankees.

The next few moments Morgan remembered as if he were a bystander, for he moved and acted on pure instinct, without conscious thought. He reached behind him and grabbed his rifle from the saddle sheath. In a smooth, swift movement, he twirled it to hold it like a club and hit the nearest man across the head. He reeled then fell hard, and Morgan heard a sickening crack as his head hit a rock.

Directly behind the first man, the second soldier raised his rifle and fired point-blank at Morgan's stomach, but either the rifle was not loaded or it misfired. To see that rifle barrel right at his gut made Morgan pause for a fatal second. The Yankee was quick, and now he grabbed his rifle barrel, reared back, and planted a vicious blow right across Morgan's left temple.

The lurid sight before his eyes instantly began to fade to black, and Morgan could feel himself falling but couldn't seem to stop himself.

He barely registered that Vulcan rushed to him, rose up, and hit the soldier with both hooves right in the chest. The man was knocked backward several feet and lay on his back, all breath gone. Vulcan moved forward to rear over him and stamp him, but the man rolled to his right and crawled away into a thick tangle of undergrowth. Vulcan neighed, a screaming trumpet sound, nose pointed to the sky, galloped headlong into the jungle of vines and shrubs, and disappeared from the death scene.

The blackness finally claimed Morgan.

❧

It seemed to Morgan that he regained consciousness in one heartbeat, because the blood pushed through his head was hot and burning as if he had liquid lava in his veins. Each throb of his pulse was a second of agony. He lay still and motionless, thinking that if he didn't move, the pain would lessen. But it did not.

Resignedly he decided to open his eyes and try to sit up, for he was uncomfortable lying on the rocky ground. He opened his eyes. At least, he thought he had opened his eyes. But he saw nothing at all but featureless black, no shadows, no murky outlines of trees and boulders. He squeezed his eyes shut, which felt like an explosion in his head, then opened them again. Still nothing.

Panicky now, he scrabbled with his feet and pushed up with his hands until he was kneeling. He reached up to feel his eyelids, frantically thinking that they would not open, and his fingers gouged right into his eyeballs.

His eyes were wide open, and he was blind.

For an eternity, it seemed, he knelt there, his eyes straining and popping out of his head. He swiveled his head around in a futile effort to see. His brain said, "You're blind," but his body fought it. Every muscle was as rigid as stone, his mind was a single energy screaming a single word over and over: "See! See! See!"

But the strain overtaxed Morgan's shocked system, and he grew weak and limp, and his thoughts became thick and murky. He drew in a deep shuddering breath and began to feel again the horrendous pain in his head. He put his shaking hands to his temples, then slowly his fingers went to his eyes, and he deliberately closed his eyelids. With a jaw-hardening effort of will, he made himself calm down and concentrate.

Morgan had always been a man of action, but in different ways than that term usually denotes. He was a fixer. If he faced a problem, he formulated a plan then went to work and fixed the problem. If he had a monumental project, he broke it down into manageable steps and worked until he had finished completely. He could not bear passivity. To him it was the same as stagnation, and he must always be moving forward to accomplish the task in front of him. That was why, with no combat experience and no natural aggressiveness to speak of, he had instantly attacked the Union soldiers the moment he saw them. They were a problem, and he fixed it.

As these thoughts slowly plodded through his mind, Morgan decided to shift into a more comfortable sitting position, and he put his hands down to steady himself. His hands rested on a man's chest.

Morgan shot up and took a step backward, tripped over a rock, and fell sprawling on his back. It knocked the breath out of him, and again he panicked as he struggled to pull air into his chest. But as he started breathing the panic subsided. *I killed him*, Morgan thought with a strange indifference. *He's dead. I killed him.*

And now Morgan's tidy, efficient mind simply took over and compartmentalized all the jumbled thoughts and shocking images and deep fears, even the pain. It was as if a shutter closed, hiding all the confusion in another part of his brain, leaving him in a small, tightly controlled and clear and logical place.

He sat up and felt around him for a support, but there was nothing but small rocks and ground-covering vines surrounding him. He crossed his legs and thought, *I'm in the Wilderness. I was scouting for the pickets, and I came upon those two soldiers.* He could remember hitting the one and hearing his head crack savagely on a rock. But he remembered little after that. He wondered why the other soldier hadn't killed him. Then he wondered if he had killed the other soldier, too, but he wasn't about to go crawling around, feeling his way, trying to find another dead body. It wouldn't help anything. He was alive, and he was alone in the Wilderness.

He thought of Vulcan, but after considering it, he wasn't at all surprised that the horse had bolted. Vulcan was high-strung, but he was smart, and after all, they were only about three miles from Rapidan Run.

That thought took Morgan's breath away even quicker than his headlong fall had done.

Only three miles. Only three miles! It might as well be three hundred, or three thousand! I am blind. I cannot find my way home!

Perilous weakness hit him again, his head felt as if it were splitting into little jagged pieces, and he was nauseated. Trembling, he got to his hands and knees, crawled a couple of feet, and vomited. And then he was sick again and again until he knew his system was completely empty.

He half-fell as he turned away, then went down and crawled on his belly a few feet. Letting his head fall into his hands, he thought with anguish, *I always did something. I always figured out how to make things right, how to make them work, how to accomplish everything I set out to do. But now my worst fears have come to me, I'm helpless. Utterly, completely helpless.*

Morgan wandered in the darkness, both physical and spiritual, for a long time. He found himself praying with a desperation he had never known. *Oh God, what can I do? Please, please, tell me.*

Show me something, anything! Please, let me see a way out!

Very gently, as if God had barely touched his shoulder, Morgan felt the answer. There was no task he could accomplish. There was no way out. There was nothing he could do.

Nothing except surrender. For the first time in his life, scalding tears sprang to his sightless eyes and fell into his hands as they cupped his face. It was the hardest thing he had ever done, to do nothing. Calmly now he prayed, *I am in Your hands, Lord. Thy will be done.*

Morgan marveled at the feeling of the presence of God, a sharper, more vivid sense than sight alone could ever give. He rested and meditated and prayed and was completely at ease.

Only a few miles away, he heard the opening salvo of big guns and the sharp constant crackle of musket fire began. Abruptly Morgan remembered that he was in the Wilderness, and probably less than a mile to his left was the flank of a force of about seventy-five thousand Yankees. It was daytime, he suddenly realized. Because he saw only darkness, he had, quite naturally he supposed, assumed it was still night. *I may not be able to see where they are, but I can sure run away from the sound of the guns.*

But no, he couldn't run anywhere, he would surely fall with each step. Morgan could find his way in the dark, certainly, but only if he was walking or on horseback, scanning the entire scene in view. He didn't know every rock and ravine in the Wilderness.

In another reluctant surrender, he thought, *I guess it would only be sensible to sit here and hope I don't get shot and let the Yanks take me prisoner.* But on reflection he saw that would not be a sensible course at all. Coming from the east, assuming that the battle even swung this far over, the Union soldiers would see their dead comrade first, and there would be Morgan, sitting placidly by, an easy target for a soldier in heated battle mode. "The term 'sitting duck' comes to mind," Morgan said ruefully to himself. Aside from that, it went utterly against Morgan's every instinct to let himself be taken prisoner.

SURRÉNDER

I know, Lord, that I can't solve this situation, that by myself I can't fix this. But I don't think You just want me to sit here and die. Isn't there some way, something You could do to help me?

This humble plea was much more heartfelt than his indignant demands to God before. But there was still no answer. Morgan decided to crawl. He got up on his hands and knees, turned so that he was facing away from the nearby battle din, and began. He cut his hand on the first rock, but he kept crawling. He knew he was moving so slowly that it was just about hopeless, but doggedly he kept on.

Morgan was already aware that his hearing had sharpened since he couldn't see, and he heard the soft tread of a shoed horse. Then a warm muzzle hit him on the shoulder so hard he fell over. Lying on the rocks, he murmured, "Vulcan? Is that you?"

Vulcan answered with a sarcastic snort and another blow to the shoulder. "Okay, okay," Morgan muttered, "take it easy. I'm blind, you know. It's not going to do you any good to knock me around."

Vulcan shifted his front hooves and impatiently bobbed his head. Morgan could hear the jingle of the bridle rings and the creaks of the leather very close to his ear. "Don't step on me, you big ninny. Let me think." Morgan pictured himself standing up, feeling for the stirrup, and swinging up into the saddle. And then he would be sitting there on a feisty horse, blind. That was crazy.

But it was better than crawling.

He pushed Vulcan's insistent nose away then, teetering a little, managed to stand up. He reached out with both hands and felt the horse's hot, muscular shoulder. He kept on. He felt the stirrup strap. In a move he had done thousands of times, he grabbed the saddle horn, put his left foot in the stirrup, kicked up and over with his right foot, and he was on horseback.

The minute he was sitting up there he felt horribly vulnerable, not only to bullets but to low tree branches and overhanging rocks. Helplessly he bent over and clasped his arms around Vulcan's strong neck. "I can't do it, boy. You're going to have to do this by yourself.

Please just take me somewhere, away from here."

Vulcan started walking slowly along, picking his way. Morgan's head began to pound again, and the sickening rolling of his stomach started up. He felt as if his whole body was spinning around, like a child's top, and vaguely he thought how odd it was that being dizzy felt so different when he couldn't see. The whirling sensation grew stronger, and Morgan fell unconscious again. This time he welcomed it.

CHAPTER TWENTY-FOUR

Morgan opened his eyes and said sadly, "Still nighttime. . ."

A low-timbred, rich voice answered, "Yes, it is." He felt a cool, soft hand smooth back his hair and smelled a faint, poignantly familiar scent of chamomile.

"Am I dead?" he asked curiously.

"No, no, no, Morgan, you're not dead. You're just injured."

He digested this for a while. "Are you Jolie?" he finally asked.

"What?" she exclaimed, though she kept her voice low and calm. "Of course it's Jolie. Don't you recognize me, Morgan dear?"

"I can't see you," he said quietly. "I'm blind."

The hand stroking his forehead stopped for only a moment then resumed. "I didn't know," she said simply. "You've been unconscious since you got here. This is the first time you've opened your eyes."

"Since I got here. . . You mean Vulcan brought me home?" he said, weakly incredulous.

"Yes, he did. And I cannot imagine how you stayed in the saddle. You were collapsed over his neck, arms hanging down. He must have come very slowly and carefully from wherever you were."

"We were in the Wilderness," he said wearily. "What day is it?"

"It's Thursday," she answered. Then seeing that it meant nothing to him, she added, "It's May 5th. The battle in the Wilderness started this morning and went on all day long until about an hour ago. It's about nine o'clock at night now."

"May 4th," he said, "that night. That's when we rode into the Wilderness, and I—there were some Yankees, and—something happened. I can't remember—"

"Ssshh, don't worry about that right now," Jolie said. "You'll remember in time."

"My head hurts," he said, reaching up and feeling the enormous swelling on the left side of his head.

Jolie took his hand in both of hers, settled it onto his chest, and patted it. "I'm going to get you some medicine."

He heard the tinkling of a glass and smelled it even before she pressed the glass to his lips. "Laudanum," he said, wrinkling his nose. "Don't we have any brandy left?"

"No, I'm sorry, we don't," she said. The two bottles of brandy that Jolie had stored away in the pantry had disappeared back in December, the day the Bledsoes left Rapidan Run. "But laudanum is better for severe pain, anyway. Drink it, please, Morgan. You'll rest, and that's what you need."

Obediently he took two gulps of the strong medicine. With a heavy sigh he lay back on the pillow and closed his eyes. His right hand groped for her, and Jolie took it and held it. "I'm so tired," he murmured.

"I know. You just relax and sleep, Morgan dear. You're home now, and you're safe."

This time, when the blackness overtook him, it brought a peaceful rest.

❧

Jolie held his hand until he was taking long even breaths and his grip on her hand relaxed. Silently she rose and went downstairs, leaving Morgan's bedroom door open.

Amon, Evetta, Ketura, Rosh, and Santo all sat at the dining room table, waiting.

When she entered, she put her finger to her lips to stop the questions she saw coming. "He's sleeping, and I left the door open so we can hear if he wakes up." She slid into her chair and stared down at the table. "He doesn't remember what happened. He just said that he was in the Wilderness last night."

"Last night?" Amon echoed. "Oh, ain't no tellin' about him. But Evetta says he wasn't shot or anything." Evetta and Jolie had taken off his filthy clothes, quickly bathed him, and put him in a comfortable, light linen nightshirt. His hands and knees were scratched and scraped, but other than the appalling bruise on his head, he didn't appear to be seriously injured.

"No, he wasn't shot," Jolie said. "But obviously something, or someone, hit his head hard. It's swelling up and turning bluer every minute. And—and—" She swallowed hard then continued, "He's blind."

A stunned silence lay heavy on the room.

Evetta said, "We gotta get a doctor."

"There's no doctor," Jolie said painfully. "There won't be any doctor, except in the field hospitals and then in Fredericksburg, or wherever the army ends up after this battle."

"Then what are we gonna do?" Amon asked worriedly.

"There's nothing we can do, except watch him and give him laudanum to help him rest so he can recover," Jolie said firmly.

No one said it, but the thought was almost tangible and audible in the quiet room: *If he recovers.*

❧

Jolie and Ketura took turns sitting with Morgan throughout the night. Evetta was willing, but all three of the women decided that it would be best for Jolie and Ketura to take care of Morgan.

Evetta was a magnificent cook, but she was a dismal nurse. In her kitchen she moved quickly and purposefully without a wasted moment or movement. In the sickroom she fumbled and ran into the bed and almost hit Morgan's ear when she was adjusting his pillow. Gladly she banished herself to the kitchen.

At about three o'clock in the morning, Jolie was sitting in the easy chair Amon had moved upstairs to Morgan's bedside. It was a tattered old armchair that had been in the corner of the study, unused except when Jolie wanted to snuggle up in it on winter nights. But it was soft and comfortable, the contours of her body well worn into it, and she could sleep in it.

Now she awoke from a light doze and stared at Morgan. All through the night he had been sleeping so heavily that she began to worry that he was unconscious again. She tensed up because she wanted to shake him awake, but then she realized how foolish that was. If he woke up, he woke up. If he was unconscious, shaking him wouldn't do any good anyway. After a while she dozed again, uneasily.

At four o'clock, Ketura came in and whispered, "I'll sit with him now, Jolie. Go get some good sleep."

Morgan still slept soundly. He hadn't even moved.

Jolie was still worried, but she knew she would have to get some sleep if she was going to be able to take good care of Morgan, so she went to bed.

Just an hour later, the roar of cannon shattered the quiet sunrise. Jolie jumped up and ran to Morgan's room without even pulling on her dressing gown.

Ketura, too, had stood up in alarm at the sudden crashing booms. "That's closer than yesterday," she said, her eyes big and round.

Morgan turned his head toward the west and the Wilderness. His eyes opened, but it was obvious from their emptiness that he wasn't seeing. "Artillery," he murmured dully.

Ketura went across the room to look out the window, but

it faced north. Even if it had faced west, she couldn't have seen anything except a dingy gray smoke from the cannon rising.

Jolie hurried to his bedside and, seeing the condition of his face, didn't want to even touch his forehead. She took his hand and stroked it. It felt cold, and Jolie herself felt a chill, for it was a warm morning. "Yes, it's sunrise, Morgan. It's begun again."

He licked his dry, swollen lips.

Jolie berated herself, for he obviously had a raging thirst. Quickly she poured him a glass of water then gingerly slipped her hand behind his neck. "If you can raise your head just a little, I have some water,"

"It hurts so badly," he whispered, but he did manage, with Jolie's help, to get up just enough to drink.

"Small sips, Morgan. Don't gulp," she warned him.

But it was too late. Jolie grabbed the basin just in time for Morgan to be helplessly sick.

Ketura rushed back but then stood there, unable to do anything.

"He's falling, help me," Jolie grunted, pushing on Morgan's shoulder.

He had leaned over the bed when he knew he was going to throw up, and he was so weak he was sliding out of the bed head-first.

Ketura grabbed his other shoulder, and between them they managed to push him back onto the bed.

"So. . .so sorry," he whispered, squeezing his eyes shut.

"No," Jolie said firmly. "No. Don't be sorry. Don't ever apologize. Now I want you to just lie back and relax, Morgan. Try to make yourself relax." She sat down in the chair and took his hand, then began lightly stroking it and murmuring softly to him, "It's me, Jolie, dear Morgan. You're home, and we're all going to take very good care of you. Just be calm, clear your mind, take nice even breaths. . . ." She kept up the soothing undertones until it seemed that he slept. But now it was different from the night before. He twitched, and he frowned. She saw his eyes moving erratically underneath his eyelids. "Oh, Morgan," she whispered to herself with anguish.

Jolie had forgotten about Ketura, but now the girl touched her shoulder lightly and bent down to whisper, "Jolie, you slept less than an hour before the cannon woke you up. Go on, go back to bed and at least get another hour or two of sleep. Go on, you're still in your nightdress."

"It doesn't matter," she said distantly. "He can't see me anyway."

"It does matter," Ketura said firmly, "and you know it. Besides, it won't do Mr. Tremayne one bit of good for you to sit here and pass out in that chair, which is what you'll do if you don't get some rest. Now is as good a time as any. I'll come wake you if there's any change."

"Come get me if he wakes up," Jolie insisted. "I don't care if it's ten minutes from now."

"All right, I will," Ketura promised.

Jolie tried to go back to sleep, but it was impossible. Battle raged near, and something was wrong with Morgan, she knew it. Something new. After about half an hour, she gave up, rose, and dressed. She went downstairs and out to the kitchen, where she knew Evetta and Amon would be. The boys were there, too.

"How is he?" Amon instantly demanded.

"I—I don't know. Something's wrong," Jolie said hesitantly. "I mean, of course something's wrong, but I mean he's not resting as well as last night, and it worries me."

Evetta's face was grim. "Jolie, we don't know how bad his injury is, really. It may be that—"

"No, don't say it!" Jolie said loudly. "I know it, Evetta. Just please don't say it."

Evetta nodded with understanding.

Amon shook his head. "Y'know, those guns there is closer than they was yesterday. We might end up in the middle of a big ol' bloody mess."

"I know, but what can we do?" Jolie said. Then her face changed. "Oh, Amon, Amon. Of course you need to get your family out of here. You all take the wagon and go now, before they get any closer."

Amon frowned darkly. "We thought of that, but we ain't gonna do any such thing. First place, I know you wouldn't let us move Mr. Tremayne, and you'd stay here with him, and that can't be. Second place, Mr. Tremayne, he'd kill us if we runned off and left his horses. And where are we gonna go, anyways? 'Crost the river? There's a big bunch of Yankees over there, and prob'ly in Fredericksburg and everywhere else 'round here they're crawlin' around. Onliest reason I said anything is to ask if you want us to hole up somewheres else, like the barn or the stables, maybe."

Jolie frowned. "I don't know, Amon," she said at last. "You and Evetta would be able to decide that a lot better than I could."

Amon's fierce visage softened. He, like everyone else, had forgotten that Jolie was only eighteen years old. "I think the Lord's going to have to watch over us whatever comes, and we might as well be comfortable in our houses as in a barn."

"Good," Jolie said heartily. "Maybe they won't get this far east," she said hopefully. "But if they do, you're right, Amon. I can pray for protection here as well as somewhere else." She hurried to the door.

Evetta sternly called after her, "I'm bringin' you up some breakfast, missy, and you're going to eat it."

"Yes, ma'am," she called over her shoulder.

The battle did not rage at Rapidan Run. The two armies clashed all day long in the Wilderness. Jolie reflected that she wasn't getting used to the continuous thunder of cannon and the spiking racket of thousands of muskets, but somehow she shut it out of her mind, and so she didn't really hear it. Besides, she was so concentrated on Morgan that she was barely aware of anything else at all.

At about noon, he suddenly started shivering uncontrollably. As lightly as a snowflake, she laid her hand on his forehead and knew that he had a fever. She started laying cool, wet cloths on his forehead, though he still shivered convulsively. His fever got so high, and the heat given off him was so intense that the cloths were too warm only seconds after she had applied them to his forehead. She worked steadily, methodically, continually wetting a cloth and wringing it out and replacing the warm one and starting again. Ketura came in, and Jolie only looked up at her and said darkly, "No."

After about an hour he stopped shivering, but then he started talking and thrashing about. "Not going to cold-shoe him. I've got to set up that forge," he said clearly, his eyes open and glaring but obviously unseeing. "Have to move that mare. She's too restless for Traveler." He was restlessly making odd motions in the air with both hands, and fitfully he tossed his head from side to side.

Jolie held his wrists and began to wonder desperately if she might be able to force some laudanum down his throat when he abruptly calmed down. His arms dropped limply to the bed, and he lay still against the pillow. After a few moments, his eyes slowly closed. He began to murmur, but he spoke so weakly and softly that Jolie couldn't understand anything he was saying.

Like an automaton, she began putting wet cloths on his forehead again, for he still gave off waves of heat from his entire body. She could feel it emanating from him when she bent over. Though outwardly she looked calm and controlled, inwardly she was ravaged by fear.

Is this brain fever? I've heard of it, and don't people always die from it? Oh, God, no, no, no! If he dies I'll kill myself!

No such dire thought had ever entered Jolie's mind, and she drew herself up with alarm. "That's not true," she whispered to herself. "I'm so sorry, Lord. I'm so sorry. . . ."

It was hard for her to gather her thoughts, but finally she was able to pray. *Oh Lord, You know my heart, You know how much I love him and how much it frightens me to think that he might die. I don't know if I even really mean this, Lord, but I say now to You: Your will be done. I pray for his healing, I pray that he will live, I pray that I'll have the chance to tell him how much he means to me, how he is my whole life. But if. . .if. . .You take him. . .Your will be done.*

She repeated these words and variations of them many times over, all afternoon into the evening. Ketura came in every half hour or so, but Jolie rarely even looked up, she was so absorbed in her prayers and attending Morgan. When Amon came in as night fell, she looked up and said with wonder, "They've stopped firing."

He nodded. "Artillery stopped after only coupla hours. The onliest reason we could hear the muskets this far is 'cause there must have been 'bout a hunnerd thousand of 'em blasting all at the same time. He crossed his muscular arms and said quietly, "The Wilderness, it's on fire."

"Is it close?" she asked anxiously.

"No, thank the Lord Jesus for another mercy on this day," he said fervently. "Them two armies stayed all bunched up 'bout four miles over, and that's where the fire is. I guess it might get over this far, but I doubt it. Calm night tonight, no wind, and it'd have to jump a coupla pretty good streams, Rosh and Santo tells me."

"Thank You, Lord," she said simply.

She had not thought it possible, but Morgan's fever seemed to go even higher as night fell. Every once in a while his whole body jerked, and he would say something she could hear, though his voice was thick and sluggish. Once he blurted out, "Tell Ketura I was wrong. It is haunted." Mostly he muttered things about caring for horses. An hour later he said, "Scout from headquarters, here's my pass." Still later, "Meredith, Perry, we've got to strike the tent."

Finally he got so quiet and still that Jolie, for a heartwrenching moment, thought that he had died. She knelt by his bedside and grabbed his hand, which still burned, to her great relief. Tiredly she laid her head down beside their clasped hands. *If he lives, I'm going to tell him. I have to. I won't while he's feverish and not able to understand. I'll wait until he's better. He'll get better. . .and I'll tell him, first thing.*

His fever lessened, but he sank visibly into a deep stupor. Jolie watched him hour after hour, clinging to his hand. She thought that she could actually see him wasting away. He seemed to be getting thinner, his jawbones and cheekbones on the uninjured right side of his head appeared to be more prominent. She was afraid to leave him, because she was terrified that each long breath was his last.

When the north windows grew into a light gray instead of charcoal gray, she knew it was dawn, and she thought that she was so agitated that she might be getting a fever herself.

The sun rose again, and the light now streaming through the windows seemed offensively bright and cheerful. Jolie rubbed her gritty eyes and stared back at Morgan. Then she leaned forward and laid her hand on his forehead then against his chest. There was no mistake, he was definitely cooler. In fact, he felt a little clammy, so she pulled the sheet up and gently arranged his arms outside it with his hands resting on his chest. He looked more natural that way.

Ketura came and went a couple of times.

Jolie thought it had been a couple of hours since dawn when Morgan slowly opened his eyes and then licked his lips. "Here, Morgan," she said, lifting his head and holding the glass to his lips. He took several small sips then laid back, seemingly content.

Jolie set down the glass and leaned over close to him. "Morgan, dear, it's Jolie. Can you hear me?"

"Sure," he whispered weakly. "Hi, Jolie."

"Hi," she said awkwardly. "I need to tell you something."

"Okay."

She stood up, leaned over, and cradled his face between her hands. She looked straight into his eyes, though she knew he couldn't see her. "Morgan, I love you. I love you so very much, with everything that is in me. I loved you when I first met you, when I was nine years old. I loved you with a child's love for years, until I knew that I loved you as a woman loves the man of her dreams. That's what you are to me, Morgan. You always have been. The best man I could ever dream of."

His eyes widened as she talked. When she finished, she let go, sat down in her easy chair, and took a deep breath. *I did it, Lord, and no matter what he says to me, I'm glad I did.*

Morgan turned his head as if he were watching her. "Jolie, are you sure?" he asked in a deep voice, much stronger than before.

"I'm sure. I've been sure for a long time."

"But I'm blind," he said darkly. "How could you love a blind man?"

"I don't love some blind man. I love you."

Her simplicity delighted him, and he managed a small smile. "I love you, too, Jolie."

"You do?" she said, astonished. "But how do you know? When did you know?"

"I'm not too sure about how I know," he admitted. "But I knew it for sure and certain when I woke up and you were there. I was so happy. I was so thankful that I loved you and you were with me that I thought I had died and gone to heaven."

She dropped to her knees by his bedside and pressed her lips to his hand. "No, you didn't die, and you didn't go to heaven. You just came home. Home to me."

❧

That day they heard no artillery, and if there were muskets firing, there weren't enough of them for the sound to travel to Rapidan Run. Morgan slept off and on all day and slept soundly and quietly for twelve hours that night. Two mighty armies only four miles away marched south.

The next day the armies clashed again at Spotsylvania. For two weeks, combat would rage all around Spotsylvania Court House.

Morgan was able to sit up enough to sip some beef broth boiled fortified with red wine.

Evetta had brought up a bowl and spoon, and Jolie started to feed Morgan.

A quick spasm of pain crossed his face, and he said, "Please, no, please don't feed me. Put it in a mug." He managed quite well.

For the next two days, fighting raged in a salient that came to be called the Bloody Angle. The men in blue and the men in gray locked in vicious hand-to-hand combat for twenty hours.

Morgan was able to sit up longer and gained strength to talk more. He asked Jolie to read *Great Expectations* to him. On the fourth night he was there, he didn't need any laudanum to help him sleep. The next day he asked Amon to help him get out of bed, and he sat in Jolie's chair for nearly an hour. He continued to improve daily.

On May 21st, Ulysses S. Grant, after battering futilely against the entrenched and fortified Army of Northern Virginia, disengaged from Spotsylvania and continued his advance south, toward Richmond. Lee parried him again at Cold Harbor. On June 3rd, the Union lost seven thousand men in one assault, a hopeless and needless engagement that Grant later heartily regretted. By June 15th, he had seen that the approaches to Richmond were too well defended, and so he shifted his army south toward Petersburg.

On that day, Morgan and Jolie sat outside on the front porch steps, holding hands.

"Morgan," she said decisively, "we have to get married."

He turned to her. Even though he still could see nothing at all, he always responded by turning to the speaker. "What?" he stammered. "Get married?"

"I am speaking English, you know," Jolie said very slowly and deliberately. "Yes. We have to get married. As soon as possible."

"But—but why do we have to get married?" Morgan said, bewildered.

"Don't make it sound like I'm telling you that you have to dig a ditch or something," Jolie said impatiently. "Don't you want to marry me?"

"Well, well, yes, sure. You just kind of took me by surprise. Uh—okay. But what's the hurry?"

Jolie rolled her eyes heavenward. "You know. I told you that I loved you, and you told me that you loved me. So that means that we want to be together forever and ever. And that means that we're engaged to be married. But I'm living with you, in your house, and that used to be all right, but now it's not. So we need to get married *fast.*"

Morgan listened to this undeniable progression of logic with amazement. Then he threw back his head and laughed. It felt good, and he thought that he couldn't remember the last time he had laughed out loud. "Hm, I'm beginning to see that you're going to be way ahead of me on some things."

"A lot of things, probably."

"A lot of things. So I guess you don't want to take a little time and think about it?"

"No, I don't have to because I've been dreaming about it since I was thirteen years old. And you can't use that excuse either. You've always been a man to go ahead and get done whatever you've decided to do."

"Like digging ditches," he said, "and now getting married. Okay. But I'm also a man that wants to do things right." He reached around to get his bearings, half stood, then groped until he could figure out how to kneel in front of Jolie on the step below her. He took her hand in his and said, "Jolie DeForge, I, too, love you with my whole heart. Even though I'm in darkness, when I'm with you I feel as if I'm standing in radiant light. Would you do me the very great honor of consenting to be my wife?"

And now Jolie was speechless.

Morgan leaned forward, and Jolie clasped him to her eagerly to kiss him for the first time. All the desire and longing coursed through her, and Morgan responded with his own long-denied passion. The kiss lasted for a long, long time.

❧

They were married on July 1, 1864, at Rapidan Run. The Reverend Melzi Chancellor, whose family owned the big house that had given its name to Chancellorsville, consented to come to the house to perform the ceremony. Their only witnesses were Amon and his family, and Jolie and Morgan couldn't have been happier.

"My family's going to kill me," he had said, "but they're just going to have to come to understand, as I did, that it was an emergency."

They were blissfully happy. It seemed that they were on an island, with their closest friends and their horses. War and sorrow and fear seemed far away.

In the middle of the month, they were in the stables early in the morning. Jolie was happily mucking out Rowena's stall, and Morgan sat on a stool. He faced her, and Jolie thought that if she hadn't known he was blind, she could swear he was watching her. He had lost that stark glare he'd had when he first came home. It had slowly gone away, along with the terrible swelling and bruising on the left side of his face. Now, a month and a half later, the only remnant was a slight swelling just on Morgan's left temple, behind the hairline.

As if he were reading her mind, he asked abruptly, "What do I look like?"

She smiled as she looked up, and she noted with interest that Morgan's frown lightened and the corner of his mouth twitched upward. *Maybe he is watching me,* she thought with amusement. *Somehow, in some way we don't understand. It's a miracle that he's here, and that I'm his wife. I'll believe in any gift You give me, Lord.*

"When I was nine years old, I remember the first day you came to DeForge House. That night I told Mr. DeForge that you were pretty."

"Pretty? No man wants to be pretty!" Morgan exploded.

"That's what he told me, but he was nicer and quieter about it," Jolie said severely. "But you are, in a way, you know. What I mean is that your face is fine, your features are clean-cut and clear, not heavy and thick like so many other men. You're not feminine, Morgan, but you are pretty."

"I'm not—oh, forget it," Morgan grumbled. "All I meant was did I still have bruising around my eye and cheekbone."

"No, you don't. Now get off that stool and get over here and help me curry Rowena," she said bossily.

He got up, felt his way over to the stall, found a curry brush hanging on a peg, and started on Rowena's right side while Jolie did her left. "I've wished a thousand times that I had seen you sometime during that year and a half I was away. I've still got stuck in my mind a little girl, looking up at me wide eyed and worried. And that Christmas day, when you were sitting in that raggedy old armchair, hugging your knees, looking out at the snow. . . You looked like a little girl then, too, peeping through a window out onto a fairytale land. I know you're no little girl, Jolie. I know you're a grown woman, and I know you must be beautiful," he said wistfully.

"Four hundred ninety-five days," she said. "I didn't see you for four hundred ninety-five days. Anyway, you can picture me in your mind, Morgan. And it will probably be better than I actually am."

"I doubt that," he said.

"Hand me the mane comb, would you? I'm going to really give her a going-over today," Jolie said. "And you're going to help me."

"Yes, ma'am," he said obediently, handing her the comb.

"You know, I was so worried about being black that I asked Evetta if it was even legal for us to get married," she said conversationally. "Everyone says I don't look—what's the matter?"

Morgan had stopped brushing the horse, and his eyes seemed to be focused on her face. He had an odd expression, half puzzlement, half amusement. "I forgot. I had forgotten that you are an octoroon."

"Had you? I'm not surprised," Jolie said airily. "I forget sometimes that you're blind."

"I don't, but I'm learning to live with it. But this reminds me, Jolie. I didn't marry some woman with black blood. I married you."

❧

In the first week of August, Will Green came riding up on his old mule, Geneva. They all greeted him joyously, for he was the first person they'd seen since April.

After a flurry of welcomes, Morgan said, "Come on, let's sit out here where it's cool, and Evetta will bring us something cool to drink. We're all starving for news."

Morgan had a cane now, hand-carved by Santo, who was turning into a skilled wood sculptor. He had formed the head of the cane into an eagle. Morgan took Will's arm and led him up the drive onto the grounds. "I can tell as soon as I get under this shed roof. The temperature drops about twenty degrees," he said.

Will stopped and looked around in wonder. Amon and the boys had built a low shed roof onto the front of the kitchen, which faced east. They had also built a long, heavy oak table and benches. "This here's new," Will said.

"Yes, we never really had a good place to sit in the back of the house," Morgan explained. "And I don't like to sit in the front yard. I like it back here, where I'm close to everything."

"But I mean, you still got nails? And planed boards and everything?" Will asked, slowly sliding onto the bench facing Morgan and Jolie.

"Yes, we've still got a lot of supplies and food, too," Jolie said. "Thanks to Morgan. People thought he was a coward because he didn't join the army right when the war started, but he spent that year traveling all over, getting everything we'd need."

Will shook his grizzly head. "You mean you ain't had no Yankees out here to clean you out? That's a miracle, pure and plain."

"The Lord's worked a lot of miracles in my life lately," Morgan said. "I'll tell you all about it, but first we'd like to hear all the news."

In his picturesque way, the saddler told him about the series of battles beginning with the Wilderness. "Caught on fire that second day of fightin'," he said, his old rugged face grieved. "Some men, they had their legs busted up and couldn't git out of the woods."

"Oh, no," Jolie said with horror.

"Thank God I got out of there the night before," Morgan said fervently. "Thank God."

Will went on to tell them of Spotsylvania, of the Bloody Angle, of Cold Harbor. "Now Marse Robert's dug in at Petersburg, and the bluebellies are diggin' in all around it. Looks like it's going to be a long time, them snipin' at each other in ditches."

Morgan sighed. "I feel so guilty because I haven't reported that I was wounded and unfit for duty. We just haven't had any way to communicate. I was afraid to let Amon or the boys go into town."

"You was listed as missing at the Wilderness when the lists come out last month. That's why I was real s'prised to hear Reverend Chancellor telling me all 'bout how he married up you and Miss Jolie. Don't blame you for bein' missin', and I mean that, Mr. Tremayne. Even if you sent one of the boys to town, it's occupied now by the bluebellies. They ain't carin' where you are, long as you ain't behind them earthworks at Petersburg."

"I can't say that I wish I was, exactly," Morgan told Will, his brow wrinkling. "But I do feel like I should be."

Jolie put her arm through his. "And you would be, if you weren't blind," she said quietly. "I'm sorry, Morgan. I wouldn't wish it on you, but as long as this war is on, I'm not going to be very regretful that you are."

"Y'know, it's a funny thing," Will said, staring at Morgan. "You look like you can see. You look at a body when they're talkin' to you, and it just seems like you're lookin' 'em straight in the eyes. I keep forgettin' that you're blind."

"That's funny," Jolie said with a smile. "So do I."

CHAPTER TWENTY-FIVE

The winter that year was hard and grim. Cold weather and icy rains set in the very first day of September, and it was winter, with no joyous autumn season. It snowed a lot that winter. Most of the time it was dark, portenous days with heavy merciless snow piling up in drifts sometimes six feet deep.

The men, including Morgan, worked hard to keep the snow at bay. Morgan could find his way all around the farm. He had begun by memorizing the number of steps to take, but after a couple of months, it became instinctive.

Rosh and Santo went into Fredericksburg once a week, unless the snowstorms were too bad. News from Petersburg wasn't good. The armies were stalemated. Still, battles erupted as Grant kept attacking, attacking, always pushing to try to finally defeat Robert E. Lee. But now, as before, it seemed he could not beat even the starving, ragged, decimated Army of Northern Virginia.

One freezing night in February, Morgan and Jolie sat in their favorite chairs close to a hearty comforting fire in the study. The boys had brought back some newspapers that day, and Jolie had been reading them to Morgan. She had just read that they estimated that Ulysses S. Grant now had about 125,000 men around Petersburg, while General Lee had 52,000.

Morgan said sadly, "It's all going to come down to the numbers in the end. There's just too many of them. They could probably go on replacing every casualty for the next ten years. But I guess we can't replace even one anymore. At Fredericksburg, I realized then that this was going to happen."

"Really? But that was such a great victory for us," Jolie said.

"It was. But I watched it from the hills above the battlefield, so I could see it, but I wasn't really in it. I saw lots of blue dots, long lines of them, come across that field of death, again and again. Tens of thousands of them marching, standing up proud, aiming, firing. . .falling. Then thousands more would come, marching right over the ones who'd been killed and wounded, marching slowly, aiming, firing. Sometimes they would even get to reload, but they all fell. At the end we found bodies piled up seven and eight deep.

"But then I saw, as clearly as if it was a painting in front of my eyes, that if they had just thrown that whole army at us then, and all eighty thousand of them had rushed up those hills in a bayonet charge, they might have just overrun us by sheer weight and momentum. They would have died, yes, but I doubt that their casualties would have been much higher than they were. They probably would have been lower. But no general had the guts to do that. . .until General Grant came along."

"But he hasn't done that at Petersburg," Jolie argued.

"No, but once again General Lee outsmarted him. Fighting against an enemy that's on a level plain with you, behind earthworks, is different from storming a hill. Those trenches are about thirty miles long. Even General Grant doesn't have enough men to rush a thirty-mile line." He sighed deeply. "But what he does have is enough men to eventually encircle General Lee and the army. It will happen. I know it. I can see it."

"You said you can see it," Jolie said softly. "And I know that's true."

"Mm. Jolie?"

"Yes?"

"It is truer than you know. I can see red," he said almost casually. "I can see the fire."

❧

Meredith and Perry, for the first and last times, came to the front of the tent and stood by the flap opening to watch General Lee. The date was April 9, 1865.

Lee came out, bowing to get through the low opening, then naturally resumed his stately erect posture. He looked at his two servants and nodded courteously to them but said nothing. His face was a study of sadness.

He wore a new uniform, Confederate gray with the graceful sleeve insignia of a general and the embroidered gold stars on his collar. His trousers were pressed to perfection with a gold stripe down the sides and a ruler-straight crease front and back and tucked into his glossy black cavalry boots with heavy gold spurs. His gauntlets were spotless white. His hat had new gold braid and tassels surrounding the brim. At his waist was a gold satin sash. At his side was a heavy sword, with jewels on the hilt and an icy blue steel scabbard that glittered in the weak sunlight as if it had been fashioned from sapphires.

An aide brought Traveler. Lee mounted, and without a backward glance, he rode down the dusty road that was lined with thousands of silent soldiers.

Perry had stayed up all night long readying General Lee's uniform and boots and sword. His face was tired and tragic.

Meredith was openly crying. "I'd give my right arm and right leg if Marse Robert didn't have to give hisself up," he said miserably.

"Me, too," Perry said quietly. "But one thing I've found, that the Lord don't want arms and legs. He wants sacrifice and surrender.

Marse Robert's done sacrificed all his life, and now it's time for him to give up and let the Lord take keer of him."

&

When General Lee reached the McLean house, the agreed-upon meeting place, General Grant had not yet arrived. Lee went inside and entered a parlor with fine but plain furniture typical of a middle-class farmhouse. He selected a marble-topped table and cane chair that was in front of the window. He would be able to see Grant arrive.

There was a flurry of horses and heavy boots on the porch. Grant came in dressed for the field. He was about five eight and sturdily built but slightly stooped. His hair and beard were thick and nut brown, with no sign of gray. He wore a plain blue coat with only shoulder straps to indicate his rank, a dark blue flannel shirt, unbuttoned and showing a black waistcoat underneath. His trousers were tucked into ordinary top boots, mud-spattered and worn.

General Lee stood and crossed the room to shake his hand. The contrast between the two men was remarkable. General Lee was six feet tall, fifty-nine years old, and immaculate. Grant was much shorter, he was fully sixteen years Lee's junior, and he was untidy. If it had not been for the gravity with which he conducted himself, he would have looked like a careless, rowdy second lieutenant.

General Grant took a seat at a small table in the middle of the room, while General Lee resumed his seat across from him. General Grant opened the conversation. "I met you once before, General Lee, while we were serving in Mexico, when you came over to General Scott's headquarters to visit Garland's brigade, to which I then belonged. I have always remembered your appearance, and I think I should have recognized you anywhere."

Politely, Lee said, "Yes, I know I met you on that occasion, and I have often thought of it and tried to recollect how you looked, but I have never been able to recall a single feature."

Grant went on reminiscing about Mexico, seeming to enjoy his recollections and encouraging Lee to talk of it, too.

General Lee was, as always, courteous, but finally he determined to bring the conversation around, though he dreaded saying the words more than anything he had ever done in his life. Still, he spoke in the most natural manner, in the soundest tones, and his deep smooth voice seemed to echo in the somberly quiet room. "I suppose, General Grant, that the object of our present meeting is fully understood. I asked to see you to ascertain upon what terms you would receive the surrender of my army."

CHAPTER TWENTY-SIX

Morgan came around the corner of the kitchen porch, and for a moment Jolie was horrified because she saw that he was using his cane again. But then she saw that he was stumping along with a limp, trying not to put any weight on his left foot. Heavily he sat down on the bench.

"What happened?" Jolie demanded.

"That horse stepped on my foot. Again. And good this time. I think he did it on purpose," Morgan grumbled.

"He's tired of everybody else riding him, you know that. He blows out his sides like a great fat man when they try to cinch him, and if they can get him saddled, he deliberately runs right against the fenceposts to try to shuck them off," Jolie said with frustration. "He's getting worse every day. You know you're the only one who can control him, Morgan."

"I'm doing a real good job at that. My broken foot is a sure sign."

"Is it really broken?" Jolie asked with sudden alarm.

"No, but it really hurts."

"Shame on you, you big baby-muffin. You scared me. You need to stop this whining, Morgan, and get on that horse and ride him. That's all there is to it."

Morgan frowned. "Am I really whining?"

"Well, kind of."

"I'm sorry about that. I'll try not to whine anymore, but really, Jolie, it scares me. I can see up close, yes, but far off everything's blurred, and it makes me a little bit dizzy. I just don't want to fall off and—and—"

"Hit your head," Jolie completed the sentence for him. "And maybe go blind again."

"Yes," Morgan said resignedly.

Jolie came around the table and sat down in Morgan's lap. She put one finger under his chin and tilted his head up to look straight at her. "Look at me, Morgan."

"With pleasure," he said, lightly kissing her lips. "You're even more beautiful than I imagined. You're alluring and exotic and radiant. Since spring has come, it seems that you've bloomed along with the flowers."

She smiled, and it was indeed dazzling. Jolie had grown into a gorgeous woman, with smooth rich olive skin with a golden cast, dark eyes slightly uptilted at the corners, a wide generous mouth, and perfect white teeth. "Evetta tells me that's another symptom. She said ladies always glow."

"What? What are you talking about?"

"You know that thing we've been hoping for, and praying for, ever since we got married?" Jolie asked with a hint of mischief.

"You—you mean, for a baby? That we'd get pregnant?" Morgan asked with excitement.

"Morgan, I was horribly sick yesterday morning and this morning! Evetta said it's got to be a baby!" she cried, throwing her arms around Morgan and pulling him close.

He almost smothered her, returning the hug, and finally she pulled back, breathless. "Don't smush me. You might smush little

SURRENDER

Jeannetta," she warned him.

"Or little Lee," he reminded her, his face lit with a foolish grin.

"Or little Lee," she agreed placidly. Then she grew grave and said, "So, what are you going to tell him, Morgan? That your big bad horse is too scary to ride? No, no, Morgan. You've never been scared of a horse in your entire life. Horses, and in particular Vulcan, are like a part of you. I may not really understand the kind of love that you have for them, but I see it, and I recognize it. Vulcan is missing you, and you're missing him."

"After what you told me, I feel like I could ride a storm! You're right, Jolie. As usual you're so right. Would you come with me now? I'm going to saddle up that old devil and make him see the error of his ways."

They walked to the stables hand in hand. Morgan still favored his left foot, but he could put weight on it now. He went in to saddle Vulcan, and Jolie went to stand on the fence rail around the paddock, as they had done for so many years.

It took so long that Jolie began to doubt that Morgan had been able to saddle the horse. But finally she heard Vulcan's heavy, prancing steps at the stable doors opening out into the paddock.

Morgan came out, sitting high and proud in the saddle, holding one rein in each hand, as he did when he wanted Vulcan to be collected. Stamping, tossing his head, snorting, Vulcan took two steps out into the paddock and then, with a slight movement of Morgan's hands, stopped completely still.

The great black stallion reared, pawed the air once, twice. He landed neatly then began a perfect gaited trot to the far end of the paddock. There he turned, a quick smooth whisk around, reared, and came back to a collected stance.

Morgan dismounted, took the reins, and led him to Jolie.

And then Morgan and Vulcan both bowed.

～

Robert E. Lee was revered in the South and reviled in the North.

In the North the press was merciless and vile. But no matter whether it was a personal attack, a criticism of his tactics or strategy or leadership, or even attacks against his family, he refused to respond, not privately and especially not publicly. He was that kind of man. In all the trials, tribulations, and tragedies that he suffered throughout his life, he never lost his sense of goodwill toward others, his self-control, or his dignity.

His fame was because he was a man of war, but others remembered his excellent service at West Point. In August of 1865, the trustees nominated him for the presidency of Washington College in Lexington, Virginia. On October 2nd, he was inaugurated in a modest service, and the final phase of his life began.

It was a good life. Lee was sensible of the honor of educating the young and worked as hard to make the college an excellent place of higher learning as he had in planning any campaign. Finally he was settled with Mary, and he knew he would never have to leave her again. They had lost sweet Annie, but the six children, including the three boys that had all served the Confederacy, had come through the war and prospered.

During the Christmas holidays, they were often all together at Lexington. Lee must have felt that it was a quiet, peaceful life, and a rewarding one. But after the war, he could never again be characterized as a happy man. In many ways he was solitary and withdrawn, and though his eyes would sparkle with good humor, he rarely smiled. The phrase "grave dignity" best described his last five years.

On September 28, 1870, he went to a vestry meeting at his church on a wintry wet evening. When he came home, he fell ill, seemingly alert one minute and then dozing off into apparent unconsciousness. His final enemy had attacked.

He seemed to be aware that each moment may be his last, and he accepted it quietly and without complaint. Steadily he worsened as days went by, and October came. He rarely spoke, and often when he did it was an unintelligible murmur. By the ninth day, it was clear that he was traveling down his last road.

Mary sat by him and held his hand.

As men of war so often do, he returned to the battlefield as his time ran out. "Tell Hill he *must* come up," he said sternly, so plainly that all in the chamber could hear.

But all battles come to an end, and Robert E. Lee's long battle did, too. "Strike the tent," he said firmly. It was his last surrender, and he finally went home.

ABOUT THE AUTHOR

Award-winning, bestselling author Gilbert Morris is well known for penning numerous Christian novels for adults and children since 1984 with 6.5 million books in print. He is probably best known for the forty-book House of Winslow series, and his *Edge of Honor* was a 2001 Christy Award winner. He lives with his wife in Gulf Shores, Alabama.

Other books by Gilbert Morris

THE LAST CAVALIERS

The Crossing
The Sword

The Appomattox Saga Omnibus 1
The Appomattox Saga Omnibus 2
The Appomattox Saga Omnibus 3